The Shadow Warrior

Elizabeth Davis

Elizabeth Davis

I dedicate this book to my wonderful middle school English teacher, Proal Heartwell, for all his support. None of this would have been possible without his help.

The
The Land of Old
Wild Land
Arel
Zrid
Plain of Ran
The Dark Forests
Daril
The Lost Sea
Endir
The Fera Aqua
The Olympian Isle

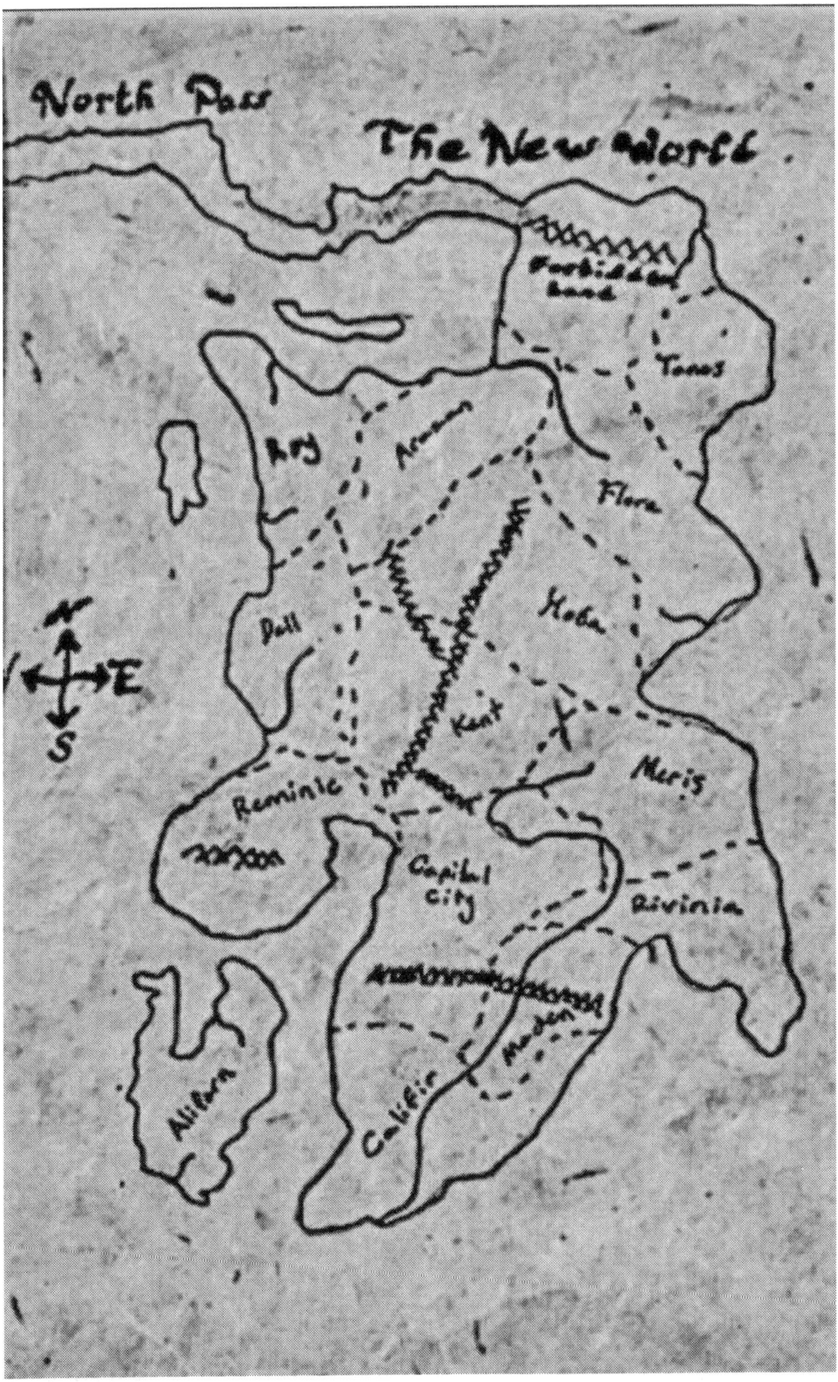
North Pass
The New World
Tonas
Roy
Flora
Hoba
Dall
N
E
S
Kent
Maris
Reminic
Capital City
Rivinia

Prologue

Two twins, aged only to the tender year of nine, stand in front of two adults, a woman and a man. Two young stallions stand behind the children like guardian angels ready to loyally protect their young masters. Both horses are muscular and lean, strong enough for war, but light enough for running. Near the girl stands the proud silver stallion that glows with a soft ice-blue light and next to the boy stands a horse whose coat pulses softly with a dark blue light. They, like the children, seem to be identical in all but color.

The woman on the throne sits as tall and proud as her husband, and she has every right to, for she is the Light. She is the one who supports the lives of all the humans on the earth. Garbed in flawless white armor and a sword at her belt, she exudes a dangerous air. The man on her right contrasts harshly to her viciously bright light. His midnight black armor seems to be darkening the corners of the room and when his magic brushes against that of his mate's, the air hums with thick tension and sporadically sparks. Neither of the two awe-inspiring beings seem to notice. However, the children eye their parents nervously. The girl grabs at her brother's arm and he holds her close as well. While the Light may be kinder, their father is the Dark, and he is wicked and cruel. Worst of all, he is the one who decides their fate.

No one speaks, but the atmosphere feels as if there is an incoming storm. A decision is being made and it is one that the parents have been unable to foresee the outcome. This one decision will change the course of the world, for it will release two powerful forces among the weak humans- Hope and Chaos. It is unclear which of the twins is to be the destroyer of an entire nation and which is to be the savior.

One will build up a whole new empire, but with that newfound strength, is destined to crush the spirits and befuddle the minds of the innocent men who will risk everything to protect their land and family. The savior will help them, but the struggle will be long and in vain, for should even one simple human believe in either Hope or Chaos, then they will never cease to exist.

One day the two children will be the greatest of enemies and it will come to a head between them. On that day, thousands of innocent humans will die. It is the way of the world. If given a push, the best of friends can become the greatest of enemies.

Will the power go to the girl, the one with the piercing ice-blue eyes and silver armor, and the one whose temper is sharper and closer to the surface then her compassion? Or should the powerful one be the boy with dark hair and deep-sea blue eyes with armor of the same color. His kindness outweighs his anger, but there is something in his countenance that has always set his mother on edge.

Today's decision is going to decide who is to become the most powerful and who will be sent to save the humans. Also, it will reveal the one who will fight to destroy them. Finally, an unspoken decision is made and a strange current rushes through the room. Unfathomable power swirls through the room and gathers in the space between the immortal parents.

Upon seeing the magic, the twins suddenly stand straight, no longer supporting each other. The boy looks at the power hungrily and suddenly the mother regrets their decision. A mistake has been made. A mistake that could bring the end of an era. Up until now she did not think of something.- something huge. *What if the most powerful child is not the savior like I thought, but the destroyer?*

Before she can say anything, the power divides. One is greater than the other. The girl watches the small portion with proud eyes, but sorrow is hidden in her stance. However well disguised it is, her mother spots it and regrets her part in this.

"Draemir Caerin, do you accept the power you are about to be given? It will reveal your true nature for better or for worse. You were given a gift as well and he will be your guide, your symbol, and your inspiration. He will be part of you, and he will reflect who you are. His name is Kelpie of the Deep." The dark blue horse bends a front leg and bows deeply when the Dark says his title.

"Girl, you were given one as well. Yours is to be known as Enbarr of the Flowing Mane." The girl's horse does not bow and grovel, but stands proudly behind the girl, steadily looking at the child below him. His expression clearly shows his promise of steadfast fidelity. The girl glances back and stares at her horse with an expression of awe equally proportioned with love. She jerks around to the front when her father addresses her brother again.

"Son, you are the chosen one, for you are the boy, and therefore the true heir of your father's power. Do you accept the power, Draemir?" The voice is deep and majestic, but also terrifying, for it contains equal amounts of pride as it does malice. Despite herself, the girl flinches and draws a disapproving frown from her father, validating his opinion of her. She is weaker than her twin. The young boy draws himself up proudly.

"I accept the power, father. I will not let you down." The Dark looks down at his son, and the look in his eyes is worrisome.

"No, I don't believe that you will." With a gesture of benediction, he gives his children their power. He sternly looks down at his daughter. "You, girl, will always be weaker than your brother. You answer to him, like you answer to me. You will speak to him with respect and do as he

3

demands. From this time on, you will faithfully serve him. He is superior to you and he has the right to punish you as he sees fit. Do you understand, girl? This is the way of the world. Women respect men, not the other way around." She does not respond, but just continues to stare ahead, her jaw set and her eyes narrowed. She is stealing herself for something.

"Elren Caerin, *am I clear?"* His voice becomes darker and the light in the room flickers dangerously. Finally the girl looks up and fire seems to dance in her ice-blue eyes, ignited by defiance and pride.

"From this day on, I will answer to no man. Neither god, nor king, nor even my father will I bow down to. If Draemir is to be more powerful than me, so be it, but that does not mean that I will answer to him. A young tree is far less powerful than the wind, but if it is strong enough, it continues to stand, and eventually the wind must go around it and the tree has become stronger than the once omnipotent gale. Do with me as you wish, but just know that I may bend, but I will never break. I will remain undefeated by the winds created solely to knock me down. Anything you do to me will only serve to make me become stronger, and eventually I will be strong enough to withstand the storm," she responds in a voice that is quiet, but firm.

The expression of the two gods are completely opposite. Pride from her mother, but her father looks as if he is about to kill his own daughter. However, before he does anything, her brother hits her with enough magic to kill a mortal. Caught by surprise, she is sent flying and lands hard on the marble floor ten feet away. Her horse rears and paws the air, immediately stepping between his master and her twin. Kelpie, his own twin brother, also rears and bares his teeth, asking for a fight. Enbarr's attention quickly shifts when his master moves.

4

Gasping for breath, she slowly gets to her feet. She looks at her twin in shock, betrayal written across her face. She stares at him for a moment more, noting his set features and the new smirk that clouds his once genuine smile. Tears fill her eyes, but she refuses to let them fall. He chose his side. His true personality was unveiled by his new power. They have reached a point of no return. This is one battle she will not win. Her hand drops to the hilt of her sword, but she does not draw it. Instead, she backs towards the door.

"One day, I will not bend. One day, maybe not tomorrow, or in a year, but one day, I will stand tall and make *you* go around me and *I* will be stronger." She contemptuously flicks her braid over her shoulder and she and her horse stalk out of the room together.

Now she must learn how to become stronger. Yes, she will be tested and sent through grueling adventures meant to drive her to madness. She will watch family and friends die and there will be nothing she can do. Her brother will hunt her relentlessly, and their father will continue to rip them apart. Every time Elren raises her sword against her brother, a part of her heart will harden. Slowly, very slowly, her walls will be built, and there will be no way in. Only one person holds the key to unlocking her frozen heart and breaching the boundaries that hold her unruly emotions captive.

The day will come when she is as strong as her brother, but if she cannot find the one holding the key, she will never know the secret to standing strong as the wind does its best to push her down. In the many years to come in Elren's life, she will face trials and if she can overcome the opposing tide, she will learn the secret to remaining undefeated. While undertaking life's hard journey, she will learn how to teach, to love, and to care, yet also how to hate, how to suffer, and she will learn the consequences that come when she allows herself to love and be happy.

Everything has consequences, but the question is simple. Are the rewards worth the sacrifices?

Five Years Later

A young warrior stands in the middle of the straight dirt road, the crowd staying well away from her. Her face is streaked with mud and her dark green tunic is in shreds. A wild look is in her ice blue eyes, like a hunted animal who knows the hunter is near, but is too tired to run any farther. Suddenly, the crowd parts and strangers cram tighter together against the buildings than they normally would and everyone stops and stares. A handsome fourteen-year-old boy strolls down the street. The crowd whispers nervously and a few of the young children begin to cry. They all know there is no running from him.

The disheveled girl in the road obviously tried and by the state of her, it was a long hunt through rough country. The boy's deep sea blue tunic is immaculate and his cruel blue eyes sparkle with dark humor. Only the girl still stands in the middle of the street. The tall warrior looks small and alone as she waits. She stares down at the little stones in the road, seeming for all the world like she doesn't know, or care, about the danger that is casually walking down the road. It is clear why he is here. He stops five meters from her and simply waits. Finally, without looking up, she speaks quietly, but in the silent street everyone hears her as clearly as if she had shouted.

"Draemir, I know why you are here and I will never allow the New Worlders to raze my home land. We may share the same blood, but we will never be true siblings. I could never claim a family member who wishes only to kill and destroy everything so that he can control the world and have all the humans in it worship him. You betrayed your right to ask anything of me. On the Decision Day, you showed who you truly are, and

6

I want nothing to do with you. I loved you once, but now you are dead to me." Her voice is as sharp and dangerous as the ice blue color of her eyes, but he just smiles coldly in response.

"You have evaded me well, Elren. You chose to abandon me and you leave me no choice, but to kill you. Such a shame you ran. You could have ruled with me. Power, fame, and glory. They all could have been yours. No one can stand against you... Except me," he amends his statement. The girl eyes him coolly, one eyebrow raised as she listens to his proposal. "Alas, I have a tight schedule to keep. Goodbye, sister. Let's make this quick, shall we?" Someone in the crowd cries a warning and the mothers cover their children's eyes as his gleaming black sword begins to rise slowly before starting its murderous overhead strike.

Finally, the girl looks up. The watching villagers are completely stunned by the expression in her eyes. There is no fear there, no uncertainty. The wild look is gone. There is grim determination written across her young face, but her eyes sparkle with kindness and humor. Even in the grave circumstances, she smiles slightly as if this is all for the villagers' entertainment. Suddenly, the black sword reaches the top of its arc and with the casual speed of a leopard, she draws her own sword in a fast and fluid movement. She easily deflects his blade and it lodges into the hard-packed ground. He yelps in surprise and for the first time ever, the people see his facade of confidence slip.

She slashes down his arm, but instead of a cut, there is a long line of ancient runes written in dark blue down the inside of his arm. He stares at it for a second before the girl swings her sword again in a deadly horizontal cut. He grabs a long dagger from its sheath at his belt and deflects her blade a hair's breadth from his neck, before reversing his grip and stabbing it deep into her chest, right below her left collar bone. The girl staggers back, but somehow, she remains standing.

7

The young warrior pulls the blade straight out without flinching and raises her sword once more, ready to continue. That expression of calm and slight humor is still maintained. As astonishing as it is that she was not killed, even more incredible is the fact that where the wound had been is now a strange series of runes like on the arm of her twin, but her's is written in ice blue. His face shows his surprise and for the first time ever, he runs from a fight. On this day, he runs from a girl.

The prey turned on the predator. His black sword appears in his hand once more and he puts it in its sheath before making a mock bow towards his most recent adversary.

"Draemir was my friend. You are a stranger now. All the humans call you Chaos and I have come to the decision that they are right. I will not stop following you and doing my best to stop all your terrible plans. I am just a shadow to you, Chaos, and I am known as the Shadow Warrior because of you. In some ways that makes life easier. It certainly makes it easier for me to surprise you and then kill you," she says softly, hate and betrayal hardening her voice.

"Better luck next time then." He fades into the lengthening shadows, a hint of what would soon be known as the town's darkest evening in many years to come. The girl glances down at her forearm and her sharp eyes widen slightly at what she reads. It is identical to the small runes on her brother's forearm. She snaps her ice blue eyes around the street once more before stumbling into a run, quickly disappearing into the woods as if she had never been there. People call out to her retreating form. Some cursing her for bringing him, others offering her a place to stop and rest. She ignores them all.

Here is what the young warrior had read on her arm. It will always remind her that there truly is no running from her brother. While once she may have trusted him, and loved him, he went too far, and when

8

she tried to stop him, he turned on her and she learned the terrible truth. There is no escaping Chaos. He will not rest until all hope is gone. Even if it takes him to the grave. A war is coming and the girl must gather as many allies as possible if she wishes to save her homeland from the New Worlders, driven by Chaos, who wish to conquer it.

The Legend of the Shadow Warrior

The people speak with one voice,
Of the war,
Which they have no choice.

To keep their hopes up,
A story they did spin.
A story that speaks of two immortal twins.

The union of the Dark and the Light,
Created the one that we all dislike.
Chaos failed to take the throne,
So, he was left alone,
to wander and roam.

New people he did find,
of a lesser kind,
Tired of following their leader,
They follow him this time.

Vanity, disorder, power, and greed,
Are the very first seed,
Of the reign,
Chaos shall lead.

Peace, prosperity, understanding, and care,

Are what the Shadow Warrior wants them to share.

But how many must die,

Before that order is revived?

Powerful the siblings are,

With sharp blue eyes that shine like stars.

Will the Shadow Warrior win?

Or will Chaos leave a path of destruction,

Wherever he has been?

No one will know until the war comes to an end.

Is it possible to defeat power, vanity, and greed?

We must wait and we will see.

Three Years Later

Chapter One

Shadow

I swear quietly as a small branch snaps under Emerald's foot, scaring away our dinner. The hare's ears snap up and it bounces away in time to avoid my arrow as it punches into the ground where it had just been grazing. I hold my breath and count to ten before turning to her as she stands behind me in the shadows. She winces slightly at the look in my eyes.

"I'm sorry, Shadow," she says in a small voice. I saved her from my brother when he killed her family, but sometimes I wonder why I chose to burden myself with caring for a child. I failed to save her family, so she was left alone in the world and now I owe it to her to protect her, but it does occasionally cross my mind that the time I spend teaching her is time lost that I could have used to gather more allies and finally make a stand against Chaos.

I look at her and wonder if I have managed to teach her anything, but before I can say anything, I hear a woodsman behind me. He makes only the slightest bit of noise, suggesting that he is familiar with stalking creatures, but it is enough to alert me of his presence.

In a sudden movement, I twist away to the right and an arrow skims across my back creating a long cut, but that is nothing to what it could have been. I cannot let Emerald see me use magic, for she is too young and the rules of magic state that she must be old enough to understand the consequences of power, but with an arrow heading straight for her, I have no choice. Gritting my teeth, I force my magic not to show up as ice blue and with the extremely suppressed magic, I can only throw her aside, out of the path of the arrow, but unfortunately, she slams into a tree head first. All the blood drains from her face so that the freckles show clearly in her fear and pain. Her green eyes are wide as she stares at the arrow that almost killed her. Her mind is in too much shock to process any of the proceedings and she drops to the ground, out cold.

I whip an arrow out of my quiver and nock it onto the string of my massive longbow. Turning, I finally get a chance to see the woodsmen and am surprised to find two strange men. They both wear long camouflage pants and shirts and their weapons are out of place. One has the strangest looking bow I have ever seen leveled at my chest and the other is armed with a spear and both have two peculiar weapons in small sheaths on their belts. The man with the bow is older and the younger man looks to be only seventeen or eighteen at the most, close to my age. New Worlders. I have never seen them this far into the Dark Woods before.

"Lower your weapon! Put it on the ground! Move! Move! Move!" The older of the two yells at me. I cock my head slightly and raise an eyebrow at his brisk manner and assumption of being in charge here. He sighs in exasperation when he takes my look to be one of incomprehension. The younger man nods wisely before speaking.

"Idiots. The whole lot of them. They all speak and act like savages. They don't even understand Remic. Look at this! Two women alone in the forest in men's clothes instead of dresses! They are even armed! The older one is probably married already. Imagine that! Kevin, you know Kevin, right? He works for the AKAL intelligence office on Indicial Street in the Capital City? His daughter would already be married! She is only thirteen!" The young man, practically still a boy, exclaims excitedly to his older companion. The other man grunts recognition of the fact, but is otherwise unimpressed.

"Didn't you read the briefing, boy? It explained all the weird customs and ideas these people believe. It even mentioned that they speak the barbaric language called Arindal." His tone is condescending and abrupt. I narrow my eyes at him and finally deign to speak to them. They both jump and stare at me when I speak in their own language. The young man has enough grace to blush in embarrassment as he realizes I understood what he had said.

"And you have not realized that your civilization is reaching a point of crumbling into confusion and insanity. I am *not* married and most likely never will be. Also, I would watch your use of the term *savages*. If we are the savages, I hate to know what your people will soon become under the leadership of Chaos." My accent is so thick that I can barely understand myself and it only serves to make me more irritated. I think for a moment before enunciating more clearly and the accent fades.

"I recommend that *you,* kind sirs, drop your own weapons or things will get messy here." Their jaws drop at my words.

"Who are you?" The young one asks with such innocent curiosity that I answer him, well, in part. Only a select few know my true name.

"I am Shadow Caerin, sometimes called the Shadow Warrior." My ice blue eyes glitter with anger as his companion tells him to shut up because he is not supposed to speak to their captive.

"I am not yours, nor anyone's captive and I never will be." I level my undrawn bow at the older man's chest. "Leave us and survive, or stay to die. It is your choice, but you do not know how fortunate you are that you have a choice after nearly killing my sister with your strange bow." Neither move, but the boy shifts his feet worriedly and I can tell that he is no longer enjoying this. The air hums with tension so thick that you could practically play it like a fiddle.

14

Given no choice but to act on my words, I draw the bowstring back until the silver and blue fletching of my arrow brushes my cheek. To my surprise, the older man simply laughs at the arrow aimed for his heart.

"I wouldn't do that if I were you," says a voice right behind me and I feel the uncomfortable sensation of a sword pressing into my back. It is the voice of a villager I helped last year when he had a problem with a bear.

"Gerald McGreylan. Fancy meeting you here," I say without turning around. My voice is full of icy daggers as I hurl them towards him. Every word reminding him of the favors that I have done for him and his family- the time I saved his daughter from a bear, and when I had rescued his wife and son from smugglers. I can hear even more men crashing through the woods behind him before they stop suddenly.

"Greetings, men. What brings you out so far from your bed tonight, Mitchell Mulligan? Oh, and Cane O'Mallia, and Connor McCarthy as well. Not enough business in your shops, oh good sirs? Or did the tavern run out of ale, cider, and mead all at once?" I speak in a condescending tone, even though they are the ones holding the swords. I hear their feet shifting uncomfortably in the leaves. They know that they will become outcasts if the villagers found out they helped New Worlders.

I smile grimly. They have no idea who they are messing with. At their urging, I slowly lower my bow and lay it on the ground. When I stand straight again, all I hold is my arrow. An ugly silence fills the air and once again, the young soldier is the only one who seems to know something is about to happen. I contemplate stepping on the dead stick an inch from the heel of my right boot to watch their surprise, but I resist the impulse. The situation is too serious.

His dark eyes dart back and forth between the men behind me, his older companion, and myself. Only one out of the six men seems to know what I am capable of.

"Put the arrow away!" Cane O'Mallia yells from behind me. I twirl it between my fingers and feel the arrows perfect balance. I mentally prepare myself for the blistering speed and strength this move will take before reaching back over my shoulder as if to put it in my quiver, but then I hurl the arrow point first at the older New World soldier.

It slices through his bow string and mechanics, rendering it useless. In the same movement, I reach over my right shoulder and grab the blade of Gerald's sword in my bare hand before he has a chance to use it. I twist it away from him, feeling the sword bite into my hand, but I give a mighty jerk anyway and out of complete shock at my stupidity to grab the edge of a sword, his grip is slack and it flies into the air, landing deep in the woods.

Swiftly, I pick up my bow and nock an arrow to the string. Quickly aiming, I send four arrows on their way. Each flies at face height into three different trees next to Cane, Mitchell, and Connor. The fourth takes Gerald McGreylan in the upper arm, only because he moved at the last second into the path of the arrow. Those four men quickly back up and bunch together. I repeat the same thing that I said earlier.

"Leave and live, or stay to die. Your families need you, so I recommend that you take the former of those options." They hesitate for a second, but when I drop my hand to the hilt of my sword threateningly, Cane starts to back up into the trees. He has a young son waiting for him at home. I am shocked he came out in the first place. The New Worlders must have paid them well. All of them are married with children. One after another they start to back away until only one still stands there, hesitantly thinking of being brave.

I unsheathe my sword and swing it through the air, marveling at the clean slicing sound of a good blade. Mitchell hastily steps back with the others. They stand there a minute longer, but then my ice blue magic suddenly dances out across the blade and they all run, with Gerald McGreylan staggering along behind them clutching his wounded arm. A strange ongoing sting echoes through my blood and I turn around curiously. The older soldier holds a strange yellow...thing. It makes a foreign humming sound and an odd current, a lot like water, shimmers in the air.

"Damn taser must be broken!" he mutters angrily before pulling out a black thing that looks like the yellow one.

"Is that where the weird current was coming from?" I ask curiously. While it may not be very painful, it was annoying.

"Wait, it was working?" he asks in sudden confusion. I shrug.

"Your-" I hesitate over the foreign word, "gun?" I add a questioning inflection to the end of the word, hoping I got it right. I have only ever heard of the New World's new *tech-nol-o-gy*, or whatever they call it. Personally, I think shields, swords, spears, bows, and lances are better than those flimsy modern inventions. Both stare at me, their expressions incredulous.

"You didn't feel the taser? That was enough electricity to kill three men!"

"E-lec-tri-ci-ty?" I repeat the foreign word in Remic, feeling it slip and slide strangely on my tongue.

"Enough of this!" the older soldier roars, startling his young companion. He pulls the trigger of the black gun. A loud pop fills the air and it feels like a hot poker is burning into my chest. It is more of a surprise than anything. I have felt worse; a sword or dagger tends to hurt more. The pain quickly dissipates and all that is there is a strange circular

17

cut and a metal ball on the ground. Finally, my irrepressible temper shows up. My form shimmers and I appear in a chainmail tunic and leggings. My sword flares with ice blue magic. *Well men, you are about to find out what you are up against.*

"I do not want to kill anyone, but it would appear that you *want* to die today." I can practically see the young soldier trembling in his boots. Only the discipline from his training keeps him from running. Allowing magic to run unchecked through my veins, my senses heighten until I can hear the ground creak as they shift their weight, and I can see every miniscule spot of tension in my adversary's stance. It is this ability, along with many thousands of hours of dedicated practice, that makes me a formidable warrior.

His forearm tenses and I raise my sword slightly. When his finger twitches slightly on the trigger, I can see the small metal bullet that shoots out the end and my eyes quickly calculate the arch and how far it will drop, using the same equation backwards as when I am shooting an arrow, before deflecting it off my blade. It ricochets off to the right and the young soldier ducks with a surprised yelp as it flies harmlessly over his head. He fires again and I change the angle of my blade and it goes left. He makes his final mistake. He fires again.

I hold my blade straight and when the bullet hits it, it comes straight back at him. Unlike his younger companion, his reflexes are not as sharp. It catches him square in the chest and his expression slowly changes from anger, to surprise, to bewilderment, and finally relaxes into one of blissful happiness as he topples over onto the ground. I stare at him in shock. So, *that* is what a gun does. The young soldier gapes at me and stares with wide eyes at his commander. It must be his first time out in the field. Slowly, even after watching his superior fail, his hand draws his own black gun. I face him calmly. His face shows such anguish of indecision that I know he cannot be all bad.

"I would not use that if I were you. You still have so much in your life to look forward to. I'm sure a strapping young lad like yourself has a girlfriend and a family waiting for you at home, wherever home may be for you." Fury suddenly sparks in his eye as I mention his family and he clicks something on the top of his gun.

"I don't have a family! No one even knows I exist! No one will ever come looking for me if I am missing or gone! You! You have a brother who is searching for you around the entire world! Even though he plans to kill you, he at least acknowledges your existence!" My temper starts to rise, but I keep my voice deadly calm.

"I wish he would perish in Hades! He has no right to call us family. Not after what he did to me. He is a liar and a murderer. He is worse than Loki!" He gives me a completely bewildered look at the name. "He is the Norse god of deceit and trickery," I explain. "He is very persuasive and will go out of his way to cause trouble."

"Ah, I see. Like the Loki from the Marvel movies. I get that reference now." I ignore his interruption and his sudden smile as if he made a joke.

"He and Dra-, I mean Chaos, would get along very well." I hesitate over my brother's name. I swore on my life that I would never speak his real name again until the final battle, so I use the name the humans gave him. Chaos lies about anything to achieve what he wants. He deserves his new name. *Am I any better though? I don't use my own real name.*

"Now, you have three options that I can see. First, you can fire that gun in your hand and force me to kill you, but it would be a pointless way for you to die since your little weapons cannot harm me. I think that both of us would rather not do that. I like you, and believe that you deserve a future, and I am sure you do not want to die today. The young never do. Your second option is to return to your side of the world. Let's review this idea- you escape me, never have to look at another female warrior, mostly because I am the only female sword master alive, but you will be hunted by Chaos and his minions because you were unsuccessful in your mission. He does not keep people that cannot get him what he wants. For your sake, I most sincerely hope you never feel his wrath."

I trace a finger across the long white scar that cuts down the left side of my face. "He gave me this when I was ten. Later, when I was fourteen, I faced him again and he nearly killed me." I shift the collar of my shirt to reveal a strange scar composed of ancient runes. His eyes widen and the blood drains from his face. "Your modern weapons will not protect you. He is stronger than I am. He will kill you with two or three times the ease than it took for me to eliminate your commander. He would most likely make someone else do it, and it would be a public execution." The young soldier licks his suddenly dry lips.

"What is the third option?" he asks, his voice cracking slightly from the tension growing within him.

"Stay here. Live on our side of the world. I cannot guarantee you will be safe, but you can... What is that word you use... Enlist! You can enlist into the warrior training here. This is probably your only option that doesn't find you dead immediately." After a few seconds of rapid thinking, he slowly puts away his gun. I sheath my sword sharply and my clothes meld back into a simple green tunic over gray riding breeches. Hanging from my leather belt are two unadorned leather sheaths. Both hold nasty surprises. A razor-sharp dagger and a long and deadly sword.

Disregarding the stunned soldier, I turn to check on Emerald. She still has not moved. To reassure myself, I check the pulse in her wrist and am relieved that it is still beating strongly.

When I look down again, I start when I see blood coating her wrist. *How did that get there?* I wonder, when suddenly, a low throb echoes from my hand. The thick gash across my palm is still bleeding. For a minute, I wonder how I got it, before remembering the moment I grabbed a sword's blade without protecting my hand. I am about to heal it with magic, but of course Emerald stirs and I sigh. I must let it heal like the humans. I tear off a piece of cloth from the sleeve of my shirt and quickly bind the cut. She cannot know who I really am, for I am not simply an orphaned seventeen-year-old from a commoner family like she believes. I am much more than that. I am the Shadow Warrior, daughter of Light and Dark, twin sister to Chaos. The one destined to set the world right or die trying.

I love her as if she were my own sister, but every time I look at her, my heart contracts and a small voice inside my head wonders how much longer until she knows. Until she hates me for not telling her. I carry the heavy burden of a secret that no one else should know. A destiny that the fates have set. It is inevitable for me, but I don't want her dragged in. She was not born into my terribly messed up family and I have hidden my history from her for many years.

When will my hand be forced? I do not know. How much time is left before she must know? Best to let her stay happy and not realize the actual dangers that surround her and how delicate our current life truly is. The fates decreed many millennia ago that a Great War would come and bring the end of an era. Leading the opposing armies would be two twins more powerful than any being to ever walk the earth, and they are the greatest of enemies, split by a betrayal.

21

I have worked hard for many years to hone my skills and gather my own army to face him and protect my world, but few are willing to follow me, due simply to the fact that I am a woman. Soon I must give my last bid to the most influential beings still left- the Olympians. Hopefully I can get them to join me and then the humans will come as well.

First, however, I must get this man to safety and from there he will hopefully spread the word of Chaos's movements. Perhaps he will be able to convince people that war is imminent and they must join forces. It is far-fetched, but I must try to do everything that I can, for if I fail, thousands of people will die.

Chapter Two

Shadow

"Come with me, but leave your strange weapons here. You will not need them where we are going," I call over my shoulder to the soldier. I gently pick Emerald up and jog through the woods with her cradled in my arms. The soldier's crashing footsteps are loud in the still woods behind me, preventing me from listening for signs of pursuit. We stop and walk into a small clearing with a small, but substantial, cabin. He regards the little structure with surprise.

"Is this where you live?" he asks curiously. I nod and kick the door open before walking through. I go to the furthest room from the door and gently set the child on her bed. I'll check on her later. When I walk back into the main room he is nervously perched on the edge of a chair. He hurriedly stands up when I come back and his face flushes when it tips over with a clatter on the floor and the back breaks off. I swirl magic around it and lift it into the air before setting it back on the ground again. It looks like nothing ever happened. I motion for him to sit again and I flop into a chair with my boots up on the table. He acknowledges my lack of proper society skills without a word.

"What is your name?" I ask in Arindal. He jumps at my voice, but responds in the same tongue.

"In the New World, they told me my new name was to be Liam Randolph."

"What is your real name?" He pauses as he tries to remember it.

"When I was born here, I was called Lendon Rander."

"What is your decision, Lendon?"

"I will remain here. Is there a village nearby that I can buy clothes and find a job? I trained with a spear when I was young and I still remember those days. Perhaps the village guard will allow me to join." With a sigh, I stand up and exit the small place I call home.

"I will show you the way and make sure they accept you." Once more we run through the forest. At the soldier barracks I give him a few last instructions. "Give them this note when you reach the guard at the gates. They will let you in and give you instructions. Good luck." After handing him the piece of parchment, I slip back through the forest and head back to my little house in the woods.

A Week Later

I jerk my thoughts back on task as a big, stocky man dressed in a tattered tunic walks up and inspects my skins. He nods a greeting and picks up a large bear hide. It took me two weeks to track the injured beast and put it out of my misery. Some stupid villager had put an arrow through its paw and was too afraid to track the wounded animal. The man looks at the price and then sets it back neatly and walks away with a downcast expression.

"Eric!" I call to his retreating form. He turns at gives me an inquiring look. I hold up the fur. "Tell your wife and children I send my regards." His eyes open wide in shock at the gift. I know how poor he is and I also know that his family will freeze this winter without proper clothes. I would hate for him to attempt to hunt down a large creature and be killed in the attempt, just because I wanted a few extra coins in my pocket.

"Thank you, may the gods bless you." He takes the warm fur in his large hands and looks at it as if it is gold as he walks back down the street. Suddenly, a few richly clothed men catch my eye. Their gold

24

embroidered purple shoulder capes flap in the biting wind. This is not a sight that you see often in this poor little village filled with farmers and mediocre merchants. They walk with a swagger like they are better than us peasants who live here. It is as if they own the world. I silently signal to my sister that we should move off before they spot us. Nobles. I know this type of men. They will do anything to get some extra gold in their pockets. I often fight them whenever I see them in smaller groups. It is always me who they are after. I doubt that has changed. I can see my brother's hand behind this. Quite often they take young boys to the New World and force them into serving in their armies.

I tried tracking one of them and had my first look at this other breed of human, but that unfortunate young boy I was searching for was gone. I still remember his parents' pleas to find him and his mother collapsing with despair upon my arrival without him. I even remember his name. Allen, it was. He was the last child left in his family. His two siblings had disappeared on a hunting trip a year before. Soon after hearing that their last child was lost forever, Allen's mother caught fever and died a week later. His father now works at the mills, refusing to acknowledge any reference to his deceased family members.

That family has a tragic fate. The days when he is not working, the father is seen spending his earnings on cheap, but potent, ale at the tavern. Most of the time the children taken are young boys. I have many sad stories of the families in this area. There are two different sides of the world. There are the people who have never changed their way of life and the people who change and advance every day. Old and New.

Dusk has fallen by the time we reach our little cabin and the house is dark. I fumble around in my pocket for a moment before finding the key to the door. Once it is open, Emerald slips by and I lock it once more. While Emerald puts away the remaining hides from market, I unclip

25

my sword from my belt and hang it neatly next to my bow, quiver, and shield. As my gaze wanders over my small armory, I notice that the fletchings of a few arrows are becoming worn and tattered. Before Emerald gets to hear her story, I need to re-fletch them.

My feet ache from the long day and I want nothing more than to simply go to bed, but earlier in the day Emerald had looked up at me with such longing and hope in her eyes when she asked me to tell her the story of the Shadow Warrior's origins. I could not refuse her request. She does not know how much that is asking of me, because she doesn't know who I really am. I am not a commoner like she believes. I am the Shadow Warrior.

The fire crackles cheerfully in the fireplace, dispelling the cold night air of late Fall. I turn around, my hand dropping to the hilt of my dagger when I hear soft footfalls in the hallway, but I relax when I see that it is just Emerald returning from her room.

"What do you want for dinner?" I ask.

"Food," she responds airily.

"I should hope so. Is that how you speak to your elders these days, little lady?" I put a hand on my hip and cock my head in an expression of mock scolding.

"Yes it is!" she responds, dissolving into a fit of giggles. I can't help smiling at her quick response. "I'm actually not hungry," she adds, in answer to my first question.

"I will tell you a story tonight, but first my arrows need refletching. If you help, it will go faster." A smile lights up her face and she hurries to fetch my quiver. I can't tell what she is more excited about; the story or helping me fix the arrows. A warm flush of happiness floods through me. Most people consider me to be cold and harsh, and they are probably right, but Emerald has always been my soft spot. She is the only one who can make me feel happy, content, and modulated, but she can also bring out my more human traits, such as guilt, shame, and fear.

My own family rejected me, my brother tried to kill me, and my father disinherited me. Perhaps I do close myself off to others, and treat them with more contempt than they deserve, but I cannot help it. Can you blame me? My brother, my *twin* brother, and I were once the closest of friends, but he betrayed me, forcing me to close off from the world, unless I wanted to go through that again. Everyone betrays someone, and I do not want to repeat the experience.

Sometimes I wonder if my brother actually did me a favor when he killed Emerald's family. He provided me with someone that keeps me grounded. Occasionally it crosses my mind that without Emerald, I could be as cruel and merciless as Chaos. I would hope not, but Emerald has taught me valuable lessons about humans. Paramount in human history is their greed and vanity, but equal to that is their kindness and compassion. The humans are not mere insects to step on like my brother believes. They are creatures important to the earth, and they have families, friends, goals, and dreams. Being around Emerald has shown me that these humans are worth saving and I will never forget it. I may have saved her life when she was young, but in her own way, she saved mine.

Emerald hurries back to me and breaks my chain of thought when she places my quiver on the table. I quickly select the four arrows I noticed earlier and pass Emerald one. This will be her first time fletching an arrow. She has watched me do this for years, but I have not shown her how to actually do it. Drawing my dagger, I quickly remove the old feathers and quickly trim a few feathers into the proper shape. Emerald watches me, then she copies me perfectly.

"First, the cock feather should be placed perpendicular to the nock and two inches in front of it. Then put the thick sticky liquid on the spine of the feather before placing it. The liquid will harden and hold it secure, but that is not enough to hold the feathers on, so now you must bind the front and the end of the feather to the shaft. Using wet sinew is best, because once it dries, it will tighten and not become undone."

She follows my movements intently as I show her how to place and bind it, before doing her own. "Then take the two hen feathers and place them one-hundred and twenty degrees from the cock feather before repeating the same steps as before." She quickly finishes the arrow's fletching and passes it to me for inspection. I look it over, searching for any irregularities, but I cannot find anything. She watches me with wide eyes, waiting to see how she did. Finally satisfied, I hand it back to her. I give her a smile.

"It is perfect." She squeals happily and dashes around the table to give me a hug, excited to have learned another skill set. I grab her and swing her in a circle, making her laugh, before setting her on her feet again. "I'll make an archer out you yet!" I exclaim. Emerald's smile is so wide that I fear her face might crack.

"Can I do the others?" she asks excitedly.

"Be my guest." I pass her the other two arrows and she begins to fletch them, her nimble fingers moving quickly. After only a few minutes, four perfect arrows are sitting on the table. She looks up at me hopefully, subtly reminding me of my promise to tell her a story. I nod in answer. We wash our hands in a bucket of water before piling a bunch of blankets and cloaks on the wooden floor in front of the fireplace. I ungracefully flop down on them and pull a giggling Emerald down with me. She curls up against me and I wrap an arm around her.

We sit in silence for a few minutes as I stare into the fire, bracing myself to tell the story of my young years. Emerald does not know who I actually am and believes that the Shadow Warrior is a mythical figure.

Little does she know, the Shadow Warrior is sitting right next to her, about to tell Emerald about her childhood. Emerald is lucky and gets to believe that it is simply a story. I am not so lucky, I had to live through it.

She does not know about my magic, nor her own hidden abilities. My destiny draws close and tomorrow morning I must leave in search of the Olympians. I need their support if I am to gather an army strong enough to defeat my brothers. If they refuse, my chances of vanquishing Chaos are gone.

I hope this story will prepare Emerald for what she is soon to learn. After tomorrow, she very well might hate me. Even if she doesn't, it will create a rift between us. There will be no more comfortable nights in front of the fire, telling stories after she learns who I truly am. I push these terrible thoughts away and begin my story.

"I suppose that the best place to start is the beginning. After all, every great warrior must start somewhere, even the Shadow Warrior." Emerald gives a small gasp and looks up at me, her expression one of extreme happiness. She has asked me many times in the past to tell her the story of the childhood of the mythical Shadow Warrior, but I have always refused, claiming that nobody knows. She always responded that I should make it up. Now she finally gets to hear it, but little does she know, this is not a fantasy, created by my imagination. This is what actually happened and it is what started the war.

"It all started with two children, aged only to the year of nine, the Dark and the Light, and of course, two young stallions. The children were named Elren and Draemir. Growing up, they were inseparable. They sparred with each other, competed, grew, and together they became fierce warriors. Both were of equal strength, even though one was a girl and the other a boy. Their parents watched them grow up in this manner and the Light loved that her daughter was just as strong and powerful as her brother. However, the Dark felt that his son should not be equal to a girl-he should be better. One day, the Dark drew Draemir aside and ordered Elren to wait in the sword arena. Curious, but obedient, she waited patiently for her brother to return.

"Every day for an entire year, the Dark pulled Draemir away from his sister and fed him with lies and hateful thoughts. Draemir would return to his sister and act like nothing had happened, but one day his sister noticed something odd- her brother was changing. When they were not training, Draemir would withdraw from his sister and sit quietly with a brooding expression. When Elren approached him about it, he snapped at her to go away. Hurt, the girl left him and went to her mother. The Light comforted her and said that Chaos was simply getting older and wanted some time to himself. The girl pointed out that she was just as old as her brother and did not need time alone. The Light solemnly turned to her daughter and said five very important words that would forever change the girl's life.

"You are not like him." This took Elren by surprise, for she and her brother were identical, except for the fact that his eyes were a deep-sea-blue and his hair a dark brown while her eyes were light blue and her hair a golden brown. Being young, she did not understand what her mother meant. It only occurred to her later that she and her brother can look similar, but on the inside, they are completely different.

"The Dark began to realize that there was only one way to make his son better than his daughter. He set the date of the Decision Day, and on that day, he would name the heir of his and his wife's power. A smaller portion would go to one, and the biggest to the other twin. The chosen one would be sent to the humans and was supposed to save them.

"The girl felt the tension in the air and immediately knew that something was about to go horribly wrong, but nobody would listen. All

30

the castle servants stopped speaking to her and eventually even Draemir was avoiding her. The only one who stayed with her was a beautiful young stallion whose coat was pure silver in color with ice blue runes across it. One day, she asked him for his name. He turned and looked at her, nobility, wisdom, and intelligence all represented in one creature. He spoke to her and he responded,

"My name is Enbarr of the Flowing Mane and I will never leave you. I am yours and you are mine." Then he dissipated into a beam of light, stunning the girl.

"Only a few minutes passed before the twins were summoned to the grand throne room. There, the Dark named Draemir to be his heir and gave him a young stallion with a coat the color of the darkest part of the sea. The horse was called Kelpie of the Deep and he and Enbarr of the Flowing Mane were twins. After the Light formally gave Elren her power and Enbarr, the Dark turned to his daughter and bluntly told her that she was now weaker than Draemir and she must faithfully serve him. In that moment, something snapped within Elren. Up until this point she had been obedient and loyal, but this was too much for her temper and her pride. She defied both her father and her brother, going past the point of return.

"On that day, her brother finished their friendship. He attacked her, attempting to kill his own twin sister who had done nothing to him except give him her loyalty."

I look down at Emerald, still curled up next to me. She is staring into the embers of the fire as if watching the Shadow Warrior's young life unfold before her eyes. I hide the bitterness from my expression and voice as I think about that terrible day. That was the day I locked all emotions away and I built walls around my mind. Only three beings have access, Emerald, Enbarr, and Enbarr's son, Stormy, who is my other battle horse.

These memories that Emerald asked for are the most painful ones that I have and she is the only one I would relive them for. After taking a deep breath, I quietly finish the story.

"Draemir hit his sister with powerful magic, enough to kill ten mortals, and when Elren slowly stood up again, she looked at him, betrayal and shock written across her face. She stared at him for a moment, noting the hard light in his deep-sea-blue eyes. It was clear that he hated her, for the Dark had told him that one day she would challenge him for that power and could possibly win. Draemir was ready to kill his twin sister to keep this power. Left with no choice, the girl and her faithful horse fled and trained on their own among the mundane humans, waiting for the day that she would become stronger than her brother so that when that day comes, she will be able to kill him." I pause for a few minutes to let the story sink in before adding the closing line.

"Emerald, always remember that it is not the beginning that matters, it is the ending that counts. The Shadow Warrior may be weaker than Chaos, but the fates decreed that one day she would be stronger than her twin." Emerald looks away from the fire and steadily looks up at me, content with her lot in life. Guilt pulls at me, making me feel ill. I wish I did not have to tell her that I am leaving tomorrow. One way or another, her life will be changing.

"I have a very important announcement to tell you," I say quietly. Emerald suddenly sits up and faces me, the tone of my voice immediately setting her on edge.

"Shadow, what is it? What is wrong?" she asks, her voice rising in pitch as her concern escalates.

"I do not know how to easily say this, but you will be given a choice. A war is coming and I must fight. First, I must go on a long journey, sailing south to find some old friends who will hopefully join me.

It will be long and hard, and I cannot guarantee that I will return. You can remain here if you want, but you would need to be careful because I will not be here to protect you. If you decide to join me, we will face many dangers, but we will face them together. I will not force you to come if you do not want to. It is completely up to you." Emerald stares at me, her face a mask of shock and fear, but she quickly nods.

"Yes! Of course I want to go! When do we leave?"

"Are you sure?" I ask.

"Yes, I am." Her voice is steady and I marvel at her courage.

"Then pack your bag. We leave at first light."

Chapter Three

Shadow

I pay the captain of the ship and signal to Emerald to lead our horses off the ship.

"Thank you," I call up to the grizzled captain once I reach the sand.

"Are you sure you don't want to be taken anywhere else? No extra charge," the captain offers, concern evident in his voice as he looks at the small island that will be underwater when high tide comes. Clearly he believes that I am crazy.

"No, sir, I am sure we will be fine. Have a safe journey back."

"Your funeral!" he yells back before the oarsmen on the starboard side give a powerful thrust and the ship pivots neatly before quickly disappearing from view.

"Um, so what *are* we doing on this tiny sandbar in the middle of the Lost Sea? I don't see anyone here." In answer, I point south again and as the wind shifts, it temporarily shows us a glimpse of a massive body of land ahead.

"How are we supposed to get there? I don't see another boat." She asks, looking doubtfully at the shoreline that appears far away, but in reality it is only about a mile away. This time I point at our horses. Stormy gives me a judgmental look that clearly says that it is rude to point. I quickly lower my hand.

"It is a good thing that Stormy and Rosy are strong swimmers." Without another word, I throw the reins over Stormy's head and vault lightly onto his bare back. After a moment of hesitation, Emerald shrugs and leads her mare, Rosy, over to a convenient rock and jumps on. The

34

horses pick their way down the beach and into the water. It is surprisingly warm, despite being late Fall and the currents aid the horses moving us along even faster. The horses' strong legs beat the water and without faltering, they carry us to the Isle of the Olympians.

There are still a few hours of light left in the day when the horses finally climb out of the surf. I slip off Stormy's back and quickly step away as he shakes all the water from his coat. When he is finished, I reach up and take his bridle off. Emerald hands me Rosy's bridle as well and I sling them over my shoulder before trudging up the beach. Stormy follows me up the beach and I pick a spot near the treeline for our camp. I neatly place my bag on the ground and pull out my bow case. I quickly pull my bow out and string it before slinging it over my shoulder. Emerald dumps her bag on the ground and looks at me questioningly, waiting for directions.

"Could you go find some herbs for a stew? I will go see if I can catch anything to eat. Stay close to the beach and do not go far in." She nods and heads off into the woods. I watch her for a few seconds before heading into the woods, going in a different direction.

Emerald

The forest is eerily quiet, no birds chirping, and no animals rustling in the underbrush. *I see why Shadow wants me to stay close to the beach. This is creepy!* I scan the ground, looking for herbs for about twenty minutes and cannot find anything.

A voice suddenly says, "There is some on your left there." I wheel around, drawing a throwing knife, to see a beautiful, tall, and lean woman in a plain gray tunic. *How did she sneak up on me? I did not hear anything!* Something's familiar about her and it takes me a moment, but then I pin it. She looks similar to Shadow, just shorter and a bit less

35

muscular. She has brown hair with golden highlights and tan skin with a serious expression, but there is a good deal of humor in her eyes.

Her eyes are a startling silver that are almost glowing in the fading light. Even as I watch though, they change color and become a kaleidoscope of different grays. I wish my green eyes would do that. I realize that I am staring and I blush. Her steady gaze looks me up and down and I fancy that I catch a gleam of something in her expression. *Is it doubt? No. Disappointment. She expected more.* This thought makes my skin crawl and I feel as if I am suddenly a foot shorter, even though I have no idea who this is.

"Who are you?" I ask, my voice quivering slightly.

"I am Artemis, the Goddess of the Hunt and the Moon. Your sister is waiting for you back at your camp. She is worried that you are lost." She turns and leads the way back to Shadow. I hurriedly grab the herbs and run after the goddess.

She looks up when she sees us and smiles at Artemis. "I should have figured you would be the first one to find us, Artemis." I look back and forth between them with wide eyes.

"You know each other?"

"Yes," Shadow replies, watching me carefully. "We are best friends. We used to go hunting together."

"In all honesty, I did not know that you went hunting with anyone. Why didn't you tell me this before, back when we were living in the woods?" I ask feeling a little hurt that there was so much I did not know.

Artemis and Shadow exchange a long look and finally Shadow gives a small nod and a shrug. Artemis turns to me and studies me as if trying to decide what to say. Shadow turns her attention to the fire she is building, not looking at me. Concern makes my stomach turn. I can't figure out what is happening. Everyone is moving too fast.

"Your sister is the Shadow Warrior, formerly known as Elren Caerin, and you, Emerald, have the ability to wield magic," Artemis says slowly and deliberately, carefully choosing her words. The world spins around me and I don't know what to think, or to say, or what to do. *Is this a good thing? Is this a bad thing? Who is she really?* Anger replaces my confusion and it dictates my words.

"Shadow, look at me," I demand. She ignores me, continuing to build the fire. *"Look at me!"* My voice rises in pitch as terror threatens to control me. Shadow slowly turns her head and steadily looks at me, her ice blue eyes piercing mine. There is a warning written in them and I lower my voice. "Is it true? Are you the Shadow Warrior?" Very slowly she nods. "Prove it." I respond instantly. *It cannot be true. If it is, she has lied and betrayed me.* In response, Shadow stands up and looks down at me.

"How would I be able to tell you those stories if it weren't me?" she asks quietly. Everything about Shadow is still and quiet. Usually her fingers are fidgeting with something, but now she is standing stock-still, like an animal trying to camouflage itself.

"You lied to me and betrayed my trust," I reply, trying to keep my voice steady. Shadow meets my angry gaze calmly and no trace of emotion shows on her face. She gives me a stern expression and I shut my mouth. The last time I spoke to her like this I had to sleep outside for a week. She continues to look at me, clearly irritated by my childish behavior. My cheeks flush with shame. I am suddenly aware of Artemis's cold look and I look down at the ground.

"I did the best I could to raise you. I could not tell you everything. You were too young and you needed to figure out your abilities on your own. I could not do that for you. I gave up freedom, and many people have suffered, simply because I saved you from a life studying needlepoint, sewing, and raising a squalling brood of little children. I stopped chasing Chaos and I also had to stop cleaning up the messes he created because I chose to take care of you instead. I see now just how grateful you are for everything I've done for you." There is that deadly calm look on her face, but her icy eyes shine with anger. I know that look to mean that she is extremely angry. *Great. Everyone seems to hate me today.* "We are sisters and I have not lied to you. I never denied that you were special. Everything I have told you is what I know. I did not reveal who I was to keep you safe and to keep you separate from my fate."

I take a half pace backward. Her face is still and emotionless as a statue, but the anger blazing in her eyes is unnerving. Her blue eyes are as cold and sharp as ice. For the first time, ever, I see a side of her that the enemies on a battlefield see. This is not the Shadow that I know. This is a tall and fierce warrior, as cold and merciless as the biting sword at her hip.

I can see her fighting to recall her temper. At this time, Artemis decides to step in. She steps up next to Shadow and starts to talk to her rapidly in a different language that I cannot understand. The next moment, she sits down again and Shadow turns on her heel and stalks off into the forest.

Chapter Four

Shadow

I try to control my temper, but I can't. The only solution is for me to get away before I say something I will regret later. As soon as I get into the forest, I start to run. *How can she accuse me of lying? It is not my fault that she was not allowed to know about her gifts and that I am the Shadow Warrior.* There are certain laws to magic that even I must obey. I run faster and faster not paying attention to where I am going. I start to climb up a steep hill, basically a small cliff. At the top I stop for a moment and sit down to collect my thoughts.

After only a minute or two I hear the angry snap of a twig being stepped on. Someone swears at its companion's big feet in a coarse voice. Instantly, I have my bow loaded and half drawn. These are ancient woods. I realize that there is a large and ancient tree four paces to my right. It should provide sufficient shelter from sight. After stuffing the arrow back into my quiver, I silently dart over to it. When the creatures come around the bend, I catch my breath. Whatever they are, they are definitely not human.

They have the bodies of men, but they are dark gray in color with eyes the color of snow as it melts and leaves the mountain tops. They don't seem to have a solid shape and they are not speaking Arindal either. For some reason, I can understand them. They have the camouflage clothes that the New World soldiers wear, just like the men I met last week. There are two of them. I select a regular arrow and nock it to the string of my bow. I stand up and quickly aim and shoot at the nearest one. The arrow just misses his heart as he jumps away just in time to ward off

39

the killing shot. I swear quietly as it only catches him in the arm. His shape becomes more distinct and he bellows in rage.

"It is that blasted hunting goddess! No other arrow can pierce our skin." I quickly load another arrow and aim at the giant. This time I do not miss. It pierces his chest and a moment later he drops dead as my ice blue magic consumes him. The other has no concern for his fallen friend. He grabs his double-bladed axe with one hand and swings it as if it weighs nothing. I duck behind the tree and then take a deep breath, gathering my courage and smoothly step into the clearing to face the mutant man. As usual, the normal surge of battle adrenaline and excitement of an upcoming fight chases away any fear. My face is emotionless, betraying nothing.

"Who are you?" I demand, my bow never wavering from my aim at his throat. I unsheathe Tíne and lower my bow and in one smooth movement, I throw it to one side and fully expose the blade as I have many times before in practice. At that time, I did not realize I would need that skill against a mutant shadow man. "Who are you?" I demand again, my voice has an edge as sharp as my blade.

"I a Maximus Umbrus. You die. Wait. You not Goddess? You look like Goddess. Who you?" he asks in rough Arindal.

"I am not the goddess, but I am far more dangerous." With that, I attack and land a glancing blow on his shoulder. I feel my strength and power rising as I call it. Tíne flickers with blue flames. His eyes widen with shock and he tries to run, but I am already upon him. I stab him in the chest and he evaporates completely into a cloud of gray. I collect my bow and head back to the camp at a run. I hear the deep rolling voices of the Maximi Umbri. There are many more coming. Once again, I duck behind the cover of a nearby tree.

"We must catch the Hunting Goddess! The masters will be furious if she gets the mysterious back up that she claims to have. Lord Chaos will torture, then kill us himself." I start when I hear my brothers name, and angrily chastise myself for fearing him. *I must be the help that they spoke of.* The shadow giants move past the tree. I cannot let them catch me. There are too many of them for me to kill all of them, but I unsling my bow and start to shoot rapidly, my hands a blur of motion. Puffs of gray and blue cover the clearing as they disintegrate, making it difficult to aim. There are ten left by the time I empty my quiver. I take off again back into the woods before they spot me. I let my feet guide me back to the camp.

Emerald and I must be the backup that was mentioned. *How do you kill a shadow?* Then it hits me. They cannot stand the light. That is how to kill them! Magic is always in the form of fire.

It isn't long before I burst out onto the beach. Artemis is instantly on her feet with her bow half drawn when she hears me running out of the woods. I stumble when I hit the soft sand.

"It's only me," I say as I get closer. I slow to a walk as I get closer to the fire Emerald built. I notice that Artemis has not lowered her bow. "It really is me," I say and pointedly look at her raised bow. To prove it, I let some of my magic pool on my hand. It's ice blue glow lights up the space around us so they can see me clearly. Only then does she lower her bow.

"Stormy! Rosy! Surefire! Time to come in closer for the night!" I call into the darkness. They come running over to the warmth of the fire. The autumn chill makes me shiver slightly and sends my thoughts to my warm cloak back in our house on the mainland. I chastise myself for forgetting to bring it. Surefire comes over and pokes me with his nose in greeting. Artemis's horse looks me over before snorting and walking

41

away. I watch his retreating form curiously. Artemis's normally energetic horse looks haggard and battle weary.

"What made you come running back so soon?" Emerald asks. I give her an icy glare before I sit with my back to the tree and recount to them what happened in the forest. Artemis sits back and stares at me. Emerald has gone pale and she glances at the forest as if they are going to come charging out any second. Finally, Artemis breaks the long silence.

"You are able to kill the Maximus Umbrus? Most of the gods were not able to kill them. Our arrows are deadly to them. Apollo and I are the only ones who could kill them. Unfortunately Apollo was captured two weeks ago."

"Emerald, you have the right to know that I have always been aware of your magic ever since the day my brother killed your family. When magic is not in use, it is in the form of fire. My fire is ice blue as you have seen. Your magic is an emerald green. If you use too much magic your fire will grow dimmer and you will be weak until your magic is recovered. Magic flows through our blood. If your fire is completely extinguished, you are dead. Ipso facto. End of story. However, if you are properly trained, you can strengthen your magic. The more often you use it, the longer it will hold out. It also depends on how strong you are. Not physically or mentally, but both together," I conclude. She struggles to digest all the important information I just threw at her.

"So, you are saying that we can kill the giant shadow things with magic-that-is-fire and *possibly* not get killed in the attempt?" Emerald finally asks. "Why aren't the other Olympians helping us?" Artemis sighs heavily.

"The Maximus Umbrus, or Maximi Umbri in the plural, have imprisoned all of the gods. As I said before, I have only lasted this long because I have waited for Shadow to help save us. You were right,

Shadow. The next time you met with the Olympians would be in a time of our great need. I have watched you your entire life, Emerald. Shadow and I have been friends for a very long time. I knew that I would need you two. I did not know that I would need your help with something this extreme. We will have to break the cages that they are in. This is my home. We must regain control of the Olympian Island, which is the seat of our power," she finishes. I turn to my empty quiver and lightly touch it with magic and a whole fresh set of arrows appears.

"Where did those come from?" Emerald asks, still awestruck by her first encounters with magic.

"Our house. I made a lot and put them in storage, so if I summon them, they are ready to go."

"Couldn't you just make a whole bunch appear, even if you did not make them yet?" I nod, appreciating the question.

"I could, but I like to know that I made them because all of mine are weighted and measured to be the exact same so there aren't any unforeseen differences, or that may be embarrassing. If I summoned them randomly, I would be taking them from random places around the world. Of course, though, in a pinch, I could do that without a problem. I have only ever accidentally summoned a quiver of crossbow quarrels once." I smile at the distant memory from my childhood. "Now that I have completely overloaded your brain, good night!" I lean back against the cold tree and find myself wishing I could simply summon a cloak.

Right before drifting off, I hear Emerald ask Artemis, "Do you do that, too? It seems overly complicated."

I wake up to the soft chirping of birds and sit up quickly. The first thing I notice is that it is *very* cold. I glance around. Emerald is still asleep and Rosy is lying next to her. Stormy is still sleeping next to me. Artemis is over by the water line with Surefire resting his head on her shoulder. She is absently staring off into the increasingly light horizon, twirling a silver arrow between her fingers. I walk over to her on silent feet. I stand next to her and Surefire and we stand in a companionable silence together, watching the sun rise over the horizon. She sighs and starts to walk back to the camp.

"We should leave soon," she says as we walk. I nod in acknowledgment of the fact. I gently nudge Emerald with the toe of my boot. She sits up quickly with her dagger unsheathed. It whips through the air where my foot had been not a moment before. She smiles sheepishly at me. Artemis practically falls over in laughter as I jump back in surprise and end up tripping over myself and landing on my backside in the sand.

"Gather your weapons and let's go!" I say trying to regain what is left of my dignity. I grab my own bow and quiver and slip them over my shoulders. My long dagger and my sword are already in their sheaths at my belt. Artemis is still chuckling as she grabs her bow and quiver. She also has her long dagger in its sheath at her belt. Stormy kicks sand over the fire and we head off into the woods with Artemis in the lead.

CRACK!

Still flighty and all my senses tuned up super high, I practically jump out of my boots.

"I think that stick wants an apology, Emerald," I say dryly over my shoulder to her. She giggles at the familiar comment from the stalking lessons, back when I attempted to teach her how to hunt. Artemis shoots Emerald a sharp look. We keep walking, a companionable silence settling over the group. In no time, we come across the camp. It is hidden deep in the very middle of the forest.

"Here is the plan, Artemis and I will send a volley of arrows into the fort on the far side. We will distract them for as long as possible. Then we will start to fight, me with my sword and Artemis with her knife. You,

Emerald, will sneak around the fort to where the gods and goddesses are being held. Light your dagger with your magic and cut the locks off. To do that, focus and envision green fire going up into your dagger. Athena will join the fight and we can destroy them once and for all.

Chapter Five

Emerald

Shadow leans down and gives me a crushing hug.

"Be safe," she whispers into my ear. Her voice is calm and cool as if she does this every day, but it suddenly hits me that this might be the last time I ever see her. She is putting her life on the line for strangers who she has never even met. At least I don't think she has ever met them. I recently discovered that there is very little that I do know about her, so she may have already met them for all I know. I close my eyes and hug her back. I struggle not to cry, but I cannot help it. I cling to her as if she is already gone. My breath comes in sobbing gasps.

"Please! Don't do this! Please!" I beg. She gently disentangles herself from me.

"I am doing this for you. I promise that I will see you again. One way or another." I look up into her vibrant blue eyes, trying to pierce the thick wall that covers all her fear. I have never noticed it before now. I have always thought her to be fearless. It is simpler to think about it like that. "Just remember this: I will always protect you. Everything I have ever done is to keep you safe. I am always with you. I have always been proud of you." She holds my gaze for a moment more. I can see the sincerity of her statement and that facade of confidence. Although, I would not be surprised if it was true courage. "Let's go," she announces calmly. She and Artemis melt off into the forest like wraiths and I stand there for a moment more before mentally shaking myself.

"She *will* live!" I say fiercely to the trees and whatever else may be listening to me. The back of my mind reminds me that she has fought harder adversaries, but I ignore it. Anything can happen when fighting is present. When I look around, I end up staring at a figure in front of me. It is my mother, but only a shade of her. She wears a leaf-green dress and when I look closer, I realize that it is *made* of leaves. She puts her hand in front of her mouth and blows a honey brown dust at me. It goes straight through me and suddenly I feel taller. Stronger. Braver. She kisses her hand and blows it to me. To my surprise, it is not a heart or anything sentimental like that, but two words.

Prepare yourself. She vanishes into the woods and after a moment of standing there stunned, I jog off towards the area where the gods are being held. My feet feel lighter. As does my heart, even though her words are permanently etched into my mind.

I light my dagger with green fire for the first time in my life, before stealthily tucking myself into a shadowy area. On the far wall, I see the first volley of arrows. Bright blue and silver flames flicker out of the sky and take out the first defenders. Every Maximus Umbrus runs over to the far wall and forms ranks in front of the two warriors.

They stand boldly in front of the force of shadow-fighters. My sister raises her sword. It burns with her wild ice blue fire and she holds it in front of her with pride. Artemis has her bow slung over her shoulders. Her long dagger glows the color of liquid moonlight. I catch my breath in awe. Despite that they are hopelessly out numbered they stand bravely without a trace of fear in their expressions. They each yell a battle cry and charge. Shadow yells something like: *dum spero, vivo.* My mind struggles through the translation. Shadow taught me the Old Language for many years and I understand it to say: *While I hope, I live.* A statement as fitting of a battle cry as I have ever heard.

As I watch, I am amazed by their skill. Shadow wipes out huge waves of the monstrous creatures with a single wave of her sword. Artemis takes out many with her dagger and stabs and slashes with

47

terrifying speed and dexterity. Her form seems to spark and I am certain that she is glowing silver. They are almost unrecognizable in the heat of the battle. Shadow has a fierce expression of fury and intense concentration written on her face. Artemis has a similar expression.

Shadow no longer looks like a regular seventeen-year-old. The years fall away until she looks ageless. Neither old nor young. Suddenly, I realize that Shadow has always been the same. Same personality, same looks, but now I am seeing a whole different person. I am not sure who it is anymore. The Shadow I thought I knew never would have kept such incredibly important secrets from me, but I guess that I have never known her as Elren.This powerful, terrifying, and awe-inspiring creature is who she really is. It isn't a comforting thought.

I look away from the fight and focus on the task at hand. I quickly cut the locks off the cells. The Olympians stand silently by the doors of their shadow prisons. The dark, marbled grey magic forms shackles and bars they cannot break, but my knife easily cuts through them. It was not forged by Hephaestus like the Olympian blades, but by Shadow herself.

"Go!" I yell as they burst out of the cells. Athena joins me in opening the cages and as the last Olympian runs from the last cage, I turn back and wordlessly point to the battle at hand. My sister and Artemis are still fighting for their lives. I hand Athena my green dagger, which immediately turns golden in her grip, and she runs screaming out into the struggling fray of monsters to help the two brave warriors. Finally, there are only five Maximi Umbri left. They are taller and stronger than the others. The two goddesses and my sister form a tight triangle. For the first time, they look uncertain.

"Fight. Well. No. Match. Original. Maximus. Umbrus. Skills. Nothing. Compared. To. Us. Crush. You. You. Not. Able. Withstand. Our.

Strength. Come. Little. Warrior. Do. You. Believe. You. Can. Take. Us. On?" they all chant together in stilted and rough Arindal. It is terrifying to hear the unvarying tones of their voices. These are monsters. Suddenly, one lunges with blinding speed at Shadow. She reacts immediately and parries his sword away. He is back upon her in a second. He fights with brute strength and she fights with speed. She dips and weaves, avoiding his deadly strength. The others are fighting around her, but I only have eyes for her.

After a while I finally manage to tear my eyes off her graceful form and glance around at the others. Artemis and Athena are fighting one of the monsters together. I have lost sight of the other three shadow men. I look back at Shadow. She is still wielding her sword in a deadly dance. She spots an opening as he takes a wild swipe where she had been only a moment ago. She stabs upward and he disintegrates into a cloud of gray dust. Suddenly, I feel a cold, cruel blade pressing against the soft skin under my chin.

"What do we have here?" the creature croons. I choke back a scream as he laughs, a deep gravelly sound that sounds quite similar to a trunk being dragged across cobblestones. "Oh!" he says quietly in surprise as a throwing knife pierces his broad chest. He disintegrates and the gray magic blows in the wind. I look up to thank my savior and I see a sight that makes my blood run cold.

In the moment that Shadow had taken to throw the knife, a Maximus Umbrus had come up behind her. She looks down in surprise as a blade protrudes from her chest, just below her right collarbone. A moment later, she crumples at his feet. Without comprehending what I had just seen, I throw one of my knives at the creature with all the fury and strength that I possess. I howl with grief, hate, and rage as I grab another knife. I charge into the fight and take on the nearest Maximus

Umbrus, fearing nothing for my own safety, a safety that Shadow sacrificed herself for me to enjoy. Everything she ever taught me about fighting comes to the fore of my mind and my body reacts immediately, both saving my life and taking the lives of others. It is a glorious and empowering sensation, but horrible and revolting when reality brings my mind down again, but the dread cannot hold down the desire to kill.

I can see nothing but green. I look down and realize that I am glowing a strong and vivid green with swirls of honey colored magic mixed in. I do not care. Nothing matters now. I kill the last Maximus Umbrus with three swift blows of my knife. Artemis and Athena have killed the other. Panting, I look around the fort to see that the other Olympians have gathered around the edge of the field. I look over at the body of my sister. All the rage I had felt disappeared. Now all I feel is shock and a peculiar numbness in my chest. My limbs shake uncontrollably as I stumble over to her lifeless body and stare in disbelief.

"Save her!" I scream and half sob to all the immortals standing in the clearing. None move. A soft breeze wafts through the clearing, it almost seems to hesitate and struggle to get through the dense layer of sorrow and silence before picking up again and passing on.

"Brother! Can you help her?" Artemis calls to Apollo. Artemis's twin brother comes over and checks for a pulse. When there isn't one, he gives me a miserable look, his golden brown eyes welling up with tears.

"I am sorry. No one can revive the dead. Not even Hades himself," he says sadly. His beautiful bay mare hangs her head mournfully. I feel as if the air has left me. *No. She cannot be dead! She is the brave older sister who is supposed to make everything alright.*

"*NO!*" I cry. "I cannot lose you! You must come back to me! I love you! You cannot die!" I kneel next to her and sob as exhaustion, pain, and grief wash over me. I am oblivious to everything around me.

"Please," I whisper in her ear. All the hurtful words that I said last night come back to me and torture my mind. Suddenly, ice blue magic covers her body and I feel a flicker of a pulse on her neck. It gets stronger and stronger and my eyes grow large. "She is alive," I whisper. It feels like an eternity, but she finally opens her eyes.

"I may have forgotten to mention that I love you, Emerald," she whispers. I hug her as hard as I can. When she sits up, there is no trace of the wound except a strange series of symbols in beautiful ice blue writing that look like ancient runes. She reads it and grimaces before pulling her collar higher to hide them from sight. I look at her curiously, but before I can ask anything, a loud cheer rings through the crowd. I help her to her feet. She immediately gives me a rib cracking hug.

"Dum speras, vivo," she whispers in my ear. The words continue to resonate through my ears like a musical note that continues to ring, even after the song ended long ago.

While you hope, I live.

The crowd parts as the three most powerful gods step through. Zeus, Poseidon, and Hades stride towards us. The first two of the three look surprised and happy, while Hades's expression is thunderous with irritation due to Shadow's escape from his realm. Athena and Artemis hastily step out of the way.

"We do not understand how this has hap-" Stormy and Rosy choose this moment to gallop in on the scene. They stop next to us before looking up expectantly at the tall gods. I had just watched my sister die, strike that, almost die and somehow come back from the brink of death. I even killed a giant shadow or two. If I thought that I could not be more surprised than I already was, I was *so* wrong.

"Please continue." A completely human voice comes from Rosy's mouth. Zeus acts as if this is completely normal and he continues as if there was never an interruption.

"Commander Caerin," he addresses my sister formally, "for your unrelenting bravery in battle, we owe you a great debt. You fought with skill that is unmatched by any mortal, or immortal, being. You faced numbers that were far superior to you and my daughters' small number of three. You stared into the face of death to protect the Olympians. You sacrificed your life to save your sister. I would normally give you the gift of immortality, but it would appear that you already possess that trait. You belong in the ranks of the most worshiped gods. Unfortunately you leave me in a difficult predicament. I cannot repay you for your great deeds. All of us are in your debt and this has never happened before. If you ever need anything, just ask and it will be as you wish," he declares. He turns to me and I find that unlike Shadow, I cannot meet his intense gaze. I peek up at him quickly and a bright red blush creeps across my cheeks upon seeing his handsome face.

"Emerald." Shadows voice is low and urgent, clearly an order. I glance at her and she nods reassuringly. Taking a deep breath, I force myself to look into his clear sky blue eyes. His gaze is calculating as he studies me. *Probably trying to see if it is worth his time to even mention me.* The corner of his mouth turns up in humor and he almost seems to have read my thoughts. I look down again at the ground, unable to meet his eyes anymore. I can feel Shadow's disapproving glare, but she doesn't say anything.

"You, Emerald Alián, also played a major part in the saving of our world. Shadow has reminded us all what sacrifice truly is. Your sister did everything she possibly could to keep you safe. When that protection was gone, you fought harder than ever. You have a heart that is made of

52

gold. For your bravery and compassion, I am glad to be able to give you immortality." I look up in surprise, forgetting my shyness. He smiles and waves his hand. All the gods and goddesses cheer and stamp. Formalities over, Artemis runs forward and gives Shadow a huge hug. I am surprised to see that she is crying.

"I thought I had lost you! Don't ever do that again!" Artemis reprimands in a shaky voice. When she pulls away she is smiling. "Welcome to the life of the Olympians."

Shadow

I look into those ever-changing silver eyes of my long standing best friend, Artemis, and the golden-brown eyes of my other best friend, Athena. I look down and see that Tíne is on the ground at my feet and I grasp the well-worn leather covered hilt of my beloved sword. I put it into its scabbard after inspecting the blade and grimacing at the deep nicks left by an Maximus Umbrus's battle axe. After using magic to fix it, I look into the eyes of Athena and Artemis and smile.

"Now what?" I ask, already looking for something to do. Artemis laughs her clear, ringing, and rare laugh and drapes one long arm around my shoulder and the other on Emerald's. The child stares up at Artemis, shock in her expression. She finally proved herself to the goddess.

"I will let you know when the time comes. For now, allow me to show you around our peaceful island." I smile to myself, but it fades when I hear Athena's question. She is staring at my newest scar as it shows above my collar.

"What does the rune mean?" Athena finally asks. I stop and turn to face them, my expression suddenly grim.

"There is not a single word in Arindal, Kreg, Talin, Remic, or any of the hundreds of languages that I know that has a single word that

exactly translates it, but it essentially is a warning." Artemis impatiently
makes a rolling gesture with her hand as she starts to become irritated by
my stalling. Her silver bow waves through the air wildly and Emerald
ducks as it whips through the space where her head had just been.

"Out with it! What does it mean?" Artemis urges. I look up from
the convenient beetle I had been pretending to study.

"It basically means that this is only the beginning." A stunned
silence falls over the little group and their expressions slowly become
grim as they realize how naive it was to believe that this battle was the
end of the matter. I reluctantly add, "There are more that go with it from
years past." I pull back the collar of my shirt and right under my left
collarbone is another ruin, but this one is very long. "This is also a
warning. It means I am too young to die. Too many are counting on me to
leave just yet. You cannot escape your destiny that easily." This time the
silence is so thick that you can see it swirl through the air. I can practically
see all the questions going through their heads.

"There are many more." I hold my breath and slowly let it out. I
allow my other runes to come back to the surface. They all gasp as my
skin is covered by little ice blue symbols that appear like beautiful and
terrible tattoos. All of them together are the same ice blue words across
Enbarr's skin. I read a random one on the back of my hand and skim
through something about a wolf warrior. I drag the ancient runes back
under the surface, but as usual, a few refuse to leave. Those that refuse to
leave are the healed wounds that should have killed me, but did not. The
most obvious, but overlooked mark is the long scar down the left side of
my face. It was given to me by a cursed blade and symbolizes a promise
of revenge.

That scar was given to me the day I decided that Elren was too weak. It was the day I became a mere shade of myself. I became a shadow of my brother as well.

A heavy silence falls over the whole group and they all stare at me. I shift my weight from foot to foot, uncomfortable under their scrutiny. The silence stretches on for another minute or two before Emerald, being totally off topic, as usual, suddenly announces,

"We need to get firewood and stock up for winter." As always, the youngest is the practical one, always moving on. I remember the flashes of memories brought to the forefront of my mind while in battle. As usual, I saw a past time when I was a youngling with a bow, quickly fast forwarding to a gangly teenager with a sword, and then a young adult right before I left for the market on the day where our lives changed forever. A day when secrets were finally revealed.

The last memory was not a moment in a fight, but of a time more peaceful. Emerald and I had been sitting by the fire laughing at a story she had told about a drunk stable boy in the village as he tried to kiss a girl, but somehow ended up with the mule. I had held her close and I still remember the long-kept promise I had whispered into her young ears. *I will always be there for you, if you never let go of Hope.* I will never get used to the sensation of dying but then abruptly being pulled back from the endless abyss. I'll never be able to die if people continue to believe in Hope. Apparently Hope still roams free. That is, for now.

Three Weeks Later

Chapter Six

Shadow

A log falls off the sled with a deafening thud as Emerald laboriously pulls it up the hill and I flinch to the left, grabbing the hilt of my sword tightly at the suddenness of the loud sound. After twenty more minutes of walking,

Crack!

This time I jump the other way and completely unsheathe my sword as yet *another* stick breaks under Emerald's foot as we walk through the foggy gloom.

"Could you be a little louder, please. I don't think everyone in the New World heard you," I reprimand irritably. The entire time we have been in the woods, it has sounded like her feet have grown to be three feet long.

Unlike in the past, no humor has accompanied our trek through the woods today. She glances at me, her expression sullen, before looking down and placing her feet carefully into the soggy mixture of melting snow and mud on the ground. "There could be ten bandits ahead and you would just be plodding along and walk straight into an ambush, keep your head up!" I bark suddenly. She winces slightly at my blunt tone. I never let her get away with anything.

"That's why you are here," she mumbles.

"I'm not always going to be there," I respond quietly. She looks away and falls silent.

She is my apprentice and I have attempted, with emphasis on *attempted*, to teach her wood craft and sword play. Any of these skills could, and probably will, save her life one day, if only she would just try harder! I would teach her archery, but she is simply unable to understand the elevation and range that you need, along with an instinctive feel for the angles. She has good aim and a great throw with her knives and she is fine with her small and low powered hunting bow, but that could never punch through armor. She has never been able to shoot a real bow with any sort of accuracy.

We are preparing for a late winter storm, should it come, but I am hoping that it will not come. Gathering the wood is both exercise to get Emerald fit and to keep ourselves, Artemis, and Athena, who share a house with us, warm through the cold nights of early spring. I signal Emerald to stop before silently sheathing my sword and bringing my bow around and nocking an arrow to the string. Any slight noise could attract any type of terrible beast. Emerald could have summoned an army of them by now.

Thanks to the battle that we fought only a few weeks ago, the woods are a dangerous place. Visibility is poor this morning with the mist and rain blowing off the ocean in icy sheets. I can scarcely see my sister who is less than five paces behind me. However, I can hear her very well. Anyone, even a half deaf bear in deep hibernation, can hear her crashing steps. Finally we reach our little house on the edge of the woods. We deposit the wood on our huge stack and cover it with canvas to ward off any late snowflakes.

It has been a little over a year since Emerald and I saved the home of the Olympians. Emerald will be turning fifteen soon. I turned eighteen some time back. Even though I am immortal, I will become older until I choose not to. Age is not really a concern to me.

My mind flips back to Emerald's waiting sword practice session later and I internally groan. My shoulder is already stiff from my own weapon sparring session with Ares earlier. He caught me in the shoulder with the flat side of his blade and a giant black, blue, and green bruise has spread across my arm from the point of my shoulder to my elbow. I leave it there without numbing it to remind me never to let it happen again.

One glance at Emerald and taking in the way her feet drag through the foliage, I automatically know that my day is far from over. All Olympians are a master of their magic and at least one weapon. Even Aphrodite, goddess of beauty and how-to-be-the-most-royal-pain-in-the-butt-possible, is incredibly dangerous with her saber and neon pink magic.

Kindly, but perhaps unfortunately, Zeus publicly announced that I was the best sword master he has ever seen after the Shadow Battle. At first I was flattered, but when Olympians started asking me to help them train, or how to master some move, or challenge me to a duel, my life has become long days of my own private sword practicing in the early morning, then my archery practice. Midday, I hunt the dangerous beasts that threaten the humans with Artemis and Athena and help others with their own issues before taking the evening off, or if someone challenges me, that is when I fight them.

I guess I'm not supposed to have so much free-time, so therefore I was given the task of training Emerald in the art of weaponry and woodcraft. My friends, Artemis and Athena, help me train her as well. Though life seems to have fallen into a rhythm, the back of my mind is constantly striving to figure out Chaos's next move. Where, when, and how will he strike next?

The door flies open, banging back on its hinges with alarming force, as Artemis and Athena hurry in. They are practically bursting to tell their message.

"Hey! Shadow! Are you here?" Their eyes quickly dart around the cabin that we all share. They finally spot me where I am leaning back in a chair with my feet up on the table. I sharply glance up at them, irritated at being bothered. Weariness pulls at me, making me even more short tempered than usual.

"No," I reply sarcastically.

"Zeus has a mission for us!" Athena announces happily, not seeming to hear my curt rejoinder.

"What's up?" Emerald asks as she walks into the room to investigate all the noise. This time Artemis blurts out the summons. *Whatever is up has them very excited,* I muse to myself. I told Zeus that war is coming, and said that he would think about it. Naturally this irritated me immensely, but there is nothing to gain by angering Zeus... Not yet at least. All I can do is figuring out a way to prove to him that the war *is* coming, and that means getting in his good books. My chair slams forward onto the wooden floor and I stand up, ignoring the creaks and groans from my limbs as I stretch and yawn.

"Alright, let's go see what he has for us," I finally respond blandly, my uncaring and slightly world weary demeanor is a sharp contrast to their flushed faces and the excitement. They all practically run out the door like young children. I take the time to slowly gather my bow and quiver off the hanging board I recently made. My sword and two daggers are strapped to my leather belt as usual. Shaking off my lethargy and ill temper like a wet horse shakes off water, I sprint out of the cabin and catch up to them easily. I slow to a jog next to Emerald.

After nearly thirty minutes of steady jogging along the treacherous path, we reach the magnificent marble palace where Zeus lives and holds all the official meetings. The marble glows in the morning light, whether just by the sun or if by magic, I have never asked. My money would be on the latter. He is waiting for us on a bench under a massive and ancient oak tree. From this point, you can see the huge clearing where most of the gods and goddesses live. A few of the others live in the woods or close to the cove. He gracefully stands up to greet us.

"Thank you for coming. Would you care to come inside?" he asks politely. We follow him into the entry hall where all big meetings are held. He sits down behind the big maple wood desk. I study him in the silence. Curly light brown hair cut short paired with a wispy beard. If you did not know otherwise, you might mistake him for a twenty-year-old human. At least until you saw his eyes. They are a beautiful, clear blue for the moment, but they change with his ever-shifting mood. Even now they turn from a clear sky-blue to gray and grim.

"I have a mission for you, Athena, and Artemis. Shadow, you will lead," he announces crisply. I nod. I expected nothing else. "You may also bring your apprentice, if you wish," he adds. He is all business today. "I choose you for this quest because I know you are more knowledgeable of the mortals than most of the other Olympians. You will need to go check on your old world. I want you to find proof that Chaos is becoming more active among your people. His men are getting bolder and now they are becoming unstoppable, taking whoever they want for their New World armies. You need to give them a good reason to leave. Let them know that we are still protecting our humans. I don't know if they operate by themselves, or if they are working for *someone* else." he looks at me pointedly, clearly letting me know it is my brother. The tips of my ears turn red. I *hate* people calling attention to my family. I renounced Chaos a very long time ago. "If they are working for Chaos, then I will mobilize the Olympian army and call a council of war. You should leave immediately." He waves a hand towards the door, dismissing us. I am lost in thought as we walk out of the door.

I finally break my silence when we get back to the house. I look up and realize that the others are all looking at me expectantly.

"What?" I ask, slightly surprised by their scrutiny.

"What is this idea you are planning?" Athena asks.

"I was thinking about heading back there anyway. Emerald and I need to get some of our winter clothes," I reply. It is their turn to look surprised. They look at each other and burst out laughing at the simplicity of the statement. I frown at them.

"What else did you expect?" I ask, my previous irritation quickly coming back to the surface.

"How about a plan to foil the invading New Worlders and gather proof for Zeus that Chaos is actually gathering an army that is already stronger than ours?" Athena asks. There is a note of amusement in her voice that sparks my already short temper.

"I am working on it. Everyone gather your travel gear and let's go. Pack light! Morningsun will be most disapproving if she has to carry too much!" I reply irritably to Athena, mentioning her palomino diva of a horse. I sling my longbow over my shoulder and strap an extra dagger into the sheath in my sleeve. Emerald grabs her healer kit and throwing knives. At least seven sheaths of different lengths and shapes hang from her belt, each for a different scenario- six for the various throwing knives, and one long dagger.

"This is for you." I hold out a beautiful sword. "It is time I gave you this. It is custom for a master to give their apprentice their sword. It is called Tréan, or Strong. I thought that it needed a name that suits the one who wields it. I am also tired of having to get rid of the nicks and sharpening Tíne's blade as you dull the edges during your training sessions. You will find this one easier than Tíne because this one is shorter and lighter." She stares at the beautiful sword with an emerald stone set deep into the cross piece for another minute before crushing me in a giant hug.

"Happy early birthday!" I manage to choke out. *She is becoming strong!* Her smile shows her gratitude. She attaches the sheathed sword to her belt like me.

"Artemis! Athena! Are you coming? Or should we leave without you?" I call. They hurry out of their rooms with their weapons. We all stand at the shore and board the little boat waiting for us. I shove it off the shore and wade in after it. I vault into the boat and a light shower of water flies into the boat after me. I reach back into the water and throw a cold wave of salt water in their faces, beaming ingeniously as they spit the water out of their mouths and glare at me. Blocking them out, I close my eyes in concentration. I can feel the current under the boat through the soles of my feet. It bends at my request and it changes direction and takes us out to sea.

"We will arrive in a few hours," I finally say as I open my eyes.

It turns out that my calculations were incorrect. The shore comes into sight within the hour. The current must be stronger than I anticipated.

"Prepare to land!" I call as I ease the boat into the shallows. Once again, I vault out of the boat and into the water. I slowly tow the boat onto the beach. Everyone quickly disembarks. "Weapons out!" I call quietly. We stealthily slip into the shadows of the woods. Surprisingly, the trip to my childhood home goes uneventfully and soon we reach the place where I grew up. It looks untouched, but that doesn't mean anything.

"Be on your guard. I am going to go in and grab the supplies." The thick scent of danger and warning is strong near the house. I have a very bad feeling about this.

I lower myself into a guard position with my sword out and to the side, ready to swing up at the first whisper of another person.

Stealthily, I creep across the room to the area that we keep our winter clothes. I grab the clothes and slip out. I check in my cloak's hidden pocket and feel the small leather pouch still undiscovered. I swing my cloak around my shoulders and head towards the door, but I pause when I look at the little fireplace. Memories of Emerald and I telling stories floods my mind and a pang of longing fills me.

"Creak!" The wooden floor, an unusual, but necessary luxury, screams a protest to the unfamiliar feet. I whip around as the floorboard groans its protest and in the same motion, I channel blue fire into my sword, Tíne. Icy blue light floods into every corner of the small room to reveal four men standing with their weapons drawn. I quickly assess them. They handle their weapons with ease. They are obviously well trained. Though they wear the clothes of a commoner, it is clear that they are nobles. One steps closer.

"It would appear that as usual you are working alone. Are you still trying to hide your sister? We will get paid well for you. Your brother has not stopped searching for you. It will be my revenge to be the one who drags you in on your knees."

"Hold it right there. What revenge are you talking about? I don't even *know* you!" I reply indignantly.

"I am one of the New Worlders, as you call us. My name is Jhonatan Keleg. You may not know me, but I know you." *Everyone in the New World seems to know my name.* I don't know if I like that or not. "You killed my group and ruined my reputation among the humans. I recommend that you lower your sword and come with us or things will get ugly here." he pauses and looks at me quizzically. He must be used to his victims begging for mercy at this point. Instead of backing down, I let out a piercing whistle with three ascending notes.

"I think you will find that I am not alone. Perhaps you should be the ones begging for mercy," I respond dryly. Suddenly, the door flies open and three wild Olympians burst in. Emerald and Athena have their swords drawn, and Artemis's bow has an arrow nocked and aimed at the leader's heart. I could have handled these pathetic little men easily, but Zeus wanted us to discourage the New Worlders, so I called them to demonstrate our power. All of our weapons glow with their master's color. Athena glows gold, Artemis is a bright silver and Emerald is a vivid green. Four Olympians against four humans. The odds are now majorly in our favor.

"You will find that my sister can take care of herself. I will, however, give *you* a chance of living. You can either stay to die, or I will allow you to go free and run away like a coward." I can see him wavering.

To prove my point, I slip my sword into its sheath, unsling my bow from my shoulder, and nock an arrow onto the string. The whole sequence only takes a second. The arrowhead bursts into the same flame that had flickered threateningly on my sword. I spare him one word, but it has many depths of malice.

"Go." They do not need any further encouragement and they stumble out of the cabin at a run. I help one out with a kick to the seat of his breeches and they start to run in earnest. Once they are a safe distance away, they turn back to face us.

"I will have my revenge!" Jhonatan Keleg yells and with that, he turns again and sprints away into the forest, his red cloak blowing behind him. I lower my bow, slowly releasing the tension on it. I resist the impulse to send one of my perfectly crafted arrows into his receding back.

"Got the cloaks," I tell them. I throw them each a heavy cloak like my own. They are the same color of the woods in the winter. Athena and Artemis glare at me.

"What?" I ask, slightly surprised by their scowls.

"There better be a real reason for coming back here!" Athena threatens, her usually mild and kind expression is stormy and irritated. I glance around to see if anyone is near. I catch a sharp look from Artemis, but ignore it.

"I will explain later. The town is not far, and we need to get away from here before the reinforcements come." I can still feel the hum of tension in the air. The danger is not gone yet. I pull my bow onto my shoulder where I can grab it easily while the others loosen their swords in their sheaths and Artemis puts her bow over her shoulder as well.

We draw our daggers and Artemis takes the lead. She knows these woods better than any of us. With our camouflage cloaks we are almost invisible as we pass through the trees. We are silent as phantoms, except for Emerald who seems to be stepping on just about every twig or fallen branch in the entire forest. Business as usual. Even though the sounds are relatively small, to my sharp ears, they are practically screaming to anything within a twenty meter radius that we are right here. I force myself to take a deep breath and to ignore the noise.

About halfway to the town, a large troop of soldiers charge past. They pass us by ten yards, but they don't seem to notice us. Apart from that, the trip to the town of Weatherford goes smoothly. Hovering at the edge of town we change the color of the cloaks to dull grays before casually stepping out of the shadows. The town is busy as always, but there is a hurried air to everyone. No one loiters in the streets for a leisurely mid-morning chat these days. I can't blame them. Even the mundane humans sense the impending danger that the king of the Olympians refuses to notice.

"Split up. Emerald, you and Athena go to the west side of the market and pick up some supplies. Rope, food, things like that. Artemis and I will head to the east side. If you get into any trouble, whistle loudly and Stormy will come help. Last I saw him, he was grazing in the meadow." I figure that I should keep Artemis and Emerald separate. Artemis seems to be eternally irritated with Emerald and while she has been less harsh to the girl after the Shadow Battle, it is clear that she has little patience for Emerald's petulance. Everyone's tempers are sharper than usual with the stress of the upcoming war. "I'll see if I can find any of Emerald's friends. We need someone to spread the word that the Shadow Warrior has returned. We will meet up by the old tree." We fade off into the crowd, going separate directions.

Chapter Seven

Shadow

We thread our way through the crowds towards the far side where the poorer merchant stands are. The crowds grow thinner and I don't see any sign of Emerald's old friends. The last time I was here all three of them were sharing a hut. They run a fruit stand.

"Over there!" Artemis calls, breaking my chain of thought. I glance over to where they are sitting about one hundred yards away.

"Let's go!" I break into a jog and stop before the cart. Their backs are turned as they attend to a customer.

"We would like a dozen carrots," I demand. Holly whips around at the sound of my voice.

"Shadow! You're alive!" she exclaims happily. I smile patiently as the child states the obvious. The other two younglings turn around after dealing with their customers.

"Who is this with you?" Grace asks curiously.

"I will tell you in a moment. It is not safe to talk in the open," I tell the young girl. They quickly pack their fruit into baskets and pouches.

"Where can we put these?"

"I'll get Stormy to carry them."

"*Oi! Stormy! We could use you right now!*" I telepathically call.

"*Coming!*" He shows up a moment later shoving people out of the way. He screeches to a halt in front of us.

"You called?" he asks in perfect Arindal. The other three girls stare at him in shock.

"Please tell me I am not going insane!" Julia groans. I glare at Stormy.

"You are to remain silent!" I snap at him. He huffs indignantly, his breath a foggy cloud in the air. I grab the heavy bags and baskets and sling them over his back.

"We are meeting Emerald and another friend of ours at the edge of the market. I have a request." Without saying anything further, I turn on my heel and start to briskly walk towards the woods, knowing that in their curiosity they will follow. Miraculously, we reach the edge of the market without incident, but I catch the villagers openly staring at me and my familiar horse. I give a courteous nod to those that I used to know, noting their haggard appearance and grim countenance. A few give me incredulous and irate glares. It is well known that I am usually in places where danger follows. In truth, I am the one following the danger. Some people see it as if trouble accompanies me wherever I go. They have good reason to resent my presence.

"Let's go back into the woods to talk," I recommend to the others, anxious to escape the villagers' attention and ire. When we get deep enough into the woods, I signal everyone to stop. Athena and Emerald appear from the woods off to the side. I figure that since Grace, Holly, and Julia live here, they can tell us more about what is going on in the once cheerful and prosperous village.

"Here we should be able to talk in private. Oh, I forgot, you don't know each other. This is Artemis on my left and Athena on my right. Grace is on the far left, Holly is next to her, and Julia on the far right." I fill them in on everything that has happened to us last year.

"You do know that they really want to catch you. They find it as an insult that you disgrace every troop of soldiers that you meet. You should go before they realize you are back," Grace says nervously, peering into the shadows cast by the massive trees. Emerald smiles happily and begins chatting with the child. It is the first time she has been with anyone close to her age in a long time.

"It is far too late for that, and you have also brought up the request we have for you and your sisters. Would you please spread the word that Artemis, Athena, and the Shadow Warrior have returned? The only thing more obvious to do in announcing our return is to send up a mile-high flare of magic. They also know that Artemis and Athena-"

"Shut up!" I whisper fiercely at all of them. Emerald gives me an aggrieved look for cutting her off, but I don't take notice. I close my eyes and strain my ears and listen as hard as I can. Then I hear it again- the shifting of feet moving as quietly as possible in full battle armor. As I listen, I count as many as seventy individual feet hitting the ground. That means that there are thirty-five men. They are about one mile away, give or take. Upon opening my eyes, I swear quietly in Daenlir. I quickly brief them on what I heard. They stare at me in shock. "Well, I guess that my plan will take place a lot sooner than I had expected. We have about twenty minutes until they reach us, so line up shoulder to shoulder," I declare.

They do as I say, despite many mutterings about my sanity from the three young humans. I ignore them.

"You must escape on Stormy and hide," I tell them briefly. "Olympians, hold out your weapons and be very still. Girls, go mount Stormy."

"What are you going to do to them?" Holly asks fearfully.

"Magic," I reply vaguely. My icy blue magic lights up the small area. A thin light mist floats over their weapons. In a moment, the weapons turn invisible. Including my own. "Form up. They are almost here." I can feel the vibrations of horse hooves through the soles of my feet as the grass whispers a warning to me. "Stand ready!" I call.

"Stormy, take the humans and go back to the village," I order him telepathically. I slap him on the rump to hurry him along. He disappears into the woods with the three girls desperately trying to stay on. "Artemis, take my sword and Athena, take my bow. They will find it on me."

"What about us?" Artemis asks.

"I don't intend to have you stay in their torture camps. It is me they really want," I reply tightly. They do not realize that they will be going out on their own. I myself will be in their fortress. A spy on the inside. It makes me shiver as I realize that I will be placing myself at the mercy of my brother. However, it is a risk I must take. After hours and hours, and many sleepless nights spent wandering the moonlit forests, I scoured all my ideas and this is my only option. I must know the strength of Chaos's army. To beat your enemy, you must understand their strategy and know their strength. I believe that I know his strategy, I have no idea of his strength. If I can come back to Zeus with the numbers of Chaos's army, then he will have no choice but to listen to me. As soon as Stormy leaves, the soldiers come pouring in. They quickly close ranks in a circle around us and laugh when they see us.

"I think the others exaggerated when they described them! They don't even have their weapons!" their leader jeers. A cruel smile lights his face and sends a shiver down my spine.

"Seize them! But leave the tall one. They call her *The Shadow Warrior*. She is the leader. Leave her for me," he orders. Emerald squeezes my hand hard and I actually feel a few bones buckle and crack. I look down into her bright green eyes questioningly. She is afraid.

"Be brave," I whisper. I press a small emerald stone into her hand and switch from verbal to telepathic speech. *"If you get into a hopeless situation, the stone will bring help."* I pass down similar stones to Artemis

70

and Athena. A silver one for Artemis and a bright gold for Athena. I repeat my silent message to them as well. A moment later the soldiers grab an unresisting Emerald and tie her hands together. They do the same for the other two Olympians as well. As ordered, they leave me alone.

"Who, may I ask, are you?" I politely ask the leader who is still sitting on his horse.

"I am Jhonatan Keleg." I start in surprise. This is the man I met earlier. He looks completely when different dressed in his New World finery and on a horse. He dismounts and walks all around me. Sizing me up, probably. He is a big man, tall and strong with a commanding presence. Suddenly, he shoves me in the back and I fall to my knees. I don't try to catch myself, even though I long to retaliate. "I told you I would have my revenge," he hisses in my ear. *Great. Exactly how many people want revenge from me? I seem to keep finding more and more friends.* He tightly ties my hands together behind my back and I do not resist in the slightest. "I have wanted to see you like this for the past year. Now to make it perfect, you must beg for mercy."

"I will do no such thing," I reply calmly. He whips his dagger through the air so fast I don't realize what he is doing until the last moment. I hurl myself backwards too late and his blade slices lengthwise down my face, on top of the thick scar given to me by Chaos.

"You may do what you want to me and you cannot hurt me," I say, making my voice sound bored. I can tell that he is not used to getting that type of response from his victims. He stares down into my defiant eyes that blaze with an icy blue fire.

"You will break. And I will be the one there to see it." They march us down to their waiting ship.

We are all shoved into the same holding room. The door slams shut and a heavy deadbolt is shoved shut with a bang that echoes with finality. It is not completely dark and I can see the three Olympians all huddled together. I clumsily get onto my feet and look around. There is nothing but a few stray bits of straw and dust. I quickly untie the knot holding the rope tight around my wrists. With my hands free, I quickly untie the others.

"Gather round," I quietly order to everyone. "Based on our current coordinates and the speed of the water we will reach the New World in two hours. I want all of you to pretend that you are still tied. Tie the rope loosely and when I yell, take out your weapons and fight the men around you. When you are all free, run down the street and find cover. Now you should all rest and eat." I reach into Emerald's hidden backpack and pull out a few twists of dried and hardened venison and hand them over to the others, taking none for myself. My appetite disappeared the minute I decided to hand myself over to my brother's minions. Though the venison is tough to eat, it has a good flavor and will give them energy. I walk over to the wall and slump down against it. Emerald sits down next to me.

"How deep is that cut?" she asks. I had completely forgotten about it.

"Relatively shallow. It doesn't hurt. It should be fine." She reaches up and wipes a trickle of blood from the cut off my cheek.

"We will get out of this, right?" she asks uncertainly.

"Yes, you will. I promise. I'll make sure of it. Now get some rest." I shut my eyes and allow the rocking of the boat put me to sleep.

I wake up suddenly. I don't know why, but I know better than to ignore such an obvious warning. I listen outside of the room. There are many feet trudging outside the door. Something big is happening.

"Everyone up!" I shout. The three Olympians jump to their feet, immediately awake. I loosely tie their hands and everyone sits on the ground pretending to not have moved. I sit between Emerald and Artemis. Despite what I have told the others, I know differently. I know that I am the main target. They know that some of us are Olympians, but I am not described so easily. I am much more than that. The door flies open with a loud crash. Ten heavily armed guards pour into the room. Two grab my arms in a vice like grip. I twist and kick against them to no avail. They are far too strong for me to fight without a weapon. The others are grabbed, but they do not fight.

The guards yank me out of the hold of the ship and out onto the deck. Despite myself, I am awed by their huge harbor-side city. It is bigger than I remember. The tall buildings dwarf even a king's castle with its huge spires. Unlike a castle, however, these rise straight up and are made from some strange metal that gleams richly in the winter sunlight. There are huge crowds watching, hundreds and hundreds of them.

They wear the strangest clothes, all bright colors. There are no trees or forests in sight. The crowd stares at me as strangely as I stare at them. The others are brought out after me, squinting slightly before their eyes adjust. Emerald gasps as she finally sees the fabled New World. It makes me want to laugh as a peculiar thought crosses my mind. Something that never occurred to me: they may be fabled by the bards in our world, but it is the same for them. We are the ones that they tell stories about. We are as much of a legend to them as they are to us.

"We have caught the elusive Shadow Warrior!" Jhonatin Keleg shouts triumphantly to the silent crowd. I happen to know the language they call Remic. They roar and stamp their feet at his statement. I draw myself up to my intimidating height and glare at the crowd with eyes as cold and forbidding as a glacier. I radiate power. They suddenly go silent and I detect a shiver of fear run through the crowd.

73

"We are caught, but not defeated!" I shout with my unique accent, different even to that of my countrymen, but my meaning is clear. The people are holding up strange devices and turning them towards us "Now!" I shout to my comrades in Arindal. A wave of ice blue magic floods over my friends. Their weapons suddenly become visible. Athena and Emerald wave their swords in quick little arcs, taking out the soldiers holding them captive. Artemis stabs her guard and breaks free. Momentarily distracted, my guards loosen their hold on me. I slip a dagger out of my sleeve sheath and kill three of them.

"Go!" I yell to the others. Blue fire lights up my dagger as I distract the guards. I glow with power. There are too many for me to hold off for long, but enough time to allow the others to escape. They quickly circle me. One pounces and knocks the legs out from under me, while another grabs my arms. Though I struggle, their numbers are too many and their combined strength is enough to conquer mine. They finally pin me down. One soldier slams the pommel of his strange black weapon to the side of my head as I struggle against them. My world goes black.

Chapter Eight

Emerald

We run wildly through the crowds. The strange people hastily create a path for us as we wave our weapons and shout. I look back to where Shadow is fighting. As I watch, they pounce on her and drive her to the ground.

"No!" I shout desperately and try to run back but Athena grabs my wrist and drags me along. I struggle to break her grip, but it is like iron from decades of wielding a sword, spear, and shield. "Shadow!" I cry. We run on until we find ourselves in a narrow alley.

"We'll stop here," Artemis decides. Athena cautiously lets go of my arm. I slump down onto the ground. Artemis sits down next to me and simply puts her arm around me and I grab onto her almost desperately. Suddenly I realize something that is enough to shake me from my grief. Artemis is being nice to me. Athena starts to take stock. We still have all our weapons, including Shadow's.

"What now? How are we supposed to get her out?" I ask thickly. No one has an answer. The silence is broken by a loud whooping noise. I look up to see a huge machine fly overhead. We stare at it in shock. "These people are insane," I whisper quietly in awe. They shout something in a language I do not understand. Artemis responds in the same language.

"Run!" she yells in Arindal to us. We sprint out into view of a huge facility.

"What does that sign say?" I ask Athena.

75

"It says, **WARNING! STAY AWAY! GOVERNMENT BUILDING!**" As we speak, two of the flying machines turn into the building. We shelter behind some thick bushes.

"I originally thought that we should create a diversion, but this place is too big. We will have to sneak in. I am sure that there will be a vent system that we can slip in through," Athena proposes.

"Let's go."

Shadow

I awake with a terrible headache. Gods in Olympus! It did not hurt this much to be run through with a sword! The piercing throb from my head brings me fully conscious. I keep my eyes closed and struggle to remember what happened. It comes back in pieces at first, then it all floods back. *The others! Are they alright? Did they get away?* I open my eyes and look around. I am in a bare, white room with only one heavy, metal door, not unlike others that I have escaped from.

My shoulder aches just thinking about breaking it down like I have in the past. There is a vent above my bed. I try to sit up and find that I can't. My hands and ankles are chained to the sides of the bed and a chain across my waist holds me down. Furious, I struggle against the chains trying in vain to break them. I lie back with a groan. Moving makes my head pound more than ever. The pitiful human chains would be easy to break, but these are made of blackiron, the metal that Chaos learned how to create from our father. I am far too weak right now to mentally put myself against them. It surprisingly takes a lot of strength to force myself to break my wrists and the small bones in my hands.

I close my eyes and shift my focus to my other senses. Danger circulates the room. It clogs the air, threatening to choke me with its potency. I listen carefully. There are four men at my door. They are all locked into an intense discussion about this weird device called a phone number fifteen, or something. I don't know what it is and neither do I care. I shift into my magical vision. It is cool and refreshing and better yet, it wipes out the pain. I am not a healer, but I have learned that my magic can numb almost any pain. My magic is like a fire made up of ice, so cold that it burns enemies, but can be cool and refreshing for my friends.

Magic is built around a person's personality. Emerald's green magic is like the spring sunshine melting the snow and ice, creating warmth and happiness. Gentle and kind, it is the essence of her personality. We are complete opposites. I am cold, she is warm. I am winter, she is summer. *We are nothing alike. She is not a warrior. I have tried and yet I still failed. If she should die, it would be my fault. I am the reason her parents died and I should never have taken her in after that. I had already messed up her life enough.*

The lock on the door turns with a rattle. Drawn from my thoughts, I watch the door open and three men walk in. I study them as they talk by the door. They are wearing the modern clothes of these strange humans. I watch them with amusement. They obviously do not know that I can clearly hear them.

"Add extra soldiers to the perimeter. Watch out for a distraction. Pretend that everyone is flocking to them, but keep back some." I really hope that the goddess of war and wisdom has a better plan than that! They finally stop talking and direct their attention towards me.

"What do you want?" I ask in Arindal. Two of the men stare at me, perplexed. Jhonatin Keleg is about to translate when I correct myself, "What is it that you want?" I ask again in heavily accented Remic. They all look at me in shock.

"Information," the oldest man responds, after he recovers his wits.

"Regarding what?" I decide that I should wait before I start to test them. Now is the time to investigate.

"Magic and more on your friends," he promptly orders. The humans make no attempt to hide their surprise at my cooperation.

"If you so wish," I answer without hesitation. I don't think I've ever been this amiable and complacent in my life. Often, once they think you have given them the truth, they will believe the lies. One of them holds a strange little black box thing like the other humans. He types something in and then speaks into it.

"This is Agent Alexander reporting on the elusive Shadow Warrior. Alright, start with your magic," the one called Alexander requests in a voice that sounds more like a demand.

"Magic is a not a rare gift. Many humans do possess it. It would appear that no one of your world can wield it," I lie to them in Remic.

"Keleg, you are not needed as a translator. You may leave," the agent informs him. He shoots an evil glare at me before stalking out of the room.

"You are not worthy of hearing the information that I may or may not tell," I say to his retreating back in Arindal. He fixes me with a look of pure loathing.

"I will personally ensure that they torture you to insanity," he responds back in Arindal. I look evenly back at him.

"If you mean to make me fear you, you are sadly mistaken, pathetic man. You may leave now," I dismiss him. He strides out of the room and slams the door behind him. As I turn away from him I am aware that the other two men still in the room have been watching me. They did not understand a word of the conversation. "None of my traveling companions have any magic," I revert to Remic.

"What are their names?" one asks.

"We have heard rumors that you, your sister, and the ones whom you call Artemis and Athena are goddesses." I did not know that they knew about Artemis and Athena. Well, that trick failed miserably.

"Your rumors are true," I agree. I turn and give them a furious glare, giving up on being reasonable. I don't know how these New Worlders are such subservient creatures. It only took my brother a year and a half to completely gain their trust and overthrow all of their previous leaders. I wish he could just settle on controlling these humans. I don't see why he needs to take mine. They take a wary step back away from me after finding themselves burned by the ice blue fire in my eyes. To them, I am a mad, wild animal. Caged, but still full of unbroken pride.

"I will not tell you anything of me or my friends! No matter what you do to me." I glare at them with utmost contempt. They have yet to mention anything of importance yet, but I must know how they plan to gather information. Are they powerful enough to harm an immortal being?

"I know how to make the renown Shadow Warrior speak. Torture can loosen anyone's tongue. Have at it men," he briefly orders to the guards standing by the doorway. As the guards come over, the other two men step away. I hurriedly light my hands with icy fire. While I want more information, I would rather not get killed. The magic tingles on my palms and sparks brightly as it cuts through my brother's magical chains. The chains on my wrists melt off. I burn the chain on my waist off as well. Hurriedly, I sever the ones on my ankles too. I stand up in time to meet the first of the guards.

His giant hand comes flying in a huge arc. I lean back and his fist whistles through the air. While he is off balance, I jab with a lightning fast punch towards the sensitive area between the two lowest ribs. He falls back, staggering from the force of it and wheezes as he tries to get his breath back. I hate hand fighting. It is my weakness in a battle. I step back and feel an arm thick with muscle wrap around my waist. The other guard picks me up and throws me across the room. I hit the wall with the force of a charging horse. No human is that strong! My magical vision shows me that they have magic. *Figures.* It is a harsh red and they both have the same color.

Every real magical person has their own color. Icy blue magic surrounds me, swirling with legendary power. Without warning, one shoots a spell at me. I sweep my magic in and the collision of the powerful spells feels like being run through with a sword. I direct my magic high in the air and engulf him in a thick cloud of blue. He screams and writhes around in agony as it burns him. I withdraw from the spell and feel as if the wind has been knocked out of my lungs. As I come out of the spell, I realize that my ribs feel as if they are on fire. Despite a few broken ribs, I scramble to my feet. Pain can wait until later when I have time to think about it. The other guard is trying to get to his feet. The guard I just fought could not handle the force of my magic. He doesn't get up.

When the other one comes at me, I don't do anything to stop him from grabbing my arms and pinning them behind my back. I throw some of my magic in his face. He drops me and grabs his face in pain and shock. On the floor, I scuttle backwards like a crab, trying to put distance between us. His hands blaze with red power. Exhausted as I am, I call on my magic again. He attacks me with a blast of power. I deflect it to the side. He then attacks with all his power. Faced with no choice, I lock against his. I have never been this challenged in strength of magic before by one who is not my brother. I suddenly heave with whatever magic I have left. He staggers back a pace.

"What are you?" I ask in Arindal. That should have killed him! He smiles, but it is the smile of a snake.

"I am a Storm Spirit. We are here because you have insulted and invoked the Storm God's wrath! Your brother, Chaos, will stop at nothing to capture you, Elren! You have bested his efforts every time! We teamed up with these humans because they also have a score to settle with you." I scowl at the mention of my brother and my real name. I can see his next blow coming, but I am helpless to stop it. The sound of my real name and the mention of my brother breaks my concentration. Red, burning hot fire streaks at me. I just manage to put up a thin line of my icy magic up before it hits me.

It tears through the thin line of defense, hesitating for a brief minute before it strikes. I feel the effects immediately. It burns fire through my veins. My pride will not allow me to yell. With a distant thought, I realize that the only reason I am still alive is because of my magic. Even immortality cannot stop us from dying in battle. With any remaining strength that I have, I stand up. I refuse be beaten by this beast. He gawks at me.

"You should be dead!" he says in surprise.

"Thanks for the concern," I reply sarcastically. As the fire burns through my veins. I do the one thing that he never expected me to do. I charge him. We hit the floor hard. His head snaps back and slams on the floor. I move in to finish him, but a fresh wave of pain hits. I turn around to see who else is here when one of the human guards slam into me. Almost in slow motion, I fall and my head strikes the floor hard. It is too much. Blackness takes over once again.

Chapter Nine

Emerald

"Watch out!" Athena hisses at me. I duck back behind the bush.

"The guards are just pouring over to one side of the building. They are all in a hurry!" I report to the others. "We should wait for the cover of night to move. How are we even going to find her? The place is giant!" Artemis slides in next to me.

"The west flank of the building is almost empty," she says quietly, startling me. I know she did that on purpose.

"Do you ever make *any* noise?" I ask, not caring that I sound petulant.

"Only if I want to," she replies easily and fixes me with a quick look clearly pointing out that I always manage to be loud.. I settle back against the prickly bush and don't show how much her comment irritates me.

"I wonder if she has found any information yet?" I wonder aloud.

"I know her better than I know myself. She has a plan. Otherwise she would not have stopped fighting. She meant to be captured," Artemis informs me icily, immediately on the defensive.

"You may not have faith in my plan, but I do. You do not know what is at stake here! This new world will take over our Land of Old!" Athena's voice is as dark as midnight. I stare at her in horror.

"Could they actually do that?" I finally ask. They nod gravely. We lean back against the bushes and wait in silence for the sun to set.

"What is that?" Athena suddenly exclaims. I look where she is pointing and my heart leaps when I see a cloud of icy blue magic threading its way through the trees. It stops in front of us and turns into the lean form of Shadow.

"Thank goodness I found you guys! I was starting to wonder if you left me! Listen closely, for I do not have long before my energy and magic runs out. I am in the southwest wing, room three-hundred and fifty-five, last door on the right. They have storm spirits so be careful. I have rarely felt so much magic before. Except maybe the most powerful gods. I must leave this spell, but first beware, they are expecting a diversion. You may see a lot of soldiers going one way, but there are a ton of them still in the halls. Just be cautious. One more thing, GET ME OUT OF HERE! Please, and thank you." The magic vanishes. We stare at the place where Shadow's magic form just vanished.

"So, when do we attack?" Artemis asks.

Shadow

I regain consciousness and don't even try to move. *I really need to stop getting whacked in the head.* I send my message to Emerald and the others. Magic is the only thing that does not hurt. Even though I am sore and tired, my endless magic is replenished and fresh.

My thoughts drift to the time before I rescued Emerald and gave her a home. In the many years prior to that, I lived by different rules. Freedom sang through my veins, but I willingly gave myself chains in order from Emerald to have a chance to live a good life instead of the horrible life of a typical orphan. Sometimes I wish I had not, but she provides a unique light to my life. It is the only reason I still tolerate the chains that bind me to a normal life and not rip them off.

I slip into my magical vision. Glancing around, I notice that there are few guards at my door. There are, however, two Storm Spirits with one human. I let go of the scanning spell and immediately the pain hits

83

with renewed force. The door creaks open. I force my eyes open as I drag myself into a sitting position, fighting against the dizziness. The same two men who were questioning me yesterday walk in. I fix them with a look that is way beyond fury.

"How dare you treat me like this!" I yell at them in Arindal. They look at me blankly. I am far too furious to translate into Remic, nor do they wish to hear the curses I am hurling at them. Finally, I control myself enough to speak in their complicated language. Without noticing, they had backed off a couple paces. "One day, hopefully soon, you will find yourselves in the Field of Punishments in Hades realm." My voice is a deadly calm, rather like the calm before and after the storm. Agent Alexander steps closer.

"How are you going to stop us? You are one pitiful girl against seven warriors."

"Empty threats are not capable of getting me to speak," I respond archly in return. The men exchange meaningful glances before turning their cold gaze back to me.

"Who says they are empty?" another man responds in a dangerous tone. I slowly look each one over and put on an unimpressed expression.

"I think I will take my chances," I respond airily. *This will be fun.*

Emerald

"Darkness has fallen! Let's go!" I call quietly to the others. We sprint across the short clearing in a crouch and I quickly yank the vent free then crawl in. The others follow and Artemis closes the vent behind us. Athena, Artemis and I light our hands and we move as quickly as we dare. Luckily, we choose the right path and we reach the hallway with Shadow's room at the end of the hall. There are now four guards at the door. Suddenly, two men angrily stride out from the room.

"All of that for nothing! All we got were her taunts. Dammit! What will Lord Chaos say?" I hear one mutter furiously to his companion. I glance sideways at my companions worriedly. *What have they done?*

"We need to take out the guards. They are probably storm spirits." I slip into my magical vision with slight difficulty, doing like Shadow said and slowly releasing my mental boundaries and allowing my senses to expand. It is awful and leaves me feeling vulnerable and open. When I asked the others about it they seemed surprised. They spoke of it as if it is a wonderful gift. To them it is an escape, and to me it is being thrown off a cliff.

"The two on the end are storm spirits. Artemis, Athena, can you get rid of them? Your magic is stronger than mine." They nod. "On three we-" I hear a faint voice through the vent,

"You will need more than one Olympian to kill the storm spirits and not exhaust yourself. Come and get me out first. I can help."

"That was Shadow," Artemis confirms.

"We should do as she says," Athena agrees. We all hurry toward the vent her voice was coming from. I kick the vent cover off and jump out. The others quickly follow.

Shadow

I hear them in the vent system as they come over my way, but it surprises me at the strength with which Emerald kicks the vent open. As they pour out of the vent, I reflect that I have rarely been happier to see anyone, as I am to see them now. I carefully sit up, grimacing slightly as the movement reopens the long deep cuts given to me by their whips and knives as they attempted to pry information from me. They may as well have tried to squeeze blood from a rock. I gained more information from them than they realize. Emerald has a furious scowl as she watches my slow movements.

"Not so much as a hello?" I joke lightly. Emerald does not smile.

"Who did this to you?" she demands, furiously looking around as if looking for the enemy.

"The storm spirits. I killed them," I reply calmly. She settles down a little bit, but she is still scowling. I turn my attention to the others. Athena and Artemis have expressions close to Emerald's. "I recommend that you take your anger out on the guards outside." I keep my voice low, but it cuts like a barbed whip. They look suitably chastised. "There are four guards outside. It will take two Olympians to fight one storm spirit. Artemis and I can take on one, while Athena and Emerald get the other," I direct them. Athena is the only one with an objection.

"What do you mean that *you* are going to help fight?" I look at her as if she has grown horns and turned into a statue.

"Do you not know me? How could I let you fight while I sit here invalid, just because of a few little scratches and a broken rib or two?" My tone is neutral, but Athena backs down from the argument.

"Just making sure!" she grumbles.

"Weapons out! I will take my own weapons back, please." Athena hands me my bow and quiver. I slip both over my shoulder. "Sword." I hold my hand out to Artemis and she passes it to me. I strap it to my belt. "Let's go!" I heave my legs over the side of the bed. Just that simple movement sets my ribs on fire. I grit my teeth and set my mind to ignore it for now. I have dealt with worse pain than this.

"Positions!" I call softly. My voice is steady, despite the flaring pain from my side. Artemis and I pull out our bows.

"Go!" Athena forces her magic against the door. It flies off its hinges and soars across the hall where it lands with a crash loud enough to wake the whole city of Roy. We pour out into the hallway. Emerald and Athena sprint a short way down the hall to draw the guards away. As they start to chase them, they turn back and pounce on the human guards from the back. With four swift blows the guards are dead. Artemis and I light an arrow each.

"*Now!*" she yells telepathically. One Storm Spirit throws Athena against the wall. I wince in sympathy at the hard hit. We both aim for the Storm Spirit that is advancing on Emerald. However, he whips around in time to avoid the arrows. He shoots one more bolt of magic at Emerald then charges at us. My mind slows everything down allowing me to take everything in at once. Emerald tries to swipe the magic aside with her sword in panic. A maneuver that takes a lot of strength and concentration that she has not mastered yet. The sword gets blown out of her hand and the magic starts to move faster. She cannot do anything except watch in fear as it streaks towards her. Without any conscious thought, I load an arrow and release. It bursts into flame and strikes the magic away. As my magic hits it away, the red magic dissipates. Everything comes back into real-time speed

"Help Athena!" I yell to her. She scoops her sword up and moves over to check on Athena where she is slumped against the wall. I focus my attention on the immediate threat. He and Artemis are locked in a deadly strength match. Artemis is using her long, jagged dagger, while he has a heavy broadsword. I pull out my sword and join the fray. With two of us, the storm spirit does not stand a chance. Artemis finishes him.

"Let's get out of here before reinforcements arrive. Keep your weapons out," she calls. Emerald scoops her sword up from the ground. We run down the hall towards the big-moving-box-that-goes-up-and-down. Artemis presses the button that summons it and we stand ready, waiting to see if the reinforcements are coming yet. I hear feet rumbling on the tile floor as the soldiers pelt down the hall in pursuit. They have strange metal things. The front row kneels with the things pointed at us.

"Don't move!" one calls, his voice quavering slightly. I snort disdainfully.

"As if we will listen to you!" Artemis and I pull out our bows. The box doors open behind us with a pleasant *ding*. "Go! Get in! We will cover!" Emerald and Athena hurry into the box. We back in. As soon as we move, they pull some sort of trigger and the air is filled with a strange popping noise. Feathered darts strike me in the legs and torso. *What insanity*! I rip them out and throw them back at the men. Some strike home and those men topple to the floor. Artemis starts to return fire. All the sudden I feel like a hot poker was driven into my leg. It goes away almost immediately.

"Ouch!" Emerald exclaims as she is also struck. They have started to shoot little black metal balls at us. I sling my bow over my shoulder and grab my sword.

"Get in the box!" I call over to Artemis. We retreat into it as I continue to deflect the metal balls off my sword while Artemis shoots her bow. They cannot hurt us other than a moment of pain, but they must be able to kill mortals. The doors shut and I turn around to make sure there were not any problems getting in. As the battle adrenaline leaves me, the pain hits full on. My knees buckle and I lean against the wall for support. Dimly, I register that the others are asking if I am alright.

"Back up," I warn them, trying not to sound breathless. I allow my magic to surround me. I can feel the ice cold magic surging through my veins, revitalizing me. It numbs all the pain and as I call off the magic all I feel is a cool tingling all throughout my body. "Is everyone alright?" I ask. They look at me in surprise then look at each other as if to see if they were all here, with all limbs attached.

"It's you that we are worried about!" Athena replies.

"Don't you worry about me! I can handle myself!" I say with mock severity. She laughs at my quick response. We draw our weapons and form a tight semi-circle almost like a wedge. *Ding!* The doors open smoothly and we step out.

There is no one there. Just an open entry hall. We dash for the doors and head out, jumping over the threshold.

"Ack!" Emerald squawks in surprise. I look over to see her teeter on the edge of the top step. That would be a long fall. I grab her by her collar and haul her back. We run down the long flight of steps and into a secluded alley. I quickly brief them on what I found.

"If we stop the Storm God, we stop the uprising, the smugglers, and that government building and we weaken Chaos's army. However, Chaos will not stop at anything. First though, we must dress like these humans," I tell them.

"What is wrong with our clothes?" Emerald asks and looks down at our tunics of dull greens, grays, and browns and breeches. "I see your point," she finally agrees as I remain silent.

"We stand out like a horse in a cow herd. I think I saw a place just down there with the clothes that these people wear." We walk into the brightly lit room. "Go and find something you like, but please keep it subtle." Athena and Emerald run off in different directions with delighted expressions. This is their first time shopping in the modern world. Artemis and I are the only ones who have been here before. We all meet up at the front desk. I pay in the gold coins of my homeland. There is a pretty woman, dressed in a strange dress of a gauzy blue material that complements her dark colored hair and skin. The young woman at the counter looks at me oddly when she sees the heavy gold coins.

"Sorry. I do not have anything else," I apologize in Remic. She opens her mouth to speak and then notices the bow and quiver. Her gaze is then directed to the silvery-blue engravings on the hilt of my sword as it glints in the harsh lighting and the casual way my left-hand rests on top of it. She just nods and takes the coins off the counter. We hurry out of the shops and back to the alley. As I glance back, I see her staring at the coins with a peculiar expression, before looking at us again.

"Let's see what you got," I say after we go about four blocks away. Emerald chose blue jeans and a deep purple shirt. Artemis, Athena and I chose the same attire of dark green cargo pants with a mottled green and brown shirt that was on a rack called, 'camo', whatever that means.

"Now we just need to find a storm. I think I know someone who can help us," I say cryptically. Animals, particularly horses, are excellent at foretelling the weather.

"Hey, Stormy, Rosy! Care to join us?" I call telepathically. A moment later, they appear out of thin air next to us. The others jump back in surprise. Stormy lets out a loud snort of laughter as Emerald falls over in surprise. Athena, Artemis, and I join him as Emerald glares up at Stormy from the concrete ground. Athena helps her to her feet. I look up to judge the time. The half-moon is high in the starry sky. It is around one o'clock.

"Alright, that's enough." I finally stop the laughter for Emeralds sake. "We don't have all night. Let's get a move on. Stormy, use one of your few skills other than scaring the immortality out of Emerald. Tell me when you sense a storm nearby or coming." He looks offended.

"I have *many* skills! For instance, I am very fast. I can outrun all of the other immortal horses!" he replies heatedly, his brown eyes flashing with indignation.

"You have yet to beat Enbarr in a race," I remind him dryly. He opens his mouth to retort, then closes it as he realizes that he has no counter argument.

We all head off into the maze of tall buildings and twisting alleys. Inadvertently, I speed up to try to outrun the buildings that feel like great looming predators. Rosy stops suddenly and sniffs the air. She looks ahead, alarmed.

"There are fifteen armed soldiers headed our way," she warns us. There is the distant sound of the dull rasp of fifteen steel blades as they are pulled out of their scabbards.

"Well, there is not a chance of the element of surprise from them," Athena says trying to remain optimistic. Of course, as soon as those words are out of her mouth, I hear a most unwelcome sound- more feet behind us. I turn around to make out fifteen more armed soldiers. I swear quietly as I realize just how outnumbered we are.

"We might still manage this." I think it over. First, I think of sending Emerald up to a thin ledge on the building, but she cannot shoot a bow.

"Emerald, you face the back and *draw your weapon for Pete's sake!* Now is not a wonderful time to gawk! Athena, take the front. Artemis and I will climb up onto the ledge and even up the odds." They nod, each person understanding their role. Emerald finally has her sword drawn. "Stormy, you and Rosy help where you can." Without further instructions, Artemis and I swiftly climb up to the ledge.

We both balance easily on the narrow footholds. Together, we sling our bows off our shoulders. Holding it with my left hand, I deftly pull an arrow out of my quiver with my right.

"I think that it is about time to use some invented arrows." I tell her in a light and conversational tone. She grins at me, the excitement of a

91

fight sending energy and extra magic through our veins. I light my arrow and she lights hers. The dazzling icy blue and bright silver fires intermix and everyone turns to look where the sudden blaze of light is coming from. I launch mine into the side where Athena is. Bright blue flames ignite as the arrow pierces through the hardened and shaped metal of a man's breastplate. As he falls, a wave of magic fire burns through the forces. I notice with half a mind that Artemis is doing the same thing on the other side. We both stop the magic and any remaining soldiers flee for their lives.

Lightly, we jump down to the ground from the story high ledge. We land softly and as a group we run through the streets, leaving caution to the wind. After hitting a couple dead ends we come across a break in the usual buildings and winding streets. A huge area of only trees and clearings appears in front of us. This must be what they call a 'park.'

"Come on! This way!" I call to them. We head off into the woods. After about a mile, I finally allow the others to stop.

"Let's make camp here," I suggest. The others nod and go about to their chores. Athena starts the fire, Artemis lays out the bed rolls, and Emerald gathers firewood and gets the packs off the horses. I slip off into the woods to hunt for something to eat. Before long, I spot a deer. By sheer luck, I happen to come across it from downwind. I silently nock an arrow onto my bow string, aim, take a breath, relax my muscles, and smoothly release the string. The arrow hits the deer right behind its left foreleg. The deer falls to the ground, instantly dead. I lightly run over to retrieve it. As I kneel, I sense a presence nearby. It may be some sixth sense or whatever, but I don't think about it. A harsh wind blows through the trees. I quickly sling the deer over my shoulder and sprint into the camp. They look up at me, startled by my sudden appearance.

"Get your weapons out! There is something coming!" I call as I draw my sword. As an afterthought I throw some magic over the deer and it suddenly disappears. In its place is the meat, already dried and hardened and the cleaned skin. The sinews lie there as well, ready to be made into anything we might need. I gesture to Emerald and she stuffs them into her knapsack.

"Um... I think you might want to know that a storm is coming," Stormy says unhelpfully.

"Oh really? I did not notice," I reply sarcastically. I choose my bow over the sword and after slamming Tíne into its scabbard, I shift into my magical vision and I can see the wind howling in an unnatural way. Almost as if it is fighting itself. Instead of the lazy rolls and playful dips of the earthy green wind mixing with the browns of the trees, they whip by in a unified force to try to fight the strange magic that has come to invade. The natural forest colors fight against the red intruders. I hesitantly reach a small tendril of my magic into the fray. Before I can withdraw, a sharp, hot bolt streaks down my magic. It is a short blow, but powerful. I stagger backwards from the sheer strength of the spell. Blinking out of the magic vision, I turn to the others.

"It is the Storm Spirits in the wind. They are not in solid form. We cannot fight with force. They are much stronger than us. We must fight with magic. Emerald, stay in your magical vision, but stay out of the fight. The rest of us will do our best to help the anemoi." The others nod. "Be warned, one storm spirit easily shoved me aside." We all slip into our magical visions. Athena, Emerald, and Artemis glow their bright and distinct colors. I unleash a torrent of icy blue magic. It takes the form of a horse.

My horse, my heart, my guide. Enbarr of the Flowing Mane. He is most commonly known as the only one who traverses both the land and the sea. Nobility and courage all represented in one animal.

The Storm Spirits are also starting to fight in the form of the horse. Something is warped about their horses though. They're all varying shades of red, for starters. But their eyes are jet black and are set in the front of their hideous heads. They are hunters.

A magnificent silver stag for Artemis and a downy gold owl for Athena appears alongside my magic. Athena leads the charge and the anemoi drop behind their support. The Storm Spirits are over run by the onslaught of magic and the surprise of the attack, losing their forward momentum. They are either trampled by the ice crystal horse, mauled by the terrible talons of the owl, or stabbed by the sharp antlers of the silver stag. More just seem to keep coming. Eventually we begin to tire. Before I know it, the odds are against us. The anemoi flee, leaving us on our own.

I glance over at Emerald and frown in irritation when I spot her green eagle in the air. She defied my direct order. However, she is holding her own, but even as I watch, one sweeps the magnificent green eagle out of the sky. It disappears into the air. The storm spirit horse morphs into a young man. He presses the sharp blade of his knife to her neck.

"Surrender and she shall live... For now." I swear angrily at him in response and he recoils slightly before regaining his composure. The other storm spirits take the shape of men. To make his point he presses the dagger harder. I point my bow down. I gesture to the others to lower their weapons. We store them in our scabbards and sling the bows over our shoulders.

"Now let her go," I demand.

"Please? I don't think I heard a please?" he muses to his companions.

"You try to kill my sister and you expect me to say *please*?" I ask incredulously.

"Our master appreciates manners. It may just be the difference between you living or dying." I spit at the ground between his boots.

"I'd take dying over showing your '*master*' any respect," I reply in a voice so cold it could freeze the Mare cum Ferā Aquā, or as the mortals know it, the Ocean with Wild Water.

"I think it is time you met the Storm God. He has waited a long time for the honor of speaking with The Shadow Warrior." Without any other warning, the fiery magic surrounds each of us. The others scream in agony as it burns them. Since my magic is ice, I do not feel it. However, Emerald, Athena, and Artemis are feeling the heat. They are immortal, but even that does not stop the searing pain from the burns. I spiral my cool magic around them and it is enough protection to stop the worst of it. It eases the pain and they are now slightly protected. I am sure it still burns, but probably not as painfully.

"Where are you taking us?" I lace the words with restrained fury.

"The throne room, of course! Where else would we take esteemed guests like yourself?" the one holding Emerald replies. The world dissolves into a red, hot blur.

The trip to the throne room lasted the longest of eternities, or as short as seconds. What I do know is that it is as if the world turned on end and spins out of control. All the sudden, it stops. We all stagger back in a desperate attempt to regain balance. Emerald barrels straight into Athena and me. We all fall over in a heap. I finally regain enough sense to look around. We are in a huge antechamber. There is a pair of massive arched doorways, each on opposite sides of the room.

"Send them in," a voice that is as slick as oil and arrogant as a conceded noble, booms from behind the closed door

Chapter Ten

Shadow

"Form up," I order quietly. Athena and Artemis go to my direct left and right. Emerald takes the rear where she is most protected. All our swords and daggers remain sheathed, but they can be whipped out in less than a fraction of a second. Artemis and I have our bows strung and over our shoulders. We can nock and shoot in half a second. As I look around the magnificent hall, my gaze lands on the throne in the center of the huge room. It stands out in the sparsely furnished room. On closer inspection, it looks like it is made of oak wood and trimmed with intertwined gold and silver. The only thing greater than the throne is the man sitting in the chair.

He is surprisingly small in stature, but make no mistake, that doesn't make him any less powerful. He looks to be about twenty years in age, light hair cut short. The most noticeable thing about his appearance is he has a swarthy and unpleasant face and merciless black eyes.

"You have given us a great chase. It is time that this ended. I received a great prophecy many years ago. It entailed a woman who is a great warrior, who carries the hopes and beliefs of the Olympians and the people in the Land of Old. However, this person is said not to be an Olympian. It is foretold that she is far greater than any Olympian. From a race far earlier than the Olympians. From a time where there were only two things. The Light and the Dark. Born from these are two great heroes. Given the power of both, she was to protect the future generations. As every hero must come with, she holds one fatal flaw. Her pure pride will be her downfall one day. Nothing will stop the Shadow Warrior from the goal she has set. She will stop only if she is killed in the process. She is unable to kill those whom she loves, even if they are attempting to kill her. I have searched for years and around the world for this warrior. Now that I have you, I see nothing special. How do I even know if it is you, *Elren Caerin*?" he asks me viciously, watching with pleasure as I flinch at hearing my real name. The runes on my forearm tingle. He just summarized them.

"What do you think you can gain from me?" I think I already know, but I must hear it all the same.

"With you out of the way, there is nothing to stop me from taking over the entire human world with Chaos *Caerin*," he adds emphasis on our last name, trying to bait me. I stifle a growl with effort and struggle to regain my temper as he benevolently smiles at me, as if he had just given me the greatest present possible.

"What of the Olympians?" Athena growls like a dog with her hackles up.

"You have fought against my warriors. You all know you will fall to them. You know that there is not any chance for the Olympians to withstand the onslaught without the Shadow Warrior."

"What are you going to do with us?" Emerald quietly asks. Her voice quivers slightly with fear. I am surprised she spoke at all.

"I will test how long you last in the true test of mental and physical strength. Well it was nice meeting you, Shadow Warrior. Goodbye! Oh yes, there is one last thing, there is no such thing as friendship in the labyrinth. Chaos, your bro-," I lunge forward at him, my temper finally breaking loose.

Everything dissolves into mist.

When it reappears, I am on my knees in a stone room. I hear something crunch under my foot and I jump backwards as a skull stares back. *Great! I am in a room full of dead people!* As I slowly stand up, I take stock of the situation. My backpack and a torch are with me. All of the bones look like they have been down here for ages. There is even a skeleton of some strange beast as well.

In the backpack, there are squares of ambrosia and a canteen of nectar; along with that, there is the food that the new humans like to eat that looks as if it might be poisonous because it is so bright. Doubtfully, I pull the silver wrapper off one that reads YORK. I gingerly bite into it and recoil in surprise. Not because it is bad, just strange. The brown outside is very foreign to me, but the inside tastes like crushed mint leaves.

There are two big leather skins filled with water. Now that I know I have food, I must get out of this room without doors. Slipping the pack over my shoulder, I stalk to the closest wall. It is just a stupid stone wall. I look up in frustration. There are ancient runes from the age before the gods. My vision swims. I blink rapidly to clear my eyes and read the complex series of symbols that are my native tongue.

The tree of life,

The river cool.

The battle of good.

Stranger beware,

Truth will be revealed,

Lies shall get you nowhere.

Only darkness will await you in there.

The walls form a square and they are six feet by six feet. I light my right-hand with blue fire before throwing it into the air where it forms a light mist of ice blue above me. My head is within an inch of the ceiling and I repress the urge to duck. *Wait, what is that?* I look closer at an etching on the upper right corner of the wall. A squiggly line. A river. The River Cool. My heart beats faster. With a spark of excitement, I hurry over to the next wall. It also looks blank. There! On the lower left corner!

A tree! Moving faster now, I spot two crossed swords in the bottom right corner. It is the symbol for combat. On the last one it is a single knife stained with blood on the top left corner. I don't like the look of that.

I shut my eyes and force myself to concentrate. I prefer to leave the riddles for others to solve, but I am alone now and it is up to me. The tree, the river, the swords, and the knife. The river gives life to the tree. The bloody knife can mean death. The swords mean combat, many die in combat. Life and death. It is a strange sort of riddle, unlike any that the traveling bards used to tell, but I was always terrible at figuring them out. It is going be either the tree or the knife. I will choose the tree. The tree means life. Life means friends and family. Unfortunately, my life includes combat, and where combat lies, is also where death is closest. I press the symbol into the wall. The stone cracks and a gap opens.

"Here we go," I say to myself, before I duck into the tunnel.

Artemis

"Whoa!" I stumble as I land on hard stone. We are in a completely enclosed stone pathway. It is lit every ten feet and the magical red fire in the torches throw eerie shadows flitting around.

"Artemis, where are we?" Athena asks me, her voice bouncing off the walls.

"The labyrinth," I reply absently. "Who is missing? I only count three of us. Where is Shadow?" My voice suddenly sharpens with alarm.

"You mean our *Shadow Warrior,* Elren Caerin? The twin sister to Chaos? That Shadow?" Emerald replies bitterly. "I have a few questions for her." Athena and I quickly exchange a look. I know it must hurt Emerald the most. Emerald has had a hard life. First, she lost her family, then in the past battle, her sister was revealed to be someone else, and now her sister is a huge figure that carries the fate of the world on her shoulders and is directly related to the one killing countless lives. How do you expect a fifteen-year-old to understand that? However, she has a special talent for irritating me. She is petulant and bratty and expects life to be easier.

We both know that a divided group will not cooperate, and a group who doesn't work together is a group that does not survive. Instead of harshly answering her I look around. There are two backpacks. I grab one and hand the other to Emerald before I suddenly stiffen. Athena also stands stock-still. I listen as hard as I can.

"What is it?" Emerald asks urgently. Athena holds up a hand to ward off the questions. It sounds like a big animal. I strain my ears further. It is at the very edge of my range of hearing. It makes the hair on the back of my neck stand on end. I have been hunting in ancient forests for ages and only once have I heard that sound. I am tasked with keeping the monsters at bay. This monster is the only one I have ever truly feared. She came down from the stars to get revenge on Hera, but Zeus sent us to intercept it.

It took three centaurs, Athena, Shadow, and myself to kill it. Even with all our power combined, one centaur was killed and everyone else was severely wounded. Athena finally threw her dagger and blinded it as I sent a volley of arrows down it's throat as it roared in agony. I can still remember the terror we felt facing it. Twenty-seven silver arrows and one golden dagger to take it down.

"Move! We need to get out of here!" I whisper urgently. We sprint down the corridor. Whipping around corners and plunging down further into the dark, we run. We run as if there is a horde of demons behind us. Although, the one behind us is as strong as an army of mortal men. Despite our frantic running, I can hear it getting closer and closer and before I know it, it is right behind us. This is supposed to be my area of expertise, yet I run with great fear. I can tell that Emerald is doing her best not to panic.

I hear a brief cry of pain and a nasty thud. I skid to a halt just in time to stop a headlong run into a wall. I light my hand with some of my silver fire to push the pressing darkness back. *Oh no! Please no!* This is what I feared. A dead end with a monster on our tails. As I look closer, I see two things. In an unspoken word, Athena and Emerald draw their swords. Athena has a mask of blood running down her face from the gash on her forehead. I take one arrow from my quiver. With deliberate and precise movements, I nock an arrow onto the string of my bow, I am prepared to die fighting. Emerald and Athena are as well.

I throw a mist of silver magic high into the air. It shimmers like moonlight in a dark forest. That thought gives me a sense of comfort, despite the dire situation. Almost immediately, a vivid green and gold joins it. Probably our last stand together, but the most depressing part is that our whole group is not here.

Before long, the giant horror fills the path. It is bear-like in shape and stance, but that is where the similarities of a mortal bear end. The eyes dance with a maniacal fire. Its claws are as sharp and long as daggers, thickly coated in poison. The bear is black as midnight, and the fur is as strong as armor. Thick and matted, it is impenetrable. It is an Ursa Major, or I guess this one is the Ursa Minor. However, there is nothing small about it.

Some think the defeat of it was done heroically, unflinching, and without fear. They could not be more wrong. I was the one given credit, but I would have died many times over without my friends. All of those with me that day were far more powerful than me and the two immortals next to me. Now, here is her cub, he has come down from the stars and wishes for blood. He demands revenge.

The bear lets loose a massive roar and swipes its giant claw through the air. I duck and roll as it whistles over my head. I feel the rush of battle adrenaline coursing through me. I am not going to cower in fear. I will die fighting. Emerald does not duck in time, and the huge paw rakes across her chest and face. She slams into the wall and slides to the floor. The gashes smoke ominously.

As the bear shuffles forward to finish its work, I shoot a volley of arrows into the thick fur protecting its throat. While the bear's fur is hard as armor, my arrows are made to go through the full body armor that knights wear. I assume that the arrows have the effect of a bee sting to the beast. Painful for a second, but gone the next, leaving the bear even more angry. The Ursa Minor roars and whips around to face me. Athena positions herself between it and Emerald. It stands up on its hind legs and towers high above us. All defiant thoughts leave me. There is no chance of us killing this thing.

The giant paw comes at us again and it swipes the bow from my hand. I guess I will use my dagger instead, then. Athena and I raise our weapons and let loose our own war cries before charging to our deaths. We are only immortal to time. Any of us can be killed in battle. Right now, that is what we are running towards.

Shadow

I stop for a minute to try to gauge the distance I have covered. Many miles have steadily passed under my boots. Without the echos made by my steps blocking out small noises, I hear a very faint sound. It almost sounds like screaming. I mentally shrug. I know that there are monsters and other people in this maze. When monsters and men meet it is generally accompanied by plenty of screaming. As I'm walking, something in my pocket gets hot.

"Ouch!" I mutter as I bring my blue stone out of my pocket. It is glowing extremely bright, but most surprising is that it is no longer an icy blue. The gem is a mixture of green, gold, and silver. They swirl around and as I watch, I see a picture of carnage and destruction- the Ursa Minor. It finally found us.

As further images flash across the stone, I catch glimpses of Emerald thrown against the wall. Athena and Artemis are doing their best, but their efforts are in vain. Instinctively, I spiral some of my magic into the gem as if it might help them. With a startled yelp, I feel myself hurtled into space, pulled by my own magic.

Chapter Eleven

Artemis

The bear stands on its hind legs and roars in pleasure as we start our hopeless charge. Without warning, the bear suddenly drops onto his front legs and its roar turns into something more of a question than a threat. All the sudden, there is a giant explosion of blue. It is so strong it blows Athena and me into the wall. I stagger slightly against impact and blink away the black spots. The bear was thrown against the wall of the wide pathway with staggering force. Out of the remaining fog of powerful magic, a tall figure steps into the clear. The magnificent form flickers in and out of focus due to the immense power radiating from it- a sight that would send an army running and kill a mortal with just a stray glance.

I do not recognize her at first because she looks completely different, but it is Shadow, and she is dressed for war and extremely angry. Her torso is covered in plate armor, with shoulder protection, but her arms and legs are protected only by thin and light silver chainmail. On the left side of her breastplate is a rearing stallion. Her sword, Tine, is a bright ice blue and her shield also has that same fearsome symbol, a rearing stallion with ice blue fire radiating power. Never have I seen her look so terrifying. Her light brown hair is pulled back into a braid and her face is covered in grime and dirt. Her eyes are blazing with power and determination. She is truly fearless.

The bear can only watch as she steps in front of us all. Athena and I exchange fearful glances. The bear backs away uncertainly at this appearance. She shouts a challenge in a foreign tongue that I have never heard before. The bear is either incredibly stupid, or bold, but whatever she said, he did not like it. He lets out a huge roar and charges straight at Shadow.

She refuses to back off. Instead, she braces her feet and holds her kite shaped shield in front of her with her sword bristling and ready. The bear slams into the shield with the force of eight charging oxen. That is enough to kill ten men. It is stopped dead. Shadow does not even seem to feel the impact. Her shield does not even have a scratch. Calmly, she stabs her sword deep into the bear's heart. It is as if the bear did not have any armor at all. She shoves the bear backwards and withdraws her sword in one fluid motion. The bear disappears with a sparkling flare of orange. Now he is returned to the stars, where he ought to be.

The blue glow slowly dims and her armor melts back into her clothes. She is once more back into her gray breeches and a dull green shirt. She is no longer surrounded by an aura of blue, but her eyes still dance with a dangerous light.

"Who is down?" Shadow asks with a surprisingly calm and modulated voice after fighting the bear. Without noticing, we backed up when she appeared.

"Emerald," I hasten to reply. The image of her still burns in my memory. It always will. As does the fear of seeing one so powerful, even if you know they are on your side. It is hard not to think about the fact that if she wanted to, Shadow could have killed all of us without even breaking a sweat. I have never seen even Zeus look that terrifying.

She hurries towards Emerald before I had even finished my sentence. After a moment of hesitation, Athena and I follow. Shadow gently props Emerald up against the wall. She carefully wipes the blood away from the deep cuts across her face. The cuts themselves are healing, but they are going to hurt later. Her shirt is totally shredded and blood coats it, but like the cuts on her face, they are already healing. Although, she is going to have scars for the rest of her life. If she were not a healer, she would have been killed by the poisons in the claws. The magic that runs through her veins keeps her from injuries and illnesses.

"I can numb the wounds until they are fully healed. I think it is getting a bit dark in here," she randomly adds with an air of mild detachment. She throws a mist of ice blue magic high into the air along with the green, gold, and silver that are already mixed. The room brightens as if the night had left and day had come. I never knew my friend had such power. *How much strength does it take to keep that power hidden and in control?*

One would not expect the colors to mix, but somehow, they do. As I watch them, they swirl and dance around making joyful patterns against the stark black rocks that form the ceiling of this wretched maze. Funny how they only just started to do that. Earlier they were just looming above us like a cloud. It is as if they are either joyful at being reunited, or happy that we defeated the bear. I shake my head to get rid of those fanciful notions. It is magic. It is unable to do anything until we ask for it. I still cannot suppress a slight doubt that I am wrong.

Shadow

"You might want to step back," I request quietly to Artemis and Athena. I know they watch me cautiously and even flinch as I speak, but I pretend not to notice. My heart drops in my chest at their fear. This is one reason I have not shown anyone the extent of my magic, but I did what I had to do to save them. As they step back, I allow my magic to pool in the palm of my hand. I will it to thin out and become a light mist before it encircles Emerald and then disappears. I step away and turn to face Athena and Artemis.

"So, I guess we lived to fight one more day and have to spend more time in this vile maze," a voice behind me says. The others all startle and turn to look at Emerald who is sitting against the wall. I turn slowly to face her. Of all the others, Emerald is the hardest for me to face. Athena and Artemis always knew that there were many prophecies about me. Emerald was the only one who did not know. It is as if her sister is suddenly slipping away and becoming a total stranger to her. *I knew this day would eventually come.* The brick wall she has leaned on since she was small has crumbled away to reveal what she was really propped up against- a stranger, a monster even. She looks at me for a moment and then at the others. "Please help me up." Athena grips her forearm and helps her to her feet. She sways lightly for a minute and then steadies herself. Athena quickly releases her grip and gives me an odd look.

"How did you get here, Shadow?" Athena persists.

"A bit of magic," I say evasively again, but that would only work once. Artemis elegantly raises an eyebrow.

"Do you seriously think we believe that?"

"Fine," I sigh. I really don't feel like explaining anything right now. Exhaustion pulls at me, but I quickly start talking because I know that they won't leave me alone until I explain. "I was walking and my stone burned me. When I pulled it out, it was not its customary ice blue, but it was the colors in the mist above us. Silver, gold, and green. I saw flashes of what was happening here. I saw the bear, and I saw Artemis and Athena preparing to run a headlong charge that would lead to their deaths. I spiraled some of my magic into the stone, and then I was here." I shrug. It is best that they did not know the details. "Let's all rest for a little bit, then we really do need to get out of here before another monster is sent to kill us. We have a wall to our backs so we don't need to worry about an attack from behind... Hopefully. I'll set a guard. Each is for one hour, me, Artemis, and Athena. Wake me if you hear anything."

"What about me?" Emerald asks.

"You need to rest and recover. Get some food from the packs and sleep," Athena orders. Emerald nods her understanding and Athena heads over to the wall with Artemis. After a moment's hesitation Emerald follows. As she goes to move past me I put my hand on her shoulder. She tries to shrug it off but I hold on.

"I need to speak with you," I say quietly in her ear. Using the hand that I have on her shoulder, I firmly steer her a good distance down the hallway. If Athena and Artemis wanted to, they could hear us, but they already know what is coming. I throw up all my mental shields in a futile attempt not to feel what Emerald calls me out on. I stop and she faces me.

"Why did you not tell me? You knew about this." Although I had braced myself, the words still sting like those little black bullets the New Worlders use. I hesitate for a long second to organize my thoughts and then start speaking slowly.

"I am sorry that I have dragged you through all of this. If I had a choice, you would still be at home, not running for your life through a monster filled prison. This is the life that *I* am supposed to live. You are only fifteen. You shouldn't have to worry about whether you live or die tomorrow. You still have your whole life ahead of you, unlike me. If you lived a normal life, you would be more concerned about things like whether the boy who runs the leather cart likes your new tunic? Or, you would be hanging out with your friends in the village. I am sorry. If it weren't for that one unfortunate day when Chaos killed your family, you could still be living happily in the woods. I did not want you to become wrapped in this perilous fate of mine." Emerald listens to my explanation with her arms crossed over her chest and her face emotionless. I know she does not believe me. She has come to realize that I would have been drawn in some other way to the Isle of the Olympians. This is my fate. There is not an escape from it. Anyone who even tries is wasting time.

"Why, Shadow? Why did you lie to me? I trusted you beyond anyone in the world and you betrayed me. You led me to believe that you actually cared about me. I looked up to you. Why shouldn't I have? You were perfect. You were strong, confident, kind, and compassionate. I gave you all my love and devotion as an abandoned child would to a parent or a lost sibling. Any time I was with my friends, I was bragging about how you are so much better than a parent. You did not make me clean my room, or care when I walked through the house with mud on my boots. When I needed you, you were there. I could tell you all my problems and you would help me. Then suddenly all of that was gone. I feel like I blinked and then you had disappeared. Sure, you would be away for a few days without warning, but you would always return with apologies and make it up to me. This time it is different. There is no going back after this, *Elren Caerin.*"

I flinch violently at the sound of my name, but Emerald doesn't seem to notice and if she does, she doesn't care. She continues, her voice becoming harder and angrier.

"While you may have saved me from your brother, you condemned me nonetheless and I will never forgive you for that. You took away the life I should have had and dragged me through all this hell, and I never saw it coming. I bought it all when I was young. I *never* suspected that you could do this to me, but here we are. You are a stranger and now I am lost. What now? What can I possibly say that can make you understand? You are more like your brother than you think. While he may be known to the world for his cruelty, you keep your black streak hidden from view. I hadn't seen it before, but now it is showing up. Dammit

Shadow! Why did you hide yourself from me? You failed to keep me safe and to love me. You *failed* me."

I flinch again at her words. Each word rips off part of my shield and now I am defenseless. Her words hurt more than any wound. I can face an army alone without the slightest qualm, but having Emerald yelling at me is like a dull sword being thrust through my heart, especially because it is the truth. Something inside me hardens and my heart turns to steel. My eyes become icy and I draw myself up tall and look down at the small girl.

"I took care of you! I practically raised you! I have looked after you for your whole life. Before even you knew! You are special! Do you not realize this? You are still my apprentice and my little sister, whether you like it or not. I sheltered you from the cruelty of life. Without me, you would most likely be married and stuck inside a house scrubbing your life away for a man who doesn't give a damn! Don't blame me for ruining your life, child, because I am the only one who cared enough to try and help you."

"I don't *want* a swordmaster! All I want is my sister back!" she screams at me and tugs at her braid, clearly full of anger and uncontainable energy.

"After I get you out of here, I am not taking you anywhere ever again. You are going to be apprenticed to someone else. They can deal with you better than I. Although, they will not tolerate this childlike insolence like I might. They will tan your hide for simply talking back. I hope you get what you always wished for." My voice is icy cold and uncompromising as I tell her what I plan. She finally pushed me too far. Tears well up in her bright green eyes and she looks completely shocked. She never expected that I would renounce her. I soften my voice a little bit. "You will get to live your life." I hesitate before adding softly, "Live your life for me. It is almost impossible for me to live until my twentieth birthday."

"Then die a painful death!" she shouts at me before sprinting down the hallway back to where the others are sleeping, leaving me where I stand alone against the wall. I briefly give the stone wall a rueful grin. *I walked straight into that one.* The dry humor quickly fades as I unintentionally think about the harsh words that we traded. Mentally, I feel like I'm slowly dissolving and crumbling away. Perhaps what hurts most though, is that what she said is true. *I am more like my brother than I thought.*

Guilt is the worst feeling. While anger may give energy, and sorrow will give inspiration, guilt drains you and leaves you devoid of any other emotions or thoughts. It is one of the worst punishments- a self-induced torture.

Athena

I lay awake in my sleeping roll and listen to Shadow and Emerald's argument. I know that Artemis next to me is doing the same. Emerald stalks over and throws herself onto her blankets, mumbling and cursing to herself. I wait a few minutes and her breathing slowly evens out. When I judge the moment right, I speak to her softly, even though I want to slap her across the face for what she said to Shadow. She has no idea how hard Shadow has worked for her. She doesn't know how many sacrifices were made for her to live a better life than most. Shadow gave up total freedom to help give Emerald a roof over her head and a warm hearth in the winter. It makes my blood boil to hear those ungrateful and horrible words.

"She really does only want you to be safe. She dragged herself here by magic to save you. Your sister is extremely powerful. Some might use it for bad. The ones who use it for domination are the ones who cannot control it, so it controls them. It takes them over. Shadow has always been very disciplined and in control, but she has a fierce temper. That has nothing to do with the magic, but more to do with the responsibility of keeping it under control. I have never met anyone who has a quarter the power that she possesses. She knows what can happen if she goes too far with it."

I hesitate for a minute to gather my thoughts and then continue.

"The Storm God and Chaos live among discord and they stoke the fire. They would like nothing more than for Shadow to be pushed to the breaking point, and believe me, both will try to get her there. It is proof that she has one if she felt that she had to reveal her immortal side. They will try to break her.

"Use too much magic and it will kill you. Your heart is the core of your magic. Without magic flowing through your blood, the heart cannot function and you *will* die. You need to know this information. She has kept this part of herself from you for a reason. She did not want you to be afraid of her. Chaos and the Storm God separated her from our group because they wanted her to lose herself and then they could use her power for evil purposes." I do not want to tell Emerald this, but it is something she must know.

"Okay. Thank you, Athena. I am just tired of being left in the dark," she replies in a very small voice. She sounds like she suddenly got a head cold. I know she feels terrible about what she just said. Even though she said those horrible things, she did not want a new sword master. She must have known how deep that cut her sister, even if Shadow did not show it. It startles me when Artemis suddenly speaks from the corner.

112

"You have no idea what Shadow has done for you. She gave up absolutely *everything* for you. She had freedom where she could help hundreds of people and live how she chose. Sometimes she would just strike out without warning and venture all the way to the other side of the land. Only one person has ever been through the North Pass and returned. That person is down the hall, shielding us from danger so we can shut our eyes and sleep soundly. She ventured to places around the world that no one will ever lay eyes on again. Do you know why it has only been in the past few years the Chaos has been able to rise to power? Do you know, Emerald? Can't you see it? I see it in your eyes. You know the answer," Artemis growls from the darkness.

There is a tone in her voice that makes the hair on the back of my neck stand straight up. A horrified silence is all that resonates from the child as the terrible answer comes to her. Artemis continues to speak in that dark voice, sending shivers down my spine.

"Hundreds of people have suffered because Shadow allowed *one* person to soften her unbreakable shell. Before you came along, she was the one who kept Chaos from gaining control over the humans. She hunted him and hounded him from place to place and kept him chasing her. Then she saw it as her duty to protect you, because she failed to stop Chaos from killing your family. You are a debt that she has carried for over nine years. Perhaps by now it would have been paid off, but she grew to love you, and trust you. Now you want to throw all of that away with your selfish words.

"You underestimate the strength of your words, Emerald Alían. You prance around in armor you don't deserve with weapons fit for a king, hand wrought by none other than the Shadow Warrior herself, but you are nothing more than a silly girl who ought to be learning how to clean and cook. In Olympus, we had begun treating you as one of us, but

113

you have proved yourself to just be an ignorant child. Everyone would have been better off if you had not been a distraction to her. We warned her and suggested that she should send you to another place, but she insisted that she would be the one to take care of you. She saw something special in you. I thought I had seen a glimpse of it before, but right now, all I see is an ungrateful child who is unworthy to call herself the Shadow Warrior's apprentice." Artemis sits up straight and her silver eyes burn through the darkness like a wolf, transfixing Emerald like a cornered prey animal. The youngling squirms under the terrifying gaze. In a soft voice Emerald says something I never expected.

"I do not want to be a warrior, or to have Shadow as my swordmaster. All I have wanted is to have my sister back. You stole her from me." Artemis's cold glare does not soften in the slightest.

"Perhaps you should have said that earlier instead of yelling at her."

I have never seen my friend, normally cool and collected, this angry before. I tense my muscles slightly, prepared to spring between the prey and the predator if the need arises. Artemis' hard eyes turn to me and I can see the burning fury there, and the clear warning not to interfere. *This has been a long time in coming.* Emerald has put her foot in a deep hole with a wolf nipping at her heels.

"Be careful of your words child, for you know not of their power. If I *ever* hear you speak like that again, you will be very sorry," Artemis concludes softly, her voice deadly composed and quiet, which is somehow more terrifying than her anger. She leans back against the wall and closes her eyes once again. I can see Emerald trembling violently in complete fear and horror. I offer no sympathy. She got what she deserved.

Chapter Twelve

Shadow

I spiral my blue magic high into the air and, *poof*! It explodes into a fine blue dust. Immediately, I reform it into a rearing stallion-Enbarr of the Flowing Mane. He is my guide and my symbol. I frown at it and the horse comes to life. He gallops back and forth. Where his hooves strike the ground, a bolt of blue fire flares into life before simmering down again. As I watch him, I start to get a sense of foreboding. Something is amiss. Enbarr is trying to warn me.

"What is it?" He just looks at me. I remember he dislikes the new languages. "What is it?" I ask in the ancient language known as Daenlir. It is the language Chaos and I grew up speaking.

"Danger! Something's coming. Something powerful! We are trapped!" he responds.

"Go warn the others. They will understand Remic, Arindal, and Tinal," I direct him. He gallops down the hall and soon I cannot hear his hoofbeats. I do, however, hear something coming down the hall from the opposite direction. *Oh great, something else is here to kill us.* After switching to my immortal form, I can feel that it is just under the surface. Some part of me has awoken. It is not necessarily good or evil, but I am different. I have shown who I really am. There is no going back now. I am thrown into a race with destiny and I am not sure if I will finish.

I can hear whatever it is getting closer. After a moment of rummaging through my backpack, I find what I am looking for- a coil of rope. I wind it back and forth like a giant vertical spider web. I have a vague suspicion as to what is after us. This should slow it down just a little bit. After making sure it is tight, I shoulder my knapsack and run. I sprint the entire way back to the camp. The others are already packed up.

"How are we getting out? We are in a dead end!" Emerald asks me fearfully. I guess she is speaking to me again, although I notice her pale face and wide eyes. She looks deeply shaken and she refuses to look me in the eye.

"Nowhere is truly impossible to escape," I respond absently as I inspect the wall. There are small etchings on the wall, runes. Very few are still alive who can read the obscure symbols. I taught Emerald a few simple words, but it is very hard if it is not your first language. I am fluent in many languages, but Daenlir is my first tongue. They read,

Blood meets blood,

Lies and truth.

Together it can get done,

What one alone could not.

May the wind be at your back.

Well, that's helpful. Why does this person like riddles so much? I am seriously tired of them. They all seem to have my life in the balance. Suddenly, I hear a crash and the angry bellow of a bull. The Minotaur is here.

I look at Athena and Artemis to see if they heard it as well. They both nod. The trap I set will only stop it for minute or two. There is no time to lose. I read the runes aloud for the others. Emerald, Athena, and Artemis look thoughtful as they try to figure it out.

I know what it means, but I do not want them to know. They must be brave for this to work. None of us will die without it going through me first. I am going to take on the Minotaur.

Most people think that there is only one Minotaur, but they are very wrong. There is one in the heart of every labyrinth. Just like the guards in front of the royal gates, he is the protector of the end of the labyrinth. You cannot escape without going through him first. Theseus is the most famous Minotaur slayer, known for his bold rescue of the trapped people in the maze and heroic killing of the Minotaur, but he is not the only one who has encountered the beast. That isn't to say that any others have survived their battle. The skulls of the skeletons nearby seem to grimace grotesquely at my predicament.

"Get against the wall. If the Minotaur gets through me, do your best to kill it. Do not try to help me, because if you do it may mean that your demise will come sooner than the fates had planned. Powerful magic will be flying and I don't want anyone caught in the crossfire. All of the monsters are at their most powerful here. This one lives here. It makes the Ursa Minor look like a cub."

Another angry bellow echoes down the corridor. The Minotaur is coming. I put my hands on Emerald's shoulders and keep my intense gaze locked on her until she reluctantly looks me in the eye. The fear and horror in them seem to make the different greens in her eyes swirl around. I'm not sure why, but it makes me speak softer than I had planned.

"No matter what you see, I am forever your sister. Nothing can change that." I walk a few yards forward and wait for the Minotaur. The half bull and half man lumbers around the corner. With the head of a bull and the torso of a man, he is a demon from the underworld.

He lets loose a triumphant roar as he sees me without my sword drawn and simply waiting for him. I allow my battle adrenaline to fuel me. My senses heighten and I can hear everything. I can smell the rich and dark scent of the dirt pressing down on us. I can see every little detail. I flicker with power. In a flash of light I am encased in my custom armor. I need the freedom that you cannot have in full plate armor. I glance at the ice blue and silver horse, Enbarr of the Flowing Mane, on my breastplate- the symbol of bravery and intelligence.

I draw my sword and glance down the long silver-blue blade. The sword is perfectly balanced with a hilt of silver that is as light as a feather. The grip is a beautiful silver leather. My blade has a name worthy of its legend- Tíne, or Fire. I shrug my shield higher onto my left arm. My symbol is also etched there in an icy blue. Upon seeing my sword he hesitates, but with an angry bellow, he charges. I jump aside and then aim a straight thrust at his chest. He easily dances aside. In a flash of red light, a broadsword appears in one of his giant hands. The other holds a double-sided battle axe. We begin to circle each other, occasionally fainting a thrust or a side hand cut.

I watch his eyes as he moves. He suddenly darts in with a fast strike. Caught slightly off guard, I parry the blade away, but not before it scores a long gash down my arm. I quickly duck the wild backswing of the axe and swear as the blood courses down my armor. It is merely an irritation, but could become deadly should it distract me. He cuts and slashes in a vicious frontal attack and I am forced to stubbornly give ground as he tries to catch me off balance. His strokes are powerful, but they are wild.

"Fight strength with speed!" I reprimand myself. I stay light on my feet and I dart around him and force him to meet my lightning thrusts. He moves fast though and launches a huge overhead blow at me. I throw my shield up to block the strike. The sheer force of it sends me to my knees onto the hard rock floor. He draws the axe back for a killing shot when I launch myself into a forward roll that takes me under his legs and I jump to my feet. It is time I go onto the attack.

I find a new source of strength and launch a bewildering series of lightning fast strokes. Overhand, side hand, thrust, underhand, overhand. I give myself over to the muscle memory drilled into me by years of hard practice. To the eye, my sword is just a flash of ice blue magic. He struggles to keep up with the rapid strikes. He catches me in the ribs with the flat side of the axe once, but I cannot feel anything. The only reason I noticed it was because of the sweet note that my armor sang as the metal crashed against the silver. The world is tinged with blue. I fight with such fury that the Minotaur cannot stand the pressure of my terrible blows. He stumbles and almost with a life of its own, my sword darts in and buries itself deep in his heart. He disappears in a mist of red.

I will never be able to tell you what made me do it, but I suddenly drop to the ground and roll to the left. Right where I had just stood, a sword whistles through empty space. A man slightly taller than me stands behind the spot where I had just been. His eyes glow with a demonic red light. He wears a black and gray tunic with a lightning bolt on the left side of his chest. He slashes down to where I am kneeling on the ground. *Where did he spring from?* I do not have time to think about it as he launches an assault of flashing strikes. I don't even have a chance to regain my footing. I just dodge and parry the blade with my sword and catch the rain of hard blows on my shield. This cannot go on for long. I do the only option I have left. I throw the shield at him. He does not duck fast enough and the sharp metal rim catches him in the forehead. I hurry and get to my feet before he recovers from the wound.

"Who are you?" I ask in the brief pause. He smiles grimly.

"Your enemy." Without another word, he launches into a rapid pattern of forehand and backhand strokes. Something is not right. I can feel the very traces of a memory hidden deeply at the edge of my mind. I should not be fighting him. Taking advantage of my loss of concentration, he swings an overhead strike. I only have time to lean to one side before I feel a searing pain down my side. The man's sword slices through a chink in my armor and the sword bites deeply into my side. I wince slightly, but I show no other signs of the pain. A wound like that ought to be fatal, yet I feel no different. I am not a human, nor am I an Olympian. I am a creature far beyond them. I am the Shadow Warrior. Suddenly, out of the blue, a memory surfaces and the missing puzzle piece clicks into place.

"Stop!" I shout and step back a few strides. He stops immediately as if I had frozen him. I look deep into the man's red eyes. When I blink into my magical vision, I can see red magic- the magic of the Storm God. More memories from my past flood into my mind.

A man is laughing at a joke that a young girl of seven just told him as they sit in front of a cabin mending some arrow's fletching. The same girl and man are sitting together by the hearth in the winter. A man and a beautiful woman are sitting quietly at the kitchen table sipping their morning coffee. The same young girl comes storming through the door, covered in mud. She had obviously slipped in the mud during her practice session on a rainy day, the man laughs at the furious expression on her face. Despite her anger, she grudgingly smiles too. I snap out of the memories. The man stares back at me with those demonic red eyes. I stumble back a few steps in shock and despair. That man is none other than my own foster father, Will O'Conghalaigh. I force myself to look into those red, blank eyes.

"Drop your sword," I command quietly. To my surprise, he does. I send some of my cool and light magic into his head. Holding down my frantic emotions, I desperately shut my eyes and send my memories and one word with the magic. *Will.* The armor melds back into my clothes. I still have Tíne and the shield with me and both give me energy and power. I hold the mind spell until the red magic leaves. It forms a great cloud and the cloud forms a young man. He flies at me and when he comes near me, he rams my shoulder with his shield and his sword flashes a scant inch from my neck as he unintentionally saves me from the bite of his blade as I fall to the ground.

Stunned, and slightly breathless from the mind magic, my strength is diminished. I look up at the high ceiling hoping to see the stars for the last time before the storm spirit kills me. *What a pointless death.* Instead of everything growing dark, it gets lighter until everything is white. There is nothing but a strange white stone ceiling high above. My soul will be trapped down here forever. I shall never join the stars. I can see the smiling face of an unearthly beautiful woman, who I realize now to be my mother. She smiles gently at me like she used to when I was young and had just done something stupid.

"*Silly child! You know that breaking your ribs in a fight is a stupid way to die!*"

"*I know. Sorry, Mother.*"

"*The humans still need you. Your job is not finished yet. You cannot die now, you cannot die ever. You are far beyond immortal.*" The face disappears. I look around. The storm spirit is advancing on me. He looks disappointed that I am not dead.

"I guess I have to finish you off myself." He glides over to me.

"Be gone! Never come back again!" I try to shout, but my voice fades when my fractured ribs move and steal my breath. I slowly draw my dagger and send as much magic as I can into it before throwing it as hard as possible. Years and years of practice make my throw perfect. He howls and vanishes. My knife clatters to the ground. After glancing over at Will, I sink back down to the floor, totally spent. Emerald sprints towards me. She kneels next to me. Her hands shake as she seals the wound in my side and on my arm. The cracked ribs start to mend.

"Please don't leave me!" she cries. I open my eyes again and raise an eyebrow at her in a well-known expression.

"Where is there to go?" I reply dryly. "Do you seriously think that I would miss an upcoming war?" Despite my light-hearted comments, I know how close of a brush I had with Death. I hate it when I do that! Mind magic is very difficult for me. It takes three times the magic. For some, that would have been very easy and the physical magic would be hard. Artemis and Athena look down at me fearfully. "Seriously? You *all* thought I would leave you stuck in this mess? I cannot leave our world hanging you know! There is a war to be fought and I do not plan on missing it. I still have to convince Zeus to listen to me."

"You know, I really think you need to stop getting nearly killed," Artemis lectures me.

"Yeah, it might be better. I bet it hurts less to. Help me up."

"You really should not stand up, but what are we going to do with him?" Athena jerks her head at my surrogate father. Despite Emerald and Artemis's concerns, I grab Athena's extended hand. As she hauls me to my feet, I wince as pain shears through my ribcage. I look over to where Athena is standing guard over my father. I shake my head to clear it and organize my thoughts.

"Emerald, come over here please," I order quietly.

"Would you all give us a moment?" They all go a little way down the hall. My father is sitting on the floor watching us. Pain is written clearly on his face as he struggles to remember what happened.

"Emerald, this is my father," I tell her gently. She gives me a look that is clearly wondering about my sanity. I catch her looking at both of us and noticing the lack of resemblance. His hair is dark and his eyes are hazel.

"My surrogate father," I add in explanation. "I am not joking. He was taken over by a Storm Spirit. That means that he has been in the maze for a long time. He stopped fighting it, so it took him. The Storm God was going to use him. He was sent to kill me because the Storm God knew that I would not kill him and he could make him kill me without the slightest qualm." She looks at me and then at the helpless man at our feet, for once at a loss of words.

"What is wrong with him? Why does he not speak?" she finally asks.

"His mind is in shock. I had to help him find what little resistance he had left. I sent him the few memories I had." My father moans and mumbles something inarticulate. We both look down. At that moment, he opens his eyes again. I look into his hazel brown eyes. This time there are no more traces of the red magic. I slowly sink to my knees beside him. He looks at me, unable to comprehend what he is seeing.

"What happened?" He sees the newly healed injuries and gasps.

"Shadow! What have I done?" There are tears in his eyes as the confusing memories flood in. I watch his thoughts as they flash through his head.

I was fighting... Shadow? Everything was red. Then an ice blue came in and tried to take over the red. Memories came and went. Emily. The Goddess of the Light and his best friend. Shadow sitting with him the night before he left for an ill-fated mission. He and Shadow laughing as they repair the fletching on some arrows. Times from long ago when life was calm and happy. A clear memory surfaced- Shadow on the ground helpless, without her weapons as the cursed Storm Spirit comes at her.

I clear my throat to get his attention. He looks at me with pain-filled eyes as he remembers trying to kill me. I am his adopted daughter, but he loved me like I was his real daughter. His pride and joy. Emerald became an orphan when Chaos came and killed her family and left me torn. For the first time, I had to choose between what was right and what was necessary. I knew that I owed the child, but could I actually care for the girl? I did not have time for her, but I felt sympathetic towards her when I remembered how hard it was to wander through life alone. Against my better judgement, I took Emerald in and she became my sister. My parents had disappeared two years before I saved her. Now I have found my foster father. My mother is the goddess of the Light and I rarely see her anymore. My true father, the God of the Dark, disappeared from my life when he began teaching my brother the ways of the cruel and the evil.

"I tried to kill you," he whispers.

"No, you did not. The Storm God did. This is not your fault. If anything, it is a blessing. You found us and now we are together again. Let's get out of here! Athena! Artemis! Come on! You do want to get out of here right?" They jog over to us.

"This is my foster father. His name is Will O'Conghalaigh, or if you prefer to say Connolly, that works, too." I let them greet each other as I stand up again. I walk over to the wall that is blocking our way. The message on the wall said that I would find what we need. That means that we need him. Blood meets blood, at least by word of mouth, if not biologically related.

"Hé! Come over here guys! Will, can you read this?" He looks at it and nods.

"Daenlir, the Language of Old. I am not fluent, but I know enough to get by."

"Then you know what to do?" I ask. He nods. I draw Tíne from the sheath at my belt. The sword's blue blade and silver hilt glimmers with a light of its own. The super sharp edge of the blade will serve the purpose. Without further warning, I cut a shallow gash on my arm. I pass the blade to Will and he does the same. The blood mixes on the sword. It glows brighter and brighter. Suddenly, the wall is gone.

Chapter Thirteen

Evan

I do not know who I am and neither do I care. The dark presses in against me and I long to scream, but the strength necessary disappeared a long time ago. A brief flicker of a memory flits across my mind, but it is gone the moment I try to focus in on it. I can feel the presence of something evil nearby. It continues to come closer as I grow weaker. The harsh red magic slides into my mind for the hundredth time and I shove it out with my dark blue magic. Oh, how I wish I were still in the forest with Ma and Pa! Years later after being taken away by that mysterious girl to the warrior school on that fateful night, I still long for them. That will never be. They were killed and I was taken to this dark chamber of stone.

I used to believe in Hope, but now I know how naive that notion was. Hope abandoned me a long time ago. I just want to give up. To allow myself to be taken by the warm and welcoming red, but something stops me and gives me a little bit more strength. That strength is nearly gone.

The taunting ice blue memory flits closer. I make a halfhearted grab at it with my magic, but it just moves away again. I wish that I could remember anything. I barely even know my name. That makes it worse, humiliating even. Dying without even remembering your name or history. With a supreme effort, I think hard and try to remember anything. A name floats lazily across my mind. Evan. Evan Faelin. I am... Nineteen? The memory comes into focus as if that were a trigger.

Four Years Prior

I am standing behind a tree watching a girl continue with an unbelievable sword practice. She is strikingly familiar, but I do not dare to

126

show myself. Her sword is an icy-blue blur as she practices different sequences, the sword seeming to be an extension of her right arm as she flows through the motions. She suddenly throws the sword up in the air, spins to the side, drawing her long dagger with her right hand and stabbing at a warrior that only she can see. With barely a glance, she stretches out her left hand and catches the sword. I watch her muscles in fascination as they powerfully maneuver from one movement to another.

My ears turn bright red as I notice her flawless figure with awesome musculature showing, due to her short tunic and breeches. However, while chivalry demands that I look away, I cannot. She obviously doesn't care that she is seen in men's clothes with far more than a single man's strength, but I cannot help the hot blood from rushing to my face. Women wear dresses to conceal their forms. It almost seems indecent for a woman to wear such attire, but I could never imagine this warrior in anything other than a man's clothes. I suppose if you live and fight like a warrior, you may as well as dress the part, too.

After an hour or so of the best swordsmanship I've ever seen, she throws the sword aside in frustration as she fails to get a tiny twist of her sword in a maneuver to go the way she wants. I turn to leave and accidentally step on a branch. The noise is loud to my ears, but there is no response from the girl in the clearing.

Women are not allowed to become knights. They stay at home and tend to the house and the children. In only a year or two, she will most likely be married and wearing dresses and an apron instead of a sword belt. A far extreme from the fierce and noble girl in front of me. A voice deep in my mind tells me I am wrong. This warrior's heart is one that will remain free. It will never be captured. Especially not by one who is as lowly as an orphaned battle school apprentice. There is no way that one of such remarkable beauty and poise would even so much as look at me twice. However, while her heart may remain uncaptured, mine is already stuck fast in that trap. That is what drew me out to this remote clearing in the dangerous woods.

I cautiously take another step deeper into the woods, away from the girl. An arrow splits the air an inch above my head with a sinister whisper. I freeze in terror. My heart beats loudly in my ears and I am surprised that I can even hear what she says. Her voice has its own cadence to it, unlike any way of speech that I have ever heard before. Almost like a different accent, but less abrupt than that. It reminds me of the magnificent feeling when a wild song grows stronger and stronger, making your heart soar. The type of song that gives energy and fortitude with every beat of the sonorous hand drum and the clear notes of the bone flute. No voice I have ever heard has that much magic flowing within it.

My heart beats faster, but not from fear. A strange, new feeling has taken its place next to the fear. Who is this person who has successfully stolen my heart and terrified the living daylights out of me at the same time? This is not someone to mess with.

"I wouldn't move if I were you." I didn't see her move and her back is still turned, but there is another arrow already nocked on the string of her massive longbow. My mouth grows dry with fear. "Come out where I can see you." Her voice sounds young, but there is a ring of authority to it that allows for no refusal. I nervously step into the clearing and she finally turns around. I recoil as her ice blue eyes pierce me like a dagger. The girl looks about seventeen years old. She is around the same age as me. She looks me up and down, taking note of the battered sword scabbard that I wear at my belt. She stoops to retrieve her sword, but her eyes never look away. Like the way a wolf watches its prey. There is something unsettling about her that I cannot place. Her eyes are a startling ice blue. They crackle with intensity, yet they are not cruel. I can even make out a light of humor in them. "What is your name?" I jump slightly at the pure confidence that resonates in her clear, exotic, and enchanting voice.

"My name is Evan Faelin. I am seventeen years old. Who are you?" I ask in return. My voice cracks slightly from the tension. I am slightly embarrassed about being afraid of a girl, but one look at her sword, held easily in her right hand and the powerful bow in her left, changes my mind. She hesitates for a long minute before answering.

"Some have called me Shadow. You may address me by that name. I am sixteen, if we are speaking in your human years. It is not a good idea to wander so far from the Ludus Praelii." She reads my blank look and clarifies, "The School of Battle. They will be looking for you. Why have you strayed so far into the Dark Woods?" I meet those level blue eyes with my own defiantly, daring her to make fun of me. I hold my head up high as I explain why I am here, terrified and staring at an arrow that could easily have been through my heart instead of embedded in a tree next to me.

"The other boys were beating me up because I am smaller than they are." Now that I think about it, I realize just how tall the girl is. She must be at least six feet. I am about two whole inches shorter than her! There is a calculating look in her eyes as she appraises me again, this time her piercing gaze quickly takes in my demeanor and it lingers briefly on the black and purple bruises covering my limbs. She glances at the sun as it abruptly drops below the tree line to gage the time.

"The sun will be gone soon. This is the most dangerous time. I will take you back." I look at her. Even though she is a year younger than me, I get the sense that she is a far more accomplished warrior than a simple fifth year apprentice.

"What about you? Will you be alright on your own?" She smiles at me, but it is a sad half smile. My heart throbs in my chest and the tips of my ears turn bright red. Fortunately the darkness hides my flushed features. I want to help this strange girl, but I don't know how.

"I have wandered this forest since I was four. I am more concerned about you finding your way back and not blundering through my woods." She starts to walk briskly to the other side of the clearing. I jog to catch up with her.

"Won't your parents wonder where you are?" I ask her. Her shoulders and back suddenly stiffen up, and I can't help noticing the intense muscles across her shoulders, arms, and back once more. It does nothing to help my furiously flushed features.

"They are gone," she replies shortly. I am instantly sorry that I asked. That sharp edge to her voice is back.

"My parents are missing too," I tell her hurriedly, hoping to placate her sudden sharpness.

"Your parents are the Faelins, correct?" she asks. As we have been speaking, her accent has been slowly becoming more prominent with every word she says, threatening to make my heart jump out of my chest with the call of the music.

"Yes... Why do you ask?" There is a brief flicker of uncertainty as she looks at me before covering it up. I thought for a moment I saw a flicker of guilt, but that quickly disappears leaving me to wonder if I actually saw anything.

"You know they are dead," she replies bluntly. I stop as what she said hits me.

"How did you know?" I ask in amazement and hope as I run to catch up to her. *Maybe she could tell me about them and give me the details of their heroic deaths!*

"I know many things about your past, Evan Faelin," she retorts, but while her words are harsh in meaning, she says them gently. "I know all of the things that go on in the village and even further beyond. I know that the Carrigan's youngest son is deathly ill with the pox. In Severenth village, the great river, Quintillun, is going to overflow its banks tonight and they will need my help to keep the people safe. Mykel Flin's wife and two children have gone missing in Stellap village. Even now they have sent a messenger that will arrive tomorrow and beg for my assistance. Now, enough of this talk. Come on or it will be totally dark and you will get in trouble for being out alone in the Dark Woods. I also don't want my sister to worry about me."

Without saying anything else, she takes off into a ground-covering run. She runs swiftly and with sure-footed steps through the deepening shadows. I stumble on at least ten different roots in the first five minutes. As we run, I watch her. I have a feeling that I know her from somewhere before and not too long ago either. I saw her in the clearing and I was more fascinated by her skills, but now I notice another thing. She is more than striking; she is beautiful. Her light brown hair shimmers with many different colors as it sways back and forth in time with her long and easy strides. She has high cheekbones and a defined, but not quite angular face. Her clear eyes are guarded, but not hostile.

She is not someone to mess with; countless scars line her arms and one long scar streaks down her face from just above her left eye to the bottom of her jaw. Just like a sword cut. Those are scars that only people get if they have fought many battles. Rather than taking away from her beauty, it adds a bit of mystery to her countenance. She is tall and slim, with hard muscle that continues to catch my eye, but lithe and light like a distance runner. We soon reach the apprentice knight dormitory.

"Farewell. This is where I leave you. The woods are dangerous, but not everyone there wants to hurt you. If you ever get into trouble with those other boys, turn this in your hand once and I will come. May the road rise to meet you." She fades into the shadows of the trees as if she had never been here. I open my hand to see what she gave me. It is a smooth river stone, but unlike any I have ever seen. This one is the color of ice blue.

"And may the wind be at your back," I whisper into the darkness to finish the traditional farewell. There is no answer. The mysterious girl is gone.

As the days pass into months and the months pass into years, there is no sign of her. Sometimes in the early morning runs and exercises I can spot a tall figure running effortlessly through the trees near the running trail, but it is gone the moment I look again. I deal with the taunts and the beatings as they come. It has been nearly two years since that night in the forest. She would be eighteen. Every morning, I look towards the woods to see if she has miraculously come back. Every night, I think about the mysterious girl who wields a sword better than any man. There is something about her that draws my thoughts to her. It must have been the look on her face and the expression in her eyes. Her eyes, despite the humor masking it, hide a sadness that comes from being in more than one battle and seeing more than one ought to in a lifetime, let alone a sixteen-year-old. They had shone with intelligence and seriousness. Her face was aged by seriousness and the weight of responsibility.

All of this drives my curiosity and sends my mind working in overtime to figure out her backstory. While it may not be a happy history, it is one that would explain who she is.

As I lay in bed thinking about her and shivering under the inadequate blankets, I hear feet on the floor near me. Rough hands grab me and hurl me to the floor. Then I feel myself dragged out the door and towards the edge of the woods where the person drops me like a sack of potatoes. I scramble to my feet and turn to face my attackers, shivering in the cold. I groan when I see who it is. It is Trevor, Devin, and Ron. In the evening combats, I had beaten them all so badly that the other apprentices had laughed and teased them about being beaten by the Runt, as I am called. I had used some of the moves that I had seen that one night in the clearing of the Dark Woods. They are not in anyone else's repertoire and they did not have any way to counter them. While I can beat them one on one, three to one... They will kill me.

"The Runt thinks he is *so* great."

"We are going to kill you for what you have done." I look at each of them as they speak. I know that they really would do it. With a sick feeling, I draw my sword, but it is the most graceless standard issue lump of iron ever made. One boy uses a thick-shafted spear and slams it into my knees. I let go an involuntary cry of pain as another cracks across my bare back. I drop the sword and curl up into a ball on the ground as they rain blow after blow on me. I feel something smooth in my hand. Hoping against hope that it is what I think it is, I turn it in my hand. Nothing happens. I sob in despair and pain.

"Time for the Runt to go night, night!" Trevor says viciously still using the taunting litany. I wait for the final blow. All I hear is a startled cry from him. I risk a look and I painfully sit up in surprise. My bruises burn. Trevor is stunned by a heavy, blunted arrow head. Devin and Ron look up in shock to find a slim eighteen-year-old *girl* slinging her bow back into the woods. As their eyes involuntarily watch the bow fly out into the woods, a hand reaches out and catches it. Another girl steps out. She looks about the same age.

Shadow and the other girl look remarkably similar. With the same golden brown hair and confident stance of an archer, they could be twins, but the girl in the woods is shorter and there is a different vibe from her. She lacks the mysterious grandeur of my tall legend of a warrior.

One more girl steps into the clear. She looks around fifteen with strawberry blonde hair. A shadow falls over me and I look up to see Shadow standing behind me, the light of the moon behind her makes her glow like a goddess. Her graceful sword swings in quick little arcs. As I study her closer, I notice that she seems more haggard and drawn with a new scar standing out vividly as the collar of her shirt shifts slightly.

It somehow catches me by surprise, even though countless other smaller scars map out her mysterious history. For some reason, I did not think it was possible for her to be given a serious wound. Everyone in the battle school considers the Shadow Warrior to be a legend, yet here she stands, liberally marked with evidence of old wounds. Legends do not bleed. They feel no pain, fear no one, and can't ever be touched by anyone. A legend is invincible.

"May I ask what you are doing here, boys? Isn't it past your bedtime?" she asks, using a patronizing tone as if speaking to children. Once again, I notice her eyes. This time however, they are hard and sharp like ice. Not the eyes that shine with warmth that comes from a kind disposition, not the ones I have thought of every night before I fall asleep. They flash as she glares at the three older boys. "You do not wish to tell me? Very well. I do not really need a reason to kill you. You would not be anywhere *near* the hardest that I have fought. Actually... I think a deer I caught yesterday was a harder fight than it would be to defeat *you*. Although, I do not like the way that you planned to kill my friend. One on one, I would not have intervened, three to one is cowardice."

She steps forward and towers above them. They both step forward to accept her challenge, their blood riled from her accusation, and that a *girl* would dare to threaten them and insult them like that, but then they hesitate. Shadow laughs at their expressions.

"So, now you realize who I am. It is really not a good idea for two half-trained boys to take on the Shadow Warrior, is it?" Her sword sweeps out and knocks the spears out of their hands. She turns it into a smooth backhand swing and turns the blade to the flat side and knocks them to the ground. She hesitates and stops to face Devin. The big boy looks ready for a fight. His expensive and beautifully crafted sword is drawn and ready. Devin shoots a rapid thrust that is so fast I blinked and almost missed it.

"That's more like it!" she cries happily as she catches his sword on her own blade, sending it gliding harmlessly past her slim waist. I am suddenly struck by the thought of how similar she is to the elves in the stories I have read. Her power, speed, beauty, and lithe grace is exactly how the fair folk were described.

She laughs merrily out of pure humor; her voice is as clear and wild as a sleigh bell.

"Good try. Perhaps you should move a little faster next ti-" before she even finished her sentence, her sword, seeming to have a life of its own, slams into his blade and in a complicated circle move, her sword is on top and she flicks his sword out of his hand. Her sword tip lightly touches his throat and he freezes instinctively at the terrible sensation of being completely at someone else's mercy. "You ought to work on your reflexes. I will have to inform your sword master, Bevel Hardstriker. Well!" she claps her hands together judiciously. "Now that you are all warmed up, Master Devin Webber. I'm curious to watch you fight Evan. Why don't you two pair off? He might be a bit better of a match up than me. I am far out of your league, boy, so I would take the offer if I were you," she suggests to Devin.

I draw my sword in answer. She holds up her hand. "Wait just a second. Can I see your blade?" Mystified by everything that is happening tonight, I pass her the terrible sword. She takes it and grimaces. "This is useless! How do you even fight with this?" I shrug unhappily.

"It is all I have," I say defensively. She raises an eyebrow at me. Before I get a chance to protest, she draws her own sword and I bite off my words. I will not forget who the sword master is here. To my surprise, instead of cutting me in half, she switches the direction of the blade and offers me to take the hilt. Cautiously, I grab the silver leather grip. It is soft and molded. The sword in my hand feels graceful and agile. Unlike my sword, this one does not pull on my wrist trying to drag my hand down.

"This is amazing!" I exclaim in delight, marveling at the way the beautiful sword catches the moonlight.

"It is called Tíne. Let's see you against Master Webber." I turn and look at Devin. He has been slowly backing away. Shadow snaps her fingers and it sounds abnormally loud in the very cold midnight air. Suddenly, another girl is behind him with a sword drawn. Her blade is gold. And I mean *pure gold*.

"I would not try that if I were you," the stranger says mildly. Devin glances at me again and with a look of pure black rage, he draws his sword and charges at me. I glance down at Tíne and yelp. The blade flickers with ice blue fire inside the metal as if the sword has fire coursing through it. Shadow mutters a few words in a language I don't understand and the blade goes back to a normal blued steel, with perhaps a little more blue than normal. She nods reassuringly at me and I swallow nervously.

Devin is still coming closer. My throat is suddenly parched. It is one thing to have mock combat with wooden swords where the worst that will happen is you get a few bruises or a broken limb, but these are real swords with edges and I know Devin will kill me if he can. He suddenly lunges at me with a straight thrust and I almost lose the fight before it can begin. Hastily, I jump to the side and swear as my bare foot steps on a sharp rock and as I duck down to pluck it out of my heel, his back-cut whistles over my head by a scant inch.

I notice that Shadow's friend has her bow ready to help. An arrow is already set on the string and halfway drawn. This really angers me. I can handle this bilge rat on my own. Just because he is a few years older, a lot taller, and a good deal stronger doesn't mean he is better. *Wait, aren't those all qualities that* make *him better than me?* A small voice queries from the very back of my mind. Shadow leans casually against a tree, still eyeing my sword with disgust, as if she is more concerned with the thought of how terrible its balance is, versus the fact that I am about to be skewered. Devin raises his sword and shoots it forward with the speed of a striking snake. I leap to the side and let out an undignified squeak as it surprises me and my cheeks grow bright red as I realize it was a feint.

The sword starts to feel warm in my hand and I am not entirely sure why. It seems to be getting irritated with my terrible fighting. Ron and Trevor laugh nastily from where they are watching the one-sided duel. I sneak another glance at Shadow and notice that she is straight faced, but the corners of her mouth are twitching. She makes a gesture like swinging a sword and I understand her meaning. The sword in my hands reacts without me asking and I swing a full overhead strike and I am not faking it. Devin leaps back and instantly goes onto the attack. Overhead, side cut, thrust, overhead. They come rapidly and give me no chance to do anything except block his sword.

Again, the sword in my hand seems to be reacting on its own accord. At the edge of my hearing, Shadow mutters something and the sword suddenly feels heavier in my hands, but my confidence has never been lighter. Suddenly, everything slows down. His strikes that once seemed so fast are now slow. I can see through his form and where he leaves himself open. Finally, he makes a big swipe and loses his balance. Acting purely on impulse, I slash at him and open a massive wound in his side. He gives a cry of pain and surprise and falls to his knees trying to staunch the blood. *What have I done?*

I hurry forward to see if I can help him. Even though he had been trying to kill me, I would never have intentionally killed him. Shadow gracefully drops to her knees next to Devin and I and looks at him for a minute, her eyes hard, cold, and merciless, before asking the most obvious question I have ever heard in my life:

"Do you wish to live?" Devin nods, unable to speak from the waves of pain I know are flooding through his body. "Will you leave Evan alone?" Once more he nods. Without any other warning of what is to come, she cups her hands like she would to scoop water from a creek, but instead of water, there is ice blue mist. It floats gently into Devin's wound. Within a second, there is a neat row of ice blue stitches where the gash had been. He collapses and his two friends hurry forward to take him back to the eighth-year bunks.

In equal parts, I feel like I am about to either gape at Shadow, or be sick. Suddenly, I am conscious of the fact that I only wearing my breeches and am not wearing a shirt or tunic. She seems to read my mind and gives me a critical once over before smiling slightly at my embarrassment. She makes a quiet gesture. *This never happened.* She takes back her sword and leaves mine on the ground between us.

"I have kept an eye on you for the past few years and shielded you from as many of the dangers as possible. I am going on a long journey soon. I have recently fought in a great battle, but it was only the first of many to come. Most will be battles that I alone can fight. I will be very busy and it is possible that you and I will not meet again. It was very nice to know you. I really hope you continue your dream of becoming a knight, for we will need your courage. Keep the stone. It will give you luck. Oh, yes, I almost forgot. Make sure that you keep your sword with you always. They will not be able to mess with you if you keep it with you. Have faith in your abilities, for you are greater than you believe." I glance down at my standard issued sword. It is poorly balanced and difficult to handle, but I keep the edge sharp and dangerous.

She follows my gaze and as I watch, the sword is coated with a soft icy blue light, the same shade of blue as her eyes. I look at it in surprise. The blue stone she gave me is embedded in the crosspiece of the hilt. A second later, a whole new sword is sitting on the ground. It is beautiful. A straight, slightly blued steel blade and the dark blue and silver adorned hilt glints in the moonlight. There is a sapphire stone set into the pommel. It is the exact color of my own eyes and the strange mist that I can wield when no one is around. It occurs to me that she can do the same thing. Only the children of the rich nobles get nice swords from their families.

Before I can even begin to try and find words to express my thanks, she says, "I will miss you. This is also for luck." She leans down and kisses me on the cheek softly. I see the deep sadness in her eyes revealed along with the pain she bares on her shoulders. I blush and feel as if I intruded on something personal. She steps away and starts to walk into the woods. With the moonlight streaming down on her she looks ageless. I notice, not for the first time, that she is truly beautiful in her wild and mysterious way.

"Goodbye, Wolf!" She raises one hand in farewell, before disappearing into the forest. I will never know why she called me Wolf. What I feel is that I've lost her forever this time.

The memory fades back into black. That was the most vivid and longest memory that I have had in a long time. I realize that my cheeks are wet with tears. I suddenly feel stronger and more hopeful. I open my eyes for the first time in what feels like years and feel for the hilt of my sword. That was only one year ago. Before I became a knight. Before I was imprisoned in stone. I have still thought about her every day.

I did not know it was possible to be more surprised, but when a wall that was completely solid only a moment ago, is suddenly gone in a flash of multicolored light, I was proven wrong. On the other side of the opening is someone I never expected to see ever again. Those piercing ice blue eyes have not changed at all.

Shadow

When the wall is gone, the sword's light diminishes. I step through and the others all follow. I hear something move and then see someone appear in the sword light. My sword swings up into a guard position immediately. I instantly regret the sudden movement as it sets my ribs on fire again. I lower it slowly as I see a boy who is no older than nineteen.

"Come out where I can see you," I call sharply. He hesitantly steps forward. I look him over warily. There is a sword in his hand, but the sword is pointed to the ground and he sways in exhaustion and starvation as he stands. I sense no threat from this skinny kid who looks like he has not eaten in weeks. "What is your name, boy?"

"Evan. Evan Faelin." He seems to wonder at the sound of his voice. I start at the name and look at him more closely. I have often thought about him.

"Wolf?" He looks at me with something close to shock.

"You know, I have wondered for a long time why you called me that. I have wondered about you, Shadow. I was starting to think that it was all a dream." I now remember my old friend. It feels like it was ages ago- a happier time. So much has happened since then. I have wondered about the boy I had saved. First as an eleven-year-old, then as a gangly fifteen-year-old, and then a broad shouldered and well-muscled seventeen year old, now an even more refined nineteen year old.

"I am glad that we found you, my friend." That is all I can say, even though I would like to give voice to my other thoughts.

"As am I. I'm not sure how much longer I was going to last. A man in red kept trying to kill me. The stone you gave me sent me a memory. I had given up. I was about to surrender to him. Then I remembered you. I remembered the time in the woods and when you saved my life. You have now saved my life three times." I hold my hand up sharply to stop his babbling. The others' quiet conversations go silent at my abrupt gesture and they all stare at me intently, ready for orders.

Evan stops talking a moment later than the others and blushes. I hear a slight noise in the dark. My clothes ruffle with a slight breeze. It can barely be called even that, more of an alteration in the still air. It picks up and becomes a stiff wind. It smells earthy and rich, like a cruel reminder that we are trapped in the maze made of stone and destined never to see the light world again. The others are all turning in different directions trying to figure out where it is coming from. I close my eyes and listen. It seems to echo back and forth down the hall.

"The wall," Evan whispers. I open my eyes and look at him. His eyes shine with a dark blue light in the semi-darkness. He is looking at the wall that is nearest to us. I step over to it. Looking at it I cannot see anything. He stares at it through those intense dark blue eyes and I glance at him curiously. It is only visible by magic and he obviously has magic. "What does it mean?" he asks.

"It says,

You have come to the end.

A place that none have ever been.

Answer my riddle and you shall go free,

Otherwise you will sit here and remain.

Just like the others who have come before thee.

What always runs and never walks,

Often murmurs, never talks,

Has a bed, but never sleeps,

Has a mouth, but never eats."

"Well, at least it does not have to do with one of us getting killed," Artemis says brightly.

"Yeah, but this is the only way out, so same difference really." After waving nonchalantly at the skeletons nearby to make my point, I walk away from where Athena and Emerald are talking quietly. I hate riddles. I lack the patience for them. I pace back and forth a few times, deep in thought, before gesturing for them to sit. I sit down next to Artemis and make a quick gesture to Evan to sit if he would like.

"Let's take this apart and try to figure it out. What runs and never walks?" I recite the line.

"Someone being chased by a monster?" Evan suggests. I shoot him a hard look. I can't tell if he is joking or not.

"Maybe... Let's move on to the next one. Often murmurs, but never talks."

"The wind! It murmurs, but cannot speak," Emerald says.

"The wind speaks if you listen," Athena points out.

"Oh, I guess so." Emerald stops and thinks about that.

"Wait, what about water? It murmurs over stones and doesn't talk," Will points out.

"That sounds right, and water runs, it does not walk!" Athena chimes in.

"Has a bed, but never sleeps. A river or a stream does not stop. It just keeps going on until it mixes with the Lost Sea," Evan suddenly says.

"A river does not have a mouth," Emerald protests. "It also does not eat!" she quickly adds.

"Wait. Back home the fishermen used to say that they like to hunt salmon at the mouth of the river. That is the start of a river," Artemis recalls suddenly.

"The answer is River. A river runs and never walks, it murmurs, but never talks. A river has a bed, but never sleeps. It also has a mouth, but never eats," Athena sums it all up.

"What are we waiting for! Let's get out of this terrible maze filled with death! So how exactly are we getting out?" Evan asks.

"May the wind be at your back," I whisper. Hurriedly, I turn my back to the wall where the strange wind is coming from. I study the riddle etched on the wall. As I look at it, I figure out what I am supposed to do.

I unsheathe my dagger. It glows slightly with a faint ice blue light. I carve the word river into the wall directly across from the riddle. I automatically translate it into my native tongue, Daenlir, before writing it in. The words are ice blue and they show up as a stark contrast to the black stone. It fades into the wall slowly. Glancing down at my dagger, I swear quietly as I see the deep nicks in the blade from the rock.

I hear a loud crack and the walls feel like they are contracting and releasing. Again, and again, the floor heaves up and down. I grab Artemis and Evan's hands. Everyone grabs each other as everything crumbles around us. Faintly, I hear a scream of rage as we get away. The Storm God will get his revenge one day, but that day is not going to be today.

Chapter Fourteen

Shadow

The black slowly recedes to reveal that we are lying sprawled in a beautiful golden meadow. The golden grass waves gently in a soft breeze. The sky is a beautiful clear blue. A warm ray of sunshine smiles down on us.

"Are we dead?" Evan asks curiously.

"No, we are home!" I jump to my feet in joy. I release a shower of ice blue mist into the air. It rains down gently. This is the Enchanted Meadow. We are safe right now. My energy and unrestrained happiness is infectious. Emerald, Athena, Will, and Artemis are all smiling broadly.

"Um, where is home for you?" Evan asks warily.

"Olympus. Welcome to Olympus, Evan. By the way, we never formally introduced ourselves," Athena says. "I am Athena. Goddess of Wisdom and War," she introduces herself.

"I am Artemis, Goddess of the Hunt and the Moon."

"I am Emerald, Shadow's apprentice."

"And I am Commander Shadow Caerin, Hero of Olympus, and I have also been called The Shadow Warrior." I give him my full title, but leave out my real name. It is my greatest secret and he has not earned the right to know it. Not yet.

"I am Will Connolly, Shadow's surrogate father. I also happen to be Zeus's lieutenant." Evan looks at us in awe.

"I am Evan Faelin, a knight for Lord Philip Alistair of Greenway Castle." I feel sorry for him. He goes from being hopelessly imprisoned in stone and is now standing among some of the most powerful Olympians in a place that looks like Elysium.

"Well, I guess we should probably report to Zeus." I whistle loudly before Rose and Stormy come galloping out of the trees with some horses from the immortal herd. This should officially freak Evan out.

"Thank goodness you came back! We have been searching and searching for you. Zeus was about to send out a team of centaurs looking for you," Rose tells me as she skids to a stop. Stormy tries to copy the motion but trips and falls over. Everyone laughs as he stands up indignantly and kicks the root that tripped him.

"Nobody saw that," he comments, that mischievous expression evident in his eyes.

"The horses talk and there are centaurs," Evan says faintly to no one in particular.

"You will get used to it. Now I assume that even a short knight can ride, right?" I jest. To be honest he is not short anymore. He is only an inch or two smaller than me.

"I am sure that I can ride better than a giant!" he retorts heartily. Everyone mounts a horse. I ride Stormy and Emerald rides Rose. Athena, Artemis, and Will get on their respective mounts and Evan borrows another horse named Rivermist. A gorgeous dappled grey with dark blue eyes and different blue streaks in his coat. I gently press my heels into Stormy's side. He takes off with a whinny of joy and I shout with excitement.

He and I always love a good run. We race into the nearby woods. The others thunder after us in pursuit. In the distance, I can hear other hooves. I drop the reins to his neck and steer with my knees and unsling my bow. Nocking an arrow on the string, I turn and shoot at an old oak tree that is near Artemis. She sits up in surprise then loads her own bow and shoots two arrows in rapid succession at a young spruce tree in front of me. I nod and take a sharp left. The others turn after me. I make a hand gesture for silence. We gallop on- the horses' hooves are unnaturally silent over the debris strewn ground. The kilometers fly by with impossible speed. Stormy's ears twitch back to me.

"We are being followed," he warns me quietly.

"I know. Artemis confirmed it. We have been followed since we left the meadow," I reply. I do not know whether by friend or foe. Always assume that it is the enemy. I stand straight up in my stirrups, balancing easily with the familiar movement of his gallop, and I raise my bow in the air in the well-known symbol of weapons out. I hear the whisper of swords coming out of scabbards. Artemis holds her bow. I slow my mount to a slow canter. The others follow suit. At an unspoken word, we all halt and form a tight circle to confer.

"What is happening?" Evan asks worriedly, glancing around and gripping his sword tightly.

"We are being followed. All of you, follow Athena to Zeus's palace. Artemis and I will hold them back. Now go!" I shout the last two words. They all turn their horses and flat out gallop through the trees. No mortal animal can catch any of the horses at that pace. However, there is a distinct possibility that our pursuers are not mortal. Artemis sits on her war horse, Surefire. Both Stormy and Surefire are some of the fastest horses in the world. If the numbers are too great for us, we can simply meld into the forest with our camouflage cloaks while continuing to lessen their numbers. I can hear the rumbling of hooves through the ground. Surefire snorts.

"They stopped trying to move silently," he points this out as if we could not tell.

Surefire is a dark gray with silver dapples. He has a thin stripe of silver down his face and silver on the lower part of his legs as well. He looks the part of an immortal horse. Stormy is bay, a reddish brown with a

146

black mane and tail. He has white on the lower part of left hind leg and clips of it on his heels, finished off with a crescent moon on his forehead. Both horses are our friends and war partners.

Gregory

Two riders appear one hundred meters in front of us. They are armed with powerful bows, one of them a massive longbow, but they hold them non-threateningly down by their sides.

"Company, halt!" I call to my men. They all stop uncertainly as they see the two riders appear on the trail in front of us. We have been tracking a large group of people, but now there are only these two. *Where did the others go?* We were sent to scout the Land of Old by none other than Lord Chaos himself. I do not know who these people are. I just do as I'm told. Upon first sight, these riders look intimidating, but a closer look reveals that they are just two young girls. They are not even adults!

"We have you outnumbered twenty-five to two. Step aside." I am taken aback when the rider on the bay horse sits up tall and has a look of defiance in her piercing blue eyes.

"No," she answers bluntly, clearly not in the mood to parley with words. They both raise their bows in the air in an obvious threat. "I would not come any closer if I were you. Do you even have any idea where you were sent, human?" The girl who is speaking to us has a look of total disdain as she takes in our short recurve bows and crossbows. Compared to her longbow, they are nothing but toys.

Her Remic has a thick accent. This is not an opponent to take lightly. There is an air of someone who knows how to fight, and knows the strain of leadership. The long scar across her face catches my eye. She has obviously fought in many battles and lived to tell the tale. Despite what I have gathered, we would be worse off if we went back empty handed. I start my horse forward and in a blur of motion both girls have an arrow on the string and are at full draw aimed at my throat. They both release at the same time. I wait for the searing pain of death to come at any second. I flinch as two arrows land in the same spot between my horse's feet. My mare rears and dances backwards a few steps before I can get her back under control.

"This is your last warning," says the girl on the silvery gray horse. All the training that I have ever had is screaming at me to take the momentum and take charge of the situation. The only problem is, I do not know how. I feel the uncertainty radiating off my men. They are looking to me for leadership. I cannot go back without information unless I wish to die.

I put my big shield on my arm and draw my two-handed broadsword from the scabbard. The men all do the same. Dismounting smoothly, I prepare to attack. The girls speak softly in a language that I vaguely understand from a time long ago, before slowly lowering their bows. I feel a momentary surge of victory. They are simple archers. Before I can feel too confident, the girl with the ice blue eyes tosses her beautifully crafted bow to the other before swinging a small round shield onto her left arm. She gracefully dismounts her bay horse and unsheathes a beautiful straight cavalry sword. She wields it with one hand as if it weighs nothing.

One of my men rushes forward to challenge her. She watches him, completely unconcerned, as he runs at her with his sword extended. My men all cheer him on and shout encouragement. He goes for a powerful overhead swing that would split her in half... If she were still there. She moved a few steps away and stands there with a look of amusement. Confused, he tries for a straight thrust. Instead of moving away, she allows the blade to glance off her shield. He stumbles forward a few steps and she had already moved a few more steps over. She easily could have killed him right then. *She is toying with him!* That thought flits through my mind and I am shocked. That man is the best swordsman in our group. Now enraged, my warrior attacks full out.

She simply darts away and allows him to come again. Eventually, he tires and she finally steps in. I turn away. I don't want to see one of my men killed. I hear the sword fall with a muffled thud on the ground. When I dare to look up again, I realize that she only disarmed him. She grabs him by the back of his shirt and with baffling strength, she throws the man back towards us. He flies for about ten meters before crashing back down to the ground.

"Anyone else?" she asks mildly. She plants her sword into the ground and leans on it impassively.

"Who are you?" I ask in awe. I have never seen anyone move that fast, or be that strong. She seems to contemplate on the best way to answer.

"I am Commander Shadow Caerin, the hero of Olympus and most commonly referred to as the Shadow Warrior. My friend here is Artemis, Goddess of the Hunt and the Moon. Who are you, human?" I barely hear the last bit after hearing that she is the fabled Shadow Warrior. This warrior is the only one who rivals Chaos. We mere humans cannot dare to go up against her and hope to win.

"Gregory, Gregory Arand," I introduce myself.

"Drop your weapon, Gregory Arand, and join us on our ride. You may be just who I was looking for. Come closer." Faced with no choice, I signal to my men to drop their weapons. Fearing a trick, I mount and slowly ride up to where she is standing. Her blade is sheathed and the shield is slung over her back.

149

As we draw level with her, I notice for the first time just how tall she is. A shade under six foot, yet lean and purely muscle. She has an aura of power.

"You need not fear me. I just have someone who I am sure would like to meet you." Her voice has lost the cold edge and now I can see that there is a look of sadness and the weight of responsibility in her eyes. However, there is also a bright spark of humor that is stronger and keeps her to who she is. It keeps away ruthlessness and arrogance, along with the power craze that has sunk its talons deep into Chaos. Respect blots out my fear. This warrior may be terrifying and horrible in our legends, but the warrior standing in front of me appears to be honest in her intentions. Although, I am certain that her terrible and wild side is simply hidden for now. *Two faced. This is not someone I could easily trust.*

Shadow

I can tell that Gregory is studying me with interest. It would appear that I have quite a reputation in the New World. I ignore him and speak to Artemis in our language.

"Let's take them to Zeus and see what he has to say. This should be the proof of war that he wants. Ride in the back to ensure that none try to escape," I tell her in Arindal. She nods and goes to the back. I nudge Stormy with my heel and we fly into a kilometer-eating canter. The others follow. Before long, we reach the base of the hill where the steps of Zeus's palace start. A few Olympians had followed curiously as we had galloped through the village. I gesture to a few centaurs who are playing a game with long sticks with weaved grass netting and they throw a leather ball back and forth.

"Watch them, please," I ask them.

150

"Sure," Gildin responds enthusiastically and trots over. I gesture for Gregory to dismount and I slip down from Stormy's back. Artemis walks over from where she was organizing the centaurs. The half human, half horse warriors all carry a recurve bow and a light saber. They will escort the humans to the prison. Although, to be honest, it is not much of a prison. It is a bunch of thick trees that Demeter grew together, forming a yard on the inside. There is a lean-to in the middle. When a few gods or goddesses combine powers around it, it is a perfect holding place. Artemis lightly jumps off Surefire next to us.

"Hold out your hands," she orders. When Gregory complies, she ties a light rope loosely around them. It is more for show and pomp than anything else. None of us fear him and we know that our skills far surpass those of a mundane human. With Artemis on one side of him and me on the other, we start up the long staircase. About halfway up the giant hill, Gregory breaks the thick silence that had fallen over us.

"What are you going to do to me?" The fear is clear on his face as he finally gains enough courage to ask. I stop and study him. He wears a scruffy beard and his hair is a mundane shade of brown frosted with gray. He is dressed in the fashion of that terrible future world, yet there is a different feel off him. Most of the men that I met from there are arrogant and power crazy. They cannot show emotion without being scorned and ridiculed by their peers. This man in front of me is upfront and clear. Effectively, he is simpler. He is not held down by those expectations.

"Where are you from?" I ask curiously.

"The land of Arél. I was taken as an eleven-year-old to the New World. I have lived there for thirty years, now I am home, well, closer to home." He looks wistful as he remembers those days. "You did not answer my question," he reminds me suddenly. I turn to fully face him.

"That is up to you. Would you rather fight with the New World and destroy the world that I work very hard to protect? Wipe out thousands of innocent people just so you have room to build more of those monstrous buildings? Would you do that to your home land?" I demand sharply. His face fills with pain as he hears what he was helping to do.

"Don't you see? I have to do this! Lord Chaos has my family. If I do not obey, he will kill my wife and two children," he whispers. I can see the pain and desperation that is written clearly on his face. I glance at him, emotionless, once more before starting upwards again. It is time for me to report to Zeus, but I stop for a second and allow sympathy to show on my face before gently telling him his worst nightmare. As much as I don't want too, it is my obligation to him. It is another trace of blood on my name. My brother's terrible deeds fall to me through our shared blood. *Why must I always be the one to deal with the aftermath of his crimes?*

"I am very sorry, but I know he has killed them already. It was swift and painless, because in his rage he just wanted to kill. If it helps, a painless death is more than most warriors can hope for. I cannot ask for such a reward." I have to turn away. I cannot stand the pain on his face and the flood of tears that catch in his scruffy beard.

It is not long before we reach the top. As we enter the antechamber to Zeus's throne room, the fat and lazy chamberlain gestures for us to wait. A guard steps forward and roughly seizes Gregory by the arm. Gregory looks at me in alarm as the guard starts to march him towards the door.

"Leave him," I order the guard. He hesitates for a second, before I casually let my hand drop to the hilt of the sword at my hip. Making a decision, he shoves Gregory back towards us before stalking out after shooting me a resentful look. I technically cannot tell him what to do, but most people have heard of my skill at arms… And my quick temper.

"The Lord of the Sky will see you now," Carlos tells us. The Chamberlain had waddled back in while we were not paying attention. I lead the way into the room. Immediately, I sense a forbidding atmosphere in the room. One look at Zeus confirms the suspicion. His normally bright blue eyes are a dark gray with black thunder clouds scuttling by. I notice that Artemis and Athena are the only ones who are standing with me. Evan looks like he is ready to flee the room. My father and Emerald are not quite as fearful, but I can see Emerald's pale face, and the way Will is clenching and unclenching his hands. My father warily walks up and takes his post next to The Lord of the Sky. Next to me I can feel Gregory practically shaking. We stand silently as he casts a furious glare over us.

Finally, he breaks the terrible silence, "How *dare* you bring humans to my realm, Shadow Caerin! Artemis and Athena! My own daughters! I thought that I taught you the laws of Olympus. No human is ever allowed to set foot on our sacred ground-"

"Unless in the great time of the deciding war," I cut him off. "This rule is based off the ancient prophecy that was made millenniums ago, by the Oracle at Delphi. It basically said that when a human sets foot on the sacred ground of Olympus, it means that a war of epic proportions is afoot. It means that the Olympians would fall from power. That law was set because you were afraid- afraid of the humans that you knew were only biding their time before they rose against you. The only reason they have not risen against us sooner is because they lacked a leader. In case you did not notice, they have one now.

"Chaos will take your place on the throne and the Storm God, Leucetios, will be lieutenant, taking Will's place. The Olympians will become extinct. You will all be hunted until there is no one left. It is time for you to face that and to stop cowering away and brushing these things aside! When will you finally understand? Do you not get it? The side of the world that changes, they are fighting and changing *because* they cannot stand for one person to have too much power. That breed of people can never be content because they constantly want and need power! They will try to eliminate it so they can become something greater than it. It is how they progress onto new eras. They had the Revolutionary War, the Trojan War, the World Wars, the Napoleonic Wars, and all of those Civil Wars *because* a group of people wanted more power! War is here, Zeus, and it is time for you to stop hiding."

As I speak, Zeus's face contorts with rage as he hears my daring speech. The air around me sparks and crackles. I continue nonetheless. By the time I finish, the pressure in the room drops so fast that my ears pop. A second before he blasts me, I raise my sword. The lightning arcs down towards me and I easily slash through it. Tíne absorbs the blow without a problem. It blows my arm backwards with the force, but I did not get blasted into a tiny scorch mark on the marble floor which is something that I generally try to avoid. Zeus is generally a fair and just leader, but his abrupt temper and impulsive actions have turned many allies into enemies. Artemis, Emerald, and Athena had backed up as I was speaking. I shove Gregory back with the others. I am about to poke an already angry bear with a sharp stick. Sometimes that is the only way to get people to do anything.

"Face it. You need them, and you need me. Everyone here knows that my power is far greater than your own, and you fear me, but in a way I am one of the reasons they feel safe. Should you fail them, there is someone who can take your place." My eyes narrow dangerously and my temper flits too close for comfort to the surface.

"I could wipe every single one of the Olympians out and no one could stand against me. Imagine that. I could single-handedly rule everything. Fortunately for you and the rest of the world, I have no ambition for power, but I know someone who has the strength and plans to do what I will not. My brother's power far exceeds mine, and he even has an army ready to kill us all. He can kill me as easily as I could kill you. There is nowhere else for you to turn except to me. I am your last chance. If *I* say that these humans can save our world, then believe me, they can. You have trusted me to this point, can't you trust me to make the call for war?" With a scream of rage Zeus stands up, glowing with power.

I quickly throw up a wall of magic to protect the others from his rage. He throws lightning bolt after lightning bolt at me and the others, but they simply dissipate upon contact with my sword and my magic. My eyes sharpen with concentration and I watch each bolt leave his hand. As each one comes towards me, I catch it on my sword.

After seven, my arm begins to tingle and ache, but I cannot afford to allow him to harm the others. It doesn't take long for my irrepressible temper to surface. I throw a bolt of my own magic at the king of the gods and his magic is too weak to stop it. He is thrown back down onto his throne. He struggles for a moment, but then his eyes clear and the terrible rage disappears. He looks around in shock and then at me. Regret for his impulsive actions fills him and deciding that his anger is spent, I sheathe my sword and release the wall of magic. Many long minutes pass and Zeus finally comes to a decision.

"Guards! Take the humans and throw them off the cliffs!" I sigh. *Seriously? He could not come to the right decision?*

"No. You will not. They are under my protection. No harm will come to them. Also, the boy is not human. He is a duoanimus. A shape shifter. You know his name." It is a statement, not a question. His eyebrows contract further together and the air compresses again. I cock my head slightly and raise an eyebrow, challenging him to try and blow me up again. To my immense amusement, the pressure returns to normal and Zeus himself looks surprised, but it quickly fades away to be replaced once more by anger. A deep weariness fills me. *Why must I deal with this childish behavior?*

"You dare to go against me? The all-powerful Lord of the Sky? The King of the Olympians? Who are you to disobey your king?"

"You are not my king. I serve no man, and I answer only to the needs of those who are in trouble. You already know this. I am the daughter of the Dark and the Light, the Shadow Warrior. I am also Elren Caerin, the twin sister of Draemir Caerin who is known as Chaos." He stares at me, aghast.

"Show me your true form and only then will I believe you and summon the war council. Prove yours-." Before he can finish the sentence I throw some ice blue magic high into the air. It swirls around me, faster and faster, then it is gone.

Evan

I watch Shadow with awe along with a deep sense of foreboding. I do not think she is making this better. *What did she call me?* A duoanimus. Two formed. Shape shifter. Is she lying? My thoughts are interrupted by a tornado of blue. I slowly look up to see that Shadow has been replaced with a warrior. Soft leather knee high boots, hide leggings under her awesome custom armor. A blazing blue stallion is emblazed on the left side of her breastplate. A long, flowing, ice blue side cape is on her right shoulder so it does not interfere with her quiver. Suddenly her symbol appears in full size next to her. He is unlike any horse I have ever seen. Apart from being silver in color, he has runes in a language I cannot understand written in ice blue all over its body.

He is a giant of a horse, but fine boned and athletic. The warrior, I cannot see her as Shadow right now, speaks to him in a language I have never heard before, but I can guess that it is the same as the writing on the stallion. Zeus slowly reads the words on the stallion before speaking. His eyes widen with shock and fear, but to my chagrin he does not read it aloud. *What could be so terrible that it would strike fear in a god?*

Chapter Fifteen

Shadow

"Aonbarr Mhanannáin. *Enbarr of the Flowing Mane,*" Zeus whispers, saying both forms of the stallion's name. "So, it *is* true." He sits back in wonder as he realizes that I really am who I say that I am and that this means that war is really coming.

"Can we move on now?" I ask impatiently, not in the mood to wait for him to figure it out. "There are more important things that we need to focus on right now." He nods slowly in agreement.

"I apologize that you saw my bad decisions today," he addresses Evan and Gregory. They shuffle their feet awkwardly and mumble an incomprehensible response.

"Meet me back at the cabin, everyone. Emerald, lead Evan and Gregory there," I order. They turn and walk out of the great hall. Now it is just Artemis, Athena, Will, and myself.

"My Lord, we must prepare for war. If the Land of Old is taken over, it means that they will also take Olympus, seeing as we are part of the old ways," Athena starts the conversation bluntly.

"We need to rally the battle schools and assemble the army. I propose that we send my traveling group to the Arélian king to gather their enemies. Zeus, you will need to go with Hades and Poseidon to alert the other humans. Also, send some more groups out so we can gather more people faster. Artemis's twin, Apollo, and Hermes, Demeter, Hestia, and send a few minor gods or goddesses with them," I rattle off orders quickly, hoping that he won't interrupt me. However, I am not fast enough. I've never been great at talking.

"Wait! We should call a council of the major gods and goddesses," Zeus interrupts. I sigh, I had been trying to avoid this. It will take more time and there is a chance that they will refuse.

"Alright. But we need them to start on this immediately."

"Done. Be back in one day. I will summon them." He dismisses us with a wave of his hand. I allow my magic to surround me and at the last second I change my mind on what to change to. When the magic recedes, I am in a hunter's clothes. Hide breeches, arm guards, the boots stay the same, and a dark green tunic finishes off the look. My cloak is a mixture of different greens and some brown. It helps me to blend in with the forest. Much better.

My weapons look like simple utilitarian weapons, but the sword is sharp enough to shear off an opponent's broadsword. It's simple leather grip and an unadorned hilt, hides a vicious bite. Tíne, my sword's name, means fire, the last thing that many demons and monsters have seen. It will be a sad day when more human blood must fall from its edges. I turn to leave and the others follow. Enbarr walks next to me. I twine my fingers through his long silken mane, before vaulting up.

"I'll meet back at the cabin!" I call as Enbarr leaps away like an arrow from my bow. He effortlessly runs across the meadow. His feet barely touch the ground and soon we enter the woods. I can feel his joy at being able to run freely once more, under his true master. I let go of his mane and with my legs, I steer him towards the cabin that is off to the west. He shakes his head violently before swerving to the right, away from the cabin. Puzzled, I allow him to lead the way. We move like wraiths in the forest. Enbarr's hooves are silent, even through the thickets of undergrowth. Stormy is trained to be very quiet, but cannot move as silently as this. I live in the thickest and darkest part of the woods and I can barely see the cabin through the trees.

"Blend in," I whisper into Enbarr's ear before sliding off to land silently on the leaf-strewn ground. I look up in time to see his hair turn from silver with blue writing on it, to the many shades of green and brown that are in a forest. "Stay close. I will be back."

As I creep towards the house, I hear the soft murmur of unfamiliar voices. Cautiously, I move to the edge of the small clearing and stand in the shade of a tree where the light is uncertain. From there I can clearly watch four men as they stand guard around the sides of the cabin. Five men are inside the cabin. They are all armed with swords and shields. As I look closer, I make out the people sitting at the table. I sigh as I see Emerald and Evan.

Their hands are tied in front of them. I assume that their weapons were taken. Quickly, I make my decision. I grab a low tree branch and scale the tree quickly. As I climb, I unsling my bow from my shoulder and deftly nock and shoot an arrow in the space of a second. My target is the middle of the large wooden shield of the sentry nearest to me. Only twenty meters away, and three feet wide, it is an incredibly easy shot. A second after shooting my arrow, I hear his shout of surprise and all of the others turn to look at him. The one on the other side of the house comes over with his sword drawn.

Now that I have their attention, I jump from the branch where I had been crouching. I bend my knees to absorb the shock. Though I am tall, these men make me look small. They are all far over six feet. Maybe even seven feet tall! Now what have I gotten myself into? An arrow flies out of nowhere and I twist to the side only just in time for the arrow that was aimed at my heart, to get my upper arm instead. Without pausing to pull out the arrow, I nock and shoot instantly. My arrow flies true and the offending man falls to the ground out of a tree like a stone. I pull the arrow out of my arm and throw it aside. Silver blue tinged blood flows down my arm. I frown for a moment; normally it would not bleed so much. *No time to think about it now.* I hear the sinister whisper of steel on leather as four swords are drawn out as the guards abandon their posts around the house to discover what is happening. I bring my bow up in an obvious threat.

"Untie my friends and I will spare you a painful death." My voice is cool and confident, but I know that the odds are not in my favor. They do not even bother to answer. They start to advance towards me. The string of my bow thrums as the heavy draw weight releases. Without realizing it, I had grabbed a shattering arrow. With astounding reflexes, the man in front throws up his shield. Upon contact, the tip of the arrow throws thin, but wicked, strips of stone and the shaft splinters into deadly projectiles to anyone in the way. Three of them cry out as they are cut by the vicious shards.

The guards inside the house start to file out as they see the three men taken out with a single arrow. My friends look up as they hear the guards yell. I make eye contact with Emerald before subtly tapping my wrist. I have always insisted on her having a small knife in a hidden sheath under the cuff of her sleeve. She looks confused, but there is a light of understanding in her eyes as she realizes that I am drawing the guards out to give her and Evan a chance to escape. With the guards vigilantly watching them, there was never a chance for them to even attempt to get free of the ropes around their wrists and ankles. I would be cornering myself if I just charged into the house.

"Hey, you! Stop!" one yells as I turn to run, hoping to draw the guards away. I shoot two of them and they both fall to the ground clutching arrow wounds to the legs. Zeus may want them later. I am hoping that they will all chase after me. Unfortunately, two stay and two follow. They know better than to bunch together. They dart between the trees and present a minimal sized target. They are obviously well trained.

I quickly scale a tree and after getting a few meters up, I find a solid enough branch where, if I must, I can shoot. The men are blundering closer. I whistle loudly, three ascending notes and one lower. This gives away my position, but I was not trying for concealment. There is a slight movement in the nearby woods. I catch a glimpse of what looks like a moving bush or tree for a second, before they walk out of the foliage on the opposite side. Enbarr is listening. The men have rounds shields on their arms and a broadsword in their other hand. One of them is left handed. This should prove to be interesting. I stand on the branch and walk fearlessly across it so I do not need to shout.

"Looking for me?" I jump easily to the ground far below. To reduce the impact of the hard ground, I launch into a forward roll. When the maneuver is finished and I am on my feet, they notice that my bow is fully drawn and an arrow is nocked on the string. Jumping from that height would either break a regular human's legs, or kill them in an extreme case. I bet they were hoping for the latter.

"What are y-" I dodge his sudden attack. I can feel the edge if his sword just barely graze my ribs. It is the oldest trick known to a swordsman, to catch your opponent off guard by talking to him and then thrusting in at him. Lucky for me, I already know that trick and I was ready for it. The speed of the thrust is surprising though. Not many humans are that fast.

Samuel

Her reflexes are incredible! I realize that this is no mere girl with a bow. She throws the bow aside and an instant later the sword that was in its scabbard a millisecond ago is out. She holds it deftly in her right hand.

Instead of the red blood of all men, there is silvery blue blood soaking her sleeve from the arrow. We were sent to capture humans and torture them for information before bringing them to Lord Chaos and the Storm God. We saw that others lived there, but did not think they would be immortal. Now we are faced by an enraged Olympian. I gesture towards my second in command to face her. I can feel my confidence flowing back as I realize she is not even an adult. At first sight, she looked huge and terrifying, but now that I am closer I can see that she is still very young. Only a few years older than my younger brother, Allen.

She is tanned from years of hard work under the sun and remarkably strong. Her light brown hair is pulled back into a braid. The only thing that is unnerving is her eyes. She could pass as a normal human if she chose, but there is an aura of something different. She holds herself with a self-assurance that sets her apart. Most eighteen-year-old girls in the Capital City all blush and giggle at the sight of some cute boy. They primp and preen all day and worry if they don't look good enough. This girl in front of me is travel stained with dirt on her face and still walks with confidence. The eyes are what set her apart from most. The light blue is as sharp as ice and a shiver forces its way down my spine when I see a light of contained irritation in them. No turning back now.

"Go!" I yell and both of us charge in to attack, our swords and shields raised and ready.

Shadow

One of the men, I assume he is the leader, studies me. I stare right back, calm and cool, but I cannot believe that they would have the nerve to take my friends. At a word from the leader they both charge at me. Once again I whistle, but this time I go up five notes and then down two. A streak of silver comes out of the woods. Enbarr of The Flowing

Mane stands next to me in the blink of an eye. The two men stop in confusion, giving me a moment to prepare myself for the duel about to come. My reflexes are primed and ready for whatever they may try. I smoothly step forward to meet them

They both come slower now as they put aside their surprise. The leader stays further back as he waits to assess my skill. The advancing swordsman and I leap into a deadly dance of sword work. As I predicted, he has a huge amount of strength. It is rather like dancing. I dart around and the shriek of swords is the music. My feet move to their own beat. The flicker of swords are like the arms in a twirl, twisting and turning at light's speed to stay on beat. My feet are flying in intricate steps and patterns that keep me away from the sharp point of my adversary's sword. Unlike in a real dance, where the worst thing that can happen is stepping on your partner's toes, in this dance I either stay on beat, or the music stops and I lose my life before the bow.

I suddenly hear the slightest crunch of a fallen twig behind me. I jump in the air, pulling my knees up high above the scything movement of his sword as he cuts for the tendons behind my knees, a crippling blow if it had landed, and as soon as my feet hit the ground, I lower my shoulder and slam the soldier in the chest before spinning away. The second man behind me is taken by surprise and his intended overhand blow slams into the ground next to me. I could really use my shield about now. My move has taken me away from them so that I can face them both. This time they both close in on me. My world closes in on the sword in my hand and the two men's swords.

Overhand, parry, stab, overhand, TURN! Underhand, backhand. A flashing blur of blued metal to my eyes. Neither pose a huge problem on their own, but they attack together like a pack of hounds working to take down a stag. I cannot go on the attack with them both pressing me like this, so I must wait and patiently parry their blades until I spot an opening in the second in commands guard and aim a straight thrust. He twists away and I catch him in shoulder instead. He sinks to the ground clutching the painful, but not mortal wound.

I can sense the other man's sword as he swipes at me in rage. With my back turned, I cannot see him, but I can hear his grunt of exertion as he swings his heavy sword in an arc towards me. The flat side slams into ribs. I feel two start to buckle. *Luck.* That easily could have sliced through my lungs. I grimace in pain and irritation as he yanks it around and goes in for a killing shot. I duck his blade and jump back to buy myself some time but before I move out of reach, his sword somehow pierces deep into my right shoulder, close to the puncture wound from the arrow earlier. I never saw it coming.

Silently I berate myself for that slip up. He sets the point of his sword into the dirt after pulling it out and he waits for me to fall. I look down at the wound to see if it is bad. Blood flows from it, but it is tinged with an icy blue. I swirl magic into my hand and send it into the wounds. Within seconds the bleeding stops and the wound closes, though it does still ache. His expectant expression turns to something close to awe as I glare at him with calm and clear eyes.

"Who are you? You should be dead right now. There is poison on our weapons and even some on that arrow that we shot at you!"

"Your mortal weapons cannot kill me. I am not an Olympian, I am far more powerful than any of them could ever hope to be. I am the Shadow Warrior, and I am sworn against Chaos and the Storm God. Therefore, I am an enemy of you." My sword, Tíne, suddenly blazes with icy blue fire. "You have one chance to surrender or else you will face my sword. This time I will not hold back from killing you. Take your choice." I will give him one chance, but one chance only. He snarls in rage.

"I will not back down to a *woman*. Fancy title or not, you are nothing more than a strange girl with some talent with a sword." My eyes blaze with a cold fury. The fastest way to infuriate me is to claim that a girl is unable to be better than a man. A fury that has been crawling under my skin is close to bursting out of my control. Just like a wild horse, you can only hold it so long before it breaks loose.

"You may wish to believe that, but I am glad you said that. I am tired of holding myself back. You have given me a reason to kill you. You trying to kill me was not enough to cross the boundaries I set in killing humans, but implying that men are better than women is more than enough to do it. My own father refused me my birthright, only because I am a girl. Your comment is not one that I take lightly." My voice is as hard and cold as the ice in my eyes. He recoils as I show the thin and fraying strings of my self-restraint. I have never allowed all my magic to be full strength. I have had to hold myself back for many years. I can feel the magic growing stronger and stronger. That wild horse is reaching the end of its tether. I'm not totally sure what will happen when it is loose.

Samuel

Suddenly it doesn't seem like such a great idea to challenge her. I watch fearfully as she makes a supreme effort to reign in her temper. Her form seems to shimmer. Even as I watch she starts to glow with an ice blue light.

"I gave you a chance. You will wish that you had taken it," she states ominously. *Am I seriously afraid of this teenager?* My fear turns to fury at this confident tall girl. With a snarl of fury, I launch a wicked fast frontal attack. I have great strength and the young warrior is forced to give ground. Though she is slowly moving backward, she blocks my best strokes with an almost contemptuous ease. Slowly, I regain some control

166

of myself. I withdraw and we circle warily. I faint a thrust at her and she doesn't even flinch. She launches herself with the suddenness of a hurricane. One moment it is calm and quiet, the next second the wind is whirling and the sky and water are one. I desperately throw my sword up to block hers.

My mouth goes dry with fear as I realize that this is how my life will end. I will die at the hand of a young girl. Suddenly, her face has a look of surprise. She whirls around to the side and narrowly misses another thrust from a silver, blue, and red stained sword. As she turns, I catch sight of a terrible wound. The sword had been driven straight through her right shoulder again. Her sword arm. Most warriors cannot fight with their non-dominant hand unless they are totally dedicated, so she should be weaker on that side.

The fallen warrior swings a wild roundabout side cut to finish her, but there is a drawn-out shriek of her sword meeting his in a powerful parry. She switched the sword to her left hand. She meets his thrusts and wild swings. With a last-ditch effort, he puts all his strength into an incredibly strong and incredibly fast side-cut swing. If she takes the blow on her sword, it will shear the blade right off or rip the hilt out of her hand. She is not left handed, so it would be weaker.

His tactic would have split her in half, if she were still there. His sword lands with a dull thud into the hard-packed earth. She steps in and finishes him. He looks up in surprise before falling to the ground. He will never rise again. She turns to me and her sword is still swinging in small arcs. The blood flies from the blade and makes me feel sick from fear and desperation. She has been wielding the long sword with her weaker hand for a long time, but she shows no signs of tiring.

What have I done?

Shadow

"Do you want the same fate? If you surrender now, your life may be hard, but you will not end up with your head on the end of my sword," I threaten him. As I watch, he struggles with the decision. I already know what his response will be. This man has had prime treatment his whole life. He will not be a servant for someone else. He has lived on the top of society his whole life. That much is obvious.

"I will demolish you, girl!" he responds, his voice laced with venom. I shrug philosophically. I expected nothing less.

"Very well. I would like you to try. It should prove to be entertaining to see you fail-" I launch into a rapid attack. He desperately throws up his shield to take the blows. I had the element of surprise on my side, but if I let up he will regain his balance and the battle will become chancier. Before long, his reflexes start to slow down due to the typical human fatigue. I thrust in and I feel the sword penetrate deep into his chest. He sinks down onto his knees as he tries unsuccessfully to stanch the blood.

"Please, I beg you! Take me where I can see the stars. If I die in the dark my soul will wander forever. Please!" he begs. I look down into his eyes. There is great fear there. I hesitate before nodding assent. A dying wish should never go unanswered.

"I will do that." I lift him into my arms as if he weighs nothing. I run quickly through the trees until I come upon a moonlit clearing. Gently, I set him down onto the ground. He weakly opens his eyes.

"Thank you. You have freed me. This is my only escape from a world of torture and obedience. I was taken from the town of Irid when I was younger. My sister and I were ambushed by superior numbers and I never saw my family again." A shadow flickers across my face.

168

Recognition, horror, and guilt are in my eyes for a brief second, but I shake my head and my eyes reveal nothing more. I was sent to track them and find them, but I was unable to reach them in time.

"Rest easy now, friend. I am sorry you tried to kill me. If you had a chance to live and do good in your new life, would you do it? I could not offer you that path before. It was your choice to either follow my brother or run. If it got you away from the evil clutches of the Storm God and Chaos's hands, would you follow me? I am sorry, but I cannot give you your life back. However, if you renounce Chaos I can ease your suffering. All I need to know is the number of men Chaos has gathered." He stares up at me sadly.

"Yes, I would. I do not have that chance. I am dying. Nothing can change the fact that I have acted so wrongly, but I can tell you a rough estimate of the size of his army. It is approximately one million soldiers all totaled." He stops and stares up at the trees high above and for a moment I wonder if his soul has passed on, but then he suddenly speaks again.

"I deserve to die. At least I was killed by one so pure and dedicated to keeping this doomed world straight that it purged my soul of the blackness that has inhabited it for many years," he eloquently states. There is a calm that is settling over him that always comes to those who are about to die and have accepted it.

"Close your eyes and die a hero's death." Ice blue magic gathers into my hands. He opens his eyes in surprise as the pain suddenly disappears.

"Why did you do that? I deserve the pain." There is almost a pleading note in his voice. He truly regrets the terrible things he has done.

"I know how to treat a respectable opponent. What are the names of your family members? I swear I will make sure they are safe." I see a light of fear and regret recede and disappear from his face, to be replaced with the swift and relaxing cloud of relief and calm that always announces the coming of Death.

"My younger brother is called Allen. I am Samuel. My sister is Ann. Please save them if you can," he asks, his voice fading to a whisper.

Chapter Sixteen

Shadow

"May you find peace." I step away and run lightly towards my cabin.

"Do you need me, or can I leave?" I nod distractedly to Enbarr's request.

"Don't go too far. I will need you soon." He gallops a few more strides before disappearing into a silver and ice blue mist. I lengthen my running stride until the trees turn into a haze of greens and browns. My feet skim the ground and I fly through the woods, dodging in and out of the shadows. Running with joy that's tinged with sorrow. I have killed many in my years. I have been a murderer since before my seventh birthday.

Only a few kills do I feel guilty about. I have always known what side is right and I have always gone with that instinctive feeling. In the heat of battle, you are faced without a choice. There is not another option. Whether the man is good or evil, you cannot run the risk of finding out. Lies are a powerful thing. If people know you will respect their tale, you will always end up with people handing you falsehoods that you accept. After all these years, I still wear some of their names on my heart. A constant presence that will never leave you. It is a slow torture you can never escape. Though you can scream and beat at the walls containing you, you can never break them down. This is the price you pay to be a warrior. There is always a price. This is the one I must pay.

The wind whips my face as I run. Low tree branches grab for my braid. Still I run. Faster than the wind that I am racing. I must get back before my sister and friends are harmed.

Emerald

The guards that stayed behind turn and watch as Shadow disappears into the woods. I know I am ashen in the face as I stare at the grains of wood in the rough table, fear and horror conjuring horrible images in my mind. Alone among us, Evan looks totally unfazed, even bored. He leans his chair back on its back legs and stares out the window with a thoughtful expression. As if sensing my fearful gaze, he turns his head and smiles at me as if he does this every day. *How can he be so calm at a time like this?* Even after what we know they will do to us for information?

I still do not know what Shadow's cryptic message means. Why did she tap her wrist? Then it hits me. My small sleeve dagger. I keep it hidden in a sheath under the cuff of my shirt. If I plan on ever attempting this, I guess now is the time. While the guards are distracted, I twist my wrist in an awkward position to try to get the knife out. The rope bites deep into the soft skin on the inside of my forearm, causing hot tears in the back of my eyes to spring up. I manage to get to the cuff of the sleeve, but my wrist will not go any further. Now what? The guards still have not come back inside, but I am out of ideas.

"Need some help?" Artemis is suddenly behind me. I would have jumped straight out of my chair if I weren't tied to it. She pulls out her dagger and brings it towards the rope to cut it, but it starts to vibrate in her hand. She brings it within a centimeter of the rope and it won't go any closer. Her blade, just like mine, is magical. Nothing can break it or dull it and it can cut through anything, except apparently these ropes. "There is strong magic here. Have you tried to use any magic to get out?"

"Yes, and it obviously did not work. Where did the guards go? They will come back and find you here!"

172

"The ropes are magical. That is why my dagger will not work," she mutters to herself again, trying to figure it out. It is the same story when she tries to cut Evan's ropes. The long dagger starts to violently shake. It lets out an almost inaudible hum. Artemis puts all of her strength down on the knife, but it will not move any closer. It starts to bend and she finally gives up and releases the pressure before the unbreakable knife breaks. "I have never encountered magic that is this strong before. Hephaestus's blades are meant to go through any spell. The Storm God does not have that much power! This is the doing of Chaos."

"What are you going to do?" Evan asks, his unruffled manner giving way to curiosity.

"I don't know," Artemis replies truthfully.

"Thanks for the rescue," I mutter under my breath. Evan shoots me an irritated glance.

"Hopefully, Shadow will be back soon. I think that she may be the only one who can counter his magic. She is the only one who is as strong as he. Her blade is not the same make as yours, right?"

"No." Artemis shakes her head. "Tíne was made by her mother. Just like Chaos's blade was made for him by their father." Artemis suddenly whisks out the back entrance without warning. Not a moment after she is out of sight, the guards come traipsing back in. One glances at Evan and I before resuming his post. Suddenly, I can see every muscle in his back stiffen. He whips around to face us again. Artemis left her knife on the table. Evan is still in the same nonchalant position with his chair resting on its back legs. He gives the guard a lazy smile.

The guard yells to his fellows in his own tongue that Shadow had called *Remic* and they all turn to look at us where we have not moved. Though I do not understand the language, their panic is clear. The panic turns to rage as the one left in charge stalks over to me. Evan sits up suddenly in his chair, his normally calm sapphire eyes are hard and they shine with intensity.

"Do not go near her!" he orders in Arindal. When the guard keeps coming he tries again. This time in Remic. "Do-not-go-near-her." *When did he learn Remic?* Sometimes he reminds me so much of Shadow. She can be relaxed and seem like a normal older sister. She will joke and make me laugh, but the moment something threatens me, or anyone she cares about, she can be a terrifying sight. Right now, Evan's mask of calm and relaxation is gone. The guard ignores him and continues on. Three steps away. Two steps. One. He grabs a coil of leather from an inner pocket of his jacket. I can't do anything except watch through horrified eyes as the whip descends.

Evan

She does nothing to stop the tears in her eyes as the whip repeatedly strikes her, but she does not shout like most would. It breaks my heart to see her like this. In the short time that I have known her she is like a sister to me. I cannot bear to see her like this.

"Leave her alone!" I shout as I strain at the ropes. What is it that Shadow had called me? A duoanimus? Shape shifter. Something clicks deep in my mind. Emerald needs help. My dark blue magic takes over my vision. Everything is tinged sapphire blue. More magic than I have ever dared to summon. In the blink of an eye I am on all fours.

I look down at myself in shock. What did I just do? My feet... Wait no, my *paws*, are braced to lunge at the man. My coat is shaggy and dark blue with white streaks. Without any further wait, I launch off the ground and clear the long table easily. I land between the man with the whip and Emerald. A feral growl rises from my throat. Foolishly, he cracks the whip at me. I jump onto him and my powerful jaws clamp down on the arm holding the whip. He screams in pain and I release him. With the threat gone, I relax my hackles and turn to look at Emerald.

"Wolf," she whispers quietly. Suddenly something else clicks. This is why Shadow calls me Wolf. I can turn into one. How did I not see this before? The other guards fearfully back away a few steps as I chew through the ropes holding Emerald. They have a sharp and metallic taste that makes me want to gag. I turn back to my human form and quickly look down to make sure I still have my clothes on. That would be rather embarrassing. My fears allayed, I quickly walk to the back of the small room and scoop up my sword. I toss Emerald her light sword as well.

The remaining men are very big, easily over two meters high and broad across the chest. *Hope she knows what she is doing.* I hold my sword in a light grip. I do not have long to wait before the one who attacked Emerald challenges me. The other attacks Emerald. A second before the guard attacks me, I have a moment of fear when I realize that Emerald is sure to be far overmatched. Then the only thing I see is the whirling sword of the massive man in front of me.

Shadow

I burst out of the woods and slow down to a jog as I take stock. I see Artemis and Athena hiding in the outer fringes of the woods, furiously debating what to do. Moving on, I spot Emerald and Evan sizing up two more giant guards. I slip in through the back door and loosen my sword in its scabbard. I hang my bow and quiver up on the special rack I had built for them, almost as if I had been coming back from a regular day of hunting. Emerald's low powered hunting bow is hanging there as well, dwarfed in comparison with my longbow.

In the tight conditions of the cabin, the bow would be nothing but a hindrance. I hear the clash of steel on wood as swords are met by shields. Casually, I lean against the wall. I manage not to yelp as my injured shoulder presses against the rough timber of the house walls. There is no time to heal it and I don't have any energy to waste on it. I watch Evan curiously as he faces off. Every swordmaster, and Evan is definitely a swordmaster, has his own style. I am one of the only female swordmasters currently alive. Most noble or wealthy women if they choose to have a weapon, it tends to be a saber or a knife for safety. I prefer using speed and agility mixed with my strength to devastating results. Many men are stronger than me, but none are faster.

An apprentice generally carries the style of their master. Out of curiosity, I grab two shields off the weapon rack. I whistle quietly before moving unobtrusively alongside him with my sword drawn. I do not wish to startle him. I cross swords with the guard in a rapid move and motion with my right hand for Evan to step back and take the shield. He nods and drops back to slip the shallow bowl shaped shield over his left arm. The man tries to uncross the swords, but I counter the movement easily. I must fight with my left, but that is not a problem. Even just the weight of the shield on my injured right arm makes my shoulder snap with pain. Evan is ready now and in one fluid movement I disengage and step back.

I turn and look over at Emerald as she gives a shrill yelp of pain. There is a long scratch on her arm, but it is not deep. I am confused as to why she would yelp at that. Then I see a long and deep cut on her left side. She jumps to the side quickly to avoid the sharp thrust from her opponent. I can see that he is just toying with her now. Emerald is overmatched and in danger.

In three long steps, I am right behind her. She is tiring quickly at this point. Her expression gives away her desperation. All of the sudden, he kicks out at her shin. I can hear the crack of bone as his heavy boot hits the fine bone of her lower leg. She hits the ground hard and the man takes his time finishing the unfair fight and those few chance seconds are what saves her life and gives me time to throw myself in front of the blade and twist my right arm so the sword glances off the shield. My shoulder and now the whole arm throbs from twisting the muscles and straining the joints. The man moves back in surprise as a new opponent faces him. I disarm him and he looks down at his blade that flew under the table. He throws his hands up in surrender. I turn and check on Emerald. Her face is pale and she looks like she is about to be sick.

Some sixth sense alerts me of movement behind me. I turn just in time to avoid a knife to the back. Instead, it catches me in my right shoulder again. I swear so violently that even he steps back a few steps and Emerald gives me a scandalized look from her seat on the floor. Evan and his adversary both stop, their swords in the air still, and stare at me in shock.

"Can't say I hear many ladies speak like that!" Evan's newest enemy comments in surprise. Evan nods in whole-hearted agreement. They both look at each other and shrug.

"Oh, shut up the whole lot of you! Aren't you both supposed to be trying to kill each other or something?" My voice is a good deal more high pitched than usual. They both look at each other again and leap back into their duel. Evan throws the shield like a discus and it hits him in the head so hard that his adversary is instantly knocked out. That arm is really killing me now. Blood pours from the wounds. I step in with a lightning thrust and the blade takes Emerald's opponent in the center of his chest. He falls back, dead before he hits the floor. I should have known better than to turn away. Even for a second. "Can you heal yourself?" Emerald shakes her head.

"Can't concentrate," she grunts through clenched teeth. I nod in understanding. Without warning, I grab her leg in an iron grip and pull the bone back into the correct position. She screams and thrashes for a second before I let go. I set the bone and send some icy magic to numb it. "Why didn't you warn me?" she demands.

"You would not have let me do it if you knew what was coming," I reply with calm logic. She glares at me.

"At least it stopped hurting now," she grudgingly admits.

"You are welcome. Now come on! We still have to get the war council to agree on my plans for battle. You'll have to numb that again later until it is healed. Now that my magic has already protected the bone, you will be able to speed up the healing process." She gives me the evil eye. After taking a moment to numb my damaged shoulder, I grab my bow and quiver off the weapons rack.

"Thank you so much," she replies icily as I return. I shrug. I will never be able to win a verbal battle with my sister, even though I fluently speak one hundred and sixty-eight languages.

"Let's go." Artemis and Athena lead the way out towards the woods. Evan and Emerald follow behind. I hesitate at the edge of the clearing and turn back. Something is not right. I drop back and head towards the house. Artemis gives me a curious look, but I wave her on.

"I'll meet you there. Don't follow me," I order. She gives me a concerned look, but does as I ordered. The hair on the back of my neck stands straight up and my heart starts to beat faster and faster. *Stop it!* I tell myself and wait for it to slow down before moving again. I can sense the dark and slimy presence of evil lurking nearby.

I instinctively duck into the shadows nearby. My magical cloak shimmers slightly and changes to exactly match the colors. Not a moment later, a strange creature stalks by. With red eyes and a shuffling gait, I recognize it as a wild boar. In general, they are vicious and merciless killers if you are near them, but this is a whole different category of dangerous. This one happens to be five feet tall with pure muscle and the sharp tusks are a crimson colored metal. Those haunting eyes gleam with a mad light. It is hunting.

I suck in my breath in an attempt to curb my rising fear. A Calydonian boar. I have never fought one before, but I have heard stories of the damage they inflict. Even the great huntress, Atalanta, the greatest hunter of her time, was unable to slay it on her own. For the first time, I feel as if a sword and a quiver of arrows may not be adequate weapons. For once, I do not know what I am up against. The beast stops and stares directly where I stand frozen. As I stare into those demonic eyes, I know that he can sense me there. Cloak, or no cloak, it knows I'm here, and it knows who I am. Perhaps in the way I can sense an evil presence, it can sense a non-evil presence. Despite being aware of my presence, he turns and follows my friends instead.

I stand there for a moment longer before something starts to nag at me again. Torn between helping my friends and following the feeling of something not right, I hesitate for a second, thinking rapidly. Even though I worry for my friends, I know they are not helpless. They have a better chance of defeating it together than I would alone. I silently sprint past the house and continue through the woods on the other side of the clearing. Whatever it is that continues to draw me closer, I am near. I sprint on, even though blaringly obvious and all but persuasive warning signs are flying through my head. The smell of evil clogs the air, threatening to choke me. The one who I had promised I would protect is in danger. I had only known him for a few hours, but in those hours, I made a promise and I do not break promises.

I force myself to skid to a halt and take stock. There are voices ahead, but my ears are listening for only one: Gregory Arand. I had nearly forgotten about the New World human who agreed to help us. Moving

179

more cautiously, I come closer to the noises. They fall silent. Before I have a chance to get over the surprise of the sudden decrease in noise, an echoing scream resonates through the air. It flows and bounces off everything around me. The trees and bushes all recoil and the animals hurry into hiding. Reaching higher and higher in pitch, it is an animal reaction. That is the sound of the highest levels of mortal agony and pain. Without pausing to think, or even draw my sword, I foolishly sprint headlong into the clearing ahead.

On the ground, Gregory is writhing in pain. My eyes are drawn upwards to the one who is behind such torture. I freeze as I see the man standing above him. Dressed in a deep-sea blue tunic and armor of the same color is the most terrifying warrior anyone will ever see. The strangest thing about him is not that he is ugly, but that he is incredibly handsome. His arms are ripped with muscle and he stands well over six feet tall. He has a strong face and dark hair, with high cheekbones and sharp dark blue eyes. A long scar marks the left side of his face. When he looks up, I see who he truly is. His eyes are a glowing dark blue like the tunic, but they are cold and pitiless. There is no compassion and no mercy. You live simply because he doesn't care enough to kill you.

"Hello, Brother," I practically spit out the words. The title 'brother' feels like acid in my mouth and it burns my tongue. He turns his attention to me. Gregory stops writhing around, but he does not rise.

"Well, well, well. What do we have here? Has the Shadow Warrior decided to confront me already? Did I finally scare the devious fox out of hiding?" He smiles, but it is the smile of a snake before eating its prey. His voice sends shivers down my spine. It is so familiar, but as I strive to remember where it is from, it slips away from me. Looking back later, I would realize that it is like my own- same pronunciations and different accent than any others in the area.

"Better to be a devious fox, than a marauding bear intent on stealing more than simply gold. You steal lives. So, call me a fox. There are far worse things that I can call you." He laughs and it takes me back to when I was younger and smaller. My hands tremble, but not out of fear. I watched this man kill a whole village of innocent people. I watched him cut down children and women. He killed all of Emerald's family and Evan's family as well. I was nine years old when I first confronted him. The last thing I remember from that fight was excruciating pain and then only pure blackness. When I woke up, I was surrounded by death and destruction. That scene has never left me alone. It haunts me in my sleep nine years later. I met him again when I was fourteen years old and he wanted me to join him. After defying him, I was nearly killed and I received my greatest burden. Now I face him once more.

"Let the human go. It is not him you wish to punish. I believe that I still hold that honor," I say mildly. My voice is calm and the command is without argument.

"Does a *human's* life mean enough to you to face me? This whelp was unable to complete a reconnaissance mission. He deserves the punishment due to him, brought on by his desertion and incompetence. I am the only one who you fear. The *only* one you have ever feared. You know that I am the only one who can defeat you. Despite your bold words, I know you are terrified. Your eyes betray you as always. Will you deny that you are afraid?" he taunts, like he is fourteen again. *Boys!* I raise an eyebrow at his pitiful taunts before answering calmly.

"Any life matters, powerful or not. I have promised to protect the humans of this world and I will succeed, or die trying. I will not deny your words, but I will add something else. I not only fear you, I hate you with every fiber of my being. The fear continues to fuel that fire, creating a larger reserve of power to use when I finally get to kill you."

"Bold words, little sister. Can you hold to them?" A glossy black sword appears in his massive hand. Suddenly, a searing pain resounds across my shoulder blades and cascades down my right arm. I gasp in pain and alarm as my knees threaten to buckle and I hear blood roaring in my ears. He continues to apply greater pressure on the wound with his magic, easily overpowering the magic that was protecting it. Far beyond all pain I have ever felt, it seems to circulate in my blood. Black spots dance across my vision and I frantically blink them away. I will not allow myself to get lost in the comfort of the welcoming hands of oblivion. I yell with pain mixed with defiance as I refuse the welcoming arms of blackness. His cruel laugh fills my ears and I retch from the pain and horror.

"Shadow!" a voice yells, cracking at the end of my name. I slowly look up see my friends ready for battle. My heart sinks. *If anything happens to them it is because of me.*

Chapter Seventeen

Artemis

A strange man dressed in dark blue, as deep as the darkest part of the ocean, holds Shadow by the color of her shirt in a vice-like grip. He drops her and turns to face us. She doesn't move and lies where she had fallen as she tries to catch her breath. He looks directly at me and I shiver at the pure evil I feel radiating off him. I allow my silver magic to spiral around me and in a second I am coated in silver armor that glows with a mythical light. Next to me, Athena is coated in bright gold armor as well.

It is Chaos, and if he chose to, he could easily kill us with a flick of his finger. Shadow opens her eyes and I can read the raw pain that shows up and looks like broken glass. Her ice blue eyes look shattered. It rips my heart out to see my friend with so much agony clearly written upon her face.

"Artemis! Behind you! It is coming!" she yells. Her voice is strained, but I know better than to ignore the warning she has given. The superior smirk on Chaos's face wipes off in an instant. He kicks Shadow in the ribs, but she is not done yet. "Finish what I started. Mobilize the army!" she shouts. Chaos's face is contorted in rage as his surprise is foiled and he plants a vicious kick on her injured shoulder. An inhuman howl from Shadow follows and my heart skips a beat as a terrible fear fills me. All the blood drains from my face. One who can inflict such pain on the most powerful person I know is beyond anyone I could ever fight. He actually is stronger than Shadow. Up until now I refused to believe it.

I feel all the hairs on the back of my neck stand straight up as an unearthly roar comes from behind me. I slowly turn and stare up at the huge boar that looks down at me, it's foul breath smells sickly sweet like death and decay.

Slowly, I take one arrow from my quiver and place it on the string of my bow. I can hear, rather than see the others next to me drawing their weapons. As if on cue, everyone charges fearlessly at the boar, screaming their own battle cries.

"Wolf formation!" Athena shouts desperately, her voice cracking in the fear of the moment. Everyone follows her orders without question, seeing as she *is* the goddess of warfare strategies. All of us are very familiar with her battle codes and follow her orders seamlessly.

The wolf formation is when you surround the beast or person and attack as a mass from all sides; therefore, the unfortunate beast does not know where to turn to defend itself. I cannot reach Shadow without confronting Chaos and that would be suicide. Chaos watches all of this with interest. He obviously wants to see us get killed by his little pet. Shadow is clearly not a concern to him. Judging by his expression, he already knows that he has her in his control. There is nothing she can do. She is as good as dead at this point. He could kill her whenever he wants. Shadow is completely at his questionable mercy.

I release arrow after arrow. As soon as one is released, I shoot again. The boar turns to me in rage as the arrows stick out of its hide like a pincushion. I have enough time for a quick curse as it swipes at me with the glowing crimson tusk and I am forced to roll so as not to be skewered on the sharp point. In my heart, I can feel my bow scream as the wood fractures. My heart jumps into my throat as the tusk flies harmlessly over my head by only a few scant inches. That was too close.

He grunts and spins around indignantly as Emerald sticks her sword into his buttock. Athena darts in and aims a strike at his throat. He kicks out with a viciously sharp front hoof that catches her in the ribs. The ring of her armor is loud in the silence of the woods. Athena staggers off to the woods clutching her side. From the cracking sound that came to me all the way across the clearing, I am guessing that more than one rib is broken. I throw a rope to Evan out of my pack and grab another length for myself. Emerald is holding her own against the boar for now, weaving between the tusks and flying hooves. I meet Evan's calm eyes with my own and without a second thought, I loop the rope around the boar's back legs and tie the remainder to a tree nearby. Evan had tied the end to another tree and suddenly darts under the boar's belly and trails the rope behind him as he makes his daring run.

The boar spots him coming and gets ready to kick. Evan shimmers and in a heartbeat, he is suddenly a wolf holding the rope in his mouth. His sapphire blue and white coat is a streak as he runs through the legs, dodging the kicks aimed at him. When he makes it across he turns back into a human and ties the rope to a tree with a few deft knots. I shoot a few arrows into the growing pincushion that I have made of his rump. My bow creaks with its last efforts and my heart wrenches. Again, the beast bellows and tries to turn. The boar is wickedly fast, but his haste is his undoing.

The ropes on his hind legs grow taut and the ones Evan had tied around the front tighten at the same moment. The beast flounders for a moment before, almost in slow motion, he begins to fall. He hits the ground with a colossal thud and thrashes around before lying still on the ground. I cautiously draw my long dagger and move closer to the giant head. His eyes are shut. I am about to step forward and thrust my dagger into the bottom of his neck when suddenly a faint voice shouts a warning.

"He is faking! Watch-" the voice is cut off and I hear dull thud, followed by a sharp cracking sound. Shadow gives an inarticulate yell as his boot catches her in the shoulder with a well-placed kick. At her yell, the boar's eyes snap open and he thrusts his tusk up at me with the speed of a snake. Had I been standing in the spot I was in previously, the tusk would have skewered me through the stomach. Only Shadow's warning saved my life. I curse myself for not remembering how cunning these creatures are and that it cost Shadow a good deal more pain.

I drop my knife and aim carefully with my bow, and a silver tipped arrow rips through its throat and the animal disintegrates into a maroon-brown pile of ashes. With a last scream, my bow cracks in half. Deep inside me I can feel my heart crack with it. After you work with the same bow for a few hundred years, you get to be pretty attached to it. It is as much a weapon as a partner. I quickly turn to the others. Athena limps over, still clutching her side.

"Shadow!" Someone yells. I turn, expecting the pain filled yell to belong to Emerald, but instead I see now that it is Evan. He is sprinting toward Chaos with his sword drawn. The sapphire hilt gleams a dark blue and the sword's blade is an even darker shade, as if one had mixed gray and dark blue together. Chaos watches him come closer. He casually leans over and grabs Shadow by the collar of her shirt with one hand as if she weighs nothing.

"Stop!" Chaos finally orders sharply. Evan slams into a wall of deep-sea blue magic, even darker than Evan's sapphire magic. By this time the rest of us catch up to him. I grab him by the shoulder and can barely hold him back as he tries to hurl himself at the wall of potent magic.

"Get off me!" he yells, trying to break my unrelenting grip. We stand on the other side of his magical dome barrier only five feet from our friend. He switches his hold on her to grab her shoulder once more. Her eyes fly open as the pain hits once more and the kaleidoscope of ice blue seems to fragment even more. Chaos's magic surrounds her for a second

186

before it flies at me, Athena, Evan, and Emerald. Suddenly, I feel the same pain as Shadow. It is nauseating and terrible and absolutely debilitating.

As quickly as it came, it is gone. I feel sick as I realize how much more agonizing it must be for Shadow. Emerald lurches to the side and is violently sick. Athena and Evan are shaking violently from the after effects of it. Despite her pain, Shadow's eyes are open and she is still conscious. I can practically see her fighting the dizziness and the oncoming blackness that accompanies such pain. One ought to have died before enduring such agony.

"This is only a small taste of pain she will feel. I will see to it that she feels *so* much more." Chaos drops her onto the ground as she wrenches herself out of his grip, digging deep into hidden reserves of strength. He lets her go, knowing that she cannot go far. She is completely in his power. With a flick of his finger he could make her curl up on the ground writhing in pain.

From years of training, she lands on her feet and twists away. As she turns to face us from across the clearing she grabs her sword in a left-handed grip. It would be unpractical for her to try the bow. She could never shoot with her shoulder as it is. If you did not know her, you would never know she was in pain. The only sign she shows is a reluctance to move her arm and a slight limp on that side. Her eyes have cleared and they show no sign of wavering. They seem to pierce through my own as she calmly meets my gaze, reminding me of her order to mobilize the army.

"You wish to play with swords, my little shadow? Allow me to oblige you." He sweeps his massive blackiron sword in a powerful side-cut. She gracefully leaps back to avoid the sword, but stumbles on landing and proves to us all that she is feeling the pain, despite her convincing facade. She refuses to meet his sword and continues to duck and move away from the blade. I can see Chaos getting more frustrated as she lightly dances around him. Finally, she manages to turn him in a complete circle so she is near us.

"When he takes me, run. He will be preoccupied with me and probably not chase you," she mutters out the corner of her mouth. I want to be able to tell her that she can do it, that she can beat him, but she is undoubtedly the best swordmaster here. She knows her own abilities and limitations better than anyone else. The fact that she knows that she cannot win is a bad sign. I know her shoulder is hurting more than she is letting on. Her movements are jerky and uneven as she tries not to jar her shoulder. Beads of sweat gather on her face and roll down her cheeks, something I've never seen from her before. Her forehead is furrowed and the lines around her mouth are hard.

"Evan," she addresses him directly, "make Emerald go with you. You will need to rally the different kings and have them gather all their best warriors and knights. I have spoken with them all previously and they agreed to come. Also, you must teach Emerald. There is still so much for her to learn. You will all need your skills to be as sharp as possible. I appreciate that you came, but you have put yourself in terrible danger. I will not have any of you harmed on my account. My blood trail is long enough and your blood would be too much for me bear."

She turns and faces us full on. Shadow has never expressed herself through words, or expressions. Her actions speak loud enough for all to hear and see. The trees, animals, and wind whispers as she walks across the land. Nothing anyone can ever say surpasses the eloquent words of the land. For the first time in all the years I have known her, an expression I have never seen is in her eyes. Fear. This may be the last time we ever see her.

"Hopefully I will see you again, but it is unlikely. Go now. Emerald must convince the high council. End what I started. I do not want Emerald to watch me be killed. It is time for my past to resurface and blot out my future." She looks to me and I feel a swell of pride that she would pick me to complete her mission and take position as leader in her place.

The fear and pain leave her eyes as she sees me nod and is replaced with resolve and a hard light of determination... And is that a bit of relief as well? Her shoulders seem to be lifted from an invisible burden. A rueful smile crosses her features, but hardens into a fierce and wild expression. The thick scar across her face lends a mysterious and hard edge to her appearance, hinting at the hidden side of her that we all know is there, but she has never let us see it. She is not going to go down easily.

Suddenly, she ducks and a black sword cleaves the air above her. *How did she know?* Even my ears that are accustomed to listening for the soft steps of animals in a forest did not catch the swift steps of Chaos. Shadow sweeps her legs in a circle and Chaos falls to the earth. Before Shadow can follow up on her advantage, he jumps to his feet to meet her swing. He once more digs into her shoulder with his magic and she crumples to the ground.

"Damn this wretched shoulder!" she howls, her voice breaking from the pain. *"Go! Get out of here while you still can!"* she screams telepathically. Judging from the winces from Evan, Athena, and Emerald, they also got the message. Evan grabs Emerald's hand and he starts to run, dragging a struggling and crying Emerald with him. I am not far behind and Athena follows, dragging Gregory along. I cannot help but to look back one last time at my friend, knowing that it may be the very last time I ever see her. Shadow and Chaos disappear in a whirlwind of dark and light blue.

Shadow

I watch my friends run back into the woods through a haze of pain. "Good luck," I whisper, knowing they cannot hear me. Suddenly a bigger wave of pain hits without warning and my world goes black; I cannot hold out against the pain any longer.

Consciousness returns slowly and I feel as if I am floating out of a tunnel of black. Suddenly jarred awake, I gasp as my shoulder screams at me. It was skewered not only by a sword, but by a knife, an arrow, *and* a sword again. Then I strained it, catching a sword on my shield, and *then* Chaos had grabbed it and twisted it multiple times. I can feel that the big shoulder blade bone is fractured by his well-placed kick for warning Artemis and preventing her to fall into the trap that the boar set. Definitely the worst day *ever.*

I cautiously open my eyes to try and figure out where I am. The first thing I see is stars. I blink a few times to make sure I am seeing right, but there they are. I can see the constellation of Orion chasing the Great Scorpion across the galaxy. He was killed by the scorpion when he believed himself to be the greatest hunter. Now he continues to chase the scorpion all the way around the North Star, hoping in vain for revenge. He stops and looks down at me with concern. Suddenly, he points to someone behind me before waving good luck and running off again. His body shimmers with the starlight and his unruly black hair flies behind him as he continues to chase his greatest enemy across the kingdom of starlight.

Flat on my back, I cannot see who is coming. I suppress a yelp of pain that threatens to leave my throat when my shoulder moves. My hands are bound in front of me and when I test the strength of the ropes, they are like iron. My entire right side feels limp and shaky as the wound steals my strength. I painfully sit upright and realize that there is an additional rope around my ankle trailing to a solid tree where it is securely tied. I glance down to figure out what is poking me in the ribs and spot the ice blue stone set into the hilt of my sword. They did not take it.

"They tried to take it from you, but it burned the man's hands and two of the ones who tried have frostbite and the skin on their hands resist all magical healing. Same with your bow. When Lord Chaos tried it, his hands were burned badly. He is the one who gave you that bruise on your face," a young voice says from behind me. I stiffen as I hear him walk closer before crouching in front of me so we are at the same eye level. His lantern glows softly and reflects off warm brown eyes. He looks pained as he watches my careful movements with my shoulder.

"Good. It did its job," I reply irritably. The boy looks young, maybe fourteen or fifteen. His black hair is cut short and his serious brown eyes dart back and forth as he makes sure nothing is coming. Somehow, he seems familiar.

"Who are you?" I ask in a softer tone and a quieter voice. "You are not supposed to be here." I can tell he would be in trouble if anyone knew he was here. His eyes dart around the clearing warily before coming back to meet my steady gaze.

"My name is Allen," he softly replies. All of a sudden, the name fits into my memory.

"I met your older brother, Samuel." I am rewarded with a scowl for my sudden remembrance of the name. "Did you not get along?" I add cautiously, knowing that I am not able to fight right now. Even if I could, I would not be able to make myself hurt this youngster. Even injured, it would not be a fair fight.

"No. He was supposed to take care of Ann and me. Ann is dead and it is all his fault. He never did anything for us. It all fell on me. Ann died because I-" he cuts himself off and I watch anguish cover his face. "I have to go. They treat me like a slave after my brother failed. I will be in trouble if I do not go back. This is for you. Beware all that is beautiful. In beauty is danger." *Don't I know it.* I think to myself. He throws a satchel of food to me before standing up and melting back into the forest.

Alright, first things first, I close my eyes and enter the world of my magic. The ice blue magic surges crazily all around and it takes all my effort to calm myself. As I slowly relax and calm my raging mind, the magic settles. I had not realized how tensed up I was. It is no wonder that Allen was looking at me like I was some sort of terrifying beast. I direct the icy magic into the wounds in my shoulders. After I pull the magic back and open my eyes, I feel a whole world of difference now that my shoulder no longer hurts. Now there is room for fear.

With a good deal of effort, I stuff those feelings back down and take stock of the situation. I try forcing magic into the ropes, but the dark blue magic of Chaos stops it. I stand up and start to pace. With my shoulder on the mend, I feel as if I am back to normal, albeit bored. I don't do to well with the concept of wait and see. Patience is not my strong suit. If they are going to kill me, can't they just get on with it?

I walk over to the tree and look up. The bark is rough and sharp. Out of curiosity and perhaps a good bit of boredom, I start to rub the ropes and am immediately rewarded for my efforts by a ton of splinters. I keep going and soon the rope starts to fray. Before long, the rope splits. *They may be sword, knife, and magic proof, but not tree proof!* I almost laugh at the stupidity of the thought

I flex my wrists and rub my hands to get circulation moving through them once more. There is an uncomfortable sensation of needles in my hands as the blood flows through them again. I lean down and scoop the small satchel off the ground and scurry up the tree. I try to break the long rope on the tree, but apparently, he was more concerned about that one rather than the one on my wrists. I can go up five meters before the rope pulls tight. Oh well, high enough, I guess.

After carefully plucking the splinters out of my hands, I open the satchel to see what it is. I balance a stale piece of bread on my knees along with a beautiful red apple. I know there might be poison or who knows what on the bread, but my stomach beats my head and I make fast work of it.

When I grab the apple and raise it to my mouth, I hesitate. Something is not right with it. I pull a dagger out of my sleeve. The super sharp knife cuts through the apple as easily as a soft piece of cheese. As I had suspected, the inside is tinged with dark magic. *Poison.* Irritated, I throw the apple as hard as possible away from me. Making a note to myself to never trust something that is too perfect, too nice. It will almost always come back to bite you. Then I suddenly realize that I should not need that reminder. The boy was trying to warn me.

I hear a small cry of pain followed by a rather large thud as a heavy body hits the ground. In a state of mild confusion, I scramble down from my perch to see what is happening. A heavy-set man is crawling to his feet as he rubs his head. A large bruise, rather in the shape of the apple, covers his eye in a dark shadow. I stuff my dagger into the sheath hidden under my sleeve. I pull my sword out of its scabbard and exult in the calming feel of grabbing the sword with my right hand once more. I hold the sword in a light grip as I stalk forward a few steps staying completely silent. He spots the offending apple and swears foully before saying,

"Dammit! She did not fall for it. Lord Chaos will be furious! Oh well. She is already heading for her death anyway. Chaos is going to torture her personally; it is not as if she will survive, anyway. I will blame the boy for it. Then Lord Chaos will be mad at him and not me." My temper rises as I hear how he plans to blame poor Allen. I wait with my sword ready for him to get closer. *I will show him not to mess with me or my friends.* He stumbles closer to where I stand near the tree. With a sudden impulsive thought, I stuff my sword back into my scabbard. This may be my only chance for escape, but more importantly, it my be my only chance to find out Chaos's next move. Knowing that information would be worth dying to get it. I will wait and see what happens. Calming my temper with difficulty, I wait for him to come over here.

His labored breathing alerts me that he is near. He walks into the small clearing with the lantern swinging to his uneven walk. He walks with a heavy limp and is one of the ugliest men I have ever seen. His bald head glints in the flickering moonlight as the light is filtered through the bare limbs of the trees as they dance and wave in the icy cold winter wind.

His eye is black and swollen from the flying apple assault. His expression is twisted and his eyes glint maliciously. His long, unkempt, and greasy beard shines repulsively in the light offered by the lantern. He grabs the rope and pulls out a blackiron knife and severs through the magic rope connected to the tree. It surprises me when he doesn't comment on the fact that my hands are free. *So, that is how they cut it.* He stalks over to me and I look at him curiously. Despite his large girth, he is well muscled and solidly built. He grabs my arm and ties a normal rope around my wrists, before marching off into the shadows cast by the waving trees. Still waiting for the right moment, I follow along without objection, even though all my instincts are telling me to fight him now and escape.

The wind picks up and whips my hair free of its braid and my cloak flies behind me in the wild wind and just for a moment, I feel free, free of the fear that lies deep within me, a fear I have hidden from all, a fear of failure. If I fail, the world will fall into ruin and disorder. It will fall to Chaos. Stoking that fire and pushing them further into the madness, my brother standing at the reins.

Soft singing in a different language reaches me where I stand in the forest. The wind whispers stories in my ears of far off lands. It tells me of why there still is reason to fight. It speaks of hope and lightness in the face of the oncoming dark. I know I will not come out of this unscathed, but I am never going to stop fighting. Chaos will never get anything out of me. I would never reveal anything to him. He will have to kill me first, and I don't die easily, as many have found out, much to their detriment.

"The hero of the forests,

The savior of free men.

The Shadow Warrior ventures to a place,

To be vanquished once again."

The wind shifts and the voice passes, heading to carry more messages around.

"Wait!" I call desperately as it heads back into the trees, enjoying a freedom I have never felt and never will know. I strain at the rope that holds me. The Chaos's minion pulls more insistently. *"Pass my message to my sister. Tell her I love her. I may never see her again, tell her she is my greatest treasure. My precious Emerald. Tell her I say goodbye,"* I call magically.

The wind stops and gathers to form the shape of a young woman. She nods and looks at me sadly. She knows there is little hope for me. She will carry the message. Sap-like tears streak down the dryad's cheeks and she waves farewell before dissolving back into wind to pass on my last message. I am surprised to find that my own eyes are a little bit misty as well. Her warning does not bode well for me.

Blinking back my sorrow, I follow the man once more to continue through the woods. My death heads towards me. I straighten my shoulders and hold my head high. Too soon, a clearing comes up ahead. Instinctively, I know this is where we are headed; with a hollow sense of disappointment, I enter the place where I am to die.

Chapter Eighteen

Shadow

He violently shoves me into the clearing and I gracefully step forward into the light of the flickering firelight. Coolly looking around, I spot Allen near the fire as he tends to it. I meet his eye for the fastest of seconds and give an almost imperceptible nod before I turn, glaring at my brother with utmost fury and contempt. The last time Allen had seen me, I was crippled and now I stand here without any sign of fear or pain and stare down the one whom all fear. Chaos sits in a high-backed chair and looks entirely too pleased with this whole situation.

"You may all leave now. The Shadow Warrior and I are going to have a little conversation." I glare at him before turning to Allen. I must warn him of the danger he faces. He is going to be accused of helping the greatest enemy, and Chaos will kill him for it, whether he did it or not. I lock eyes with Allen and see something I did not expect. His brown eyes shine with a new light. Looking through my magic, I can see the magic surrounding him. Faint traces of sunset orange, red, and yellow magic surrounds him. Impulsively, I send a telepathic message.

"You must escape. They are planning to kill you!" He jumps in surprise as he gets the message. Slowly he turns towards me. I notice he wears a short sword and a hunting knife on his belt with a small round shield and knapsack across his back. Chaos suddenly stands up and charges at the boy. A split second later, with a yell, I summon a blast of magic strong enough to knock Chaos over.

"Run!" I yell. Allen hesitates. "Go! Get out of here!" I yell once more. He turns and sprints away as Chaos jumps to his feet in alarm. I look at him and swear at him in all the languages I know before spitting

197

on his boots. He looks at me for a second before laughing. The laugh of a mad man.

"You will pay for that, little savage!" he promises. "Leave! Go get all the bored soldiers who wish for some entertainment," he commands the others. The beefy man holding the rope drops it and leaves as he is commanded. Chaos walks a large circle around me and I turn to face him. Then I notice the deep-sea blue magic that has formed a huge barrier that I cannot get out of. "Let me know when you wish to tell me your battle plans, after that I will kill you quickly. Until then, enjoy your torture."

He snaps his fingers and the rope binding my wrists disappears in a blue mist. Turning in a circle, I inspect this new torture. There is suddenly a huge crowd of men and judging by the mixture of chainmail tunics and clothes of the modern world, these are the bored soldiers. Then where is the entertainment? *I could use a good laugh about now.*

The modern warriors jostle closer for a better view. They have never seen a fight like this. Without warning, a huge weight slams into my back and I feel sharp claws dig deep into my back. Thrown forward by the momentum of the beast, I land and go into a forward roll throwing the creature off. Agilely springing back to my feet, I draw my sword in a fluid motion. Blood flows down my back, but I know those cuts are far from fatal. However, if I let them distract me, they will definitely become deadly.

The beast resembles a leopard, but it is dark brown with shaggy fur and red eyes. The creature has spots of light tan and a mouth full of sharp teeth. The crowd jeers and throws a few stones. Even though the barrier keeps me in, it does not keep others out. The stones sting, but they are nothing but a nuisance. A quick glance over my shoulder shows Chaos sitting on his throne once more. He watches this fight with great amusement and curiosity. The leopard charges at me once more and at the last second, I step aside and slash down with my sword. The magical sword slices the creature in half and it immediately disappears in a puff of tan. I whirl my sword in a circle through the air and turn to face Chaos. My statement is clear: *Bring it on. I will face any monster you put at me before telling you anything.*

A hush falls over the crowd and I turn and slice at the next monster. This time it is another boar, but this one is a disgusting shade of pink. What is *wrong* with this poor creature? My sword shears off one huge, pink tusk. The creature squeals in pain and rage before it swings around in a tight circle for another charge. It comes towards me slowly to ensure that I cannot dodge it and run again. My mouth goes dry with fear as I realize that I must now face it head on. The crowd goes silent as the boar advances. I would never go against a boar without a boar spear and a team of experienced warriors.

Desperately, I raise my sword once more and wave it slightly from side to side to discourage the beast. With a blood lust in its eyes, the boar comes forward with a horrible eagerness to kill the one in its way. It's only way out of this prison is to be victorious and kill me. It slices with its tusk and I try to parry with my sword, but the giant boar is way stronger than me. I drop my sword and grab its remaining tusk, and I'm forced onto my knees in the effort of holding the boar's tusk, with all the strength of its muscular body behind it. Finally, it gives a huge shove and I cannot hold any longer. Out of sheer luck, I fall in time to avoid the deadly tusk. I hurriedly grab my sword and stab upwards at the thick neck.

My wickedly sharp blade slices through the thick hide and the boar crumbles into pink dust. I wrinkle my nose at the terrible color for a boar and brush the pink dust from my tunic. One less monster in this world.

A searing pain slices across the back of my knee. I drop to my other knee as the sharp pain wracks through my leg. A scream tries and fails to force its way from my mouth as I feel each tendon and ligament being severed by the creature behind me. I desperately try to numb it, but my magic will not work in this cursed dome of evil magic. The crowd shouts, but this time it is not directed at me.

"Not fair! That one is immortal!" one shouts at Chaos

"Take that one back!" another yells. Chaos ignores them, and the yells and protests grow louder. Finally Chaos addresses them.

"SHUT UP!!! Or I will make ALL OF YOU fight the monster too!" he roars. The crowd obediently falls silent and I struggle to my feet.

I freeze when I see it. The most beautiful monster that I have laid eyes on stands in front of me. It's scales ripple with thousands of different greens. Just like grass as it waves in the sunlight. Its head is topped with short horns and it's eyes are a deep brown. I stare into those eyes and do not see any of the former hate or blood lust that was in the previous two monsters. The big eyes hold sadness and fear as it is forced to kill me.

Closer inspection reveals that this is a very young dragon, only five feet in length and four feet tall. Abruptly, I sheath my sword in my scabbard, refusing to kill such a young and good monster. The young dragon is forced to fight me, but I will not fight back. I will die before killing it.

"Chaos!" I call loudly, never taking my eyes off the dragon, "I refuse to raise my sword against this young kit. Let it go free!" The crowd of soldiers cheer my defiance. The dragon comes closer. It swipes at me again with its giant claws and I am unable to move with my leg. The claws gouge deeply from my shoulder across to my opposite hip. Numbly, I look down to see the blood spreading across my torn clothes.

"Stop! I will not hurt you! I have not, and will not, raise any weapon against you. Join me and I will get you out of here. Trust me," I whisper as I look into those conflicted eyes. It's paw is already coming down for the last time. Even if the dragon wanted to, there is not time for it to stop. The paw slams into me and throws me towards the ground. The last thing I see is the ground rushing up to meet me.

Chaos

"Lord Chaos, she is dead. Leave her for the dragon. It will save us baggage. It is clear that she would never tell you anything anyway." I thoughtfully look over at my second in charge.

"You know this, do you?" I ask. He nods emphatically.

"It disabled her knee. She won't be able to walk. If she doesn't find a doctor, or for your side of the world you call them healers, she will either bleed to death, or if she somehow manages to bind it, she will be crippled and unable to use the leg. She is no longer a concern," he says dismissively in his thick New World accent. I take one more look at the figure of the girl. Even though she is knocked out and bleeding on the ground, there is still an air of defiance and pride around her. Despite myself, I feel a distinct surge of respect. She is by far the first who has ever challenged me.

We are not born from a human family. Our parents are the Light and the Dark. She represents hope, order, and honor. Another example of how siblings can be totally different. Without her, the humans will split into fragmented parts much easier. Her little command group is soon to fall into discord, so my job should be easier after this. Athena, Evan, Emerald, and Artemis, with the human stuck in the middle will fall easily by my sword. The personalities are so different, so *eclectic*, that without the girl, they have nothing binding them all together. They were joined by her. Artemis and Athena were the only ones who are already friends. Neither of them are strong enough to control the group. They will fall prey to me by turning on each other. *A house divided cannot stand.* I repeat the old dictum in my head.

Looking down on her crippled form on the ground, I know I will face her again. She will somehow survive. I look forward to that day when we will finally duel. I know I will win, but it will be a further show of strength and killing her will crush the spirits of her warriors. She represents their hopes, dreams, and they believe she will protect them. She is the new light, I am the new dark. History always repeats itself and we are the next generation. Last time, the Dark won. A feral grin crosses my face. I would have it no other way.

I glance at her once more. Suddenly, white magic penetrates through my vision and I turn away from my men to hide the sudden swirling agony.

"Remember this girl, your *sister*- your *twin* sister. Remember the days long ago," a female voice hisses through my ears. Against my will, the memories fly back.

I am once again twelve and walking through a village in search of the family who is in one of the prophecies. The Faelins, or *the Wolves*. The humans of the village flee as I stride confidently down the cobblestone street. Those who dare to stand in front of me are struck down by my blackiron sword, *Dorcha*, which means dark in the old language.

My cold laughter rings off the walls of the small houses of the village. Suddenly, a quick flash of movement catches the corner of my vision and the moment I turn to look, it is gone. My magic tingles as I sense a strong presence nearby. I continue, but perhaps with a little bit less confidence and with a bit more urgency. A few more times I catch that quick flash of what I can now distinguish as an ice blue streak. I walk faster and faster, eventually breaking into a run as I see the street where the Faelins live coming closer.

I slow to a walk and feel a distinct surge of pleasure as I spot them standing in the deserted road speaking with another family. All thoughts of the shadow following me are gone. I silently stalk down the road and raise my sword for a short, swift, killing blow. With Joseph Faelin's back turned, this would be all too easy. Smiling grimly, I start the downward stroke.

Suddenly, the ringing crash of sword meeting sword splits the air. The four adults turn fearfully, shock in their eyes, to see a nine-year-old girl standing with a sword that looks far too heavy for her to hold, let alone wield. Ian Alián and Joseph Faelin draw their swords to help. This girl is unknown to both families, yet is helping anyway.

With an incredibly strong wrist, she turns the swords in a circle and I just barely dodge her thrust. I slam my sword in a terrible side stroke and discover that this is no mere child as she jumps aside and deflects the sword. Slashing back, I only miss her killing blow by a hair. A long, deep gash sends blood mixed with dark blue magic cascading down the left side of my face.

Despite her age, she is an impressive warrior. Ian Álaian grabs her shoulder and shoves the girl back towards his wife. If he had lived, he should have realized that it was this decision to take the fight out of her hands and try to defeat me, a god, with only two men, that killed him. I can see now that this child is not a simple mortal. With two deft strokes of my sword, both Ian and Joseph are dead on the cobblestones, with their lifeblood leaving them in torrents.

"Please, see that my son makes it safely to the battle school. He just turned of age and is strong of body, mind, and heart. He has the potential to be a great warrior and he is a true *Faelin* in blood. The gift of his ancestors runs through his veins. Please, give him a chance to live out his life if the gods allow!" Joseph's wife cries to the girl. The girl turns solemn ice blue eyes to the distraught woman and nods gravely.

"My young daughter has no place to go! She cannot go to battle school. Will you ensure her safety? Can you find somewhere safe for her to live? She would be torn apart in an orphanage and is too young for an apprenticeship." Ian's wife begs. Again, the girl nods.

"Your children will be safe," she assures them.

"Do not interfere. We will buy you time to get our children to safety. Please protect them." Both women wait for the warrior to agree. Not knowing what instinct makes them place so much trust in a young girl, they both know that this child will be true to her word. I look forward to killing the warrior-child before killing the boy, Evan Faelin. The Wolf line will finally be extinguished! The two brave mothers charge at me with their sabers drawn.

The girl darts into the house and reappears with two children, one ten, the other six. The six-year-old girl stumbles and falls as she turns to see what just happened. The warrior, with baffling strength, picks her up as if she weighs nothing and begins to run, pulling the boy with her. I chase after her with a yell. She stops and puts the young girl on her feet and whispers something to both. The boy nods and the crying girl holds his hand. As I pound closer, I can hear what she says.

"I will see you again, Emerald Alián and Evan Faelin. Hide in the woods and you will be safe. I will find you. Now run!" The boy tugs on the girl's hand and they start to run again. The girl with the ice blue eyes watches them run over the crest of the hill and disappear over the top, before slowly turning to face me.

I stop and look at the strange girl. She draws herself taller and I am shocked to see that she is incredibly tall. I stand a little under six feet at age twelve, but this girl is only five inches or so shorter than me at age nine. Even though she is tall, there is something else about her that is timeless. Her ice blue eyes shine with intelligence and a kind heart, but also speak of danger and a hard light that can only be earned by knowing Death and defying him. She is slim and well-muscled from years of hard fighting and practice. Something's familiar about her that I cannot place. A black light and a harsh white light is suddenly beside me.

"Do you not recognize her? Are you really that daft, son? You have the same features. High cheekbones, same shaped eyes, same nose. Can you not connect the dots? She is your twin sister, idiot. You grew up with her and you were best friends to boot! This is Elren Caerin. She is the one who shall keep your evil deeds in check. When you look at her, you will know real fear. You can hide it down deep, but you know it is true. She will be the one who topples your reign and vanquishes you in battle and all will be as it should."

I snap out of the memory and turn back to my men who stare at me curiously.

"Let's go!" I call, my voice harsh. "The Shadow Warrior is finished. Our way is clear. Now we must summon the army." I look at her one more time and feel my hate rising for this warrior who is the only one in the way of the great destiny I was set. My sister. It is bad enough just *having* a sibling, but throw on top that she is the highest ranked warrior and legend? Something beyond hate rises in my chest. I grab a spear from a startled young soldier near me before throwing it as hard as possible at her. It takes her in the side and pins her to the ground. I nod in satisfaction as she does not move. There is no possible way for her to survive.

Still, a nagging doubt clouds my mind. Somehow, I know this is not the last time I will see her. Choosing to ignore the voices whispering that I am making a mistake, I turn away and lead the small group of soldiers with me into the woods to go back to the modern world. I shake off the moment of weak pity and move forward, banishing all thoughts of the girl from my mind. We must gather our army to defeat the Olympian Gods. If we take out those who worship them, it will weaken their resistance until they do not have any support left. Without supporting beams, the palace will crumble and I will be the ruler of all. I will rule this new breed of humans.

Chapter Nineteen

Artemis

Our feet pound the ground in a rapid tempo as we sprint blindly through the woods. My mind is numb as the images of what just happened flashes through it. Shadow left defenseless and injured at the mercy of Chaos. The boar. Shadow disappearing to who knows where. Me, the leader. My shattered bow. All these thoughts and emotions swirl through my head. Shadow was more than my best friend. I sometimes thought she was more of my family than my twin brother, Apollo. She is definitely less annoying.

We slow down for a few minutes for the human to recover. Gregory's face is almost gray in color as he leans over trying to catch his breath. I start to gather myself back together, putting the needs of the group in front of my own fear and aching heart. I know I have a job to do, but equally strong to my sense of duty is my loyalty to my friend. Over the labored breaths of my friends, I hear a slight whispering in the woods behind me.

My hand goes immediately to my quiver before I realize that an arrow is useless without a bow. Instead, I grab my long dagger. The edges are razor sharp and it is nearly as long as the swords that Evan, Athena, and Emerald carry, although it is nothing compared to the broad sword that Gregory carries in a scabbard slung across his back. Athena also draws her sword and turns to face the same direction. Evan and Emerald are slower to react. Emerald is not as fit as she should be, and Evan's ribs show very clearly through the filthy and torn shirt. He spent weeks in the maze on strict rations of dried beef and venison and two canteens of water. Though he is regaining his strength, he is still quite weak.

My eyes search the elongated shadows of the trees and I stand, all my muscles tense, as I await the attacker. I slowly relax and just as I lower my dagger, a woman materializes out of the woods. A tree spirit. Her eyes are a leafy green color and her dress is like swirling leaves. I notice a tear of sap streaking its way down her cheek. I feel as if a stone was dropped into my stomach and great fear courses down my spine. I instinctively know whom this message is from, and gauging by the dryad's expression, it is not good news.

"What is it?" Evan asks urgently. "Who is it from?" Judging by the ashen color of his face, I can tell he already knows as well.

"This is the last message from Commander Caerin. She asked me to carry this to you immediately. She sent this to Emerald." I look at Emerald and all the blood has drained from her face. The phrase, *last message* does not have a pleasant ring to it. Emerald gives a tight nod to show that she is ready to hear it. "She says: *Pass my message to my sister. Tell her I love her. I may not see her again, so tell her she is my greatest treasure. My precious Emerald. Tell her I say goodbye.*" With the message finished, the tree spirit fades away.

Emerald starts to sob silently. Her shoulders shake and she sits on the ground with her hands over her face. Athena and I exchange a long horror-struck look. Evan lets out a long moan and mutters a few words that I do not catch before slumping down against a tree with his head clutched in his hands and running his fingers through his recently cut hair. Both Athena and I had known Shadow for an incredibly long time and to think that she is gone for forever is unbearable.

"This is all my fault," Gregory chokes out through stifled tears. "She was caught because she tried to save me. Now she is dead." At his last word, a heavy blanket of silence falls over the small group. As tempted to agree as I am, I must step up and be the leader, but how can I do that when I feel as hopeless as the others? Athena squeezes my shoulder and I look over at her. *Together.* Do not make the same mistake as Shadow. She took all the leadership and we both know how hard that was on her. Nobody should be able to bear that pressure without crumbling, but she is Shadow, there is no other explanation for it.

"How do we know she is dead?" I ask abruptly in the silence. Everyone stares at me. Even Evan picks his head up to stare at me incredulously. "The messenger never said that she was killed. We all know that Shadow is more than capable of taking care of herself." I can hear the growing conviction in my voice. "We swore that we would complete her orders, and I don't know the code of conduct for you high and mighty humans, Evan, but I was trained by a good master who taught me that when I give my word to do something, I better do it. Emerald, you are her apprentice. You understand that your training is incomplete. Evan will take over your sword training." Evan simply nods.

I know how much he likes Shadow. Ever since that one night when he found her in the woods, he has been in love. I know she also feels the same for him. However, I don't know if it is as a brother, or as something else. For his sake, I hope it is the latter.

"We will rest here for now," I abruptly decide. The sun sits low in the sky and I can tell by the angle of the light through the trees that there is less than an hour left in this horrible day. "Emerald, see if you can catch a rabbit or two and while you are out, and collect herbs to make rabbit stew. Remember, focus and do not rush the shot. I really do not feel like going hunting for rabbits after they have all been scared off by you tromping through. Keep your head up and remember the way back. I also do not want to have to track you in the dark." Emerald looks up, mildly hurt by my brisk manner.

Normally, I am not this blunt. I look away, not in the mood to apologize. After making sure her weapons are ready and her bow is strung, Emerald slings her quiver across her shoulders and grabs her bow, tiny and toy-like compared to what my bow had been.

"Have you tried a bigger bow?" Evan asks as he watches her get ready.

"Yes," she replies shortly and tries to hurry out of camp. However, Evan is not ready to let the subject drop yet. "Shadow was, I mean is," he corrects himself hastily, "an amazing shot. Didn't she teach you?"

"She tried." Emerald bites off her words.

"Oh." That is all he says in response and lets the silence grow long and awkward. I glance at him curiously wondering where this line of questions is going. He has a thoughtful expression on his face, but he says nothing further and Emerald practically runs out of the clearing from the awkward conversation. Gregory has a small smile written on his face as he listens to the conversation.

I glance up at the moon's angle and start in surprise. Tomorrow is a blue moon. The Olympians are incredibly superstitious and a blue moon is an omen. More often than not, it is bad. Rarely does it mean anything good. I decide not to mention it to the others. Can there not be a moment with bad news anymore? I cannot help but wonder when everything started to go wrong. *What would Shadow want me to do?* Her voice rings clearly through my mind.

"Forget all about me. You have a job to do. Banish all thoughts of me and rally the group. Athena and Evan will help," I hear her voice as clearly as if she were standing next to me. Suddenly, something in my pocket burns me. I swear quietly and pull out my small silver stone. It projects a thin projection of a screen. Kind of like those, oh what do they

call them.... tele-vi-sion-s. Evan, Athena, and Gregory look up at the sudden light.

I watch wordlessly as Shadow steps out of the trees in the picture with complete composure and control, even though she is walking through her greatest enemy's camp. There is no trace of fear or hesitation. She gives those around her looks of great contempt and scorn. Except one. There is a young boy in tattered clothes that tends the fire near Chaos. She catches his eye and I know her well enough to know she is sending a telepathic message. The boy jerks upright and suddenly Shadow breaks her composure.

"Run!" she yells at him. He sprints off into the woods like a startled hare. Chaos shouts and a few men break off and chase after him. The next part is confusing, but when the image comes clear again, she is facing a great leopard-like creature. As she turns, I see long and deep claw marks across her back. She kills the demon with ease and fixes a challenging glare on Chaos. *Bring it on,* she says through her body language. Suddenly, a horrid looking creature barrels towards her. A bright *pink* Calydonian boar, not unlike the one we recently faced, runs at her. She barely escapes and cuts off a tusk. This time the creature is about on top of her before she slits its throat. I feel a distinct surge of pride watching her skills.

My breath catches as I spot the next beast- a beautiful baby dragon. Judging by its coloring and diamond shaped face, it is a Denaléri dragon. The last dragon. I wish I could warn Shadow of the danger behind her, but she cannot hear me. The dragon's huge claws tear the back of her knee to shreds. I give a small cry of despair. That is a major wound. That could easily kill an Olympian. She surprises all of those watching when she rises to her other leg. She threatens the beast with her sword before stopping in shock of seeing the baby dragon. The watching men yell at

211

Chaos to take it back. He silences them with a few gestures and words. Shadow sheaths her sword and yells at Chaos.

"What is she doing!" Evan shouts, horrified that she would leave herself without her weapon against a dragon, the most terrible of all beasts, but I slowly nod when I watch her action.

"That is Shadow, alright."

"It is against all she stands for to kill something so innocent and young," Athena says quietly to Evan. Even though I agree with Shadow, I cannot bear to see her give herself up like this. Although, it is a fitting end for her, refusing to kill something innocent. Shadow speaks quietly to the dragon and the dragon tries to stop the downward rush of its paw, but it is in vain. The super sharp claws slice the side of her face across to her opposite hip, leaving long, deep wounds across her torso and face. She does not rise.

Evan gives a cry of despair and recoils, weeping into his hands. Athena stares in shock for a few minutes before turning away. I wince as Chaos throws a spear and its barbed point catches her in the side. The dragon is at the opposite side of the magic dome and paces back and forth, whining in horror and fear. I still watch the shimmering screen of magic for some time after Chaos leaves.

As I move to stop the magic, I spot something strange. Shadow is still breathing. Albeit shallow and strained, she is breathing. Still clasped in her hand, the pommel of her sword glows brightly. It seems to glow brighter and suddenly her magic form steps out of the glowing stone. A holographic shadow of herself. She sits on Enbarr. Shadow looks down at her solid form on the ground and then looks at me directly. She points to her knee and shakes her head. Even in this magic form, where she should not have any injuries, her knee is still bloody and gouged. Then I look at her closer. All her injuries are still there. She shakes her head at me. An electrical shock runs through me and I can hear her clearly.

"*You know, I don't think I will make it this time,*" she says with clarity and indifference. "*It may be difficult, seeing as I am six feet tall and occasionally glow bright blue, but please, in all seriousness, don't dwell on me. I am only one pawn in this long game of war. Do not allow grief to overtake you. You are far above that. Tell Emerald that I know just how strong she is, even if she does not know it yet. Finish my mission. Bring peace, order, and stability to the lands and lastly, Evan,*" she hesitates before plowing on, "*tell him one thing. I loved him. I always have. May the road rise to meet you, may the wind be at your back. Farewells are hard, but know I am always with you. We shall meet again someday.*"

The shadow form disappears and her breathing slows. I turn away, unable to watch my friend die. I turn the silver stone in my hand and the screen vanishes. I tell Athena what Shadow told me to tell her and turn to Evan. He looks up. I am surprised to see a strange emotion in his eyes. Disappointment, fear, and hopelessness mixed to create a need for revenge on those who took his heart from him.

"Evan," I say his name softly. He switches his glare up to me. For the first time, I see the wolfish light in them and I resist from drawing my dagger. "Shadow gave me a message for you. She said: She loved you. She always has. May the road rise to meet you, may the wind be at your back. Farewells are hard, but know she will always be with you. You will meet again someday." I watch the bitterness and need for revenge fade from his eyes to be replaced with deep sadness.

"I loved her more than anything. Now I don't know what to do. Even when she was not around, she was my guide, my North Star on the darkest and most lonely of nights," he says softly, silent tears tracing paths down his cheeks.

"We must honor our commander's last order. We must bring peace, order, and stability to the lands. We must all be strong if we are to do that. She told me to forget about her. We are all above grief. Tomorrow and the weeks after tomorrow are more important than what happened today. Focus on what is next. Dwelling on the past will not do you any good. You must teach Emerald. She will need guidance through these next weeks. Be strong." His back straightens and he wipes the tears off his face. I nod and we all sit on the logs to await Emerald.

After a while, I hear her walking through the brush nearby. A small deer and a bunch of herbs are gathered in a bundle. Emerald carries the deer over her shoulder. I step over to her and heft the considerable weight of the deer over my shoulder. I'm surprised that she was able to carry this.

I set the unfortunate creature on the ground and pull out my skinning knife. Before long, we have a haunch of meat roasting over the fire on a green wood stick. Our mouths water as the smell of roasting meat permeates the air. I use some herbs that Emerald had found and they make it smell even more amazing. Soon we cannot wait any longer. Emerald pulls out the wooden bowls and utensils and the food quickly disappears.

Sitting around the merry campfire, everything should be peaceful. Comfortably full of good food and the jumping fire warming the air around us, it could be another of our many nights in the woods. But this time something is missing. There is an empty spot by the fire. A bowl and set of utensils unused. Most of all, we are feeling the absence of Shadow's calming presence. Though she did not often engage in the idle side chatter, I felt that I could relax when she was here. Even though I am a goddess, she is the one I looked to for answers. *She is the one everyone went to for answers.* It feels so utterly *wrong* without her here with us. I look up and catch Athena's eye and I know her mind is working along the same lines.

"I've been wondering what is in this pack." I break the long silence that had stretched on for many minutes now, following our evening meal. "I might have *liberated* it from the modern world." Now that I have everyone's attention. I reach behind me and pull out a black backpack. Without further drama, I dump all the contents onto the ground. Gregory looks mildly uncomfortable.

"You know," he starts speaking slowly and deliberately, "it is very bad when people steal. In the modern world, you can get into trouble." I look up at him and stare incredulously.

"You are concerned about us getting in trouble for stealing a *backpack*," I repeat his words. "We broke into a high security government facility, killed some storm spirit guards, knocked out all the humans who came near us, and led them on a chase through the streets of their own city, and it is bad that I stole a *backpack*?" I notice the others all hiding smiles. Good. I must keep their minds away from Shadow. I raise an eyebrow at Gregory to see if there is anything else. He raises his hands in defeat, but I notice a hint of a smile, the first one since he found out that his family was killed by Chaos. Then everyone's faces become grim again when they remember the days events. I can still see the haunting images in my mind's eye. I must keep their minds off Shadow and keep them entertained. Shadow ordered us not to grieve for her and I have never disobeyed a direct order from her.

"First item. This is some type of....er.... Food?" Athena holds them up for them to see. A York, S-nick-ers, Skit-el-s, and a Ree-seeeee," Athena carefully pronounces the items names. Gregory smothers laughter behind his hand as he hears how Athena is saying the names of the items he had become familiar with in the New World. I look doubtfully at the bright and shiny wrappers. I'm not sure that they are edible, they are so brightly colored.

"Dibs on the Reese's!" Gregory finally exclaims enthusiastically as we continue to stare at the foreign foods. Now four pairs of eyes turn to land on him.

"What is *dibs*?" Emerald asks, genuinely puzzled.

"Is it a person?" Athena chimes in curiously.

"Is it something on the Reese's?" Emerald looks concerned.

"I've got it. It is a person named Dibs who lives on the Reese's." Evan's expression is guileless, but when I catch his eye, I can see the mirth and mischief as he quickly winks at me. Athena and I have been to the modern world and have heard their strange expressions and words. I have figured out most, but a few still confuse me; for instance, there is texting, hashtags, photo bombed, chillaxin, (I have no idea about that one!) confuzzled, which I have assumed is another way of saying that there is a conned fuzzy bear named Ed. Don't even get me started with their abbreviations! Lol, Igtg, yolo, ttyl, IKR, yeat, xoxo and IDK, I mean, *why* would you even say that?

Obviously, Evan has heard some of the strange expressions as well. Finally, it is too much. His expression and mischievous ways are too much to handle. I start to laugh and Athena joins in. Evan keeps his dark blue eyes steady and puzzled for another minute or so, staring at us disapprovingly, before he starts to laugh as well. An aggrieved Gregory looks at us.

"Tough crowd. I see that some of you," he pointedly looks to where Evan, Athena, and I sit across the fire, "know what the *expression* means."

216

"You sound like a New Worlder now. You may speak Arindal like a native, but you give yourself away with these expressions," Emerald chimes in.

"Anyway, I *want* the Reese's. Are we clear?"

"Clear as a fresh mountain spring. Now, you want the York, you said?" Athena gives him an ingenious look. Gregory mutters something uncomplimentary about dealing with idiots. Perhaps with a few other choice words I won't repeat.

"There is a strange, black, flat thingy here," I change the topic.

"It's called a *computer.*" Gregory in his turn, looks amused by our ignorance.

"What is that?" Evan suddenly exclaims, totally disgusted by the color of the thing he found in a pocket of the backpack. It is similar to the small black devices that most modern humans carry and look at during all hours of the day, but this one is different. This one is a vivid shade of bubblegum pink, with a weird pattern of dead leaves on it. Somewhere in that alien world, a teenage girl will be wondering where her phone is. In a world mostly filled with dull and drab colors, unless you are among the wealthy, this is a completely new experience. Athena and I exchange distasteful expressions on this overly bright color.

"I've had enough of these humans! They are becoming too advanced for their own good," Athena mutters darkly and dramatically leans against an old fallen tree, but quickly sits up again when ants suddenly pour out of the dead wood. "Anyone play an instrument or anything? Something to liven up this dark night?" Everyone shakes their head, but suddenly Athena looks up from where she is staring at the strange pink device as if trying to think of a subtle way of destroying it, even though the back of it says that it is 'LifeProof'. "Emerald, you should sing! When you used to sing at home your voice was so pretty that all the boys stopped to watch! Even Ares!" I sit up straight again as the blush rises on Emerald's fair skin.

"Yes, sing for us!" she urges. Emerald finally gives in.

"Alright, alright! I'll do it." She thinks for a minute before starting a sweet old ballad that is well known through the countryside.

"There once was a twisted old willow,
Its voice was the wind through the leaves.
But mostly it sat there in silence,
Even when the day had a breeze.

This particular tree,
Has a long and tragic history
Many sad memories it remembers,
But for only one reason does it remain.

There once a young pretty maiden,
And a kind, young gentleman,
But war had arrived and peace had died,
Calling her brave knight to the front line-"

Her voice falters and she hesitates as another voice joins in. This one is lower, but still easy and clear and she looks across the fire at Evan as he sings the lower part. He nods and she continues. To those watching they can see small bits of their bright magic light up the space. A sapphire blue, with some ice blue sprinkled in, and the light green with a small bit of ice blue magic swirl together as the verses continue.

"The night before he left her,

218

They sat and planted a tree.
He had taken her hand and told her,
To think of him after he leaves,
Whenever she looked at their tree.

Soon after he left,
She had their child,
And took him up to the small tree.

They sat there a while,
And never did the boy,
Ever cry after that first hour

When he returned,
They rejoiced happily,
And celebrated Peace's return,
Under their young willow tree.

Soon after he returned,
A war arrived,
But this was a different kind.

Illness swept in and had no mercy,
Not even the smallest bit.
With it it took,
A happy family,
And left only one,
To learn how to be happy once more.

There once was a happy young willow,

Who lived up by the stream,

But now it is old,

And that child had grown,

To become a warrior just like his father before him.

This gnarled old willow still stands,

A memento of what started as a happy story,

But one with a tragic end."

Everyone sits still and silent as the song brings back memories of our fallen commander. Suddenly, as I am thinking about times gone, something in my pocket becomes painfully hot.

Out of curiosity, I pull out my stone. Despite the chilly temperature, it is still warm in my hand. The curious gift from Shadow shimmers in the fire's wavering light and suddenly, in a fine script, there are words of a strange and foreign language that I do not know. Shadow was fluent in so many different languages that this could be anything. As I squint at it, the symbols slowly change into letters. This time, I can read it. *Vixi et speravi, quod viximus et speravimus.*

"Everyone, look at your stones." I drag them all out of their own private thoughts and they immediately reach for them. Each stone has the same message. Even Evan's stone, deeply embedded into the hilt of his sword, glows with Shadow's handwriting.

"What do they say?" Gregory asks, since he cannot read the language.

"It says, I lived and hoped, because *we* lived and hoped." Athena's voice catches as she reads it. Evan and I glance at each other, then Emerald suddenly gives a small cry. Our eyes snap back to the stones and I feel my heart jump into my throat. All the ice blue magic in the stones is slowly gathering into a thin form of Shadow.

Just like I had seen in the vision from my stone, she is astride Enbarr, but this time she dismounts carefully. Enbarr disappears and her form becomes sharper as the extra magic adds into her form. She looks around at all of us and smiles, but it holds endless fathoms of sadness. Her normally ice blue eyes are gray as the pain continues to slam through her blood with every breath. I can see the long, deep, and open gashes of the dragon's claws and silver-blue blood still seeps from the wounds across her upper body.

"Hello, again. I hoped we would not need to meet like this, but it seems as if there is not another option. I do not have much time, for in my current state this is a very hard form to hold. Yes, I am alive, but not for much longer." Her form shivers violently and for a minute I am afraid that she is gone, but it reforms and she starts to speak faster. "You must all hurry and pass along my message and battle plans. I am sorry to ask this of you all, because we have all had a rather... *exciting* day, but please push on through the night. It is dangerous in the woods, but you are all capable fighters. Evan, come here please." She beckons him over. Her form shimmers again, but she keeps it together. Even with the acute hearing that comes from being an immortal hunter, I can barely hear what she says to him.

She reaches out a tentative hand towards him and he grasps it in his own. That should not be possible. Then again, when has she ever fit in the tight boundaries of what *is* possible? Evan looks just as surprised by the strong and calloused hand within his own.

"I love you, Shadow. I always have. Ever since I saw you in the woods when I was young, you have never left my thoughts. I-" his voice breaks and he looks up to meet her eyes. "I don't know what I will do without you. You are my North Star, when you are gone, it is like clouds briefly covering it, but I always know that the storm will pass and you will return. What will I do if my guiding star is gone? I will be more lost without you than when I was in the maze." She slowly looks up at the bright stars that sit serenely in the heavens above our heads.

A warm, summer breeze wafts through the trees, even though it is the middle of winter. The distinctive smell of the summer earth after a cool drizzle simmers in the air. She smiles and this time it is her real smile. Her eyes lose the gray and return to sharp ice blue. She stands up to her full height and looks down at Evan, smiling gently.

"Often, people look to others for answers and never realize that their own might be even better. If you need a guiding star, just look up and there are always plenty in the sky." She looks around at her silent audience once more and like a warm ray of sunshine finally clearing the clouds, we see her as she really is. There is no pain and no fear. She is hope, happiness, kindness, and compassion. Most of all, she looks relieved to step off the path and fade into the woods to peace and happiness. Despite my personal grief, I am happy for her.

The wind and summery scent intensifies and she glows brighter. She slips her hand out of Evan's and spares us all a last smile. But this time I notice there is a secretive light and despite their clearness, there is still one place deep within her that remains clouded and she glances around uncertainly for a second before nodding to herself and lets go of the magic. I watch the ice blue magic float through the air until it is gone and the night's bitter wind returns. Evan opens his hand and gasps as he spots the small blue stone that is half dark blue and fades to her ice blue. At the base of his wrist there are three words, etched there like a tattoo with ice blue ink. *Believe in yourself.*

"We need to move on." There is a sudden steel in his eyes and his shoulders straighten. "We must finish her mission. Without doing that we would be dishonoring her." He grabs his pack and everyone silently follows his example. All I want to do is crawl under the covers in bed and just give up. However, I know Evan is right and Shadow would be disappointed if we failed before we even tried. I insert a metal rod into my heart and force her out of my thoughts. I reach for my bow before I remember that it was smashed. I sigh and pick up my dagger. Evan puts out the fire.

"Let's get this war started." I lead the way out of the clearing and we head to Zeus's palace. One of the million small groups who have already felt the losses of the war before the first sword has drawn blood on the final battlefield. Why was I so naive to believe that our small group would never feel the cruel touch of War?

Chapter Twenty

Shadow

My consciousness returns slowly and as the thick black wall breaks apart, the pain returns in great masses, shooting through the rapidly widening gaps and breaking them further. My knee shoots red hot bolts of fire and the spear pinning me to the ground adds to the symphony of bright assaults of pain wracking through my whole body. I moan as the pain reaches past boundaries I did not know existed. As I lie there in total agony, hoping for the relief of death, a new magic gently slides through my blood system and the pain slowly recedes until it is gone.

With a great shuddering breath, I finally figure out that I am alive. A kaleidoscope of greens relaxes all my tensed muscles that have been working for who knows how long to keep myself from writhing around and ripping my side open even more. I just focus on breathing. I never knew what being weak felt like until now. All my muscles are exhausted and start to tremble violently when I try to move them. I open my eyes as the last of the pain flees my system. A dragon looks down at me curiously from where it sits, yes *sits*, next to me. I lift my head to look at it closer and the pain hits again. I close my eyes and wait, groaning as it courses like fire through my veins. Okay, don't move. Got it.

"Lie still. You will further injure yourself. My magic is barely restraining the pain. Hold still. This is about to hurt. Rather a lot, actually," The dragon warns me. I squeeze my eyes tightly and try to mentally brace myself. I don't reply and just grit my teeth and try to think a happy thought. A scream is drawn from my throat as the spear is pulled straight out of my skin. The dragon nudges me gently. I hesitatingly try to open my eyes, but suddenly they are too heavy to lift. My entire body aches and I feel weak as a newborn kitten. I must have drifted in and out of consciousness for the rest of the night, because when I wake up again and manage to open my eyes, the sun is just peeking out between the trunks of the trees to the east.

The young dragon is fast asleep next to me and fire courses through my blood once again without the young kit's magic. A strange shadow flies overhead again and again, each time coming lower. The dragon neatly bandaged my knee and side using magic. The deep wounds across my upper body and back are now fully sealed scars. The dragon must have used a ton of magic to heal my wounds. The two major wounds snarl at me as I heave myself to my good leg. I hiss and swear before drawing my sword and lean against a convenient tree. The creature lands with a soft thump in front of me. I am the only one between this giant dragon and my smaller friend.

Carefully keeping my sword in front of me, I hop over and gently put my wounded leg down on the grass, and carefully put a small bit weight on it. It shoots another fiery burst of pain and gives out. I swear quietly again and look at the dragon in front of me. This is a fully grown female dragon. From tail to the tip of its snout, it is around twenty feet long and ten feet tall. It's iridescent scales shimmer with thousands of different colors that I did not know existed anymore. I stand on one foot facing one of the most, or *the* most powerful creatures left in the lands. I would barely stand against a puny human soldier at this moment.

"*Laedin ren nael dire ilan Relan?*" I cannot understand the old language of dragons, but they are very knowledgeable creatures who speak many languages, so the dragon ought to understand my native language.

"What do you want? I do not want to hurt you, but I will not let you hurt my friend," I say quietly in Daenlir. The dragon looks at me appraisingly before tucking its wings into its sides and walks a few long strides closer. I raise my sword higher in a more obvious threat. The adult dragon surprises me when she responds in Daenlir.

"You are wounded, child. Would you sacrifice your life to save a dragon? Look at the creature. She is so small and young. Still at the tender age where she can still be tired from too much magic. She hasn't had enough of a life to miss anything. Why risk your own life for hers?"

"I do not kill, or let someone else kill, any creature if they have good in them. This young kit has more good in her than a lot of the Olympians that I know."

"You would still sacrifice *yourself* though? Just to protect her?"

"I have done it before and they obviously found that I am harder to kill than expected. Now, are we going to stand around talking about it, or could we just get on with this please? I've already said all my goodbyes anyhow." The dragon looks at me strangely before stepping closer. This time when she speaks, her voice is different; kinder and more respectful.

"It is alright. I am not here to hurt either of you. This is my kit, Relan. She did not come back to our cave several weeks ago. I have searched everywhere for her. I finally found her. Sorry for the act I just put you through, but I had to be sure. I will do anything to keep her safe. We are the only two dragons left. However, that is a story best told later. What is your name, little warrior?" I stare at this powerful dragon in front of me. *Do I trust her?* My instinct tells me that I should, but my head reminds me that dragons are known for trickery.

Matters are taken out of my hands when I incautiously step back onto my wounded leg. It buckles under me and my side is also set alight with agony as I move. Before I hit the ground, the mother dragon catches me in her paw and grabs Relan by the scruff of her neck in the other. I unwillingly give a tiny moan that I quickly cut off as her paw brushes my knee. She flies us to a distant mountain within a few minutes. She lets go of Relan when we land in the cave. Relan wakes up with a start as she realizes that she is somewhere different. Panicked, she jumps to her feet and looks around to see her mother gently place me on the stone floor.

"Mama!" she squeals just like a small human child would. I cannot help but smile at their happy reunion, but it makes me think of my friends. Have they passed my message to Zeus? Did he listen? I can very distantly remember sending myself in magic form to speak to them, but the memory of their expressions as I said farewell is too much and I can feel deep inside me where I have buried a lifetime of tears, the dam is breaking. I close my eyes and clear my thoughts.

I carefully draw out a small bit of magic and let it rest in my palm. Carefully, I gather it into a diamond and draw my sword. The small ice blue light enters the hilt and comes to a stop square in the crosspiece of my sword. An ice blue, diamond shaped gem glitters in the weak light. That is a last resort. I look up at the sudden silence in the cave. Both dragons watch me incredulously.

"You are a magic wielder! I should have realized you were different from humans. Now I can see that you are not even a goddess! You are the one they all speak of through the woods." The mother dragon looks at me like she just found a golden mountain. "You are the only one who can help us! The gods want us killed, but you are stronger and kinder than them! Your refusal to kill Relan clearly shows that." I let out a long sad sigh and study the hard ground below me.

"Yes, I am known as the Shadow Warrior, but I doubt I am able to save you. I was not even able to save myself from my own brother. I have become weak," I reply bitterly.

"Child, look up." I draw my gaze up and meet the mother dragon's eyes. They hold eons of knowledge, suffering, sorrow, joy,

227

happiness, and humor. She seems to see through me to places that nobody has ever cared enough to find. She nods and breaks the connection. This time instead of awe, there is motherly concern and understanding. I look at her pleadingly. My eyes begging for someone who can understand the way I have felt for too many years. "Child, what is your name?" I have the feeling she already knows but I tell her anyway.

"Shadow Caerin."

"That is not your real name, Elren. Why do you present yourself under a fake name?"

"I know no other name that I can be proud of. I am a shadow. People think they see me, but they never care about anything past what they hear and see on the outside. When I was young, I was proud of my name. However, that pride was taken away when I was beaten, whipped, and tortured. I was ashamed that I could not do anything to help myself or anyone else. I almost killed myself trying to escape. Elren was not someone to be proud of, so I took the name people had given me. If people called me the Shadow Warrior, then that is who I'll be. I am a shadow of my brother. Now I am no one, because Shadow just died at the hand of her brother. Elren is all I have left to me now."

"Elren Caerin, I know you're still young and you are not used to people thinking you are some great hero. *Everyone* has flaws. Everyone feels fear, hope, sadness, joy, guilt, and shame. The question is, who can deal with it and put it past them? You and your brother, Draemir, are very similar on the outside, but the inside is totally different. You were taught very young that anger is what ruins peace and order. Emotions were supposed to be hidden and fear is a weakness." She looks away, lost in thought for a moment.

"You two are very similar in most ways. Your anger can escape from you at times. I saw in your memories that you try very hard not to let it escape from your control. Chaos feeds on his anger. It makes him vengeful and violent. You are very wise if you can put that aside and bury it deep. Humans are different. They will explode if their emotions get too bottled up. However, you are an immortal being, not a simple human. Now, I will heal your injuries as well as I can. With luck, you should be able to walk again. Close your eyes."

I do as she says and feel my heart lighten considerably as some of the burden is taken off my shoulders. Though I feel that weight gone, my heart still has a gash torn across it. My friends are still out there preparing for a one-sided war. I must join them as soon as I can. The dragon's magic courses through my veins like a waterfall down a cliff- wild, free, and refreshing- all pain is gone.

I open my eyes and unwind the bandage on my side. There is no trace of a wound. On my knee, there is a new rune, but this one has all of the colors of the dragon. I get to my feet hesitantly and carefully put weight on it. It feels completely back to normal. I walk a few steps and am overjoyed to be able to move again. There is still a limp, but there is no pain. The limp will disappear with time, probably not soon, but eventually. I am lucky that I am even able to walk.

"Thank you! Thank you so much!" Laidena gives me her toothy smile and offers for me to climb onto her back.

"We must return you to your friends. It has been a long time since I fought in a war. I think this is the right war to fight. I will leave you in a nearby village called Hearthburry. From there, you must find your friends alone. I will see you on the battlefield." I jump off her back and turn to watch Laidena and little Relan fly away into the distance. I casually walk down the road and the villagers all stare at me. For a moment I wonder why, but then I look down at myself and remember that I look like I was wrestling with the devil. My tunic is shredded by the sharp claw marks and bloodstains coat the jagged edges. My braid has come out of the constraints of my leather tie. My face is streaked with mud and blood, as are my arms. With my new limp, I must look like wild beast. I quickly turn off the road and enter the refuge of the leafy forest.

Fog shifts between the trees in great wafting sheets, obliterating the path behind me. When I get deep enough in, I surround myself with my magic and in a second my tunic is totally mended and looks like it has never been through a fight. Soon I come across a small pond in the middle of a brush patch. When I glance down at the water I am shocked at what I see. I am not eighteen years old anymore. Sometimes I do that. I can skip a year, but this time I aged more than a year. I am twenty- the same age as my brother. Just like the prophecy said and my eyes drop down to read the ancient runes on my arm again. We are twins again for the last battle, but the real question is if we are equal again.

I doubt that.

I quickly wash myself in the pond and when I dress again, I barely recognize my own hands without the dried blood and dirt caked on them. I jog through the woods, heading south, but after a few miles I hear a sound that is out of place. My sharp ears catch the soft sound of heavy soled boots among the fallen branches and leaves. My ears perk and senses heighten. I silently pull my bow off my shoulder and fit an arrow to the string. The outline of a human is in the nearby shadows.

"Show yourself, or there is an arrow here for you, and I rarely miss what I am aiming at!" With a loud crunching of twigs and dead leaves, the figure hurriedly steps into the clear. In his hands, there is a simple round shield and a short sword. Something is off though. As I curiously study him, and when I look past his awkward and unpracticed form, I figure out what it is. He is left handed. I know only a few men whose dominant hand is their left. I return my arrow to my quiver and sling my bow across my shoulders. The left-handed warrior in front of me is no bigger than a boy. I approach without much concern. However, I would have to be a fool not to stay light on my feet and expect anything.

"S-s-stay b-back!" he calls shakily. "I-I-I am a-armed!" He looks terrified as I continue to walk forward, despite his warning, or terrified plea as most would define it. When I am close enough to speak normally, I quietly call the boy's name.

"Allen, I am not here to hurt you."

"Yes, you are! Everyone is bad! They all hunt me! They come when I am asleep and try to kill me!" He suddenly lunges at me with surprising speed for a human. Refraining from instinctively drawing my sword, I step to the side and grab his hand holding onto the sword and force it point down, deep into the soft earth. He swings his right fist with the shield in a desperate attack and I don't notice in time to duck. It catches me on the cheekbone below my left eye and the rim of the shield gives me a long and deep cut. My temper flares at the sudden burst of pain. Both quickly simmer down and I grab his other wrist as well. I brutally slam his chest with my shoulder and release him as he falls back and sits on the forest floor gasping for air.

"Seriously, Allen. I didn't plan on hurting you."

"Who are you?" he wheezes, giving up the idea of fighting after seeing how easily I threw him to the ground. For a moment, I wonder if I should tell him or not, but I decide that he deserves to know the truth. Even though he gave me a nasty bruise and cut.

"I have been called many things, but you may know me as Elren. Generally, my enemies call me the Shadow Warrior, except one. You, however, are not one of my enemies. Your father will be very happy to see you. I am sorry to say that your mother died of sickness soon after you and your siblings were taken by Chaos." His mouth moves slowly like he is spelling something out as he processes the huge load of information I just threw at him.

"So, you mean that my father is still alive?" The hope in his eyes is almost painful to look at it, it shines so bright.

"The last time I was home he was alive. Of course, the last time I saw him was two years ago."

"Wait. Stop right there, and back it up. You are supposed to be dead. You were killed by the dragon and Chaos skewered you with a spear. There is absolutely no way you could have lived." My knee and side twinge as he mentions them.

"Nobody thinks you are alive either," I reply dryly. He has the grace to smile.

"I guess that is fair. One question though. How do you know so much about me?" Without answering his question, I study him. He looks exhausted, cold, and half starved. I look at the position of the sun as it slips down through the sky into a bright red and orange fire and decide that I can afford a short break and will continue through the night.

"Let's get a fire going and I will tell you more." Soon we have a small fire going with the flames dancing wildly. I limp over to the fire. When I sit down, I stretch my leg out straight. It has been getting stiff and starting to ache since I stopped moving.

"I suppose I should tell you how I know so much about you. It started way back when your siblings were taken." The story unfolds through my head as I begin to tell him the sad tale. Ice blue magic spirals into the air above and figures appear out of it.

"My horse's legs were beating the mud, splashing the both of us from head to toe. I had received an urgent message from a young couple in the village. Two of their children had disappeared earlier in the week and now their third child was gone." I relive the moment as I tell him.

"It was a little after midnight when my horse skidded to a stop in front of the small inn. I had quickly slipped out of my saddle and rapped on the door. Scarcely a second had passed before it swung open with a loud crash and a sword point was quivering under my chin.

"Wh-who are you!" a man's scared voice greeted me. For a moment, I wondered if I was at the wrong inn, but a quick glance at the sign reassured me. I did not step away from the wavering sword, as much as I wanted to, I could sense that he would strike if I moved. Instead, I spoke calmly and firmly. As if *he* were the fourteen-year-old with a sword at his neck.

"My name is Shadow. I received a message that a boy named Allen was stolen from his parents and they hoped that I would be able to help. So, I am here." He looked at me for a second before abruptly sheathing his sword.

"Come in."

"Not until I know who you are," I had replied evenly. "I have many enemies and how should I know that you aren't one of them?" He swung around and glared at me for my patronizing tone of voice.

"Last time I checked, you are unarmed and young, whereas I am an adult with a long and sharp sword. Watch your mouth, missy." Without warning, I drew my sword and it glowed menacingly with a faint ice blue light.

"Look again. I may be young, but I am more than capable with a sword," I replied irritably. I had had a very long day chasing bandits and criminals and I was very happy sleeping in my house before the frantic messenger came and banged on my door like he wanted to break it down. Just as abruptly as I had drawn it, I sheathed my sword and stood with my arms crossed. "Do you want Allen to be found? You are wasting precious time. Each minute you squander, he gets farther away. Either quit the shenanigans, or I can just as easily get on my horse again and go back to sleep without another thought." The man was totally taken aback by my words. His face spasmed with anger.

"Get out of my sight, you conceited little girl! I never want to see you here again!" He slammed the door shut. I had scratched a small rune, a bird's claw with a slash through it, on the top part of the door before turning away and wearily mounting my horse, Stormy. The symbol marked his dishonor. I looked up at the inn and had spotted a woman standing by an upstairs window.

Tears coursed down her cheeks in great rivers. I halted my horse and pulled out a piece of parchment. I quickly scribbled that I will do my best to find her youngest son and bring him home safely. With my magic, I lifted it into the air and it gently floated to your mother's hand. She read it and looked at me hopefully. A small voice had whispered in my ears, *The mother will die from sorrow if you fail. Do not fail.* I nodded to her and galloped out of the village. The only signs of my presence there was a regretful man, an anguished woman, dishonor on the door, and hoof prints beaten into the mud.

"I was able to track you as far as the coast and saw where the ship's prow had left a deep trench in the sand, but you were gone with the ship. I cursed the man who had delayed my search, or else I would have caught you before you had left. I cursed myself for not finding you. I have for the past few years."

"What happened to my mother? I mean, I know she is dead, but how did she die?" he asks hesitantly, dreading my answer, but needing to hear it all the same.

"She was so upset that she became very ill and did not have the will to live anymore." His soft brown eyes fill with tears. "Your father will be very happy to see you." I hesitate for a second before plowing on.

"Your older brother Samuel is dead. I am pretty sure you knew that, but what you do not know is that he died by this sword." Tíne glows faintly in its scabbard as I mention it. "He was left handed too. He realized in the end that he was wrong to side with Chaos. He last wish was that I would find and protect his younger siblings. You found me. I've been looking for you, but I got sidetracked due to the preparations necessary for the upcoming war. The Olympians have not been cooperative. It is a bit of a big undertaking to get all of those damn idiots to agree on battle tactics." He looks around fearfully as if expecting to see me get zapped into a pile of ashes.

"Umm, I don't think it is a good idea to insult the gods." He clears his throat uncomfortably as his voice cracks. "Even if you are a goddess, they get very mad, right? I would think that Lord Zeus would zap you to ashes for saying that." I laugh in genuine amusement.

"For one, they are all afraid of me. Second, Zeus gave up trying to zap me for my comments a long time ago." He relaxes slightly and the grip on his sword lessens.

"What are you? Human or goddess?" I frown thoughtfully before slowly answering.

"I am not a human, but I am also not a goddess. Honestly, no one knows my strength. Not even me. There is not a name that they have come up with yet that can define who I am. If that makes any sense." He nods slowly and a puzzled frown furrows his brow. Suddenly his expression clears and a smile lights up his face like a beam of sunshine.

"I think the only title that fits you is Legendary. You and Chaos are legends." I smile at the title.

"Alright then. However, you need to head home. Your father needs someone to help him. I can get you a ride and send you with food and a blanket, but I cannot accompany you. I need to get to my friends and let them know that I'm alive."

"*Rosy! I need a ride! Bring food and a good blanket!*" I call her telepathically.

"*Who is that?*" Rosy asks back pugnaciously.

"*Oh, come on! It is Elren!*"

"*Aren't you dead?*" she asks.

"*Not yet. I need you to give this boy a ride and bring supplies so he can make it home.*

"*Okay, okay. I'm coming.*" Approximately two seconds later, a small and petite bay horse crashes out of the fog.

"You called?" Rosy asks in clear Arindal. Allen's jaw drops. He stares at Emerald's horse in shock.

"The horse talks," he says faintly. Rosy walks forward and shoves him with her nose for his rudeness.

"A lot of horses speak, you just haven't been around us long enough to hear it," Rosy reprimands him. With an obvious effort, Allen pulls himself back together. I rummage through the saddle packs to see what she brought. It is the same stuff that my friends and I had bought in the market a long time ago. I pause for a second and try to count the weeks that have passed. With a shock, I realize that it has almost been four months since we left Olympus for this awful quest. Soon the flowers will be poking their heads out of the thawing ground and animals will be out and about. This spring there will be more than just blooming flowers and innocent young creatures. Many will die this spring.

Her head whips around and I feel my blood freeze. There are others here. They are watching us. My knee groaning at me, I quickly draw my bow and an ice blue arrow appears on my bow string. Tíne also dances with ice blue fire in its sheath. Something feels so incredibly off.

The air itself hums with tension and power. Allen also jumps to his feet and draws his sword. His plain little bowl shaped shield is on his right arm. He stares at me with a thousand questions in his eyes, but the uneasy light in my eyes discourages all conversation. The fog seems to grow denser and closer, conquering my eyesight.

"Allen," I say in a serious voice as I spot what we are up against, "are you prepared for a fight if there is one to come?" He looks at me; puzzled, but nods. "Well, looks like our opponent is here. Or should I say, *opponents*." He whips around to follow my grim gaze. Figures stand, their shapes barely discernible as they stand shrouded in fog.

Every slow step they take seems to draw the fog with them. We are surrounded. Strangely enough, they are women. As one, they draw their weapons. Still with the peaceful look given by Death, three continue to walk in a trancelike state towards us. I bite my lip as fifty million options and questions fly through my head. In agony of indecision, I hesitate to strike first. They are women who fight with long swords like me and a distant part of my mind almost wants me to put my sword down and go with them into the mist. I look at the terrified young boy next to me. I cannot leave him.

I suddenly grab him by the scruff of his neck and bodily hurl him onto the back of Rosy.

"Allen, find your father. Go somewhere safe." He looks at me, his brown eyes filled with fear. I give him his sword since he dropped it and in it is something new. Deep in the hilt is a stone the colors of a sunset and the blade glows slightly like the horizon over the ocean. The short sword is longer and sturdier, but light and easy to handle. I leave a trace of ice blue in a line on the sword.

"Let the sword guide you." I swat Rosy across the rump and she gallops off. Allen leans low over Rosy's mane, riding instinctively, as she dashes off into the woods. Gritting my teeth, I level my bow and steady my hand. The threat is obvious, but completely unheeded as they advance. Suddenly, I realize where all the great female warriors have gone. Put to the side after their great deeds, they disappeared from history. Now they are here.

Studying their faces, I recognize Joan of Arc from the lost kingdom of France, Urduja, the beautiful Filipino war leader, and Han E. Lee from the other lost kingdom of China. Each woman is of a different time and place, but why are they here and why show up to fight me? One by one, they line up. Joan of Arc steps forward first. She looks to be only seventeen years of age. She is of medium height, but stocky and muscular.

It is slightly surprising to me because in all the portraits of her, she is tall and super slim. Her dark brown hair is French braided and a tattered purple ribbon is still tied in. She smiles at me and lays her sword at my feet. In the hilt is a deep purple stone.

"My magic is here. I give you all I have left. With it comes wisdom in battle." Her voice has a strong accent and fades in and out as her magical form wavers in the light breeze.

"Thank you," I reply in French, still not entirely sure what is happening. Her smile grows larger and she shakes my hand before stepping back. Urduja leaves her lance. In it holds the brightest yellow I have ever seen. Her form shimmers and she appears as if she were still in flesh form, not the last essence of her magic. Her dark hair is braided with gold and she wears gold bangles crisscrossing her arms and her tunic is gold and white as well. All of it complements her tall, beautiful form and bronze colored skin.

"I give leadership. You have much, but need more." Her Arindal is missing parts, but her voice is like music, making up for the gaps.

"Thank you for your gift. Leadership is a skill that always needs to be strengthened," I reply in Tagalog. She nods gravely and steps back with Joan. Han E. Lee steps forward. She is slim of build and graceful in her movements, only a little taller than five feet, but the casual way her left hand rests on the hilt of the sword at her hip, along with the athletic movements, shows that she is an experienced warrior. Her bronze and red robes flutter behind her as she quickly steps forward. She had been a soldier in the Chinese army under the male name, Han. She carries a long cavalry sword with the faintest hint of bronze magic surrounding it. The fog seems to be trying to draw her back, but she resists and lays the blade with the others.

"For cunning," she whispers as all her strength is focused on holding her form here and not passing on. I nod my gratitude. Chinese is an ancient language I have not yet learned, but it has always fascinated me.

"Thank you all. Your gifts are greatly appreciated, but why give them to me?" I ask in complete bewilderment and slight shock. Joan's bright purple eyes smile. The only extrovert in the group, she steps up as the spokeswoman.

"You are the greatest warrior who will ever walk this Earth. It is time we shed our mantles and move on. We wish to sacrifice our greatest strengths for you to use. Without them, we will fade and die, but the time is right for us to leave this world for good. Call the stones to you. They will come."

I summon them with my magic and all three suddenly fly at me. I catch two, but the third one nails me straight between the eyes. I raise an eyebrow at Urduja when I notice the bright yellow color of the offending stone. She stifles laughter behind her hand. I carefully place them in Tíne's hilt. Joan's goes straight into the pommel of the sword moving mine to the cross section, while Urduja's and Han's are on the very ends of the hilt.

"We only require one favor from you. Could you give us some magic to help us leave this life? We need it to finally move on," Han E. Lee asks. I nod instantly.

"Of course." I summon a large mist of ice blue magic into the air and it splits into three equal parts before surrounding them. When the mist is gone, the fog surrounding them disappears. Their forms are solid and they all wear full armor. I catch my breath as I stand before these magnificent warriors. Each shimmers in her own bright colors. Suddenly, I see how they got the portraits of Joan wrong. She stands as tall as me now and her brilliant armor glows with a strong royal purple color.

She smiles at me as I gawk at them, for once losing my composure. Urduja is very hard to look at since her armor shines as bright as the sun. Her armor is made of pure gold and magic which is probably how she got her name. In my language, it translates to Rising Sun. Her bronze skin glows as if rubbed with oils. Her black hair is braided back with thin gold strands. She looks like a goddess. Han wears gold and red armor. Her hair is tied back and shines in the dull light of the forest. All three of them stand tall and proud.

Four horses walk out of the fog and three of them stand by their masters as the fourth stays back. A great gray horse, almost white, stands by Joan's shoulder. A tall, spindly animal, but built for speed and stamina. A beautiful buckskin mare stands next to Urduja. Her coat glows with so many shifting shades of gold, yellow, creams, and tan that like her rider, she is hard to look at for too long. Her bold black and dark brown stripes barring her legs and the dorsal stripe from mane to tail shimmer as if you had poured stardust all over the brown. The dark tips of her ears and her dark brown nose glitter as well. Han's horse is dwarfed by these two giants, and looks to be a mere pony in comparison. It is jet black without any white anywhere. In place of white though, there is a glowing bronze star in the middle of his forehead. His eyes are bronze with a hard light in them. He is as deadly as his rider in battle, but he playfully nibbles on Han's cloak, showing his hidden playfulness.

The fourth horse steps out into the clear. Full night has fallen, but Enbarr glows a mythical silver and the ice blue writing shows clearly across his body. Words that I know too well. The words symbolize everything that will happen in my life. They explain my prophecy, my fate, and my destiny. All of them revolve around one person- my brother. We will meet again and I cannot afford to lose that battle. He is the only one who has the power to defeat me, and I will never surrender.

I look up, expecting the others to have left by now, but they watch me sympathetically. My expression must have given away my thoughts, because their eyes are understanding, but they also know that I am not afraid of how my legend will end.

"You will never actually die. You represent something that can be carried through the hearts of all generations. While they carry your memory, you will never be gone. You are hope. While people continue to hope, you cannot die. Therefore, you are the most powerful of us all. I will stand with you in the final battle before I leave," Joan declares abruptly.

"I will stand with you," Urduja replies as well.

"We will all stand with you," Han confirms. I can only nod my appreciation. With these warriors helping us, we stand a better chance against Chaos's army. However, we still only stand a slim chance. Although, that is far better than no chance at all.

"The army will assemble in the Plain of Ren. Hopefully, if fate allows, I will see you there with all limbs attached." With a quick grin, I step forward and clasp hands with each legendary warrior before mounting Enbarr. Each horse bows to Enbarr as he passes and he nods to them as well. I turn him back with slight pressure from my left knee and watch as the three figures disappear into the thick fog. Whirling Enbarr around, we fly through the trees with a reckless abandon. My heart beats in time to the sound of his galloping hooves. In my thoughts, one flies through. *Home. I am heading home.* When Chaos had captured me, I never believed I would ever have the chance to say that. I savor the sweet taste of those words on my tongue.

"Home. I am heading home," I whisper to the trees.

Chapter Twenty-One

Emerald

My gut has twisted itself into knots with nerves. I am suddenly conscious of all of the mud and blood smeared on my face and the ratty shape of my once beautiful tunic. My fingers run through my hair once more to try and get rid of the countless knots. Artemis and Athena look immaculate. Artemis's light brown hair is loose and it shines in the early morning light. Her green and brown tunic is perfect. Athena also looks gorgeous. Her dark brown hair is in a perfect ponytail. They watch me sympathetically as I fuss with my clothes and hair. Evan is also miraculously cleaned up. His sapphire tunic is belted at the waist and reminds me just how lean he is. His face is clean shaven and his hair cropped short. I wonder if he would have survived any longer before we came. Somehow, I know that he would have. He has something to live for.

His arms are folded across his chest and he is staring at the door with a deep and serious frown, a far cry from the first time we were here with him. His expression is fierce and almost wolfish, but when he turns and meets my eyes I can see all the sadness that he has been wrestling with. He is a man on a mission. He will not settle until Chaos has seen his revenge. My heart beats faster, but sadness slams through me once more as Shadow resurfaces in my mind. I remember her and Evan the first time we met. Suddenly, unbidden memories fly through my head.

A strange girl stands in the doorway, looking in. I can hear the screams and shouting outside and the boy named Evan tries to keep me calm, even though fear and panic rim his dark blue eyes. She comes in and takes both of us by the arms. I have never seen the girl before, but her presence is calming, even though she is so hurried in her desperate rescue attempt. Tension flows through her muscles and her hands are so hard that her grip is almost painful. She drags both of us out of the house like we are dolls, even though Evan is a year older than she.

When she finally speaks, I am surprised by her voice. Her accent is so different from everyone else's, but her voice is calm and quiet. I wonder whether she is even a human. Surely this lean and muscular girl is a goddess? Her eyes intrigue me, but she does not meet my gaze.

We run a few steps and I glance back to see where my parents were standing and when I spot them dead on the ground, my eyes are drawn up to the one who killed them. A boy, who looks almost identical to the girl leading us, stands there with a glossy black sword that is dripping with blood. It is dripping with the blood of my family. I begin to cry uncontrollably, every possible emotion boiling through me. Anguish, horror, hate, and sadness. Nothing matters anymore. All my memories of good times with my family are beyond painful- they are torture. I have lost everything, absolutely everything.

I trip and the girl effortlessly lifts me to my feet and puts my hand into Evan's. She tells Evan to run and hide. She would find us later. I look at her and force her to meet my eyes. I resist the urge to flinch when her ice blue eyes seem to pierce my own. Fear freezes my blood at the strength and weight that her gaze holds.

For a heartbeat, I simply look at her and take in her appearance, momentarily forgetting my anguish. Her light brown hair is tightly French-braided and tied with a faded ice blue ribbon. She wears a bright ice blue tunic and the silver scabbard and sword hilt shows by her left hip. Her face is lean like the rest of her form with high and sharp cheekbones. Angular features give her a mythical and slightly exotic look. She is far more muscular than a boy could ever dream to be, but also tall and lean. Once more, my eyes return to hers. They hold confidence, but not arrogance. As far as heroes come, in my eyes, she is better than anything my imagination could ever come up with. She is a girl, yet it never held her back. I chose her to be my hero that day. She never wavered from that image for many years. I had been content only knowing that small part of her.

When she turned back to the boy with the bloody sword and raised her own to attack him for us to survive, I was stunned by her bravery. I have never forgotten this. Whenever I revisit it, I am not looking at my parents as they lie dead on the cobblestones like some might expect. I use it to boost my courage. I think about Shadow as she turned, a young girl, to the older boy with the bloody sword. If she was able to face her greatest enemy, just to save two children, I am able to hide my fear and be courageous, just like her. Now, years later, I cannot count the brave miracles she has managed to pull out, but the biggest thing I have come to realize is that I am now my own hero. I've always heard that Fortune favors the brave, now I believe it.

My palms are beaded with nervous sweat and I wipe them on my filthy light green tunic. Isn't there anything else that I can wear? Again, my fingers tear through my hair. Finally, Artemis takes pity on me. She slowly gets up and walks over to me. It is so hard to see her without her bow. She still wears her quiver and even as I watch her hand reaches up to grab an arrow. She pulls it out with practiced ease and I notice that this one is different than the others. Instead of silver, it is light green. It is perfectly crafted and when I look at the fletching, I know who made it. One feather is ice blue. Written in a fine, curvy script is a short note from Shadow.

"This appeared in my quiver when Shadow sent her last message. It says, *I know that you, Athena, and Evan know how to summon clean outfits and clean yourselves up, but unfortunately, Emerald's magic is*

245

limited due to her age. I hope you will teach her the trick later when she is experienced enough. However, I managed to put this together in a spare moment. Hope I got the sizes right... That could be awkward... Anyway, trace the point of the arrow deep enough to create a mark and write the word 'pulchra'. I am sorry I am not there. That is my speech to give, but it fell onto you, Emerald. This is the least I could do to help. I hope you can get the counsel to agree with my plan of action. If they do not, please try anyway." We all look at the arrow, then Artemis, and then the arrow again.

"It feels like she is still alive. How was she so prepared for her death?" No one knows the answer to the question, but Evan had not been paying much attention to the conversation and breaks the awkward silence.

"Well, time's getting short. They will call us in any moment now. We did not gallop wildly through the woods all night to simply stand here." He peeks around the wall into the court. Almost everyone is seated. "Artemis, Athena, you need to go to your seats. It would be rather embarrassing if Apollo beat you there, Artemis. Guys, even Dionysus is seated. They need their Goddess of Wisdom and Goddess of the Hunt and Moon." Artemis holds up her hand to cut off his urging.

"My pride can be re-built. I want to see this." At a gesture from Artemis, I take the arrow. I carefully scratch the word into my forearm, biting my lip as it draws blood, and immediately green magic swirls around me until I can't see anything except magic. Ice blue magic is mixed in and stirs it all faster. Suddenly, it clears.

They all stare at me and I cautiously look down and gasp. My tunic is replaced with a perfectly fitted light green tunic and light brown stitches make the symbol of an eagle in flight on my chest. It is held at the waist by a strong leather belt with light green stitches. Treán's scabbard is a stiff and beautiful light brown leather with swirling patterns in green threads. All my daggers and throwing knives are covered in the same fashion. My hair is perfectly brushed out and in a tight French braid, just like how Shadow did her hair for battles. Even a light green hair ribbon is braided through. Immaculate tan breeches to my knee, where after that they are hidden by new soft leather tall boots. These are beautifully crafted and molded straight to my calves and feet as if I had worn them for years. The light brown leather is smooth and soft to the touch. On the outside of each boot, another green eagle flies across them.

Somehow it makes me feel older and less like a child. I am fifteen, but when you are around Shadow for many years, you begin to feel very young and childlike, even though there is only three years or so between us. She was so serious and recently seeming more of a parent than a sister. How can I be expected to give a speech that Shadow was supposed to say? Her own little shadow that never gets noticed, and often likes it that way, now must appear in front of the most powerful Olympians and propose an action for war. She had prepared me for something like this, so I know how to compose myself, but that does not mean I am ready to do it on my own.

Artemis and Athena run into the giant marble court to their seats. Suddenly, I feel smaller than ever. Evan drops a hand onto my shoulder and when I look up at him he gives me an encouraging smile. *You are not doing this alone.* I nod my gratitude, but my nerves don't listen. A conch horn is blown from somewhere inside the open court. That's our cue. I straighten my shoulders and think how Shadow would have entered. I throw my braid back over my shoulder and put on my most serious face with a small frown creasing my forehead and my eyebrows raised in a haughty manner.

"You look like you were just forced to eat a pickled lizard," Evan whispers in my ear. I immediately stop trying. He laughs softly. "Just be you. Nobody can be Shadow. You will know what to say." Taking a deep breath, I step through the giant marble arch and stride up the long walkway to the stage. I can hear Evan's soft footfalls behind me. All the Olympians turn and stare in surprise when it is little me and not the tall, composed, and muscular Shadow Warrior they expected.

Confused, angry, and derisive muttering ripples around the twelve most powerful Olympians in the war committee and the large crowd who came to listen. A lump forms in my throat as I realize that none of them know that Shadow is dead. I stop in my tracks and am about to turn and run when Evan steps up beside me and gives me a steadying look. Suddenly I am aware how grateful I am for his calm and reassuring presence. There is something protective and almost paternal in his eyes. It takes me by surprise, since he is only a year older than Shadow had been, but then again, Shadow had always seemed ageless.

He gently shoves me forward and as the inside of his wrist grazes my neck, a strange jolt of self-assurance and confidence flows through me. *I know what to say.* I feel a sting on the inside of my wrist and when I look down, I see one word in runes. *Confidence.* He has one just like it that reads, *believe in yourself.* Two minor gods get up to confront me as I near the stage. When I look up at them, I frown in irritation. It is clear they don't want to hear me out.

"Go home, human. You do not belong here." They step forward as if to escort me away. In a few long strides, Evan stands in front of me with his arms crossed.

"Neither do you, *godlings.*" Their faces contort with rage at his rebuke. Mostly because it is true. "This is Emerald, the apprentice of Commander Caerin, assisted in slaying the Ursa Major and Minor, helped

248

kill a magical boar the size of small house, and used her ingenuity to rescue her friends from the clutches of a labyrinth. Though she may be young, and not as powerful as the commander, she is her apprentice and is speaking for her today, so you will respect her and let her pass. If not, I have had a few very, *very*, long few weeks. You do not want to mess with me. Let this goddess through, *or else*." There is a definite challenge in his voice and it makes me look up at him in shock. His face is as hard and cold as his voice. I shoot him an alarmed look and a warning, but he simply stands there, an impassable wall between them and me. One of them laughs.

"Who are you to challenge us?" he questions and takes an aggressive step forward, expecting him to step back, but Evan doesn't move. He has had his share of dealing with bullies. Never back down to them. All races, even the Olympians, have their heroes, but they also have villains and bullies. The Olympians have kind people like Athena and Apollo, but also evil ones like the Storm God and Nemesis.

"I am Evan Faelin, The Wolf Warrior." To prove his point, his form flickers and for just an instant you can see the wolf form before it is gone. "I'll say it one more time before things get ugly. Let-her-through-NOW!" Each word is a punch and I delightedly watch the two gods crumble. Evan grabs my wrist and pulls me closer to him to protect me from the two minor gods as he shoves between them.

Suddenly, he whips around and a shield materializes in his hand. Half a second later, an ugly crack echoes around the room and an arrow harmlessly falls to the ground. An arrow that was aimed at my head. To my surprise, an icy and wolfish smile lights up his face. It is not pretty. He swiftly bends down and orders me to go up to the stage and he will be there in a minute. He quickly draws his sword in time to deflect the next arrow aimed at me. I jog the rest of the way to the stage and look back when I reach the base of the steps.

The bowstring is sliced, the bow itself is shattered, and its owner, who I recognize to be Eros, lies beside it unconscious, while his companion is in the process of being bruised a thousand times by the flat side of Evan's sword before finally yielding. Evan lightly runs over to me and we slowly walk up the steps. *Not the entrance I had hoped for.* The minute we stop in the middle, I can feel all their eyes on me. It is not a very comfortable feeling, being far younger and considerably less powerful than any of them. I take another deep breath and begin, working very hard to keep my voice steady.

"I am here today to propose an action in the upcoming war. This will be short, so I beg that you listen closely and open your minds to new ideas." My throat is dry as I wait for the muttering to die down. "If we Olympians stand alone against the New World led by Chaos, we will be destroyed. We are without our senior war commander, Shadow Caerin. She was, without a doubt, the most powerful warrior we ever knew. She was also a great master and sister to me. I beg that you listen to the words that she had prepared for this as I say them in her place, even if it just out of respect for her memory."

Shock covers their faces and silence falls as this grave news hits them. Zeus covers his face in his hands and Hera next to him quietly comforts him. Shadow meant more to them then I knew. She was part of their wild, loud, often violent, but incredibly loyal family. Tears prick my eyes and I quickly stuff my feelings back down before my weakness can be seen. This is the most important speech I will ever give. I cannot stop now, or else I'd be failing to follow through on Shadow's last wish.

"We must get over our proud nature and realize that we cannot do this alone. We all know that Chaos and the Storm God have managed to gain the support of many of the other gods and goddesses, along with so many different cultures from different nationalities. Commander Caerin believed that it was time that we gained all the allies we could. She wanted to call upon the people and kings of Arél, Endir, Irid, Daril, Aiden, Liré, -" I hesitate before adding in the last one, "and the Dírinians." A loud uproar echoes from all sides of the open courtyard at my last declaration.

"The Dírinians?" Hades yells. "Those who defiled our names, and even went so far as to change what we are known for? Those Dírinians?" More voices join in until I feel as if I am about to be blown away. I find myself thanking Evan so much for just being there. Finally, he steps out of the shadows and stands next to me. Without speaking louder than a normal level, he brings sense to a room full of hot-headed immortals.

"Don't they still fully devote themselves to you all? Even under different names you are their reasons for everything." All the voices fall silent and they stare at the skinny boy standing in their midst. "Sure, the names changed, but so what? What is a name but something to earn?" A heavy and thick silence blankets the room as they all stare at Evan. I cannot believe his bravery. Gathering my own courage, I continue to speak to the assembly.

"Chaos has managed to get all of the vengeful, merciless, violent, and ruthless people onto his side. He has built up his own army by taking control of the modern humans and ruling them, instilling more confusion and disorder until they overthrew their previous leaders who we had peace agreements with. Now they follow Chaos. I do not know how our warriors will stand against the modern weapons and different strategies, but the more people we have helping, men and women alike, the stronger we stand. If we want to keep that slim chance, I can tell you exactly how we should make a stand."

The room echoes with my words and puzzlement reflects to me from everyone. I look out at the twelve most powerful gods and goddesses sitting in their thrones. They are the ones whom I must impress. "The only way we can stand is if we stand together. The only way we can stand together is to make peace with old rivals and when we put our differences aside, we will finally be unified into a strong enough force that can withstand the onslaught of Chaos!"

My voice rises in volume as my conviction grows and I allow my passion to show through my words. "I speak for those who cannot. Shadow perished at the hand of her brother- her *twin* brother. I speak for her! Chaos slaughtered Evan's family, my family, my surrogate family, and destroyed hundreds of innocent families that did not deserve such a horrid fate. I speak for them!!" My voice is a roar, strong as a great dragon, and it throws aside all self-doubt and fear that had threatened to overwhelm me. A loud shout echoes around the room as they all yell in unison.

"We fight for those who no longer can!" Loud voices hurl themselves across the court and rebound back off anything as they fly unchecked around the open area like dangerous missiles. I catch Artemis's eye and am shocked to see silent tears falling down her cheeks. Athena meets my eyes and nods gravely. For the first time, I realize that while she appears young, she has seen many generations of humans come and go. She has experienced the deaths of many good friends, but right now, it is Shadow's death that is killing her on the inside. Now that heavy weariness seems to press down on her as it never has before. Instinctively, I know that it is because of the recent hardships we faced.

Focus! I berate myself as tears gather in my eyes. Without warning, a memory of Shadow rises to the forefront of my mind, just a frozen image in time: I had been hunting near the seaside cliffs when I had spotted Shadow standing at the very edge, completely undaunted by the huge drop inches from her boots, a tall and proud figure. One that I both knew very well, yet did not ever truly understand. She stared out at the sunrise with an incredibly peaceful expression, even though the massive longbow across her shoulders and sword hanging at her belt spoke of the upcoming war.

The fall leaves are scattered around and the different shades of red and brown accentuate the gold streaks through her light brown hair and her forest green tunic and gray breeches. Tears cascade down my face without consent as the image fades. *I am doing what she strived to do. I will not fail her.* With effort, I stuff all my emotions down deep and swear not to let them get away from me until this is over. The Olympians would see it as weakness. Zeus suddenly stands up.

"Silence!" he booms, the word resonating through his barrel of a chest. The room suddenly falls silent. "The Council has decided. We will follow Commander Shadow Caerin's battle plan." I don't know what to do. *Should I be happy, or should I be grave?* My thoughts fly through my head and I decide on the latter.

"We must start immediately. War is already wiping his boots on the welcome mat. We cannot pretend that we did not hear his knock, for he already has us in his sight. I need parties of seven warriors and three people, women and men, who are good enough with words to be messengers and diplomats. I leave it to Ares and Athena to organize these groups. Wisdom and Fighting must know how to cooperate for us to be prepared to open the door for War as he prepares to enter and watch men tear each other apart because of one man's terrible greed. Our army must be on their way to the Plain of Ren in one week's time. To a human, this would be an impossible feat, but we are not humans. We are Olympians!" I hold my breath and hope that my magic won't fail me now. I allow my magic to change my clothes into heavy plate armor and Treán is on my belt. A strong green glow flares from the armor and I draw my sword. It flares with fire like the Hills of Spring as the sun rises. Flourishing Treán above my head, I yell my closing statement.

"We are not the simple and mundane humans! We are the great and powerful Olympians!" I step off the dais and leave the building. The crowd falls away as we walk through the woods, Artemis trailing behind Evan and I back to the cabin. Athena and Ares waste no time in assigning the groups and cajoling them to hurry and grab their necessary belongings before hurrying to form another group. Soon the glade is filled with urgent bustling as groups of ten sprint down different paths through the woods to gather their packs and prepare for their journeys. Ironically, part of me finally relaxes. One less hurdle on the rough path leading to the war.

When the door slams shut behind us, I return the armor back to the clothes Shadow had prepared for me with sigh of relief that quickly turns into a muffled yelp as a terrible headache threatens to split my skull. Artemis looks down at me with minimal sympathy and badly hidden amusement.

"That should teach you very quickly not to try new magic without consulting an elder." I quietly moan into my hands as she rustles through the cabinets. Finally, she puts something down on the table in front of me. I flinch at the sudden noise.

"Drink it. You will feel better." The outside of the mug is scalding hot and after taking a cautious sip, I violently jerk back in my chair as ice cold, no, beyond ice cold liquid freezes every muscle in my body. After the effects wear off and I stop shivering, I realize that my headache is gone.

"What was that?" I ask Artemis, my voice shaking uncontrollably.

"Shadow infused some of her magic in some tea leaves, that is why it was cold and hot at the same time. She had figured that you would start investigating your magic soon and while she can do this in a blink, she seemed to know that she would not always be around to take care of such minor wounds. However, you must be careful not to drink too much. Her magic is too strong for any of us normal Olympians to withstand for long. Just a sip will do the trick. We will leave at dawn tomorrow morning." Artemis heads to the back of the cabin to her room and slams the door shut just as an exhausted Athena slips through the door and flops into a chair.

"That moved smoother than I expected. Wait, where is Gregory?" she asks in sudden alarm, obviously thinking about what happened last time the human left our sights.

"He and his men are on their way to the nearest warrior training base. They will meet us on the Plain of Ren for the final battle," I answer wearily. She nods before addressing Evan.

"Unfortunately, we don't have a spare room, but you can use Shadow's since she is not around." Abruptly she stands up, and goes to her room which is across the hall from Artemis's.

"It's the first door to the right." I point down the straight hall. "Artemis is the second door to the right, Athena is the room across the hall, and I am the first door on the left. If you are hungry, then help yourself to whatever you want." I drag myself out of my chair. "I need to gather my stuff for the trip. We are going to the Warrior School three days from my old home." He nods and tiredly picks up his bag from where he had dropped it on the floor before heading to Shadow's room.

I glance through her open door and part of me still expects her to be in there fidgeting with something or other, but the room is empty. Her bed is made and the space is immaculate. Not a speck of dust coats the shelves. It hits me again, just as hard and painfully as when she died, that I will never see her again. I will never hear her dry humor when I step on a twig, or watch her gracefully running through the woods as a creature of the forest. I will never see her rifling through letters and papers at her desk Her calm self assurance and confident demeanor are gone, and what hurts the most is that I never learned who she really was.

My heart cracks and splinters further, but also a sense of resolve and determination take its place. *I will avenge her.* I dash into my messy room before the tears start, and I throw myself onto my bed and curl up to try and hide from the pain as sobs rack through my body. Someone sits down on the bed and with a gentle hand they draw me closer to them. I open my eyes and see Evan sitting there, silent tears cascading down his face as well. I cling to him and cry as I never have before. We finally grieve for our lost friend together. I don't know how long we sit there and I slowly regain control over myself. He doesn't say anything, but words do not mean anything anyway. He gently strokes my hair and simply offers all the comfort he can.

"I know," he whispers in my ear. "I miss her as well. Chaos stole my heart from me."

"How can I ever get over this? I will never be able to forget her and that is the only way for me to stop missing her so badly."

"You can never forget those that you love. The only thing you can do is respect their memory and look to the bright side of things. Though the dark may seem impenetrable, there is always light somewhere. Sometimes the only way you can find it is to get up and just keep chasing the horizon until the sun is found once more. She has left us little memories everywhere, just like a trail leading us to the light. Look at what you are wearing! She had that prepared long before she was gone, she left little clues for us to follow.

The path has already been laid out and the trail cleared of brambles and undergrowth. Now it is up to us to stay true to it. No matter what will happen along it, just know that we will stand together. I will always stand by you. There is nothing I wouldn't do to protect you. If you don't remember any of this, just remember that. Now, dry those tears and I expect you to be ready for a hard sword lesson tomorrow, and the day after that, and the day after that." I smile despite myself and finally fall into an exhausted sleep.

Chapter Twenty-Two

Evan

I quietly let myself out of her room and silently shut the heavy oak door. It's well-oiled hinges make no noise and the house is silent. When I glance out a window, I realize how late it is. The sun crossed the sky and disappeared long ago. The moon sits high in her throne as the constellations roam around under her watchful gaze. When I was younger, I believed that the moon was my only friend and I once wished as she threw a star across the sky that I could have a friend who understood me and did not judge me by the nobility in my blood, or lack-thereof.

Two days later, I met Shadow. Never would I have believed that my wish could come true, but when I first saw her, I knew that she was far beyond any human. She even looked more like the elves in old stories than a human. She was strong and tall, but lithe and graceful. Even now, I still cannot figure out how I got the attention of one of the most powerful and beautiful goddesses ever to walk this Earth.

Cautiously, I walk through the open doorway. The room is pitch black, but ever since I first transformed into a wolf, darkness is an open book. I close the door behind me and the hinges creak and groan as it shuts, making me want to cover my ears as it breaks the silence of the night. *Well, no one will be able to catch me by surprise.* I think with a shrug. Shadow must have done that on purpose. When I light a lantern and look around, I notice how bare and organized the room is. Only a bed neatly made with a simple green quilt and a small table. There is a nondescript desk off in a corner with stacks of unopened letters.

A pile of unused parchment along with an eagle feather quill and ink is off to the side, presumably used for countless responses to letters.

Curious, I shift through the read stack. All of them are pleas for help with various problems. After reading a few of these, I look at the massive pile of unread letters. Many hold a wax seal with Zeus's signature; an eagle in flight. Another common seal holds three horses galloping out of the sea. That can be none other than Poseidon.

Suddenly, a stack of parchment catches my eye. It is sitting off to the side where I did not see it immediately. There are many pages of drawn out battle scenarios with foreign stratagems. Several pieces are just filled with neat columns of numbers detailing warriors in different countries, supplies for each place, total numbers available, and so on. I could spend hours studying the meticulous numbers, but I look at another section and encounter at least twenty pieces of parchment just filled with lines of foreign runes.

The room that at first seemed empty, actually holds many hints about her life. In the open closet, there is a pair of spare boots and a tattered, but clean, blue shirt with another pair of breeches. Several extra quivers of arrows are in the corner of the closet; all neatly stacked. There must be at least twenty separate quivers with twenty-four arrows in each.

The only other thing in the room is a shelf full of books in many languages; all are different colors. I trace my finger along the spines and feel a shiver travel the length of my own spine. My finger stops next to one book. This one is thinner and lighter. Composed of many pieces of parchment, it isn't nearly as old as the others. It is the only one that is ice blue and silver out of the entire bookshelf. I hesitate to pull it out, but curiosity beats caution and my hands tremble as I carry it over to the bed. I sit down and stare at it for several minutes before gathering myself together and flip it over to see the cover. My heart jumps to my throat when Shadow's handwriting is on the front. In a fine and curvy silver pen

against the ice blue background says, *Elren Caerin. Ler endel ril na relandir.* It
is beautiful to say, but I don't understand what it says. Who is this Elren?

Wait, no. It can't be. Shadow's name is simply Shadow Caerin.
Deep in me, I know that Elren is her real name. Why would she hide this?
What is it that is so secretive. Did nobody ever truly know her? Sadness
wells up inside me. *How lonely she must have been. Here I've been my
whole life, trying to find someone who understands me, and the only one
who did was trying to hide herself.* Suddenly the writing changes to
Arindal and says, *A book for my friends.* A series of ancient runes appear
and I recognize one of them to be my name. I shiver again and open the
book.

Instead of words, there are sketches, hundreds of them. As if
blown by a special wind, the pages flip to a section where all the pages are
marked by a sapphire blue diamond. I turn the page and gasp in
astonishment. A young wolf cub sits at the edge of a cliff overviewing a
waterfall. The father wolf stands protectively next to it, his majestic head
half turned to give the one who dared to come near a warning look. I turn
the page and am completely blown away. It is the exact same scene, but
they are humans. With a tiny bit of magic, I touch the page and they both
turn back into wolves. I am the cub in the picture.

Suddenly, a need to know more consumes me and I flip to the
next page. This time I am around ten-years-old in a village. Half turned, I
am pulling a young Emerald by the hand as we try to escape Chaos. I keep
flipping through and watch my life unfold through my encounters with the
mysterious Elren Caerin, but this time it is through her eyes. The last page
is a memory I will never forget. It jumps back many years. This one,
unlike all the others, is in full color. The others were all done in a fine
silver pen, but this one uses all colors available to one's imagination.

It was the second time we met, but at that moment, I did not know her. I was hiding among the trees to watch her as she practiced with her sword. I was unaware that she knew that I was there. In the drawing, you can only see half of me as I peer out from behind a tree. The sketch of the forest is incredible. The trees look real. To the darkest of greens, to the lightest of browns, and the darkest of greys. Not a branch is out of place.

As I'm flipping through, one catches my eye. It is of herself. She is standing shackled and bound. In the picture, she looks like she is only eleven years old. No weapons are in the picture and she leans in vain against the dark iron cuffs on her wrists and ankles. She looks very unfamiliar without a single weapon near her. Her expression is desperate and wild as she pulls against the restraints. Five words are written across the top of the page. *The day Elren was vanquished.* As I watch, magic grips me and my mind is flooded with a memory that is not mine.

A young girl, I cannot think of her as Shadow like this, is desperately running through the woods. The trees are the only reason the horsemen have not caught her. I am suddenly running too, and even though she is much faster than I could ever hope to be, I seem to keep pace without effort. Her fear is mine as we run.

The trees open into a field and she hesitates before giving a hoarse shout and taking off once more. She runs swift as the wind, but the horses are no mortal servants. These are immortal steeds. They don't gallop, they fly.

Slowly, very slowly, they begin to gain on her. She knows that they are coming closer, her face shows her despair, but she plans to make this as hard as possible. Soon we are within bow range. I yelp as an arrow harmlessly passes through me. *I guess I can't be injured in a memory.* They fly around her, but none can seem to find their mark. Until one. It flies true and catches her in the upper arm. She doesn't even wince. Just keeps running. Another buries itself in her left calf. Without a misstep, she hopelessly runs, trying to gain ground in this impossible race. To my surprise, she manages to drag out even more speed and power.

For a few minutes, it seems like she might pull this out, but the horses inevitably close the gap. I look ahead, trying to see the end of the plain. There isn't one. Her breath comes in ragged gasps. No human could run this far at this pace, but I know she is not human. Just like the horsemen pursuing her. An entire flock of arrows dives from the sky. It seems that this time, none miss her. Seven arrows to the back, three each arm, and five each leg. How she can stand, let alone run like this, surpasses the strongest man.

Blood coats her skin and clothes. Finally, one arrow cuts through the air. Different from the others, it is pure deep sea blue with blood red fletching. It hits her square behind her right knee. Tearing through the tendons and ligaments, it is a crippling blow. I feel sick at the cruel way they are hunting her. Her knees fold up under her and she hits the ground with incredible force, she tumbles a few times as momentum carries her. Her speed makes the fall worse. She lies quivering on her side for a moment as her world spins.

The pounding of hooves seems to make the earth shake. Rocks jump up and down in warning and all the small animals flee ahead of them. A family of rabbits hide behind her. More and more animals gather behind her. Within seconds, hundreds are behind her. In this magical form, I can hear them begging for her to help them. The wild and untamed fire inside her gives her the strength to stand up and ignore the pain.

"I will protect you the best that I can," she tells them. Her voice startles me. It is so different from how she speaks now. It has a completely different accent. It is beautiful to hear. It seems like a time when she spoke Daenlir more than Arindal. Suddenly, I realize that she just spoke Daenlir. It is just like listening to water as it strongly surges on its path. *Who is this person? This is not Shadow. This is a wild creature of the forest. Either a nymph or an elf.* My money would be on elf.

She nods to the animals and turns to face her attackers. She slowly pulls the bow over her shoulders. Without any visible pain, she pulls out the arrows covering her arms. She puts three in each boot, still dripping with her blood, before yanking out the one in her knee. She swears colorfully in a few different languages. The riders stop in a line before her. There are all impersonal men in full black plate armor. All the lines in the armor are blood red. The horses are coal black with glowing red eyes. The tall one in the middle pulls his visor up and dismounts.

"Draemir Caerin," she growls as if the words are the worst swear word anyone could ever say.

"Elren Caerin," he replies calmly. She raises her drawn bow and the dark blue shafted arrow is aimed between his eyes. "If she doesn't lower the bow, shoot all the little animals. Just the young ones. Start," his eyes glitter maliciously as he spots the small family of rabbits hiding behind her feet, "with the young trio of bunnies." Elren's expression is one of incredible disgust, but she does lower the bow. Put it down or they all die." Wordlessly, against all the animals cried protests, she places the arrows on the ground and is about to lay down the bow, when she looks down at the beautifully crafted weapon. She hurls it as hard as she possibly can into the long grass. Nobody should ever find it in there. He sneers at her loyalty to her weapon and her compassion for creatures weaker than her. "My best weapon against you is yourself. Shoot the animals anyway!" he orders the black knights. Fire ignites her ice blue eyes and they glow in her fury

"Why?" she yells furiously. "What have they ever done to you? Why must you kill everything that is pure and innocent?" He does not answer. Arrows arc down and the poor rabbits run to her left. Unfortunately, the archers had predicted their movement and the rabbits are helpless as the line of arrows fly towards them. The arrows all halt three feet from her little friends. I can see the faint ice blue dome around the hundreds of little animals huddled together. Prey stands next to predator as the animals unify against the greatest predator of all creatures.

Everyone's eyes are trained on the arrows that are quivering against her magic. Only I can see that she is slowly pulling out an arrow from her back. Like a streak of lightning, she hurls herself at Chaos. The arrow plunges between the greaves in his armor and he shouts at the sudden shock of pain down his arm. Following her first strike, she uses the heel of her left hand and punches him in the jaw. He flies backwards at least two meters before crashing back down onto the ground.

My own jaw drops in astonishment at the strength in that strike. She was only nine years old at this time in her life. I'm nineteen and cannot punch that hard! Elren hops backwards a few steps to avoid putting too much weight on her injured knee. Chaos slowly picks himself off the ground. I'm surprised by his age as well. He looks like he is only eleven. It still surprises me how strangely the immortals age. Chaos and Shadow are twins, but they age so differently. As he stalks over to her, rage twists his handsome features and turns him incredibly ugly. His dark blue eyes burn with the omnipotent emotion called rage. I want to run far away and hide as he comes closer, but my curiosity gets the best of me. She somehow lived through this and I really want to know how. He looms over her by at least a foot.

"They say you are beautiful among the humans. I do not see it, but I am not a simple mortal. It seems that you have become cocky since the last time I saw you. You thought you could run faster than my immortal horse, Kelpie. As your brother, it is my delight to humble you.

Perhaps ruining your supposed good looks will do the trick." I burn inside at the insults he is handing her. I want to draw my sword and slash him in half. Unfortunately, I cannot do either. I am a mere shadow here, unable to speak or move a few paces from Shadow, or I guess now Elren.

My curiosity is reaching an explosion point. I must know why she is now called Shadow, and not Elren. Cruel humor drives Chaos's actions. He draws his blackiron dagger and stops in front of her. She continues to stand and glare at him with utmost contempt. He suddenly slashes down with the knife. She simply sways to the side and the dagger passes harmlessly.

"Hold her!" he barks to one of his warriors. A knight grabs her by the shoulders and forces her to be still. He slowly, very slowly, creates a long, deep, and jagged cut. Despite all human instincts, she doesn't flinch, even as blood cascades down her face. Suddenly, I remember Elren as I knew her. She always had a long, jagged scar across her left cheek. Now I know how that came to be.

With a sudden blinding ice blue light, all her injuries are healed and her clothes are mended. Only that scar remains. The man holding her screams in sudden agony and falls to the ground dead. Elren is suddenly taller and older. Now she is around ten years old and is as tall as her twin. Again, my jaw drops at this. She eyes Chaos coldly.

"Beautiful is nothing but a word that rich noblemen use when they become fat and complacent. True beauty cannot be touched by a knife, or a sword. It is what pure and innocent creatures hold as an honorary term. You and I, we are not beautiful. You may fancy yourself that, but we are far from it. Too many secrets, too many lies and terrible mistakes. No. Neither of us are beautiful and neither of us will ever be known by our looks, but by the ringing of our blades on the field of battle."

My vision goes black, but before I can start to panic, it fades back into color. It is the exact scene from her sketch book. Elren, or Shadow, is desperately leaning against heavy blackiron chains that are around her wrists and ankles. Suddenly, there is shouting and yelling outside the dungeon door. I hesitantly move over to the door and peer out between the thick bars and I gasp. There are two girls in chains like Elren. Both look to be around the same age as well. It is Artemis and Athena. Just like Elren, they show signs of torture and stripes of blood along with tears in their clothes show where they have been whipped repeatedly. I never knew that Elren had been through so much in her life. The two goddesses across from her are not paying any attention to anything going on. They are playing a strange game with their fingers to pass the time.

The crashing of swords grows louder and the sounds of heavy bodies falling and men screaming grows louder as the fighting comes closer. Elren suddenly gives a mighty heave against the chains and I hear multiple cracks and then both chains snap like twigs. I watch her warily as she seems to be almost like a wild creature, she is so incredibly desperate to be free. Her fingers, hands, and wrists are at unnatural angles and are clearly *very* broken, but at the moment, she doesn't seem to notice. Elren breaks the chains restricting her ankles in a heartbeat before collapsing onto her knees from the pain. The chains rattle on the hard ground as she falls. *This* gets Artemis and Athena's attention. They both straighten up and come as close to their door as possible.

"What are you?" Artemis asks, her voice is hoarse and cracked from exhaustion. Elren shakes her head and struggles to regain her breath. The goddesses stare at her fearfully. She slowly picks herself up and sways for a moment. Her face is gray as she gathers herself.

"I honestly don't know," Elren answers slowly. "I am not a human, but I live near their villages. I do not think I am a beast either, though I run in the forest among them. What are you?"

"I am Artemis. Goddess of the Hunt and the Moon and daughter of Leto and Zeus." She pauses for a second. "I also do not think you are a beast."

"I am Athena. Goddess of Wisdom and I am also a daughter of Zeus. You are far from a simple mortal. What is your name, stranger?" Elren hesitates for a second, and then walks to the front of her cell, staggering slightly.

"I was once wild and free. Now I am but a shadow of that person. I have been captured and beaten. Until I earn my name back, I will remain a shadow of my former self. My name is Shadow Caerin." Shadow cocks her head as she listens to something. "Warriors are coming. I cannot stay here." She studies the solid door for a second before stepping back and grimacing. Using the least amount of magic possible, she heals her wrists to a level of being able to use them and she tears a few strips from the bottom of her already ruined tunic and binds her wrists and hands. Setting her feet and with a painful grimace, she grabs two of the bars in the center and pulls with all her strength.

At first nothing happens, but in the dark, gloomy dungeon, creaking meets my ears. It progressively gets louder until a loud crack splits the air, screeching far over the din of the clashing weapons above us. The solid iron door starts to fall. Shadow hurls herself out of the way with inhuman speed. If I had actually been there in person, I would have been crushed. Luckily for me, it simply passes through me like the arrows had.

Shadow stumbles out of the cell, the chains still trailing from her limbs. She grabs her sword from where it hangs outside the door. Her quiver hangs next to it. They had found her bow and she grabs that as well. Swinging both quiver and bow over her shoulder, she clips her sword in its sheath to her belt. Quickly, drawing her magnificent blade, she slashes first the chains on her limbs, then two bars out of the opposite cell and steps through to help the two captured goddesses. Both stare at her in awe as she severs their chains in one powerful stroke. She limps down the short dungeon and slashes out the bars in the doors. Soon a group of ten Olympians are free.

Apollo runs up to his twin sister and anxiously makes sure that she is okay. His face darkens as he hears of her apparent abuse. When all six cells are empty, Shadow jogs through the small crowd of freed warriors, including two Norse gods, Thor and Loki. When they try and stop her to give her their thanks, she just keeps going as if she can't hear them.

She stops when she is in front of the group and turns to face them, eyeing them warily. I can see her thoughts whirling as she assesses their fighting ability and if they are a threat to her. They stare back, some look at her in awe, others are closely scrutinizing her, and others are more hostile.

My jaw drops when I look at the array of people here: Artemis, Athena, Apollo, Dionysus, Aphrodite, Demeter, Ares, Chiron, the crippled Hephaestus, Thor and Loki, and to my surprise, Hera. The Queen of the Heavens is here in a dirty, gross, and damp dungeon. She looks absolutely furious.

Her normally flawless white dress is dirty and her usual perfectly assembled hair is disheveled with random places sticking straight up. I start laughing, but quickly stop when the yelling and clashing of weapons is right outside the door. Shadow turns away from the group, apparently deciding that they are not a threat to her and readies herself for a fight.

It is not long in coming as fifteen black armored knights step through. Shadow smiles. I almost feel bad for the warriors. None of them know who they are about to mess with.

"Return to your cells, prisoners!" their leader orders. Two identical silver arrows pierce through his armor and he falls dead to the floor.

"No fair!" Apollo complains to Artemis. "I wanted to make him pay for torturing you!"

"I wanted to make him pay for torturing *me*." Apollo drops the argument. All the other Olympians laugh at them. They have known the two twins since they were born. Both are fiercely loyal to one another, but they always argue whenever they are together. Unfortunately, the stunned knights think the Olympians and Norse gods are laughing at them and they silently charge, hoping to catch them by surprise. All merriment stops and the room fills with silence and ready weapons until one person starts laughing helplessly. Everyone stares in shock at the strange young girl with the sword and bow as she loses it. Hiccoughing, she finally manages to choke out,

"These fifteen humans actually plan to attack twelve immortals, and a wild girl from the woods. Are they crazy?" She starts laughing again, and soon, everyone is laughing with her. "Now, are we all going to stand here and let them down? Obviously, they want a good fight!" A roar follows her words and every one with a bow raises it and immediately takes out all the enemies except one. He is a brute of a man, over seven feet tall and ugly as a warthog with smallpox. His shield caught Shadow's ice blue shafted arrow and it sticks out, it's head completely buried in the hardwood.

"I demand trial by single combat!" he shouts to the group of immortal warriors.

"Who do you challenge?" Hera demands imperiously, readying herself for a fight. He laughs, a sound as repulsive as his face. Every one of the gods and goddesses grab their weapons, each one longing to knock this arrogant man off his proverbial high horse. Thor grips his hammer and if not for Loki holding him back, he would have attacked, abandoning the challenger's sacred rites in a duel.

"I will face your champion. Who is your greatest warrior?" After a quick, but fiery debate between Athena, Ares, and Thor, Thor steps forward.

"I accept." Without warning, he swings his legendary hammer through the air with enough power to kill ten men. However, the black armored knight just steps back and lets the heavy hammer swing Thor off balance, before he slams the Norse god with his shield and sends the muscular man flying across the dungeon as if he were nothing but a bug.

"If this is the best you have, then the Olympians stand no chance at all against my master!" he sneers.

"Good thing he isn't an Olympian, then." Hera comments, in a voice that scalds like acid.

"Who is your master?" Shadow asks, a strange tone to her voice, like she can already guess what the answer is.

"My master is Lord Chaos. He taught me and a few *select* others from the elite warriors in our lands."

"Draemir!" Shadow swears beneath her breath. She quickly turns to the Olympians and Norse Gods. "None of you can fight him and win. However, we still must honor the rules of single combat. Whoever he chooses to compete with, we simply must fight hard and die honorably."

"I challenge you, Elren Caerin. A simple hunter and mediocre warrior, I think not! I think you might be a nice challenge for me. I need to prove that Chaos's training paid off. Obviously, these people do not

270

know who you are." The man challenges Shadow, a realization dawning on him. He knew Chaos's twin sister was here. He had said that she was the one with the scar on her face. None of his interrogators could pry a single word from her. Chaos had warned him that this was not a warrior to trifle with. Was there a better way to show he was a worthy knight if he could beat the one Chaos claims no one except himself can kill?

"Shadow! Don't do it!" She turns to Artemis, an odd look in her eyes. Ice blue fire makes them dance fiercely.

"I have been challenged," she replies with a calm self-assurance. In the moment that she takes to sling her bow over her shoulders, the Olympian's most renowned fighter, Ares, loses his temper and charges Chaos's apprentice. He does not want to watch the young woodland warrior to be killed in front of them. While he may be the God of War and Fighting, he is not cold blooded.

Ares catches him by surprise and he barely has enough time to throw up his shield to block Ares crimson colored spear. He recovers quickly and jabs back with his sword. It seems like the start of a long fight, but the knight suddenly feints a thrust and then swings a side cut that would cleave the War God in half as he struggles to regain his balance. Suddenly, with a screeching of metal on metal, a strong sword blocks it.

"I accept your challenge," Shadow says softly. An abashed, yet still fuming Ares stalks away. All the Olympians look horrified as the giant and the young warrior of the woods begin to circle. I catch my breath. Rarely have I seen Shadow so intent on a fight. Normally, she only has a quarter of her attention on her own fight and the rest of her companions. Now she is one hundred percent focused.

Tíne has a faint blue tinge, but nothing compared to ice blue flames that usually flicker down its whole length. It strikes me again that

271

she must be exhausted and probably still in a ton of pain. Fighting with broken fingers, hands, wrists, and most likely broken ribs. I would not want to be her right now. Hera steps forward, about to order both to stand down, but Athena grabs her arm and speaks to her in quiet tones.

"Wait, I think it would be wise to see how good she is with a sword." Hera rounds on her frantically.

"She will be dead in a few seconds! I cannot watch this youngling die for us!"

"My Queen, I believe she can hold her own. Also, it would break all the sacred rules of single combat. They are to fight without the possibility of being helped or harmed by another person who has not been challenged," Athena responds slowly. Suddenly, the giant brute swings an impossibly fast and strong side cut and lunges all at the same time. Shadow smiles slightly and swiftly steps backwards, out of the path of the sword. With a roar, he swings again. It is powerful enough to shear off her whole torso from her legs, but only if she was still there. She stepped back again and once more the sword whistles through empty air. He stops and roars again, goaded into a killing rage.

Shadow's entire body shimmers and with a sudden blast of blinding ice blue magic, she is suddenly completely healed. Her clothes are mended and her boots are less scuffed and worn looking. Only the long scar is a reminder of what she had recently gone through. He hesitates at this change in events. It is one thing to attack an incredibly powerful person who is wounded, then one who is ready. Now Tíne is alight with bright blue fire. She smiles at him. It is clearly a challenge. *Are you still so confident?*

He snarls like a wild animal, but waits for her to make the first move. She darts her sword in and he immediately parries it away. The first moves are a series of blows intended to feel the others strength and get a feel for their speed. Then the giant warrior suddenly goes into the attack. Shadow doesn't have a shield, but she either avoids the blows or stops them with her sword and an iron wrist. Not once does his strongest or most clever attempts even seem to break through her defenses.

I have watched her fight before, but none of the breathless crowd of immortals notice the slight change in her style. Her blows start to come harder and she starts to meet his blade more often than avoiding it. Suddenly, she switches hands. Now she holds the sword in her left hand. The black-clad warrior hesitates for a second, trying to remember what Chaos had said to do if his sibling used that move. He never got a chance. He falls to the ground dead. Turning away from him, Shadow unwraps the cloth from her wrists and causally wipes the blood off her sword. All the Olympians stare at her in awe.

Suddenly, warriors rush into the room. These are clad in silver chain mail and purple armor as they march in. Shadow warily raises her sword and the warriors all stop uncertainly. None of them expected this. The leader steps forward and he also raises his sword. It is curiously shaped like a lightning bolt. An arc of pure, hot energy flies towards the tall girl. It would easily be enough to kill the strongest of immortal men, but Shadow gives him a slight half smile. Her sword blazes in an even more fierce flame and she simply slices through Zeus's power, dissolving it. This, above everything else they have seen, stuns everyone. This random girl from the woods is stronger than their king, Zeus. He raises the visor of his helmet and his expression is half furious and half incredulous. The Olympians look from the girl, to Zeus, and back to the girl.

"I mean you no harm, child." To prove it, he sheaths his sword and steps forward into the weak torchlight. Shadow raises an eyebrow at him and that one expression says, *Seriously? Do you not remember just trying to kill me?* However, she simply slams her sword into her sheath and with the utmost grace and dignity, walks out past the armor-clad Olympians.

"Wait!" She turns at Zeus's call. "Who are you? I must know who saved my wife and children." Shadow turns and gives them all a small half smile.

"When you need me again, it will be in a time of great trouble for you. At that time, there will not be any reason to stand on formalities. At that time, and if there is a time after, you may call me Shadow, for now however, I am to be known as the Shadow Warrior." She turns away to continue walking, but stops once more. "See you then!" And she is gone. A stunned silence fills the room. Every single person there is clearly in awe of her fighting skills, her courage, and her self-assurance. Nobody has ever spoken to Zeus like that before, nor have any ever shown such disregard of Zeus's powers.

I am grinning ear to ear. Never in the time that I knew her have I heard her be so abrupt with anyone. The dungeon fades back into Shadow's room and I am still smiling ridiculously.

I flip back to the page with my name in runes. All of a sudden, more writing is there.

"Evan, obviously, you found my journal. I am sorry I cannot be more help, but if you are reading this note, I have been killed or captured. Trace your name in runes with a finger and it will reveal a map. This should help you organize the army. Tell Emerald I am proud of her accomplishments and I hope that you know I am so, so sorry to have left all of you in this situation. Now you know who I really am and why I hid this from everyone. Please do not change your opinion of me for this. Often, people hide what they are ashamed of. In the end, know that I now accept that part of me, but I am still not whole. Elren was beaten. Shadow has now died. Perhaps now Elren will have come back from out of the corner and forget her wounded pride from being vanquished. It is past time that Elren stood back up for what she truly believes in. If I am still alive, I will no longer hide. It is time for my brother to see his sister again. His sister with all her power ready. I am Elren Caerin and I plan to avenge all who have been wronged by my brother, Draemir Caerin."

There is a long pause until at the bottom of the page, four words suddenly appear in ice blue magic and trail their way across the page. They stun me to my core and leave me rooted in place.

"I am still alive."

While part of me wants to yell and rejoice as loudly as I can, I know that this news would just distract everyone. We leave tomorrow and it will be a dangerous trip. Leaving those thoughts to simmer in my mind, I do as the note says and find the map. It is worn and some lines are blurred, but all the places are clear.

My eyes trace their way around the small room once more and they stop on an object in the corner. A beautifully crafted longbow stands forlornly in the corner, forgotten. It is unstrung, and looks unused. The wood glows a soft silver. *I'll show it to the others in the morning. Perhaps Artemis will want it.* Feeling better than I have in a long time, I extinguish the lantern and fall asleep.

Artemis

I watch the blood-red sun prepare to rise through the sky and scramble around to gather all my equipment. Knife? On the chair. Spare clothes? In the bag already. Quiver? Hanging on my bedpost. Bow? My heart sinks when I remember that it was smashed. It had been a gift from

275

my mother, Leto. She had given Apollo and me our identical silver bows on our tenth birthday. I miss it as much as I could miss a person.

It served me well for countless battles and hunts. I do not know how I can be the Goddess of the Hunt without it. However, I cannot stop myself from pulling on my quiver. Familiar bow or not, I will just have to pick up one from the armory. With that grim thought, I walk out of the house and slip into the forest. After jogging a good distance into the dense trees, I decide that I am far enough in. I whistle, a piercing ascent of seven notes. Surefire strolls out of the fog and walks up to me.

"Hay boss! You look rather thunderous! You must need a joke! What did the fish say when it hit the underwater wall?" I cross my arms across my chest and scowl. Without waiting for me to guess, he answers himself, "it said, DAM!" When I don't react he cocks his head and walks in a circle around me. "Something is different." He nudges me and then sticks his velvety nose directly in my face under the pretense of searching for whatever has changed. I can't help but feel my black mood lift just from being with him.

"My bow broke," I finally confess. He stops and stares at me.

"What are you going to do?" All fooling around is put aside immediately. He knows how important it is to have a good weapon and he knew how much I treasured my bow.

"I was going to get one from Hephaestus's armory. I would appreciate it if you would give me a ride since it is on the other side of the island."

"Of course!" he snorts. "There is no such thing as a command of yours that I would ever refuse." Without further conversation, I vault onto his back. I do not need a bridle or saddle with my horse. We understand each other well and he knows where I want to go. His hooves pound the ground with a rapid four beat gallop. Surefire runs straight at the trees and then dodges them at the last second, making me laugh at his antics.

The miles fly under his feet in minutes. All of our immortal companions are a caliber of horses that is far beyond the mortals' horses. They can run faster, jump higher, and cannot be killed. Of course, among them there are the stronger ones. The more powerful the Olympian, the more powerful their horse. Enbarr is the most incredible horse ever to touch the earth. I guess that sums up Shadow as well. There is also Stormy, a horse with humor, just like my Surefire.

Surefire skids to a halt at the edge of the trees, breaking my chain of thought. Up ahead, I can see the armory; however, the mile of flat ground between me and another bow is a slab of land that seems to be fighting itself. The ground is constantly shifting and bumping into itself before rebounding and bumping into another thing, just like the icebergs in the far North. To top off the entire scene, where the spaces are, red hot molten rock bubbles to the surface.

"Why can nothing ever be easy?" I roar at the molten plain. Naturally, it doesn't answer. Surefire eyes the shifting land warily.

"That-" he pauses for dramatic flair, "is a death trap meant for people who never die."

"You are not going."

"Definitely not," he adds decisively, interrupting me.

"I will meet you back here later." I unclip the sheath of my long dagger and drop it next to his feet. After a moment's pause, I lay my quiver next to it. As an afterthought, I grab one silver arrow. Without any further hesitations, I swiftly step out onto the moving slabs of earth. I jump onto another and it shifts and cracks under my weight. It is about to crumble to pieces when I leap onto another slab. After many close calls, and my tunic singed and on fire in multiple places, I reach the other side, where the ground is solid again. I quickly put out the flames and hurry into the foreboding workshop of Hephaestus.

When the giant iron door opens with a loud protest, every Cyclops stops what they are doing and stares at me. This is not a safe place for any Olympian except Hephaestus. It is especially unsafe for the small, slim goddess who spends all her days safe in the woods. The sudden silence is broken by a young Cyclop's yelp when the sword he was making suddenly begins to melt.

"Get back to work, you lazy wretches. What is the meaning of this? Who told you that you could st-" Hephaestus's roar suddenly cuts off when he sees me. I gulp. He is at least eight feet tall and a terrifying sight. His beard is on fire and his dark eyebrows are drawn together in a fierce scowl.

"I am here to request permission to have a bow from the armory." His expression lightens and is more cheerful.

"A dangerous trip only for a bow. Aren't you supposed to leave today?" I nod.

"Right this way." He turns on his heel and leads the way through the giant work tables and fiercely burning forges. I am forced to protect myself with magic as the heat and flying sparks threaten to suffocate me. Eventually we pass through and reach the armory. He points out the bows hanging on a wall and grunts once more and points to the exit door.

"Thank you!" I respond belatedly. He nods back and limps back to his workshop. There are only four bows and none of them stand out to me. None are even close to being powerful as my lost bow. There is one longbow, two recurve bows of different power, and one crossbow. All of them have a thick layer of dust and I sneeze as I pick up the longbow. When I draw it back, it feels like it may have enough power, but the old wood creaks ominously as I hold it drawn. I nock my silver arrow to the string and aim at a wooden shield one hundred yards away. The arrow flies true, but almost as soon as it is in the air, the bow splits in two. I swear as I pick the splinters out of my hand. I throw the pieces of the bow as far as I can into the massive room and hear it strike something, followed by a huge crash of metal hitting the floor.

Ignoring the loud noise, I turn back to the bows and select the larger of the two recurves. Without any effort, I summon the arrow and it flies back to my hand where I nock it onto the small bow. I can easily draw it and it spits the arrow out with reasonable power. It will have to do. Completely unsatisfied, I head out the door.

The land has not stilled and the earth continues to fight itself, but like the rising tide in the ocean, it has become more dangerous than before. The bits that hit each other, hit so hard that they both disintegrate into tiny pieces. I grit my teeth and hurry across, gathering a wonderful collection of burns and cuts that are going to scar over. Finally, I reach solid ground again and quickly put out the little fires that are eating away my tunic.

"You forgot your arrow," Surefire comments. I glare at him. The pitiful replacement bow and my newly acquired burns are putting me in a bad mood.

"You go get it then." I grab my belt with the dagger strapped to it and swing my quiver and new bow over my shoulders. I shift my shoulders uncomfortably at the different feel of the recurve bow instead of my customary longbow. After quickly repairing my tunic, I vault onto Surefire. He spins around on his haunches and darts back into the dark woods. *I hope the others are not looking for me. I should have left a note.*

"Meh. I doubt they are," Surefire reassures me. I always forget that he knows what I'm thinking about.

"Gee. Thanks."

We arrive at the cabin in less than fifteen minutes and I slide off his back and give him a quick pat.

"Thank you, my friend. Please find Stormy, and bring the entire herd of unattached horses. Athena will want Morningsun as well."

Surefire bobs his head up and down in a bow and disappears back into the woods to find his friends. I walk up the steps and push the door open. All three of them look up from their breakfast of bacon and eggs as I enter.

"Find one?" Athena asks. I grimace and pull the toy bow off my shoulder. Athena draws it back and then slowly lets it back down again. "Weren't there any other bows?" she asks distastefully. I shake my head and look at Evan as his head suddenly snaps up and he stands up excitedly before dashing to Shadow's room without a word. He comes back a minute later looking completely crestfallen.

"Last night there was a perfectly made bow in Elren- I mean Shadow's, room." He doesn't meet Athena, Emerald, and my startled looks. He makes a pretense of ruffling through his backpack to escape our surprised looks. We exchange a quick and silent conversation, but there are no answers as to how he knows who Elren was. *She must have told him.* That stings. She did not tell Emerald until last year. I let him off the hook for now, but I will come back to it later.

"Ah, well. I can't wish for something I never knew." I glare at the recurve bow with contempt. "I guess I better refresh my sword work skills." I leave the table and head back into my room. Leaning against the far wall is my spear and sword. The head of the spear is pure silver and so is my sword blade. I eye the bow with the utmost loathing and I make a snapshot decision. I am not taking it. As everyone steps out of the house, I leave it hanging on the weapons rack and grab Emerald's little hunting bow. It may be practically useless in a battle, but I cannot be the goddess of the hunt without a hunting weapon.

Surefire, Morningsun and Stormy Night stand among the small herd of immortal horses who have not chosen a rider. Horses of all colors are represented. From the darkest of blacks, to the brightest of golden palominos. Morningsun is one such golden palomino. Her mane and tail are a light golden cream while the rest of her is the same rich color, exactly like the pure gold that runs through the streams in the mountains. A thin white stripe of white on her face and two white socks are the only break in the overwhelmingly beautiful color of her coat.

She prances over to Athena. That mare is a straight on diva, but she always does exactly what Athena wants her to. She is completely devoted to her mistress. She was supposed to be Apollo's horse, since she is the color of the sun which he is the god of, and they went so far as to name her for him, but she totally rejected him, a fact that is completely awesome to me, and I usually bring it up in whenever we argue.

Stormy looks at me with dull curiosity. Ever since he heard about Shadow, no one can get him to eat anything and his spirit, once so bright and witty, is now depressed and lonely. Emerald and Rose selected each other, but it will be good for Stormy to have a job and be kept busy.

"Emerald, you are riding Stormy." Stormy walks over to her and presses his head against her, nearly knocking the small and petite girl off her feet. Immediately, he steadies her by grabbing the collar of her shirt and looks surprised by how weak she is compared to what Shadow had been. Surefire steps behind me and we back up. Evan is lost with wonder as he gazes in admiration at all the beautiful horses. Suddenly, Poseidon appears in a shimmer of sea green magic. He is here to bind Evan and his horse. Who else, but the god of horses, should oversee such a sacred rite?

"They will each come up to you and one might decide that he, or she, likes you. Then you and your horse will be bound together. There is nothing more special than the bond between you and your horse.

Understand this, though: you and your horse's lives and lifespans are directly correlated. If you are killed, your horse is now mortal and is stripped of their power and abilities, or dead. Your horse's magic will mix with yours and both of you will share the same magic. This will make you stronger and faster, while your skills will probably give him, or her, some form changing ability. What I am trying to say is, do not put your horse in undue danger, or yourself. They are putting their lives in our hands, and we put ours in their hooves," Poseidon says gravely. Evan nods. He completely understands the consequences.

As Poseidon said they would, the horses all line up and one by one. Evan talks to them and some just look at him before shaking their manes and walking away. Every horse comes to Poseidon and bows down, bending onto one knee, before leaving. Soon there are only three left. There is a buckskin, a paint, and a black-ish colored horse. The buckskin and paint both walk away after paying respect to their master.

Worry starts to flutter in my stomach. What if no horse will choose him? The last horse is a deep black color, but different shades of blue streak across his coat like a lightning storm, or a wild river. A big sapphire star is in the middle of his forehead and his eyes are a marvelous blue. He walks a circle around Evan and pokes him a few times to test his balance. He touches a large and unremarkable stone with his nose before looking at Evan.

"Pick it up and break it in half," the horse orders. Evan goes to the giant rock and strains to pick it up as the horse watches him impassively. Poseidon is smothering laughter behind his hand. Finally, Evan stops and stares at the rock. I can see an idea light up his mind and he uses his magic to lift it and break it. A large sapphire gem falls to the ground. It is the horses gift to Evan. The horse bobs his head up and down in satisfaction.

"That is fine, Shapeshifter. I accept you. I call myself Rivermist. Do you by any chance have a name?"

"Evan Faelin."

"Hmm. I don't like it. I think I will call you Wolf. It has a better ring to it than Evan. Now, step up and hold out your sword hand and place it squarely on my star." We laugh at Evans stunned expression. There isn't much that the immortal horses don't know. They are the ones to speak with if you need blackmail, gossip, or just innocent information.

"Repeat after me," Poseidon orders them. "I, Evan Faelin, am hereby ready to bind myself to Rivermist." Evan repeats him and Rivermist reverses the names and says his part. "Both of you now have to close your eyes. Gather all the magic you can and send it to the connection point. Feel it mix and meet between the both of you." Without any warning, Evan and Rivermist are thrown backwards in an explosion of sapphire blue magic. Evan lands squarely on his back several yards away and Rivermist lands on his side a little way back. "I've never seen that before!" Poseidon exclaims excitedly, clapping his hands like a young child might. Rivermist rolls over onto his belly and scrambles to his feet.

"Interesting, I can hear, smell, and see better. What is that from?" Rivermist lifts his head and his eyes glow with humor.

"Evan can change his form to be a wolf. I bet you can see in the dark as well. Those senses most likely come from that. Can you change into different forms?" Suddenly, he is gone. I look closer and can barely see his outline. He changed his coat to match the exact colors and background behind him, so he is virtually invisible. When he suddenly appears again, everyone claps. You must admit, that is cool.

Morningsun is wise like Athena, and Surefire can move silently on all terrain, which is very helpful when I am hunting, but having a camouflaged horse would be even better. Evan slowly gets to his feet with a groan. To be honest, we had forgotten about him. Poseidon starts to glow sea green again, but waits long enough for Evan to come over to his new horse.

"Never forget that if you are killed, Rivermist will be either killed at the same time as you, or will become mortal and painfully stripped of his magic." Poseidon suddenly gives Stormy grave a look. "You, young one, are lucky. You have different rules. I was not the one to create Enbarr. He is far beyond any other horse ever to walk this Earth. Don't tell Pegasus I said that! I must go now. Congratulations, Evan and Rivermist. Safe travels!" he says before disappearing. Evan looks puzzled about something.

"Doesn't that mean that Stormy should be dead, or at least mortal?" I wheel around and regard the bay horse in surprise.

"Stormy?" I ask him directly. He thinks about the best way to respond. Finally, he starts to talk slowly.

"My sire is an incredibly powerful immortal horse. I am already more powerful than most horses. I do not know what has happened to my father recently. He has disappeared." Athena gives him a curious look.

"Who is your father?" she asks. Stormy looks up at us.

"My sire is Enbarr of The Flowing Mane," he says softly. A stunned silence follows his words as the enormity of the statement soaks in.

"So, you are linked to Shadow by Enbarr and not a direct connection." He nods. "I can't imagine Enbarr being mortal." I shake my head at Athena. I can't imagine the loss Stormy must feel. A double blow.

"They are both so tightly intertwined that if Shadow was killed, I'm sure they both would die. What is your magic? I know Shadow must have bound herself to you as well. I wonder what you could have received from such strong magic," I ask. I have never known much about

284

Shadow's horse, or even Shadow herself, now that I look at it. All I really know is that he is bay with a waning crescent moon on his forehead and he has a sock on his left hind leg with little white heels on the other three feet. A black mane and tail as well. *Well this is awkward considering I have known him his entire life.*

"I have never discovered my special power. I have little things that I can do, like sense a storm coming. I can see in the dark, and run like the wind, but nothing different from any other immoral steed." He lowers his head in shame and stares at the thick mud on the ground. "There have been times when Shadow and I were in danger and there was nothing I could do. I feel like I let her down many times when I should have been able to help. If only I were there when Chaos took her. Maybe I could have done something to help. My father always said that I would know my power in a time of our great need."

"You should not be feeling sorry for yourself. Put a stop to this self-pity! Avenge them! Set your mind to something! You have nothing to lose! Fight harder than ever!" Everyone stares at Evan in shock. No one has ever heard him be so harsh. Stormy pins his ears back and stares at him.

"Excuse me?" he asks incredulously, his brown eyes flashing dangerously.

"Put this past you. Dedicate yourself to helping Emerald right now. There is nothing else you can do about it, so move on. Still hold them in your heart, but there are more things to think about. In case you did not notice, we are about to go to war." Stormy lifts his head and takes a step forward towards Evan. Now there is a spark of anger in his eyes. He draws himself to his full height. Sixteen hands and three inches of angry horse stalks over to Evan.

He watches Stormy with slight fear. I've never felt threatened by Stormy and I don't *think* he will hurt Evan, but I've never seen him this angry. Rivermist steps in front of Evan, but Stormy fixates his glare on the smaller horse and he continues to stalk forward. A silent exchange happens between the two horses and Rivermist quickly backs away. Stormy stops in front of the boy and lowers his head so their eyes are in the same level.

"Is the rumor true?" he demands. Evan gravely nods and gives Stormy a quick smile. *What just happened?* Stormy calmly walks back to Emerald and as he walks, a mist of ice blue covers his face and back. When it recedes, Shadow's beautifully crafted saddle with ice blue stitching and dark colored leather is strapped to his back. The bridle is the same style. Dark leather and ice blue stitches and a very gentle bit to help with extra maneuverability for battles and wars.

All our horses tack themselves up and I put my foot into the left stirrup and swing aboard. Evan looks in shock at his new partner before tentatively mounting him for the first time. After a last-minute check on supplies, it is assured that everyone brought a full waterskin and hard rations in their packs and it is assumed that weapons are always accompanying us.

So far, no one has noticed that I don't have that cursed bow. I'm unused to the weight of my sword as hangs from my belt and the spear is cumbersome to ride with. I end up stuffing it through the strap of my quiver. *Well, at least the quiver is good for something.* The horses start off at a rocking canter that they can hold all day without tiring. Now I just hope we can convince the knights and warriors to follow us in battle.

Apollo was sent to the Daerinians, because he is one of their favorites, along with Demeter and Dionysus. We were sent to the Arélians because Athena is not quite a favorite among the others. They believe she simply creates violence. Although, that is far from true. Evan is also a respected knight among the people of Arél, so we shouldn't run into any unforeseen issues... Hopefully.

Chapter Twenty-Three

Shadow

The trees blend together as countless miles flash by under Enbarr's hooves. The day fades to night and the night soon turns to dawn's first light. I don't know exactly where we are, but I know we have gone far. I can barely keep my eyes open from exhaustion. I have not slept in probably a few days now and my body is turning on me. My eyes feel like someone rubbed sand in them and they are so heavy that I can barely stay awake. My muscles protest as they follow the continued movement of Enbarr's canter. I can feel his concern, but he does as I wish and just keeps going.

We have never traveled this far this fast. Once a day, I get off and stretch and walk around, but I always quickly remount and we continue to send the miles flying by. It has been three days of straight travel at a full gallop. I snap out of the cloud of sleep when Enbarr starts to speak.

"Elren, there is a big village ahead. There should be a decent sized group of men at arms. If we are lucky there will be a castle with some knights. Only if we are very lucky though," Enbarr says telepathically in Daenlir. He alone, out of all the people and creatures I know, refused to call me Shadow and now I am going as my real name. Enbarr doesn't like speaking Remic, or Aríndal and Daenlir is my first language, so no one has ever noticed that he calls me Elren. I don't know how they never realized it.

"Alright, but since when is luck on our side?" I reply. We don't want our presence revealed until we know what we are dealing with. *"Change your color to that of a normal horse, please."* He snorts and like

water across wood, his coat color ripples. The silver fades to a soft gray like fresh snow and the ice blue turns to dark gray dapples across his body. He looks like a normal horse, but one of exceptional beauty. He is very tall, but fine boned and light on his feet like one of the New Worlders prized race horses, generally Thoroughbreds, while Stormy is like the graceful and fast Arabian desert horses.

We slowly walk out of the trees and take on the characters of weary and worn travelers. It is not very far from the truth for me. My shoulder and knee still ache from my most recent severe injuries. Enbarr holds his head down low and acts exhausted. I slump low in his saddle and hunch over slightly against the bitter winter wind, drawing the hood of my cloak over my head to disguise myself. At the last second I remember to change my cloak to look like a simple wool spun garment.

In the deep shadow covering my eyes, I scan the people as they calmly go about their business. They cast suspicious looks my way, but from a distance I simply look like a traveling knight. I stop in front of a group of families as they stand talking in the road. I dismount a respectful distance away and slowly limp towards them. The children squeal and run a few steps behind the adults as they catch sight of me. Four men quickly reach for their swords and the women draw long and wickedly sharp daggers and knives before standing in front of their children. I am all too aware of the image I must be giving off. A longbow and quiver across my shoulders and a sword on my belt, along with multiple daggers of various lengths.

I push the hood of the cloak off my head so they can see my face and raise my hands away from my weapons in a gesture of peace. They stare at me in shock when they see how young I am, only twenty, and an unmarried woman. Some of the wives facing me look only twenty-five and have children; they are barely older than me. Despite the nonchalant atmosphere of the village, this is a warrior community. They are ready for anything.

"Please, I don't mean any harm. I am a courier from a faraway place carrying an important message, but I became lost when I was caught in a storm. I have been wandering for a while now. I do not ask for anything. I can catch my own food and am warm enough to live. All I ask is where I am." They sheath their weapons, but their hands don't stray far from the hilts. "Can I lower my hands? I swear I mean no harm whatsoever. I have recently had a terrible injury and it continues to bother me. I am in no condition to be picking fights, especially in this town." I keep my charade of an innocent traveler and I pointedly look at the ready stances of all the bystanders eavesdropping. All of them are prepared to jump to their neighbors' aid. The unity warms my heart, which has remained cold and impassive since my brother first captured me earlier this week.

My shoulder continues to send slight shockwaves of pain and my knee echoes it until it seems like a full-on fight is raging in my body. I slowly lower my right arm and the pain immediately recedes, but suddenly, my knee decides it doesn't like the cold air and it gives out on me, forcing me to hop sideways to keep my balance. I almost swear, but remember there are children here so I end up using a few different languages instead. Finally, one of the mothers takes pity on me and steps forward.

"You are in Newbrook Village." My gaze snaps up. *Newbrook? It can't be. This is only a few miles from the Plain of Ren and the King of the Arélians!*

"Thank you for your help." I hold out my hand and after a few seconds, she grips it and shakes hands with me. Suddenly, three young girls hurry forward and talk to the mother in hurried tones. Her cheeks flush in embarrassment, but she does as they request.

"My daughters want to know what your horse is called and what your name is."

"This is Snowdancer and I am his humble servant, Elren." I kneel in the slush and mud to be on the same eye level with the little girls clinging to their mother's skirt. I smile, and it is a real and genuine smile and they shyly smile back. On the inside of myself, it feels like a stone slowly splitting; the stone that holds my emotions together. This is the first time I have genuinely smiled in a long time, perhaps even years. Their little round faces are flushed with excitement and the thrill of being young and bold.

"Remain this brave and you are going to become great warriors when you grow up," I say gently. They all look startled.

"Women can be warriors?" one asks doubtfully.

"Are you a knight?" the youngest with curly red hair asks suddenly.

"I am." They all stare at me in wonder. "Women can do anything they want if only we are brave enough to face the adversity to our decision." The adults look startled by my words. I ignore them and address the children. "Would you like to pet my horse?" They all nod enthusiastically. I slowly stand up, making sure not to put too much pressure on my knee, but it still snaps at me. I limp over to Enbarr and bring him closer. He lowers his head and the girls come forward and gently stroke him on the nose and scratch his forehead.

"You are so pretty, Snowdancer!" the oldest exclaims, and gives him a hug around his face. He puffs warm and sweet scented air from his nose on her and the girls all giggle and laugh. Finally, they turn away and return to their parents. I glance at the sun hiding behind the heavy clouds and guess it to be two or three hours past midday.

"Is there a headman to this village?" I ask an elderly man in the group. He nods his head. The gentleman points to the big house at the end of the street with distaste.

"Just beware, he is a nuisance. His name is John McNeil. All he cares about is that all the tax money is handed to him once a month. He may refuse to see you," the man warns. I drop my left hand casually to my sword hilt.

"Well, I think it would be in his best interest to speak with me. Last time I checked, a sword can be more persuasive than the tongue and I heavily despise politics. Thank you for all your help, and if this McNeil character refuses me, I certainly hope you have a replacement ready. My travels have been delayed long enough already." The group of people gathered around laugh. They liked the way that I was kind to the children. I had unintentionally stumbled upon the fastest way to their trust. I swing up into the saddle and gently tap Enbarr with my heels.

"Have a nice day. Oh, before I leave, I should tell you this." I make a snapshot decision and bring Enbarr to a halt again. "You all ought to know, the reason I am here is because there is a war coming. Soon armies will be marching onto the Plain of Ren, which is only three or four miles away. Those who are young and brave and want a good fight are welcome to join. However, to those with children and who cannot, or do not wish to fight, they should be ready to get as far away from here as possible. It will be the worst war anyone could ever imagine and the chances of us winning are small. I am sorry to leave you with such grave news, but it must be said. I came to gather each and every fighting man possible who is willing to go. I will also be going to the castles to get armies moving. The Olympian army is already there now, or at least they should be."

"Who are we even fighting?" a young man calls angrily.

Muttering breaks out through the crowd.

"The New Worlders, led by Chaos. They are brutal and ruthless."

"How do you have the power to order people to send out their armies and then they actually do it?" another man asks pugnaciously. I smile, but it is more wolfish than anything. Soft ice blue magic floats gently from my hand. The villagers gasp, but then silence falls as they look at me. Enbarr returned to his original color of silver with ice blue Daenlir written across his body. My fate is written out for all to see, but few can understand it.

I throw off my cloak to reveal my custom armor. Overlapping plates of impenetrable silver cover my torso, but my arms and legs are only protected by a light silver chainmail mesh. Unlike most knights, I cannot stand wearing a helmet. It dulls my senses and hearing. I need a full range of movement and vision. Too much armor is heavy and difficult to move in. They stare at me with wide eyes. Most of these people live the mundane lives of farmers or merchants. This is the biggest thing that has happened in years here.

"Any more questions?" When none are forthcoming, I stop next to the three young girls I was talking to earlier and dismount one more time. The oldest of the three at around eleven or twelve looks at me in awe.

"I knew women could be knights!" she exclaims happily. I smile slightly before unclipping a sheathed dagger. I draw the beautifully crafted blade and look down its short length, contemplating which gift to give her. I slice my hand, enough for my silvery-blue blood to fall onto the blade. The dagger glows for a second before returning to its normal state. The youngster watches me do this with curiosity.

"Would you hold out your right hand?" she does as I asked and I turn it palm up. With my blood, I draw a small rune in the very center of her hand. She gasps as it burns for a second before sending beams of warmth through her. Despite the cold temperature and her thin cloak, she no longer feels the cold. Her face reflects her shock. She gives her younger sisters her cloak to share. A wide and blissful smile crosses her face.

I can feel the tension radiating from every adult nearby. Something about this girl touches my very being. She draws the soft side of me out. No one has ever managed to do that. Not even Emerald. I study her curiously, trying to figure out what is so special about the girl.

"You now will never be cold or hot, no sickness or injury will ever befall you. Now, I give you my dagger. It has protected me many times. It has even saved my life a time or two. Someday, you will become a great and valiant knight. This dagger will never break or fail you. A dagger is a weapon for someone who is fast and clever. I know you will go above and beyond the standards set by men. You are incredibly special and you have a good heart." The little girl nods gravely. Finally, one man speaks.

"What is the price for this incredible gift you gave Roselyn?" I cock my head at the man who asked. My best guess is that it is her father. They have the same curly red hair.

"Why must there be a price? Does no one give free gifts anymore?"

"There is always a price," he replies firmly.

"If there must be a price, then this is the only thing I need from Rosy." Everyone stiffens at my words. "What is your full name?" I ask.

"Roselyn Wade." Her voice quivers slightly, but out of fear or excitement, I don't know.

"Alright, Roselyn Wade, do you swear, on the pain of having this blessing removed and the knife deserting you, that you will never become conceited or vengeful?" She swallows nervously, but her voice is determined as she swears by my terms. I nod. "Good. Use that dagger well."

"I will," she replies softly. I slowly stand up and limp back towards Enbarr. He suddenly pins his ears back in warning. Suddenly, I feel a razor-sharp sword tip pressing lightly into my neck. With effort, I force down my temper and instead make my expression light and pleasant.

"My king demands that the one known as the Shadow Warrior is brought to his castle and not given a chance to escape. I have twenty men with me, all of them have crossbows aimed at you now. Come quietly, and you will have a better chance of living."

"Greetings, stranger. It is such a beautiful day, isn't it?" I say pleasantly.

"Wha-" he doesn't get a chance to finish voicing his confusion as I whip around and grab the blade of his sword. I've practiced this move since I was young and know how not to cut myself. It helps when you are wearing magical chainmail gauntlets as well. With my thumb on the bottom of the blade and two fingers on top, I effortlessly hold the sword still as he tries to yank it back.

"There are children here, Knight. Allow them to remain innocent and naive if they can." I turn to the villagers who all had backed up as the knight stepped forward.

"Send the children home," I order them gently. I look at Roselyn. "Remember what I said." She nods happily. I shove the man back and draw myself to my full height and look the angry knight in the eye. He wears a crimson and gold surecoat that has a boar with wings on it. My heart races when I recognize it to be the coat of arms of the king of the Arélians. This could be my way there.

"Your king will want you back, captain. Hurry on home now, before the beasties and ghoulies come out to get you in the dark woods." I flick my hand as if to shoo him away. "You can tell your king that I'll be there tomorrow." I wink at Roselyn and she giggles. She and her parents are still standing here. She is right beside me and her parents beckon her frantically. They know that their daughter is in the line of fire.

"Shoot to disable!" he shouts to his men. True to his words, twenty bows fire at us. The girl yelps in surprise as seven bolts stop a foot away from her and drop to the ground as my gift takes effect. Rattling fills the air as they hit my armor and bounce off without a scratch. Soon they realize this, and two bolts fly towards my neck and one towards my head. I catch two of them and sway backwards to let the other fly clear.

"Head over to your parents, little one. Train hard! You have the possibility to become an incredible warrior one day. Practice, and that talent will become mastery." She runs over to her mother's side and the family vanishes from sight.

"You really want me to come with you, don't you?" I ask the knight conversationally. He nods, his face full of despair that he failed his task.

"The King will relieve me from his service if I make another mistake." He hangs his head shamefully. "I was given command of this mission, because it is supposed to be impossible. Now, here I am, faced with an opponent that cannot be killed and will not come. I-I-I just don't know what to do!" he finally cries. I step back in surprise at the sudden burst of desperation.

"Do you like being a knight?" I ask simply. In the empty street, my voice seems unnaturally loud and I wince slightly.

"Yes. I was the son of two peasant parents and have had to work every day to prove that bloodline does not matter. I was taken by the New Worlders, but was saved by you. Finally, I have reached my goal, only to have it dangling above my head, about to be snatched away any second. I don't know what I will do." I remember this man. He was tasked to bring me to Chaos. I convinced him to stay on my side of the world after I killed his commander. My armor melds back into the exact clothes I had been wearing before. Worn and tattered once again, I can also feel my energy levels take another dip lower. It takes all my skill of hiding my emotions to keep from showing my exhaustion. *If I go with them, I won't have to worry about keeping an eye open as we travel.* Abruptly, I make my decision.

"I'll go." I swing aboard Enbarr and sit there waiting.

"What?" he asks, completely caught off guard by this turn in events.

"I was heading there anyway, so I may as well go with you. A full retinue of knights to escort me there will do no harm either. Now, are we leaving or not? This is already longer than I had planned to stay in the village." They all hurry and swing onto their horses and box me in the center of them. The ones next to me eye me warily, but I ignore them.

"*Follow them. They are taking us where we want to go,*" I tell Enbarr. He snorts in agreement.

"*You sleep on the way. I'll wake you if anything happens,*" he orders. I yawn in answer, too tired to disagree.

Full dark has fallen again by the time we arrive at the castle gates, completing my fourth day of traveling. In the dark, the men stare at Enbarr and me. All the ice blue words glow and his silver coat casts ripples of light as if he were the moon, or a fallen star. My bow and sword scabbard are also silver, but the beautiful designs glow ice blue. The runes on my forearm glow as well. My mind wanders as the horses canter through the gates and over the moat bridge. *I wonder if Artemis has received the bow I made her?* I shrug. There is no way to know.

I feel bad for the loss of her most prized possession. It was my fault they were in the situation in the first place. I had made the longbow a long time ago, hoping it would be for Emerald, but it was very clear to me after her first shot with a small recurve bow, she was not going to become an archer. Hopefully Artemis will be able to use it. Enbarr suddenly stops and I look up to see eight bows drawn and aimed at me as the archers on the walls catch sight of Enbarr and me.

"Twelve o'clock," I say calmly. The others in the group look ahead as well and shout in alarm.

"Those are Garrett's archers, Captain Rander," a keen eyed young soldier informs him.

"He will order them to shoot before looking at who is there. Shields, men!" Lendon Rander orders. I raise my hand to forestall their movements.

"Don't. That is providing a perfect target. Trust me. I will protect you. You got here here safely and in return I will protect you from your own archers. I *am* immortal, you know."

"You may be, but *we* are not," one man mutters and winces under the cold look I give him. Our little group moves forward again and just as my escort said, they fire their arrows. I watch each arrow's trajectory and swipe the only three that were near being on target away with the slightest bit of magic. As each volley comes towards us, I do the same thing *over, and over* again. Don't they learn? Or at least practice hitting a moving target? Finally, we are under the torches and the archers on the walls realize who they were aiming at. They were shooting at the King's personal retinue of knights.

Oops.

I grin. Oh, how terrible they would feel to know that they were shooting at the Shadow Warrior, their kingdom's last hope of survival. Even if they do not know that yet. We dismount and Enbarr and I share a look. I snap my fingers and he disappears in an ice blue mist. The knights around me start to edge away in fear. Ignoring them, I stride towards the two guards standing in front of the door. Their faces are hidden behind impartial metal visors.

"Let me pass. I am Elren Caerin, although, people seem to know me better these days as The Shadow Warrior. They jump in surprise at the name.

"Ya don' look like a werrier ta me, lil' gurlie," one says contemptuously with the heavy drawl of someone who has had too much mead. In exasperation, I use my magic to switch my old clothes into my unusual armor. The one who had just spoken drops his spear in surprise. In a split second, I have Tíne out of its sheath and the point under his helmet, where his neck is only protected by thin chainmail.

"Perhaps you have something to say? I'm not sure I caught that? Something about a *little girl*? I am taller, faster, and stronger than you. We have very different ideas of little. Now, I will only say it one more time. Let. Us. *Through!*" I shout the last word and shove him backwards. Galvanized into action, he and his companion throw the doors open and stand at attention as I pass. The knights hurry after me, all of them are chuckling and laughing.

"Did you see Caine? He practically wet his pants! Oh, that was priceless!" the captain crows happily.

"Take me to King Rylan," I order them. They agree immediately and after multiple confusing turns and flights of stairs, we stand in the great hall with the king himself sitting on his intricate throne. The knights all kneel in front of his throne and they gesture for me to do that as well.

"Why do you not bow to your superior, -" the king's voice trails off as he waits for my name.

"Elren Caerin, *Majesty*," I add a slight mocking tone on his title. "Please do not take this the wrong way, but I serve no one, and therefore I do not kneel for anyone. Ever." He inclines his head thoughtfully, a small smile playing across his face.

"A fascinating policy, Elren, but everyone serves someone. Even the immortals bow down to their king, Zeus." I smile humorlessly.

"Oh, my liege, have you not heard? Do you honestly not recognize me from the wild descriptions floating around your kingdom? I am the Shadow Warrior. Daughter of the Dark and the Light and twin sister of Chaos Caerin. I am far beyond your general run of the mill immortals." The King heavily sits back in his chair.

"You are here to take the throne from me," he says resignedly, not even bothering to fight. I frown in sudden confusion.

"No, I do *not* want your throne! I am here to try and help you keep it! You and all the other kings are in great danger of losing your kingdoms and your lives, or whichever is more important to you. The New Worlders are coming, and they will take over everything. I have come to ask you to send out all your messengers and couriers to assemble as many warriors, men and women, to go as fast as humanly possible and assemble on the west side of The Plain of Ren. That is the only reason I am here. Allow me to remind you. I am a warrior, not a politician." His composure slips and I can see how shocked he is by my declaration of war and proposition of mobilizing the entire army in less than a week.

"I will do that and I will see you on the field of battle where all of our fates will be decided. Dare I say it, but good luck. You can count on this getting done." I incline my head, pleased with his decision.

"Thank you. I must go. My friends are soon going to be in danger. I had best be on my way."

Chapter Twenty-Four

Emerald

I wake up as dawn's first light streaks across the sky. All my muscles protest loudly as I move slightly. Many of them I did not know existed until recently. Evan has been relentlessly putting me through grueling sword drills from the past few days. He had no qualms about letting the flat side of his blade bruise me multiple times. He also told me I was not allowed to heal any injuries from the practice session to prove a point and act as a reminder. Right now, they make an excellent wake up call. To make matters worse, this humiliation was in front of Artemis and Athena, both of whom are excellent with a sword and spear. Even Artemis who is only known as an archer was incredible with her sword when she and Athena sparred last night.

I roll out from my blankets and the cold air is a slap in the face and when I look up at the sky, dark and heavy clouds obscure the sudden flare of the sunrise. Stretching my stiff muscles, I gather all my stuff and neatly organize them into my pack.

"I never knew you were an early morning person," someone behind me remarks. I whirl around in surprise. Artemis steps forward a bit so I can see her. She looks cold, but absolutely thrilled. She had the last watch and I had forgotten about her. Being a hunter, she is a master of camouflaging herself. She holds a different longbow in her hand and it is strung. I don't respond to her first comment.

"Where's that from?" I point at the bow. She beams happily in answer.

"It appeared next to me when I took my turn on watch with a note saying it was made by Elren Caerin for the Goddess of the Hunt." I frown.

"How is that possible?" She shrugs in answer.

"I don't know, but I'm not asking." She walks away and starts waking the others by stealing their blankets, and in Athena's case, by means of a pail of water. Athena undoubtedly beats everyone else in waking up and starts the day by cursing impressively.

"Good morning!" I call cheerfully, breaking her long tirade of profanity that is obviously well practiced. I whistle and the horses come out of the woods. Stormy comes over to me yawning. I sling my pack onto the saddle and reach way up to clip the bag to the saddle before starting the struggle of mounting a tall horse from the ground.

I barely manage to get my foot in the stirrup with all my joints and muscles protesting loudly. Reaching up as high as I can, I am able to grab the pommel of the saddle, but Stormy suddenly lurches forward and I lose my grip on the saddle along with my balance. With a crash that seems to make my world vibrate, I hit the ground and look up. The sound of stifled laughter fills the small campsite. My ears burn in embarrassment and I glare at Stormy angrily.

"You have no idea how long I have been waiting to pull that on someone. It never worked on Shadow," he laughs at me. I slowly pick myself off the ground. The others are all mounted and ready. Surefire, Morningsun, and Rivermist all bob their heads approvingly and it makes me wonder if bets had been made about this. Stormy carefully bends down onto his front legs, making it easy for me to mount. The minute I'm secure, he lurches up and stands again. I'm still not used to how high up I am and how long Stormy's strides are in comparison to his mother, Rose.

Why did they make me take Stormy? Nothing is wrong with Rose.
I wonder as the horses continue to gallop relentlessly. The time slowly passes as the miles fly under the horse's' hooves. The soft sound of their hooves on the ground lulls me into a trance where fantasies play out in front of my vision. I believe Shadow called it daydreaming.

Artemis pulls Surefire alongside Stormy and the two pretend to bicker as Surefire playfully nips Stormy on the neck and Stormy replies in kind. I look up from the two over at Artemis. She looks so elegant and in control on horseback. I have never been the best rider and I envy the others easy seats. They all look like centaurs they're so in tune with their mounts. Artemis holds out my hunting bow to me, ruining any hopes I had about going back to my wonderful daydreams.

"Practice!" She passes my quiver to me as well. To demonstrate, she nocks an arrow to her new beautifully engraved longbow and picks a tree ahead before firing and hitting it dead center. I look closer and realize that she hit a tiny little knot in the bark of the tree. I try it and manage to hit the very edge of it. And by *it,* I mean the tree itself. "Practice!" she calls again and lets Surefire pull ahead to the front of the group next to Athena and Morningsun. After a few shots, my shoulder and back muscles start burning. I stop for a moment to let them rest for a bit. Suddenly, Athena and Artemis raise their weapons above their heads. In our group, this means weapons ready.

I groan softly. *Really? Now? When I am already tired?* The trees open to a big clearing. Just before charging headfirst in, Artemis and Athena pull their horses to a dead halt. They rear and spin to face us.

"Dismount. Keep your weapons ready. Emerald, leave your bow with Stormy and that little quiver as well. It won't help you in a fight. Everyone, armor on." There is no sign of her previous good humor. This is not a drill.

Everyone immediately rushes to do as she ordered. Evan throws himself off Rivermist and an arrow flashes where he had been just a moment ago. He slaps his horse on the rump and urges him to run. Rivermist looks him in the eye and a private message passes between the two of them before he gallops off into the trees. Stormy gives me a long look. He has never liked me very much, but today he looks concerned.

"Watch your back. Keep both eyes open. Don't get sucked into an extended fight with one man. Always know what is happening around you. Remember what Shadow taught you. Don't die." After passing along his warning, he disappears after Rivermist. The others share a moment with their horses and send them flying after the two others.

Flashes of sapphire, gold, silver, and green fills my vision. When it recedes, we are all in armor. All my bruises and petty aches are gone. My sword, Treán, has light brown and green designs. Something I have never seen before.

Suddenly, a small army runs from the woods on the other side of the clearing. Artemis raises her new bow and shoots rapidly. Thirty men fall before she runs out of arrows. She securely puts the bow back over her shoulders and grabs her silver spear. A golden spear appears in Athena's hands as well and the owl insignia glows on her armor. Evan and I draw our swords. We all form a defensive line, Evan and Athena on the inside and Artemis and I on the outside. Athena suddenly becomes worried as she sees the numbers against us, something I've never seen from the battle-goddess, and she turns to us.

"No matter what happens, fight honorably, and remember how your fallen friends valiantly entered a battle they could not win. You are my family. I love you all. We will live and die honorably. There is nothing more glorious than dying in a battle to delay them from attacking the innocents who are fleeing the kingdom."

Just like the rising tide with a storm riding on the breaking waves, we are thrown into a one-sided battle. We are severely outnumbered, and I know now that none of us will survive this. A deep, almost inaudible thrum vibrates in my ears. It is tantalizingly familiar, but that is impossible. There is only one bow that sounds like that and it was lost with its master. Shadow is dead. Nothing can change that. There will not be a miracle at the end of this battle. She cannot somehow pull us out of this danger like she has in the past. I feel the painful emptiness and longing ache fill me. I force that away. There is not time for self-pity. That will not be how I die.

My hand steadies on Treán's hilt. I will go down fighting. Just like Shadow. Suddenly, the sound comes again and four arrows come whizzing through the air from different sides of the clearing. Four men fall and in that moment of confusion, Evan screams into the ensuing silence,

"Dum vivo, spero!" *When did he learn Tinal?* I agree with his words though. *While I live, I hope!* We echo his cry and charge to our deaths.

As we fight through the seemingly endless mass of warriors, I see Artemis taken down by a dagger thrust to the side and soon after, Athena's spear is wrenched out of her hand and before she can draw her sword, she too goes down. Evan is like watching poetry as he fights. His form fluently changes from man to wolf and back again. As a man, his sword is flying with incredible strength and precision. As a wolf, his teeth and speed take down many. After what feels like hours of fighting, five men get between us and we are forced apart. Fifteen men fall to his savage attack, but twenty take their place and he too goes down.

My mind is in total shock. Dumbfounded, I realize that I am alone. Well and truly alone. I have just watched my new family members

306

be mortally wounded and I know I cannot save them. With a pain filled scream, I wade forward into the mass of warriors, taking out anyone who is near me. Fighting as I never have before, no one stands a chance against the whirling brown and green blur of a sword in my hands. Every sequence that Shadow ever taught me clicks and is put into motion.

At last, my strength starts to falter. My blows slowly become less powerful and the sword starts to feel awkward in my hands. My breath is coming in heavy gasps as I struggle to gain enough oxygen to fuel my limbs. Suddenly, the fight is over. A giant two handed broadsword slams into mine and my grip fails. I watch my faithful sword fall onto the grass below that shines red with the freshly shed blood of my friends and enemies. Still in shock, I pull out my six throwing knives and with carefully aimed throws, six warriors fall.

A tall knight slams his shoulder into mine and my muscles give out. My vision swims as my head hits the ground. Exhausted and terrified, I roll onto my back and look up. They all look down at me without mercy. I killed their friends and comrades. Some must have had children and wives as well.

Horror fills me at what I just did. I have only ever killed beasts before. Bile rises in my throat and I feel sick. The one who knocked me down presses his heavy booted foot on my shoulder. I wince, but refrain from showing any pain from the countless bruises under my armor and the gashes that bleed through the ruined chainmail. I feel the small bones under his foot start to give and a few crack.

I close my eyes and breathe deeply. Shadow would not have given them the satisfaction of letting them see her defeat. She had far too much pride on the line than to allow that. So do I. I will die undefeated. I open my eyes and glare at them defiantly, ashamed of the tears in my eyes and the ones that trail down my cheeks.

"I am unbroken. No one will ever defeat me. I am Emerald Alián, apprentice of Shadow Caerin. She was never broken, and neither am I. Death is not defeat. In my death and my friends' deaths, there is only honor. Some of your warriors in the New World say that death is the greatest adventure. Soon, I will be fortunate enough to set foot on such a great path and I look forward to it." He slashes down with his sword and I vaguely feel pain slice through my side where his blade pierces my skin through a gap in the armor. It is curiously dull and a feeling of calm obliterates all my aches and pains.

I look back up at the wintry sky and watch the dark clouds scuttle overhead. Small snowflakes start to fall and I smile. The last snow of the year. I was able to see it once more. In the fading background, I hear more of that tantalizingly familiar sound again. A sound that reminds me of warm summer evenings and crisp mornings when Shadow had tried to teach me archery. I smile sadly as those memories float hazily through my mind. Cold magic surges through my veins and I feel like I am floating. *So this must be death. It is far more peaceful then I expected.* Suddenly, the crowd parts like an unrelenting mountain range with one wide valley. Through that valley, one person limps through. I feel myself drop back to the ground and all the pain abruptly returns. *I think that I would prefer death.*

Through a haze of pain, I see a longbow slung over the tall warrior's shoulders. Arrows are visible in the quiver on his back. The warrior fearlessly walks through the small army as they step aside. I blink my eyes frantically to see the figure better. It is a woman, not a man, like I first thought. She wears a strange set of armor. Only her torso has plate armor and her arms and legs are only protected by chainmail. Intricate designs in ice blue cover all her armor and a small horse is on the left side of her breastplate. There is something significant about that, but I can't figure it out.

A sword and dagger hang from her waist. My brain is still fuzzy and not working right from hitting the ground, but she seems *so* familiar. The warrior strides purposely towards me through the gap her presence creates. A pronounced limp accompanies her walk, but it doesn't make her any less formidable. A long, jagged scar streaks down the left side of her face. The magic running through my blood, the magic keeping me alive, sings a name through my body. A name my mind begs me to recognize. *Elren.* She stops a few feet away from where I lie helpless and when she speaks, a wave of longing floods from my empty heart. *She sounds so much like Shadow.*

"Release the girl. *Now.*" There is a dangerous edge to her voice, just as dangerous as the edge of her sword. The knight moves, but instead of moving away, he brings his sword flashing down and now that death is coming, I feel totally calm. I look at the girl again. She looks twenty years of age, but just *so* familiar. I focus on her and look at the peaceful way the snow lightly falls and sticks to her braid as death flies towards me with breathtaking strength.

Suddenly, another blade is there and with a loud screech of metal on metal, it reverses and the man falls to the ground dead, killed by his own sword.

"Leave," she orders the warriors and no one thinks to disobey and none seem to realize that there is only one of her and a hundred of them. The small army flees like a flock of sheep from a wolf back the way they came. The girl simply stands there with her sword ready until she is certain they are gone before sheathing her blade and kneeling next to me.

"Do not fear, young one. You are safe. You will be alright." Finally, I manage to speak.

"Who are you?" I manage to croak, the foreign, yet familiar, magic lending me the strength necessary to talk. She hesitates, her eyes searching mine.

"I think you already know," she says quietly. Something deep inside me clicks. My mind finally relaxes and a friendly darkness starts to cover my surroundings. Only she is still there. Her ice blue eyes hold mine here and keep me from drifting away.

"Daughter of Dark and Light. Twin to Draemir Caerin, or as he calls himself, Chaos. You, you are Elren Caerin. My sister." I sigh and allow my consciousness to slip away.

Shadow

I stand up and look around. Emerald is safe. My magic will protect her. I had forgotten how much energy it takes to send my own magic through someone else. Now I have to do it three more times. It is easy enough to pick out where my friends lie because their armor shines brightly with their magic. Artemis is closest to me and I walk over to her and put a hand on her left shoulder. She opens her eyes and stares at me for a second in shock.

"Am I dead?" she asks suddenly before passing out again. I send some magic into her and move on to Athena. Finally, when I am content that they are safe, I look for Evan. He is already standing up and waiting for me. Slowly, like a wary animal, I approach him. I do not know if he showed the others my journal, but judging by Emerald knowing my real name and who Draemir is, he most likely showed them.

That makes my life a lot easier. I stop about five feet away and hesitate. I had told him how I felt about him and I don't know if he feels the same way. *Damn! Since when did I become so hesitant?* I gather my courage and step forward purposely and don't stop until I am right next to him. I place my hand on his shoulder and he turns to look at me. He has not changed at all. We just stand there when finally, he says the words I have hoped to hear.

"I have waited a long time to say this and I was not sure how you felt about me, but when you were gone, I could not bear it." He steps closer and I can see every fleck of dark blue in his eyes. He gently kisses me and slowly pulls away. I've waited a long time for this. I throw my arms around him and give him a tight hug. Suddenly, all the exhaustion and stress of the past weeks hits me. Every emotion hits me like a punch and it slowly crumbles the already cracked wall that held them back. It starts with one tear and then ends up as a quiet sob. I give up trying to hold them back and he simply comforts me. All the faces of every person I have ever failed to save flashes through my mind, then the terrible fear I feel every time I am near my brother.

"How am I supposed to lead these men against Chaos and ask them to give their lives fighting someone even I cannot beat? I have not been able to confidently fight him since we were young. He killed Shadow, forcing me to expose myself as who I am. Who is to say that Elren is stronger? It is who I really am. I don't have anything to hide behind now. Am I strong enough? Evan, I am scared," I whisper in his ear. I have never said those words aloud before. I have never let them fall from the tip of my tongue, no matter how they tried to escape. Until today. He holds me at arm length and smiles.

"The fact that you are able to show your emotions and show your real self to everyone is what makes you stronger than Chaos. He is still hiding from himself. This is your advantage. The others already know. I showed them the memory and all of them have been in Chaos's dungeon and watched you break your wrists breaking blackiron chains. You broke an unbreakable chain when you were *eleven*. You could have crippled yourself, but you did what you had to do to help the others. I know you are strong inside and out. There is absolutely no reason why you cannot beat Chaos. You just need to believe you can." I finally manage to rein in my unruly emotions and dry my tears.

"Thank you. When I am with you, I am no longer afraid. I have lived with fear, guilt, and loneliness my entire life. I grew up with a human father and my real mother. Living among mortals taught me how to respect life. I watched the young and old die and learned there was nothing anyone could do about it. I was determined to help humans and everyone that I could. After they were "gone," I figured out the truth. My father, Will, you met him a while ago, he is Zeus's lieutenant and my mother is the Goddess of Light.

"My mother still guides me. She even appeared to me in the labyrinth. I know that my real father, the God of the Dark, is on the side with Chaos, while my mother has sided with me. My mother is the one who saw what Chaos was going to become. She was afraid that I would follow down the same path, so she separated us. My father took Chaos and taught him how to use his anger to strengthen his magic. I was taught how to value life and use hope as my strength. I grew up with the weak and learned about sacrifice and empathy. He learned power and vanity. This is how we are different. We have the same fiery temper and the exact same looks, but I do not want to be known as being like him." I realize that I am rambling on and cut off my words, even though I have much left to say. Evan nods knowingly.

"No one will ever think you are like him."

"Good. Now, we need to go to the Plain of Ren and get everything organized for the army. It will be the largest war in history and I cannot honestly say that I believe we will win this, but everyone deserves to fight for what they believe in. We must hurry. Chaos is going to come soon." I put on my business face once more and put away personal feelings. They can wait until I am dead, or about to die. I whistle loudly and five horses run out of the woods. The horses gallop across the large clearing, playfully kicking up their heels and mock fighting. Surefire, Morningsun, Stormy, Rose, and a horse I have only seen a few times before, race towards us with unnatural speed. However, I can guess who the horse's human is.

"That's Rivermist," Evan says proudly and I hide a quick smile. All of them are tacked up and ready to go. Rosy carries Emerald's little hunting bow and quiver. As a group, we walk over to the others. I click my fingers and all my magic surges back to me from the others. I back up, slightly overwhelmed by the amount of magic that suddenly returns to my blood. That surge of energy reinvigorates me and makes me a little more optimistic. The others all wake up suddenly from the loss of my magic and look around and when their eyes land on me, they stare at me in shock and disbelief.

"Elren," Athena suddenly announces my name. The others stare at me in shock. "Elren Caerin. You seem to have become old on us." I smile at her.

"Let's go youngsters, Grandma is not waiting all day! I am not going to let us stop riding until we reach the Plain of Ren tonight! Get up, and let's go!" Still in mild shock, they do as I say. We gallop the horses through the woods, throwing caution to the winds to gain time. We pass many groups of varying sizes as warriors march on their way to the battlefield. Captains call orders and they stop and stand at attention as we pass. Some even salute us. I, on my flashy bay horse, and the other horses behind us, all with surreal colors, draw quite a bit of attention. I solute them back and they smile in surprise.

"Hey, look! They are actually giving me the respect I deserve!" Stormy remarks to me before leaping and cavorting happily. I laugh at him. We reach the massive war camp right before sunset and I pull the hood of my cloak over my head. I do not have the energy to explain everything to the whole camp right now. We head straight to the command tent in the very center. Men rush around with the sergeants calling out orders. Immortal horses roam around, every last one of them looking for a way to cause trouble and to get the human soldiers blamed for it. As I watch, one buckskin stallion sneaks up behind a group of men and mimics one's voice.

"He is stupid and doesn't know what he is talking about," the horse says loudly in his voice before stepping back and watching the humans argue about it. An explosive sneeze hides his laughter. Another steals a knight's sword and shield while his back is turned. We all start laughing as we watch all the horses' different little tricks. One knocks a bucket over with magic onto the sleeping cook while a sentry walks by. The paint mare fakes a jump sideways to look scared. However, I can see the mischievous light in her eyes as the cook starts yelling at a startled sentry. Out of the corner of my eye, I spot a chestnut horse pull the bolt out of a gate. It happens to connect all the fencing that confines the mortal horses and livestock. There will be pandemonium in the morning. We hop off our horses and their tack disappears.

"Dreamer," Artemis admonishes the paint mare with mock severity.

"Go have some fun," I tell them. They gallop off as a group and I immediately start thinking of excuses to get them out of trouble later after the war counsel. Stormy is the king of tricks. Sometimes I regret naming him Stormy Night and wish I had called him Mischief Maker. Evan, Artemis, Athena, and Emerald are stopped outside the tent by the guards, but I pass unquestioned and they stand at attention with a hand on their sword hilts in a salute. Only the senior war commanders are allowed inside. I step under the low opening and the men look up from a large map on the table.

"Get out! Only senior war commanders are allowed here. You are not welcome! How did you get through the guards?" Zeus demands angrily.

"Well, they stood at attention and saluted me as I walked in, so I rather believe I have been welcomed. However, if you do not want me here, I will go. You must be informed though, I *am* a senior war commander," I respond mildly. Zeus stiffens suddenly and a puzzled expression crosses his face.

"I know that voice, but that is impossible. I was told that she was dead," he says softly to the men in the tent.

"Reveal your identity, stranger," a deep voiced knight with a dark green and tan coat of arms, demands of me. I slowly pull off my drab colored cloak and a gasp ripples around the room when they see I am a woman. My unique silver armor glows in the torch lit space.

"My name is Elren Caerin. Some may know me better as the Shadow Warrior. However, we have more important things to do than squander precious time discussing this. Chaos will be arriving with his army the day after tomorrow. I hope you will accept my assistance. If I dare say so myself, you will not regret it." They still stare at me in shock. I continue to talk while I have their attention and have not been bombarded with questions.

"The Arélian army is on their way. I have started the mobilization of their available forces. They will all be here tomorrow with a little over one hundred thousand men at arms and knights. You have my word on that. King Rylan will arrive early tomorrow. He is also their war leader, just like all of you. I have special friends who will aid me in a force that I have specifically handpicked. I hope you will not mind, but I do not stand under anyone. No one has ever been able to tell me what to do, so please do not try to order me around. I apologize in advance for any offence this might cause. I know you are all kings and I will consider what you tell me, but ultimately, I do not serve anyone. Now," I clasp my hands together, "any questions?" I don't allow my weariness to show, and heavens forbid that it surfaces, my temper. My fuse starts to grow short as they continue to stare at me like they have all lost their minds. Finally, Zeus breaks the long silence.

"Elren," he whispers. "Elren has returned to us?" I nod.

"Aye." He has been told my history and he understands what this means. He was in the dungeon as well that day. I nod a greeting to Chiron. The old centaur gravely nods back.

"My good comrades, this is the best news we could ever have hoped to receive. The one we all believed was dead, and the one who was our only hope against Chaos has miraculously come back to us." The other knights cheer loudly and rejoice.

"This is King Alonso with the bear, King Clément with the tree, King Spirus with the she-wolf, Emperor Cloepatricus with the umm... odd eye symbol, and King Androcles with the olive branch. These are all the rulers we could gather. It is terrible, but Chaos has wiped out all the other kingdoms. Only ruins are left from them. Diran and Endír have refused to help in aiding us in the war."

"Fools. Just because they live on land separate from us doesn't make them safe," I intone crossley.

"We only have three hundred fifty thousand men, four hundred thousand counting the Olympians who can fight, and the ones who cannot, such as Hestia, the Goddess of the Hearth and Home, have volunteered to help the wounded. The centaurs and the Olympians with horses will be among the cavalry." He spreads his hands. "That is as far as we have come."

"We have a lot to do then." With magic, I switch my armor into the clothes of a normal soldier. Tan breeches tucked into knee high soft leather boots with a dark gray shirt. An unadorned leather belt holds my sword and dagger while my longbow and quiver peek over my left shoulder. I stride over to the table and Zeus and the kings follow.

"I say that we should make a long line across the narrowest part about a quarter of a mile to the east from here. It is only three hundred, to four hundred yards across. Each king will have a section with all his warriors. I could take the farthest left wing point," King Clément offers. I look at the map thoughtfully. *That could work, but we need another element.* I sweep my hand across the place he had said and my magic draws each king's army and where they would be. They study it for a moment before King Alonso adds a suggestion.

"We should stagger the men so that we have a few extra lines of defense. Behind the men, the trebuchets, ballistae, and catapults could be launching over them. These New Worlders do not have defenses except maneuverability against our heavy weapons. I have a feeling that there will be a lot of weapons we are familiar fighting against, but they also have their new weapons, guns and stuff like that. Many good warriors will fall to them. Heavy weapons will crush their, um, oh, what are those infernal things called, right! Vehicles and cars! Our heavy weapons will crush those. Can those with magic assist with threats we cannot stop?" King Alonso asks and they all look at me. I nod thoughtfully.

"I should be able to take care of any threats that are major, but my attention and energy will be on different things. I must save the bulk of my energy for last resorts, but yes, if there is a crisis, I will deal with it or send someone else who is capable. I will have to face Chaos myself in the end and that will require all my strength and attention. Fortunately, the war will stop while that duel happens. If he wins, keep fighting. The idea with the catapults, ballistae, and trebuchets is excellent and should definitely be employed. Those need to be put in place tomorrow." I draw them in behind the armies. Looking at it, the kings can't seem to find anything else, but King Spirus has one more addition

"Each army should send their cavalry first before we are hit too hard." We all nod in agreement.

"Aye, we should," King Androcles says for everyone.

"I have only one more simple idea to improve this, but it may be very important. Chiron, can you afford losing two hundred centaurs? It would be an incredible asset to have one hundred archers a side firing on our enemies. Apollo and Artemis could command the companies on each side. The reason I say centaurs is because they are faster and more familiar with being in the woods should any soldiers branch off and attack them."

"It will be a loss to my force, but one that is necessary. That could help even the numbers." The archers appear on the giant map and I eye our defenses.

"We are fighting purely a defensive battle. This is our only chance. The setup we have now is as good as possible. Now we must stay to it and hope that luck is on our side." I slap a hand on the table as a thought hits me.

Just a tiny detail.

"I have befriended two dragons. They will fight on our side against the New Worlders." They stare at me with amazement, temporarily lost for words. Suddenly, shouting and yelling comes from outside the tent. I frown and turn around to leave. I can guess who is behind this and he has terrible timing. "Thank you for your time," I call as I exit the tent. They are still staring at me like I am absolutely mad.

My friends are gone, probably pitching our camp. Men are all running toward the center of the camp. I follow them and suddenly they all stop. I shove through them and wrinkle my nose at the scent of strong ale and unwashed bodies.

A giant circle is around twenty or so immortal horses and I groan when I recognize four of them and I can't find one. Angry yells come from the crowd, but some are of amazement. I follow their gazes as they look up and sigh. *Found him.*

Looks like my horse discovered his magic. He really does have awful timing. This is not what our warriors need before going into battle soon. Stormy flies above everyone, showing off to the crowd. Magical white wings sprout from his shoulders and he swoops down and steals various items from the soldiers. I angrily stride out into the cleared space and suddenly all eyes are on me. A girl in a warrior's clothes. Probably the only one they have ever seen. Hopefully not the last. I fix a glare on all of them.

"Silence!" I call. I am not very loud, but my voice cuts through the din of voices. They all suddenly fall quiet. "I am a senior war commander. My name is Elren Caerin, or as you would better know me, the Shadow Warrior. Now, I order you to tell me, *What the heck is happening here?*" I demand. After a long moment one speaks up.

"These hosses been pullin' bad jokes on us." It takes me a moment to figure out what he said, but in the end I get it. Despite the mob of angry group of armed men, I have to fight to keep a smile off my face.

"Very well. I will send them back to their owners to be punished." I turn to the group of completely unrepentant horses. "All of you, return to your owners and explain what happened here. From here on out, no more pranks." I switch to telepathic so only they can hear me.

"*If you pull any more tricks, just don't get caught!*" They gallop off in different directions.

"You four, stay here! *Freedom's Stormy Night!* Get down here! Now!" I snap, using his full name. Sensing that this time I am serious, he dives down quickly and softly lands, his wings disappear.

"Warriors, return to your tents!" They all hurry away and soon the camp is quiet again. I glance at the position of the moon and stars. It is a little past midnight. All my energy leaves in a rush and I vault onto Stormy's back.

"Let's go to our camp." Stormy suddenly lurches off the ground and wings made up of white magic unfurl from his shoulders. He soars high in the air and I can see the war camp below. An idea forms in my head.

"I am riding Enbarr into battle, because you will be my eyes from above. I want you to stay high up in the air so you can see how it is progressing. Emerald will be on your back. This will help keep her safe as well." He nods and suddenly dives straight down and I tighten my grip on his barrel with my legs to avoid falling off. The other horses are in front of a small campfire with four figures huddled next to it. Five small tents are set up on the edge of the woods.

"So, they were not exaggerating," Artemis remarks dryly, watching Stormy proudly pull the magic back.

"What is the plan?" Athena asks. I quickly sketch the map we had been looking at earlier in the dirt before bidding them goodnight and heading into my tent. I leave them there studying the plan. Soon I crawl into the low-ceilinged structure and fall asleep quickly with the thoughts of us actually being able to pull off a win. A voice deep inside of me quietly tells me that it is not possible.

I tell it to shut up.

Chapter Twenty-Five

Shadow

Before the first light of dawn even thinks about peeking over the mountains, I am already leading the teams of cyclops as they pull the heavy, long range missile launchers, four to a trebuchet and two per ballista. We have twenty trebuchets and fifty ballistae. I range them around where our men will be fighting for their lives the next day. Despite the heavy loads that the giant cyclops are pulling, Stormy has to canter for us to stay in front of them.

After a good night of solid and uninterrupted sleep, I am completely refreshed. All my muscles hum with strength and energy, while nerves bunch my stomach into knots. Everything is under way and moving smoothly, but every time I look into the distance, I can see Chaos's huge army. They are coming.

Time passes quickly and when I pause for lunch, the soldiers all edge away from me when I sit with them. I try to engage them in light conversation, but they are in awe of me and my lofty status as a commander creates an image of someone who is conceited and irritating. However, they slowly warm up to me and I find out that they are from the same area as where I grew up. One has two little girls at home and a wife. He came to protect them. His wife knows that he will not be coming home again. Tears fill his eyes and I comfort him as best as I can.

I lead the different armies into position in the afternoon. They lounge around and play different games to pass the time. I only briefly see my other friends. We are all incredibly busy. Seeing each other for the first time today, Artemis and I lead the centaurs into position in the woods in the evening. Surefire and Stormy amiably walk together as we talk.

"How are you?" she asks suddenly. I look at her. Stress weighs heavily on her. She looks older than before.

"I'm fine. How about you?" I answer carefully, knowing that any second she could explode. Artemis hesitates and gives me a side glance.

"I'm concerned about you," she finally says. When I look at her quizzically, she continues. Her silvery eyes reflect the setting sun. "I lost you once already. I can't lose you again. You have never actually beaten Chaos before. What is to say you will tomorrow?" she says the last bit in a rush. I know she has waited a long time to ask this. I look away.

"How is your side?" I ask in response.

"Don't change the subject!" she yells angrily. "What is different this time? People are counting on you! You are just going to face him because of your pride! Why is this going to be any different from the past few times, Shadow? How? Tell me this! Please! I must know!" The centaurs look at her as her voice suddenly becomes loud. I watch the sun as it dips lower behind the horizon. I can see Chaos's army as it casts dreadful shadows far ahead of them. Slowly, I begin to answer her question, weighing my words carefully.

"I am no longer Shadow, Artemis. I am Elren," I remind her softly. "Elren was beaten only once and it was a one-sided fight. She won many of her battles against Draemir. It was many archers and Chaos against me as I tried to protect innocent animals. Elren was only beaten, while Shadow was slain. I had hidden my true self, therefore weakening myself. Elren is who I am. Also, this time I will be going into a fight with him knowingly, not being surprised. I can go in believing that I will win. I am not fighting him for my pride. I am fighting Chaos for the people he has murdered, for their families, and for the young boys and girls he has robbed a future from and lastly, I am fighting for all those who could be harmed by him in future, whoever they may be. My friends and my enemies alike," I say quietly.

She takes a few minutes to process this. Finally, she says, "Alright. I think I understand. This must be done, but I will rather irritated if this goes wrong."

"You know, I don't think I will be too happy if it goes wrong either." A ghost of a smile crosses my face. "So, how is your side?"

"As good as can be. It is now just a nasty bruise, and I bet we will all have quite a few of those by this time tomorrow night." I catch the underlying message that remains unsaid. *If we are still around tomorrow.* We station the archers and head out. They will be the safest ones on the battlefield.

"Artemis, you and Apollo are leading the centaurs tomorrow. Emerald and Stormy will be above the battlefield. They are our eyes above. I also hope that this will keep her safe." Artemis nods agreement.

"I have to go. There are one thousand and one more things left to do. See you later." Surefire gallops ahead from an unspoken cue. I take a deep breath and bury my face in my hands, trying to ease a headache that's been growing throughout the day.

"Let's see how far away Chaos is." Stormy rears and jumps into the air. We fly for a few miles before we are directly above them. Cries of alarm ring through the camp when soldiers spot us. We don't respond. After a few passes, we head back. I am required to give a speech to our warriors tonight at dinner. I have no idea what I am supposed to say. It's not like they want to hear my prediction of our chances for success.

When we fly over our camp, cheers greet us and the knights clash their swords together. I jump off Stormy from about ten feet above the ground so he doesn't have to land and he goes and performs aerial tricks to entertain the men. Any grudges they had against him with the tricks he pulled are gone tonight as he takes their minds off the upcoming battle. I head to the cook and I'm surprised by the ration size. Two large chunks of chicken with cooked greens, a hard biscuit with sweet jam, and a mug of ale.

"Commander Caerin," he addresses me formally.

"Thank you, sir." The heavy-set cook grunts in reply and I move out of line for him to serve the next person. Here it seems more like a festival than the night before battle. It hits me hard that many of the men who I have spoken too or guided in sword work will not see another dinner, or remember the names of their friends. Many are destined to die. That applies to me as well. The fates made it clear that either my brother or me will survive. Not both. It is one or the other.

Later, I head to the front of the gathered men. I stand there silently and wait for them to fall quiet. While they are speaking, I study the men, it is clear who the peasants are in contrast to the wealthy noblemen and knights. All the knights and wealthy men have a horse, shiny armor, and well-crafted weapons. The peasants and commoners have scraps of older armor and have the regular utilitarian spears and swords that were handed out. There are gaps in the lines where the different armies have separated to stand under their king's standard. Finally, I have everyone's attention.

"Warriors, tomorrow we enter the last battle of this war. Look to the person on your right, and look at the one on your left. You may never see them alive again. Tonight may very well be your own last night. It could be my last night, it could be anyone's last night, it could be everyone's last night, so just remember to enjoy yourselves. Enjoy the company of your friends, or talk with someone you have never met and try and find something you can relate to. I do not want any fights tonight. Remember to be kind to everyone. Your harsh words to them may be the last thing you ever have a chance to say to them. Say what you want said to you. Now, on a happier note, I have a few instructions before you get back to your festivities." Not a sound is made as they wait to hear what I have to say. Their eyes practically beg for a more pleasant ending to my speech.

"Hope is your best friend on the battlefield. She will keep up your spirits and enable you to perform better. I am known for my unwarlike battle cry, dum vivo, spero. While I live, I hope. Hope is the guiding light that will take you out of trouble. May you all catch her, and never let her go. Good night, everyone. Positions an hour before dawn, please. I will see you there. Dum vivo, spero!" I head off to my tent, but before I can get there a young page intercepts me.

"I am sorry Commander Caerin, but the senior war council summons you. They have urgent information."

After recovering from my initial surprise and irritation, I reply calmly, "Alright, thank you. I will head there straight away." I begin to run with long, effortless strides to the command tent. Once again, the guards step aside and allow me to enter. The kings all look up and the frantic tension in the room startles me so much that my sword is out of its sheath in an instant. "What has happened here?" I ask warily. Zeus hastens to placate me.

"Oh, nothing is attacking us yet, but we have other problems. Brother? Would you care to explain your issue?" Poseidon steps forward and any less of a man would have wilted under the furious glare Zeus gives him. I can practically see the bolts of lightning flaring from his eyes.

"My greatest apologies, Commander, but I will not allow my mortal creations to fight in the war. No horses will take part in combat. That is my final word. You will simply have to make do without cavalry." I frown thoughtfully and puzzle through what he says before speaking.

"Your concern has a lot of merit. I agree with you, sir." The kings and Zeus regard me in shock.

"You *agree* with him? It will weaken our attack by a tenfold! How are we supposed to fight?"

"On the contrary, it may prove to be good strategy. They would simply have shot the horses out from under the men and we would have lost thousands of kind, loyal, gentle, and honest horses. That would have been nothing short of murder on both of our parts. We will still have our immortal horses. They cannot be injured or killed. Their riders can act as our mounted force if necessary. Now, I still have much to do, so I beg your pardon, but I must go. Good night." I disappear out the door, leaving them staring after me in surprise of my quick entrance and departure. Once outside, I feel like I can breathe again. Just like a wraith, I sprint through the maze-like setup of tents, dodging inebriated warriors. Finally, I burst out of the human and Olympian tents and enter the refuge of the dense forest.

After many miles of flying through the woods like a bird, I slow to a stop and look around the small clearing. Everything is so peaceful. As usual, whenever I find myself alone in the woods, a new energy hums through me. *Woodland Warrior, Wild Heart, and Creature of the Woods.* With all the titles I already have, why give me one more? Why must I be the Shadow Warrior? I prefer my other titles better. I kneel and redraw my sword. I give myself a small cut and with my own blood on the tip, I stick it deep into the ground point first.

"I give myself to your mercy, powerful and kind woods. Please protect me, for though I bow to no one, I give myself to you. Use me as you see fit. Whether it is for me to live or to die, it is your decision, Wise mother of all the woodland creatures, I give myself to you." Closing my eyes, I hold the pommel of my sword and breathe deeply, opening all my

senses. Slowly, my ears can catch the soft lullabies of the trees as they prepare to wake from their long slumber as spring arrives and warms them again with her gentle hand. I can smell the wood smoke in the breeze as the campfires slowly smolder into the night. The air holds many secrets. The dense and heavy smell tells me that we will be receiving the last real snow of the year soon.

"*Take your sword, Wild Heart. You have nothing to fear from me. I have watched you come and offer yourself to me your entire life, but this is the first time I have spoken to you. You are true at heart and respect those whom you should. Nature, those weaker, and those who are of strong spirit. They are the only ones that you serve. I am honored that you chose to pledge yourself to me. The air and land speak of your great deeds. Keep your eyes closed and follow my instructions.*" Almost in a trance, I stand and withdraw my sword from the soft ground. I cannot feel the cold anymore. "*Rise, my Woodland Warrior. Sword ready, up hand strike, followed by a feint side-cut, reverse it and feint a cut on the left, thrust, parry, switch hands and repeat.*" I do as ordered and the pattern becomes progressively faster and more complex.

Sweat oils my muscles and I feel like I could fly, but some place inside me continues to feel anchored to the ground. Peace is what I breathe in and it surrounds me. My sword feels light in my grip and everything feels surreal. I move faster than I ever have before while keeping my mind blank. All thoughts of the war are gone. All my fears are alleviated and resolved. There is only me, my sword, and the mother of the woods. Faster and faster. My sword and I are in a graceful dance of movement and flickering moonlight.

A story is told through movements, creating a web of lovely and deadly patterns and steps. Something wild and free has been unleashed in me. I feel as if I am dancing to the music of the woods. The beautiful and wild sounds of a bone flute mingling with a pan, the graceful strumming of a harp and a lyre create a backdrop melody while a fast and incredible beat of a hand drum sets the tempo. I am no longer grounded. Something inside of me has changed. Light as any bird, deadly as any predator, and joyful as any animal who lives under the expanse of green leaves, I am part of the forest. All too soon, on a dramatic last note, the singing forest falls silent again.

"Open your eyes, Wild One. Your people are here." I slowly open my eyes and look around. Spirits fill the woods around me. All of them are smiling with tears in their eyes and awe on their faces. In the forefront, I can see Evan and Emerald's parents. There are also other men, women, and children.

"These are all the men, women, and children who have been wrongfully slain by the evil beast called Draemir. Here we have our peace and our hope, he is disorder and discontent. We are counting on you. This is our gift from the forest." I look down at myself and gasp in shock. Right over where my heart is, a three-pronged maple leaf symbol is branded onto my skin in the green ink of the forest. A simple necklace with a small stone oak leaf hangs from my neck. *"They will protect you and prove to the world that you are a creature of the woods and that you belong to us, and us to you. The necklace will never part from you."* In a breath of wind, I am clothed in a beautifully patterned dark green tunic with soft hide leggings. Leaves are depicted in silver across the entire outfit. My leather boots also carry the patterns.

"Thank you," I reply in awe.

"Every time you enter the woods anywhere, this will magically replace whatever you are wearing and nothing will ever harm you inside my trees. You bear our mark. This has never been given before. You are our protector. Bear this burden well, Elren Caerin, The Shadow Warrior,

Wild Heart, Woodland Warrior, and the Creature of The Woods. Prepare yourself for great loss tomorrow. However, when you feel as if you have lost everything, remember us here in the woods. We will always stand behind you."

Then it is gone. The spirits vanish with a last wave and the Mother of The Woods falls quiet. I look down at Tíne and see that it too bears the mark of the forest. The leaf pattern runs down the blade. Once more, I kneel before my sword and simply close my eyes and listen, keeping my mind peaceful and blank. The forest sighs gently and I stay there all night. I am neither awake, nor asleep. I am just there... listening and breathing.

My mind wanders far afield as I slowly walk back through the woods towards the camp. Everyone is gone. Only my tent and belongings are still there. A medic tent has been set up instead of the command tent. I pack up my stuff, but leave it all just inside the trees. If things go wrong, I won't ever need it again. Quickly adjusting my quiver and bow, I head out for the field. The sky has yet to show any signs of dawn, but I know all of our warriors will be there. This is the last morning for many of these men. It could be my last morning as well. Strangely enough, this does not bother me.

Noise fades out and everything slows down. All I can hear is my heart beating in my chest and my breath as it steadily goes in and out. All my nerves are gone. For the first time, I have completely mastered myself.

Sound suddenly assaults my ears, breaking through my thin layer of peace. The clanking of armor sounds through the camp as the warriors walk around. The nervous rasp of sharpening stones against blades sounds a wakeup call. Unlike last night, there is a sad and heavy atmosphere as the men reflect upon their lives and why they are fighting. Many whisper prayers and say encouragement to themselves as they slowly trudge through the dewy fields. Too many look for courage in their flasks of ale. I can't really blame them though. Soon I find my friends where they are sitting together in a small group. No one speaks, but a companionable silence resonates between them. I silently walk up and sit between Evan and Emerald.

"It is time," I say softly. I take Emerald and Evan's hands and they take Artemis and Athena's. Together we all let magic run through us and armor covers us. I guide Emerald's magic and show her how to change her hunting clothes to armor. Impulsively, I light my hand with ice blue fire and hold it out in the middle of the circle. Evan does the same with sapphire blue magic. Emerald green, rich gold, and bright silver joins the group. The different colored magic combines and turns it all a pure white as all that power mixes. I look each one in the eyes and they all steadily look back at me.

"Tempus venit, the time has come," Evan repeats my earlier statement. We all say our goodbyes as if none of us are going to see each other again. Artemis heads off with the archers and Apollo while Athena heads to Zeus's side where she will fight and provide counsel.

Surefire and Morningsun turn and rear to us. Lyr, Apollo's dark bay mare, the one the bards all mistake for a musical instrument, also turns and rears straight up. Her thin white blaze glows in the early morning light and her lively brown eyes dance. All our horses do the same and we salute them. I fold Emerald in a crushing embrace.

"You are the best little sister anyone could ever hope to have and I am proud to say that you are my apprentice. You have more courage than you could ever need. All you have to do is believe in yourself and you are all set. If I do not return from battle, I want you to keep fighting." I tap the inside of her wrist and she looks at the runes there. "When you are in your darkest times, look at this and take heart. Courage is what comes once you have peeled away all your excuses and after you have fallen, but refuse to stop trying to get up. This is what defines you. I am so proud to call you my sister and I hope you know that. Please, whatever happens, remember that." She nods and hugs me back.

"Please come back to me. I cannot bear losing you again," she whispers in my ear. I smooth her hair back and kiss her gently on the forehead, but I do not answer her soft plea. She slowly walks over to Stormy and swings up into his saddle. I wave as Stormy takes off, unfurling his magical wings.

Finally, only Evan and I stand there. For a few seconds, we simply stare at each other, before he draws me closer. I can feel his soft breath and smell the sweet scent of horses on his tunic. He whispers quietly, "I love you, Elren. Ever since the first time I saw you, I knew I loved you. You were this beautiful and mysterious girl and you wield a sword better than any man ever could. There is something so wild, so free and untamed about you that instantly caught my heart and never left my thoughts. At school, they called me names because I had a hard time focusing on anything else. You were always in the forefront of my mind and recently, when I thought I had lost you, I was lost too. You are my North Star. My guiding light. Be safe today. I love you too much to lose you again."

"I love you too, Evan Faelin, my fierce Wolf Warrior. Let's go show Chaos that he messed with the wrong people." I smile and mount Enbarr. When I am on, his silver armor covers his vulnerable spots. Rivermist does the same thing and side-by-side, we gallop to the head of the army with Zeus, Poseidon, and Athena. Evan stops, but I keep going. Joan of Arc in her purple armor, Urduja in bright yellow armor, and Han E. Lee in gold and red armor and their majestic horses stand in the middle of the field. Enbarr puts on the brakes suddenly and slides to a stop in front of them.

"You came?" I ask in surprise, but not unhappily.

"Of course!" Joan replies enthusiastically. "Wouldn't miss a good fight!" The others nod in agreement. I look up and smile when I see two other familiar faces. Relan and Laidena appear from the sky. Relan has become much larger in a very small amount of time. They land and the earth shakes. Here are the last of the dragons, the most powerful beasts ever to walk the earth. They are fighting for us. Shouts of amazement and alarm come from the ranks of soldiers behind us at the sight of two twenty feet long dragons.

"We are here to serve, Commander," Laidena says after neatly tucking in her wings and landing in front of me. Relan, however, does not pull off the same move so well. She lands with a crash that jars my teeth and sends shock waves through my body. *Ouch.* That had to hurt. She embarrassedly gets up and shakes herself off before joining us. She is almost the same size as her mother, but doesn't have nearly the same level of grace. Her different shades of green scales shimmer in the first bleak light of a wintry dawn. We have no time for pleasantries.

"Relan, you will stay above the fighting and be my eyes above with Stormy and Emerald. You know what my magic is like. If you see any breaches in our defense or if one side starts to buckle, contact me. Laidena," I address the bigger dragon with the iridescent rainbow colored scales, "will you help in the medic tent? You are excellent at healing. This will be a two-part battle; if I know my brother well enough, he will want a midday break if it lasts that long. I will need you fresh for the second part of the day. We will have taken on massive losses by then and you will provide the men with renewed hope and courage."

She bows her head in deference before taking off. I summon Stormy and he comes galloping up, with Emerald halfway in the saddle. All of us stifle laughter as Emerald comes up swearing and making angry insults at Stormy for taking off like that. He stops next to me and affectionately nibbles at my knee. He turns and stares at Emerald innocently and jumps sideways, pretending to spook at something. She comes off with a muffled thud and a curse or two. *I think I needed to watch my language a bit more around her when she was young.* I look at her in surprise when she mutters one of my choice phrases that is not quite smiled upon in public. The irresponsible part of me is impressed by her new vocabulary, but the older sister and master part is the one that speaks.

"Guard your tongue more carefully, youngling, or I might tell Stormy to do this again when you are unsuspecting." She looks down, abashed, when she notices the three powerful warriors behind me. Her face turns a bright shade of crimson.

"Sorry," she apologizes meekly.

"Where would a beautiful young girl like yourself learn such phrases?" Joan asks curiously. I can tell that she too is impressed by Emerald's expanded vocabulary. I look away and pretend to study Chaos's army when suddenly, something actually catches my eye. I squint at the figure before my eyes focus. A lone rider gallops across the narrow girthed plain and I recognize the deep-sea-blue horse from my nightmares. It is Chaos himself.

"We must return to our positions immediately," I suddenly announce, interrupting their discussion. They follow my gaze and understand. Laidena takes off and heads to the medic tent, but swoops low over the horse and it screeches to a stop in fear until the awesome dragon is gone. Stormy takes to the sky and Relan follows. I can hear the three chatting and doing quick introductions as they hover above the army.

334

Urduja, Han, Joan, and I gallop to the head of the armies in the dead center.

I raise a hand and stop all the questions and let my new companions explain. With a small tap on Enbarr's barrel, I send him galloping out to intercept Chaos where I expect he will offer a chance of surrender and declare war, or just attempt to cut me down right then. My mouth goes dry at the idea. The only time I wanted to see that bastard was on the end of my sword. I focus my attention to my ears and block out everything else, even though my eyes still watch him approach.

Our armor rings and hums in an unnatural way. While most metals scrape and clang, our magical silver armor sings its own ethereal song and battle cry. My chainmail clinks pleasantly as it brushes against itself. The wind whispers in my ears. Scraps of music and poetry, along with quiet words of wisdom, warnings, and encouragement. The peace I discovered last night still sings in my blood and I feel calm, yet ready for action at the same time. With a twitch on my reins, Enbarr slides to a halt and we wait for my brother to arrive. I close my eyes and focus on everything around me. Enbarr stomps impatiently, shaking our armor and sending its enchanting music through me. I breathe deeply and smell the wet and cold air surrounding me.

Pounding hooves fill my ears and I feel myself start to tremble with tension and slight fear, but I quell it immediately. The sound abruptly falls off and I open my eyes and look at the man five feet across from me. Clean shaven with a thin scar on his left cheek that draws its way down to his jaw. It makes me smile.

I gave it to him.

Deep-sea-blue eyes are under slanting dark eyebrows. High cheekbones and a sharp, angular face. I recognize many of the same traits in myself. The only differences are that my eyes are ice-blue and my hair is light brown and golden, where his is dark brown and black. He is the true son of the Dark, while I am the daughter of the Light. His eyes grow large for a moment when he sees that the rumors are true. I still live.

"So, you have finally reclaimed your true name, Elren Caerin."

"I see you have not, Draemir," I reply calmly. This is the first time since I was young that I have used his real name. Enbarr of the Flowing Mane and Kelpie of the Deep stand at the same massive height and just like Draemir and I; they too are twins in everything except color and ethics. They eye each other with absolute loathing and contempt, their proud faces are fierce and wild with hate.

"You have grown up, sister. Good idea if you plan on lasting past the first blow from my sword, Dortcha." I simply look at him with one eyebrow raised in contempt until he looks away, his cheeks flushed slightly.

"What do you want?" I ask pointedly. "I'm tired of this talking."

"Surrender now and save thousands of lives. I have over one million men here who have come to take this land. If your followers stand aside, they will not be harmed and all the humans will be given a chance to live together in harmony. You and I could rule these inferior people together. No one would ever dare to oppose us."

I sigh sadly. "I was hoping you could have come up with something new. You always say that. You know, the first time we broke apart and had our first confrontation when we were young, you asked the same thing. I give you the exact wording that I used then, I will never allow the New Worlders to raze my home land. We may be siblings, but we will never be true family. I could never claim a family member who wishes only to kill and destroy everything so that he can get what he wants. So, my answer still stands and it also sounds better repeated over again than your hopeless plea. You may as well ask a wall your query. It would not give a response instead of one you have heard before." His face has been growing increasingly furious and his eyes spark and flare with fire just like mine do.

"You chose to be captain of this sinking ship, and the captain always goes down with it. I will see you later and for the last time." He throws a bolt of magic at me which I match with one of my own and the deep-sea-blue and ice-blue magic grapple with each other for a few seconds before dispersing into words that everyone on both sides can read.

LET THE BATTLE BEGIN

Chapter Twenty-Six

Shadow

We both race our horses back to our own armies. I magically amplify my voice so that all my men can hear my words.

"Stand fast and be brave of heart! Death in battle is the highest honor for a warrior. Fight for the man next to you, fight for yourself, and fight for your land. First Chaos wanted me, then he wanted my friends. Now... now he wants my world. Our world! Dum vivo, spero! Fight honorably!" I cry. As one they yell it back defiantly. Their voices reach all the way to Draemir's army as they begin their organized charge.

Strange fortified vehicles crawl on weird treads like giant lizards. I count only twenty of them and I gesture to the powerful Olympians behind me. Each sends a bolt of magic toward each vehicle and they explode into fire. All twenty are gone quickly and as each one disappears, our men cheer raucously.

Soon smaller things take their place and move around quickly on two wheels. I signal the men on the ballistae and they fire when I drop my hand. Seventeen of the two-wheel vehicles suddenly spin out and throw the riders far away. Agonized screams fill my ears and I wince.

They keep sending out different types of vehicles to no gain. Each type falls to either magic or our heavy battery of heavy projectiles. Something feels off to me. My brother is smarter than this. *What is he playing at?* I turn to consult Athena, but she wordlessly points behind me and when I turn back, I see at least five hundred thousand men charging our ranks. Suddenly, they start to fall as arrows fly from the uncanny accurate centaur bows and as Artemis and Apollo direct the fire. Arrows relentlessly pour into their ranks, but they keep coming. I unsling my bow from my shoulders and quickly pick off the faster men who had gotten ahead of the trotting group of organized soldiers.

They split into five groups, each one about one hundred thousand strong. *Dum vivo, spero.* I clap my heels to Enbarr's side and he leaps forward, charging the massive group who dared to attack my people and my land. I hear rattling as their puny guns fire at us and the small metal bullets bounce off my armor. They draw their swords too late and before the first man can get his sword unsheathed, twenty lie dead. I am the first to draw blood in this battle. They surround me, but I am unperturbed. So far, none of them have been good swordsmen. My sensitive ears can hear the cries of my men as they fall to various attacks.

An irritating buzz stings down my spine and limbs and I spot four men aiming strange yellow things at us. Tasers. Enbarr and I stride forward and easily wipe them out. Time has no meaning in a battle. All I know is that many of my men have fallen, but many of my brother's force has fallen as well. Our men are far superior in their combat skills and our armor is far better suited to protect us than theirs. My men do not fall as often as the New Worlders, but the biggest problem is that Chaos can afford these losses, we can't. Every warrior we lose makes a difference.

"Elren! Our right flank is being beaten back. They are quickly losing men and the invaders are making quick work of them!" Emerald shouts telepathically. I flinch at the noise and a bullet flies past my head, leaving a long and deep cut across my cheek in its wake. Not a mortal wound, but very irritating. I quickly heal it and Enbarr gallops through the soldiers. I watch them fall quickly as he strikes any in his path. *Such a pitiful way to die.*

Battle madness threatens to overwhelm me, but I cleanse my mind of the repulsive urge for destruction and death. It is still too early to lose myself. That is a last resort that no human army can withstand, but it is one that I could never live with after the battle has ended. I reach the far left flank and yell as loud as I can. King Clément is still fighting, but he is bleeding profusely from a mortal wound to his side. When he sees me, a look of relief crosses his face and he smiles.

"Lead them well," he says calmly, and then he falls to the ground. Two blood-streaked men proudly carry their fallen king off the field.

"Charge, men! Take heart!" I lead them and Enbarr and I surge forward against the New World soldiers. King Clément's men hesitate for a second, before one or two especially brave men join the fray of flying arrows, bullets, and hacking swords. Soon the others see how the bullets ricochet off their armor without harm and see how easily their comrades cut through their ranks. With a shout, the rest join in, savage and terrified cries mingle in the air and they make my ears throb. I fight my way over to the trees where the battle line stops.

"*How is the battle going for us?*" I ask Emerald and Stormy. In answer, they swoop down and land next to me and Enbarr.

"I can't tell. I don't have enough experience to tell how it is going. We are not caving in yet, but we are not gaining ground. Many good men have fallen." I nod slowly as I mull this over.

"Okay, thank you. You are going to be needed in the medical tent. Take a break. I will take your place in the sky. I fear the battle is not going well. While we still hold them here, one breach and they could pour in on us. Then it is only a matter of time before we are vanquished. I just hope we can hold them off long enough to reach the midday break." I look at Emerald more closely. Her face is pale and drawn and her eyes seem to be replaying the horrors that she saw on the battlefield. I force her to lock eyes with me.

Her expression relaxes as my magic swirls through her like a balm before disappearing. She shivers slightly, but her eyes clear and she gives me a shaky smile when I ask if she is alright.

"We can talk later. For now though, go get Apollo and both of you are to use your magic to heal those that you can. I will see you later. Take Enbarr and he can help give you strength." She looks up at Enbarr's back and then the stirrup, which is at the tip of her fingers if she reaches a hand up. I smile. I had forgotten that while I am over six feet tall and built with long legs, Emerald is only a shade over five feet tall and of a petite build. Enbarr is huge by horse standards, at least eighteen hands, two inches. He has a normal sized barrel, but is a long-legged beast, built to run and to be strong. He looks down at Emerald and then back at me, surprised.

"How is this pipsqueak supposed to ride me?" he asks incredulously.

"Just take care of her and get her to the healers." He snorts doubtfully. I quickly swing my bow off my shoulder and send two arrows flying away. Three shouts meet my ears as bullets are intercepted by my arrows and two of Chaos' men fall dead all at the same time. Enbarr and Stormy bob their heads up and down in appreciation of the good shots.

"I remember when you could barely hit a tree from twenty meters with a twenty pound recurve bow," Enbarr comments dryly in Daenlir.

"I also remember when you were just a young colt and could barely gallop in a straight line and spooked at bushes and birds," I retort in the same language. He shakes his mane and laughs. We have grown up together and know each other too well.

"Just go," I laugh at him and pretend to slap him on the rump. He shakes his head in mock despair, but lowers himself on his forelegs like he is bowing. Even then, Emerald struggles to mount him. I quickly shorten the stirrups and he lurches back up onto all four.

"How is it up there?" I ask hiding another huge grin. She looks tiny up on his back.

"This feels very different!" She draws her sword as Enbarr takes off into the crowd of fighting warriors.

I hear rattling on my armor and feel multiple bites of their weapons. I jump sideways as a sword whistles down from behind me. I swing around with my bow still in my hand and it catches him in the face. He reels away from me clutching his nose, which is crooked and bleeding heavily. He waves a hand and dark, marbled gray magic fixes it. *Uh, oh.* Suddenly, a horse the same color as his magic appears by his side. The huge stallion rears and trumpets a challenge to Stormy. Stormy's ears flatten and I can see how much he longs to answer, but he defers to me first. I hold up a hand to him and study the pair.

The warrior looks nervous and beads of sweat break out above his brow. The horse, on the other hand, looks completely keyed up for a fight. However, I know Stormy's strength and prowess in battle. While he may appear fine boned, maybe even fragile, he is incredibly strong and fast on his feet. His reflexes and speed are second only to Enbarr. However, this horse also looks strong. It is heavily built like a war horse. It looks like an Andalusian cross. He is bigger than Stormy, both in height and width.

"*Can you beat him?*" I ask Stormy telepathically.

"*Yes,*" he replies calmly.

"*You may respond to the challenge. Teach him what a* real *immortal horse is capable of.*" Stormy lets loose a challenge that dwarfs a simple trumpet. His response is an entire symphony. His wings disappear and he charges the other horse. I quickly draw my sword and charge the warrior. His attention had been on the two horses, but suddenly he sees me and jumps into action. His two-handed broadsword parries mine away and he rapidly swings a counter move. I step back a pace to let the sword swing him off balance. These are simply the opening gambits.

He thrusts his blade in and it is a small matter to step sideways. The momentum of his thrust carries him onto the waiting edge of my sword and he only has a second before he realizes that he is dying. Without a word, he falls to the ground dead. I turn to see how Stormy is faring and have to leap sideways as the gray horse charges me in an attempt for revenge and to escape from Stormy. I grab Stormy by the mane as he begins to give chase. After dragging me a few paces, he skids to a stop and laughs.

"That will teach him not to insult me about having wings. I think he was jealous." After lengthening the stirrups back to my length, I swing aboard and he takes off above the fighting mass. We fly up high enough to see the extent of both armies and I am dismayed to see that while we may have taken out three quarters of the force Draemir sent, we lost over half of our men. I glance up at the sun. Midday will be here soon and I hope the first round of battle will end. Relan joins us in the air.

"It is looking bad. Urduja is the only thing holding our right flank together now while Joan and Han are holding the middle and left. The Olympians are falling in waves. I can only count twenty-four or so. The storm-spirits are a tough match for them. The ones who are still fighting are scattered among our ranks. We are still holding strong, but we will not be able to hold them much longer. The men are tiring quickly," she updates us on the situation.

Looking down, I can see the bright spots of our immortal warriors. Urduja's brilliant yellow armor is like a small version of the sun and as I watch she effortlessly dispatches three storm-spirits and one of the minor gods that sided with Chaos. I watch Emerald, Enbarr, Apollo, and Lyr finally break back through our defensive line and gallop to the medical tent. Hopefully she can save many, but will there be a point to it if we don't win? I do not know our enemy as well as a good commander should. I don't know how merciful they will be to captured prisoners of war. We must win, that is all that I know for certain. As I watch, I notice a quick falter in our enemy's movements. I study them carefully and see it again.

Suddenly, a loud horn blares and they attack even more fiercely. A deep humming noise meets my ears and I look out in front of us in surprise and freeze. I recall the name of them, but it is foreign on my tongue. War planes and helicopters fly towards Relan and I with incredible speed. With loud popping noises, strange things fly at us. I catch two on my shield simultaneously and my arm is blown backwards with terrible power. Stormy is sent reeling and drops at least fifty meters before catching himself. The muscles, tendons, and ligaments in my recently healed shoulder all shriek their protests at once.

A second volley comes and three hit me in the chest, making a deep ring and sending horrible vibrations through me. I feel a rib or two crack. One brushes the side of my exposed neck and creates a massive cut, sending blood pouring down the side of my armor and down my shirt under my armor. I quickly heal myself and look at Relan to make sure the young dragon is alright. As I watch, she heals a big gash in her vulnerable wing.

"Can you breathe fire yet?" I call to her. In response, she sends a giant jet of flames that engulfs four of the small helicopters, sending them plummeting to the ground. I gather some magic and send two bolts of pure energy in the planes' engines. They both explode, forcing me to raise a barrier of icy cold magic to ward off the heat and debris from Stormy and I. The heat doesn't bother Relan at all. None come to take their places in the sky.

"Warn me if any others come," I order Stormy before turning my attention to the battle below. Our archers continue to pour arrows in from both sides of the plain with uncanny distance and accuracy.

Soon, less than a quarter of the five hundred thousand my brother sent remain. At another blast from that irritating ram horn, they flee. With pressure from my knees, Stormy swoops closer and I drop my reins onto his neck before grabbing my bow and steadily start shooting. I can hear the empty rattle of a quiver less than half full behind me. Twenty men fall as silver and blue arrows fly from the sky before I reach for my last arrow. Carefully looking at all the men, I pick one out. He is faster, stronger, and taller than the others around him. When I switch into my magical vision, I can see a strong and disgusting shade of burgundy around him. He is not human.

I light the tip with magical fire. It catches him straight between the shoulder blades and with the magic, it cuts through his armor like butter. He slowly falls and trips multiple men in a chain reaction, leaving them as prey for the blood seeking arrows of the centaurs. I refill my quiver and start shooting quickly, picking out all his immortal storm spirits and the other servants of the Storm God, Leucetios.

Suddenly, I spot the imbecile himself. I grab one arrow from my quiver and load magic into the shaft. Carefully aiming, I take a deep breath in and on the exhale, I release smoothly. I send another after it immediately, but it is unnecessary. The first arrow flies true and punches through the fleeing Storm God's armor. He falls to the ground and is trampled. *Huh. I guess we do not disappear in a puff of magic when we are killed,* a strange part of my mind thinks. I shake my head to clear it and settle my longbow across the saddle pommel to access it quickly.

While I take a moment to heal my irritated shoulder, a magically amplified voice sounds across the mile of flat ground to what is left of our combined armies. It chills my bones and freezes my blood.

"You have four hours to tend to your wounded before I will personally finish your army and vanquish your greatest hero, The Shadow Warrior." Draemir suddenly addresses me directly. "Elren Caerin, I hope you do not have anything planned for tomorrow, because you will not see the next sunrise. You better cancel any dates you have! You have until late afternoon, sister. Use the time well. They will be your last memories." He laughs menacingly.

"Right back at you, Draemir Caerin. You should treasure your breaths, Brother, instead of wasting them on blasphemy. See you soon. Love you, too!" I call back. All my men laugh at my response and the furious growl from the leader of their enemies. Stormy lands softly and the remaining warriors return to their exact starting places and stand at attention behind their kingdoms standards, showing me the level of dedication they have. They will continue to fight until the bitter end. It deeply saddens me when I look at all the gaps in the line where brave, loyal, and caring men stood just hours ago. Three kings are missing and their heirs stand in their place.

"At ease men. You have fought well and have honored your family names. This is not encouraging, but our only options are victory, death, or agreeing to live peacefully among them. I fear that we cannot win against such unending numbers, but I plan to go down with as many as possible. I am honored to have fought alongside all of you, no matter what your path will be. Now is the time to relax and talk with your new and old friends, forged and solidified by the horror of battle. All of you must keep your heads high and never look down. Honor is all anyone will ever think of when they hear your names. Even when we all fade from memories, those of your bloodline in thousands of years to come will know that they are descendants of heroes. No matter what your past was like, good or bad, you stood in the line of battle and faced these strange and terrible enemies. Those who sought to make you below them failed. You are all extraordinary. Never forget that. Death is not defeat." I walk out onto the deserted battlefield where healers run back and forth, bearing litters with wounded men and hurrying back to the medical tent.

Many thousands of good men lie dead on the ground stained red by the blood that has already been shed. The New Worlders are also caring for their wounded soldiers and carrying them out of harm's way. There is no show of hostility between the ones trying to help the wounded. I join them and add my undiminished strength to their efforts. The New World healers flee when I am near, but I help them with their wounded as well. Go ahead and let people say what they want, but on the inside, I do hate to see a good person die because no one cared to come and help them. I help both sides and am gratified to see that many others are doing the same thing around me.

Time flies by with alarming speed and when I pause to check how long it has been, I am shocked to see that three hours have quickly skipped past without being noticed. I slip off to the healer's tent to check on my friends. Athena suffered multiple broken ribs, a broken leg, and a deep gash on her arm. I hurry over to her and smile in relief when I see that Emerald, Evan, and Artemis relatively unharmed. Morningsun stands wearily next to the cot with Athena.

Emerald worriedly beckons me over. Apollo is already trying to mend Athena's broken bones, but I can tell that he is exhausted. All of the magic healers look tired and haggard from the long day. I notice that most of them are women, but there are also a good amount of men helping as well. Apollo's knees suddenly buckle and Artemis quickly steadies her

347

twin. A deep part of me twinges. I wish *my* twin brother were as kind as Apollo is to Artemis and Artemis to him. Once, long, long ago, we were not enemies, but best friends. As much as I hate him now, a part of me wishes that the times could have changed and I could have the kind and caring brother back. I shove that feeling away. In about an hour, my twin and I will be trying our very best to kill each other. I walk over to Apollo, and Artemis steps back with the others.

"Use my strength and my magic to heal her," I offer. He looks at me in alarm. I have time to notice that his golden eyes are red rimmed with fatigue.

"No, you will need it for yourself. I should be able to handle this." I shake my head and smile.

"I have plenty of strength and magic, and you have the skill. Use my offer and heal our friend." He inhales deeply and finally agrees. I put my hand on the wiry god's shoulder and send my magic through him. Apollo shivers violently at the ice-cold magic, but continues nevertheless. In seconds, all of her ailments are gone. I send another burst of powerful magic for him to keep and use for himself before withdrawing. He gapes at me.

"Your magic is very, very, very cold," he finally manages to say through chattering teeth.

"I have heard that before. Never quite experienced it being cold, but I guess it is mine, so I would not feel it," I reply cheerfully.

"How are you so powerful? Your magic feels as if it is limitless."

"You are right," I reply simply. He continues to stare at me, before I point out the other men who need help. He walks off with a new spring in his step. His tall bay horse, Lyr, follows him. I offer Athena a hand and haul her up off the cot. She shakes the stiffness from her joints and Morningsun suddenly perks up, ready to fight again.

"Ready? It is time to fight again and I fear that this is the end."
As a group, we walk with our horses behind us. Rosy is saddled and ready. Emerald is ready to fight on the ground. Treán is in its sheath at her belt. We need every warrior we have. I can no longer be selfish and protect her. Stormy's tack disappears and his wings spread open as he prepares to take flight. I hold my right hand out to him like I have ever since he was a foal. He comes to me and presses his head against mine. In that moment, there are only the two of us there with no one else around. Our minds connect and inexpressible love passes between us, a connection deeper than many could ever imagine.

"I love you, Elren."

"I love you too, my Stormy Night." We break off the connection and I ignore the curious looks from the others. Suddenly, without warning, the voice of the forest guardian enters my mind.

"Prepare for great loss." A sense of foreboding fills me and I instinctively turn and look at Evan. He looks incredibly handsome, even with dirt and blood smeared across his face and his armor.

"Rivermist, don't let him do anything stupid, please."

"I'll try my best. We decided to be bound by death. If he dies, so do I."

"A big decision. I know how that goes. I've bound myself to two horses of the same blood with the same consequences." A loud ram horn suddenly breaks any peace that may have fallen over the camp.

Here we go again.

Enbarr and I take our places next to Joan, Han E. Lee, and Urduja once more.

The ending of an era has begun.

"I sense the end is near for our time. May you keep the old ways as best that you can and attempt to keep peace, no matter what happens.

You will live as long as hope continues to burn bright. The day that hope dies is your death-day as well. A world without hope is one that can no longer be saved, and one not worth living in," Han suddenly says.

I nod in agreement and then turn to watch the last of Draemir's army as over five hundred thousand more men take on our dwindling number of two hundred fifty thousand. It would take a miracle for us to survive. I watch as the army marches towards us. Arrows start to fall from our faithful centaurs, but none come near to hitting the tall warrior in deep sea blue armor and his horse. My brother is leading them personally.

I nudge Enbarr and we stand at the front most point of our army. A glowing silver beacon, I am ready for him. I add my arrows to the fray and refill my quiver before emptying it again. Man, after man falls, but another just seems to take his place. After emptying my quiver multiple times, the army is right in front of us. Suddenly, they stop about one hundred yards away. My warriors shift uneasily and level their spears, uncertain what to expect. The army across from us ready their weapons.

"Shields up!" I shout quickly to the men as understanding dawns on me. Loud shots ring out across the field and I hear rattling on shields, punctuated by screams filled with agony as some find their mark. As each one hits my shield or my armor, I feel the bruises gather from each impact. Enbarr and the other immortal horses don't even flinch. Nothing can harm them unless their rider is killed, or mortally wounded. Our archers fire back, but are not nearly as accurate as the New World technology.

I look at my men and am distressed to see that under this direct fire we only have around fifty thousand men left standing. Bile rises in my throat as I stare at the places our brave men had been standing. Finally, hatred overcomes me. This is not war, this is slaughter. I glance at Urduja, Han, and Joan, and see the fury in their eyes as well. This is no way for our honorable warriors to die. Deep inside me, I know I cannot let this happen. Forming a diamond, we all grab each other's forearms and combine our incredibly powerful magic.

It sparks and flares, throwing massive jets of magic up through the air. The sounds fade into the background and my blood roars in my ears as I call on more magic than ever before. Suddenly, a massive wall of magic envelopes what was left of our entire army. It connects to the forest on the either side. The bullets ricochet off and nothing passes through it. We study it for a moment, marveling at what our combined magic could do. A tiny fraction of our starting army is left. Only thirty thousand men still live from the five hundred thousand that so bravely held their lines earlier today. This is a massacre.

Laidena and Relan suddenly fly out from behind the army. Roaring in unison, they attack the New World soldiers. Jets of fire kill hundreds while their sharp teeth and talons take more. Screams of terror, pain, and hate fill the air. The air almost seems tainted by death. The metallic smell of blood and the salty smell of fear takes up whatever space the blood and gore does not and the most terrible thing about the whole scenario is that I have become used to it.

Suddenly, Relan decides to attack Draemir, the one who imprisoned her and forced her to kill other innocent creatures. I long to scream at her and order her to fly away, but I know she cannot hear me. We watch in silent horror as he waits for her to come into range for him to blast her out of the sky. Then, out of nowhere, Stormy flies faster than the wind towards her. He slams into his new friend with incredible force and it sends them both reeling, but he succeeded in knocking her away.

"Laidena, you and Relan need not sacrifice yourselves for this meaningless bloodbath. Please go! Fly away and be safe!" I call to the mother dragon telepathically. She swoops over us and nods.

"Good luck!" she calls before going off to collect Relan. They quickly disappear into the growing dusk. Soon it will be dark. The heavy clouds obscure any sunset there may have been. Draemir steps forward and brandishes his sword over his head.

"Shadow Warrior! Come face me, your greatest nightmare. If you somehow beat me in single combat, my men will take your warriors prisoner, and those who agree to live among these New Worlders will go freely. Any others will be killed. If I beat you, which is likely, I know your army will attack mine, and bitterly fight to the end and earn honorable death in battle. These are my terms; if you disagree, I will personally send my large army in and wipe out everyone. Your choice," He calls across the space. I can feel the desperate, but silent pleas that I will fight Chaos. The three great warriors next to me turn and face me.

"This is where we must part. Our magic will add to your strength. I hope for everyone's sake that you win. However, don't ever forget, when people believe in you, while they believe in hope, you will still live. Dum sperant, vivas: while they hope, you live." In bursts of bright yellow, royal purple, and gold and red magic, they are gone.

In slow motion, I nudge Enbarr forward and he carefully steps over the slain brave heroes who fought for their homeland. Soon we are in the clear space where the armies have not clashed. Yet. Suddenly, a knight clad in sapphire blue armor bursts out of the ranks and my heart stops. *What is Evan doing?*

"I challenge you, Chaos! You have done nothing but kill. You have taken everything I care about. My family is gone. The men I grew up with have all been slain. Now you want to try and kill the last person left holding my heart," Evan shouts as Rivermist charges towards them.

"No!" I shout as Draemir smiles and sends an incredibly strong bolt of potent magic at Evan. I close my eyes and immediately release a huge torrent of magic. I grit my teeth and brace all my muscles in preparation for the impact. Through my magical eyesight, I watch the collision course and the two different colored forces hit. The force is so great, that I nearly fall out of my saddle and Enbarr staggers back a few steps. Kelpie and Draemir also struggle to remain upright. Evan and Rivermist are both thrown backwards fifteen yards before landing with a mighty thud. I kick Enbarr into a gallop. We stand in front of Evan and my warriors, keeping ourselves between Draemir and them.

"Chased out of hiding?" he sneers.

"I accept, but you must have your army swear on the River Styx that they will abide by the terms you stated." He elegantly waves a hand at his army and they all swear the oath in rough voices.

"Happy?" he asks.

"Not quite the word I would use right now, but close enough," I reply dryly. With wild yells from the crowds watching, we urge our horses to a full gallop. I drop the reins onto Enbarr's neck as he flies above the ground, his legs a blur. Crouching slightly in the stirrups, I draw Tíne and take a heartbeat to look down the length of my faithful sword. It has never let me down before. Shrugging my shield higher on my left arm, I loop Enbarr's reins over the saddle pommel so they stay out of the way. His shoulder muscles ripple beautifully as his magnificent strides carry me closer to Draemir.

As I look at my brother, I feel as if I am suddenly fourteen again, standing in the dirt road. Once more, the villagers are cramming to the sides of the street against the houses and shops. The young Draemir slowly walks down the road towards me once again. A thrill of anticipation and fear makes me shiver.

I look at my brother as he comes closer and I realize that every lost man, woman, and child, every sacrifice that has been made, has been leading to this very moment. Pride rushes through me when I realize that every sacrifice made, and every man, woman, and child and the ones who are trying to flee at this very moment, they chose *me* to be the one they rest their fates on. Many gave their lives so I would one day get here to this moment and help everyone. I am the one they chose. I sit taller on Enbarr and look around. Our armor sings its song of lamentation laced liberally with hope. The faces of the crowd watch me with awe and trepidation. I must not let them down.

I stand up in my stirrups and raise my sword. Three strides... Two strides... I yell wildly and send a straight thrust, using Enbarr's power, my anger and adrenaline, and all my strength in the strike. Draemir's smirk fades and he hurries to block it. The clashing of swords is deafening and I can feel the power of his block and it threatens to throw me off Enbarr completely. My twin also struggles to remain in Kelpie's saddle.

We both reel in our saddles at the power from both of us hitting. Finally, I regain my balance and manage to sit upright. I swing Enbarr around, steering with my knees and he turns with incredible speed and balance, despite his size. This time we meet shield to shield. I hold my sword under the shield and when we meet again, I slam my shield into his and Enbarr rears up high, while Kelpie mirrors his move. The two horses fight bitterly, while Draemir and I exchange blows.

Upon the initial hit, we are both sent reeling again, but I feel my sword slash through his blackiron armor, nothing that will change the fight, but an excellent moral boost for me. *He can be hit.*

We exchange powerful blows, but neither of us gain on the other. My muscles burn and my breath comes quickly. I cannot continue like this for forever. I cannot afford to make a costly mistake. Without him noticing, I free my feet from the stirrups and as Enbarr and Kelpie rise under us again, I hurl myself out of my saddle and tackle him.

He weighs more than me, but I catch him by surprise and we both fall heavily to the ground with our armor ringing like bells. I spring to my feet and dart a few steps away. I can feel my strength starting to decline and I close my eyes. Around me is the forest again. That amazing peace fills me again and I can hear the patterns that the Guardian of the Woods called out ring through my blood.

I raise my sword without opening my eyes and stop his blade. I am conscious of all the sounds around me, his footfalls, his labored breaths, everything. The nervous shuffling of feet from both sides. The horses fight furiously. Their hatred for each other is as strong as me and my brother's. In and out. I can feel my breath steadily fill and empty my lungs. A new wave of energy fills me and I open my eyes and smile into my brother's furious face as he struggles to break through my guard. His sword flies with incredible speed, but I effortlessly stop it every time.

His face shows his surprise. He has never faced me and felt this matched. I meet his blade and cut back with deadly speed. A long, jagged crack in his armor appears from his right shoulder to his left hip. Anger crosses his face and his swings inexplicably become faster and stronger. I do not have chances to strike back anymore. All my attention is focused on blocking the flickering blade of his sword as it tries to find a gap in my guard. I watch him carefully. Suddenly, I notice a pattern in his strokes, a certain cadence. I concentrate to figure out a way to exploit this weakness.

It clicks. He is relying on me to meet his blade to keep the cadence in balance. I step back and refuse to meet his black blade, Dortcha. His side cut swings him off balance and I spot my opening. Stepping in a powerful lunge, I spring forward with inhuman speed and strength and bury my sword deep into his right shoulder. He screams and jerks backwards. I withdraw my sword.

My army cheers loudly when they see him injured. He glowers at them with intense hatred. Now he knows my pain. The muscles and tendons in my shoulder still have not fully recovered since the last time we met. He switches his sword to his left hand and the fight continues, he slams me in the chest with his shield and I feel myself go weightless as I fly backwards.

His army cheers and stomps their feet. I painfully land on my side and feel multiple ribs crack when I hit the ground. My recently healed knee shrieks at me and I instinctively roll over and feel the wind of a passing dagger as it buries itself into the ground where I had just been a second ago. Pain shoots down my entire right side when I try to rise. I manage to raise myself onto one knee and look up, gasping for breath. Chaos laughs, an ugly grin on his face as he enjoys this moment. His army goes crazy.

"No!" One familiar voice rises above the clamor of the chaotic shouts. *No, no, no! Evan, stop!* I think, panic stricken, but it is too late. Chaos spots the mud and grass stained boy next to his blue streaked horse and smiles cruelly.

"Once I kill you, I will finish off your little boyfriend as well." I stab my sword into the blood-coated ground and close my eyes, blocking everything out.

"Guardian of the Woods, please share some of your strength with me so I may rise and finish him." I send out my plea and suddenly a brush of warm air caresses my cheek. Dark green magic rises through my sword and swirls inside me, healing my recent injuries. *"Thank you."* My gratitude is beyond words. I open my eyes and notice that Draemir is slowly walking towards me, enjoying the adulation of his army. Finally,

he reaches me. My ice blue eyes meet his dark blue ones and bore into them with such intense fury that he actually flinches.

"Never count the fight over until your opponent lies dead on the ground," I snarl fiercely and lunge up, drawing Tíne up from the ground. Before he can move, I stab him straight through the heart. Shock registers on his face before he falls to the ground, dead. I stare at the lifeless body of my twin brother and look at his red and dark blue blood on my sword. *I did it. I vanquished my greatest nightmare. The beast of all beasts.*

Strangely enough, to my absolute surprise, a small pang of sadness shivers through me briefly. As much evil he has wrought, he was my own flesh and blood. I shove those thoughts away. *You renounced him from yourself long ago. You have no right to be horrified by his death.* I shake myself and cast off the last of those thoughts.

His body dissolves into deep sea blue magic before reforming in a shadow form of him. Fury and mockery is written on his face. I stand in front of him boldly.

"While people still have chaotic dreams and while they still believe in chaos, I live! Perhaps not in as grand of a form, but I will still be able to whisper in men's ears chaotic thoughts and spark wars and eternally make your life difficult and dangerous. A long misery. You have taken everything from me, now I will continue to wreck any peace or hope that you manage to restore," he hisses furiously in Daenlir.

"You are a monster. The worst of beasts. The bane of all. You will live a cursed life, stripped of all your power. The memories of all that you have wrongfully killed will haunt you forever. While even I cannot stop your evil doings, I will never stop following you and I will ensure that you will never be more powerful than me. You were once the omnipotent wind and I was the small sapling, but I grew strong and now, here I stand, stronger, taller, and more powerful than you. Our father tried to crush me, but I refused to give up. Now you will know my pain. *You are now a mere shadow of me.*" As I speak, I summon all the magic that I can and I blast him with every ounce I can muster. He howls in agony before disappearing. I turn and watch the two horses continue to battle. Kelpie of the Deep seems unaffected by the loss of his master. The two horses rear up and start another round, but as I watch, Kelpie suddenly keels over dead and disappears in a puff of magic like his master. Enbarr comes down and his front hooves shake the ground.

Once I am sure that he is alright, I sprint the fifty yards back. The men in my army exchange looks and are unsure what to do. There is still an army that far outnumbers them, prepared to fight and kill the last of us, if we make a wrong move. Using magic, I send them a last speech, speaking directly into their minds.

"*Good and valiant men, you have risen far above any standard anyone could ever set. It is up to you to decide what to do next. I will not advise one way or the other. Your options are to run into the woods and attempt to escape, but I do not know where you will go. Your other choice is to go with the New Worlders and try to live among them.*

"*I know what I am going to do, but I walk a path that very few are able to follow. If you are going to try escape, now is your chance. If you are going with the soldiers, come up to me and gather into a group. I will conceal your weapons and the spell will last for five or six days. I am sorry it had to end like this, but you all just need to keep your heads high, and know inside yourselves that you were the more valiant warriors. You did not have to hide behind huge numbers. Each and every man and woman here fought with the utmost bravery. You can all walk away from here with pride. I am proud and honored to have fought alongside such magnificent warriors.*" I draw myself up and stand at attention before saluting them.

After saluting or bowing back, most of them run. They spread out into smaller clusters as friends find each other. I make a mental note to help them as much as I can. The others come together and look at me hopefully. There is nothing worse than being at an enemy's mercy without your weapon. I close my eyes and when I reopen them, my magical vision shows me everything. I can see the fear in their eyes and the exhausted way they hold themselves. Many have makeshift bandages covering a wound.

My heart breaks when I spot a young boy, barely thirteen, crying. He stands alone and I can guess that his father was killed. Man by man, I slowly conceal their weapons from sight. Finally, the army seems like they all discarded them on the field. Hope starts to impede their fear and many straighten their shoulders and look straight ahead as the soldiers come and lead them away to their strange vehicles.

"I will keep an eye over you all. If you desperately need me, whisper my name into the wind and I will come. May you never forget what is worth remembering, nor ever remember what is best forgotten," I quote an old proverb. "Remember the sacrifices that were made today and the honor your names received, but never remember the defeat, because we were never truly defeated. May the road rise up to meet you, the wind be always behind your back. May the sun shine warm upon your face, the rain fall soft on your fields. And until we meet again, may God hold you in the palm of his hand," I recite the ancient blessing and put magic in my words. The warriors all turn a salute me as they walk by. None of the New Worlders dare come near me or any of the remaining Olympians.

Out of all the Olympians that started out on the field this morning, only ten remain here. Zeus of the sky, Hera of the heavens, Poseidon of the sea, Artemis and Surefire of the moon and hunt, Apollo and Lyr of the sun, Hades of the underworld, Aphrodite of love and beauty, Athena and Morningsun of wisdom, Ares of war, and Hestia of home. They are all that is left of the old world. Hephaestus of the forge and Hermes of commerce, travelers, and thieves has fallen, never to rise again, along with many other brave Olympians and their loyal horses left on the field. We stand there until all of the soldiers are gone and we are the only living people here. I look around at all the thousands of dead men and feel a wave of nausea sweeps through me. The others seem to have similar thoughts racing through their heads. Emerald quickly dismounts Rose and is sick to her stomach. Evan walks over to her and talks to her in subdued tones.

Chapter Twenty-Seven

Shadow

Enbarr and I walk out to the middle of the field where the brunt of the fighting took place. I glance down at the tangle of bodies at my feet as I walk and suddenly feel as if the world tipped on its side. I feel sick to my stomach as well. A father and young son lie on the ground, the father trying to protect the son, even while they are in Death's indifferent embrace. Everything around me goes silent and seems to move in slow motion. All I can see are the two bodies almost buried by their comrades who tried and failed to protect them. In slow motion, I walk over to the two figures. I crouch next to them and gently roll them over to reveal their identities. Tears well up in my eyes and spill out. Young Allen finally found his father. Sadness drives through me like a dagger. Life can be both cruel and kind. It just depends on the hand that Fate dealt to you.

I gently wipe the blood from his face and my hand lingers on his tender cheek. Suddenly, his limp form trembles and a moan drags itself from the boy. His serious brown eyes meet my astonished and sorrowful gaze. I look at the spear through his side and a faint smile crosses his face.

"Life, love, hope, and happiness are the greatest gifts given to mankind. I relinquish them now to join my family up in eternal happiness. Never give up, Elren. While I may be finished, you must always believe in the best parts of your gifts. Cherish them while you can." His steady gaze holds my tearful one for a long searching moment before his eyes close for the last time. The youthful face is soft and relaxed as he begins the journey to eternal peace and happiness where his mother, father, sister, and brother await him. I dry my eyes and gaze down at his peaceful expression. Death can be a gift, and it can be a dreaded thing. For young

361

Allen, it was an escape. No more pain or suffering. I stand up and look around me. All those lives lost, and all those who still struggle to live. *Life is a gift too;* the boy's voice reminds me.

I turn in a full circle and survey the death and destruction that my brother caused. Suddenly, it strikes me that I may have caused this if the cards of fate had fallen differently. If my mother had taken Draemir and my father me, our fates would have been reversed. *So why me? Why make me the good one? How was I different?* These thoughts tear through my exhausted mind and terror rises in me. A voice angrily responds in my head and I wince at the sudden blindingly bright white magic.

"Do you have no faith in me? Do you think that I did not know what I was doing? I chose you. *You are good, and he was bad. I knew from the moment you were born that you would represent these humans and be their hope. Draemir was despair. He brought fear, hate, and chaos wherever he went. This is how it was meant to be. It could not have been anything different. The fates would not have allowed that. Now, rest easy and calm your mind and heart. The great suffering that was predicted has passed. The losses have been great. I recommend you find a way to give all these fallen men the honor they deserve."* the voice softens. *"Daughter, you did very well. I am proud of you."* The presence fades and I open my eyes again.

I use an incredible amount of magic and throw it over the entire field. All the bodies, New Worlders and our brave warriors alike, disappear in clouds of white magic. I throw it all up to the heavens and hundreds of thousands of warriors are drawn out in new constellations. Every man who fell is there. All of them serenely look down at us and seem to smile. I feel a burden seem to release inside me. A weight that has been growing inside me since the war first started is gone. Draemir Caerin has been vanquished. A huge grin crosses my face. I fear no one. I can freely tread on the earth once more without a destiny laid out for me.

"Now what?" Emerald voices the question everyone is thinking.

"What do you mean?" I ask quietly. "Have you not had enough action?" I raise an eyebrow at her. She gives me a pained look.

"I *mean*, what about Chaos? What will we do now? He can still whisper into humans' hearts and control their minds using their deepest desires and the hopeless greed and vanity that these people still have." I give her a steady look before addressing the remaining Olympians.

"Now we work to return the peace and order that is needed for prosperity. It will be a long and drawn out war, but we will fight until we are no longer needed. And we will fight together." And so we march off. Who knows how long this will take? A day? A year? One hundred years? However long, I will not stop until the people are safe, and peace returns.

Just because people support peace, honor, and bravery, does not mean that it can ever subdue chaos and disorder. There may be times when peace can win a battle, but it will never win the whole war. However, there is still a chance for your kind. Perhaps when Peace and Hope work together they will be able to defeat the chaos that threatens to control your people.

When times became hard and self-doubt crept in, I remembered a simple phrase and it reminded me that while things seem impossible and there is nowhere else to turn, Hope is always there.

Dum vivo, spero.
While I live, I hope.

363

Epilogue

Hundreds of years later, in the days where knights, archers, and warriors no longer walk the earth in human forms, if you happen to venture into the woods and glimpse a tall and slim figure with a bow and sword silently running through the trees, you might put it down to be your eyes fooling you, or perhaps a peculiar creature. I will let you in on a well-kept secret. Feel privileged to know that if you had held back a blink, you would have seen that the passing figure had a slight limp to its effortless gait- a mark that proves that no matter how kind, courageous, lucky, or skilled you are, misfortune can and will befall you. All rewards worth having must be earned for them to mean anything.

Feel protected and safe should you come across this creature of the woods, for this is the one who has been long forgotten by humans, but gave absolutely everything to save your kind. It fights the battles that none ever know about. Battles against unimaginable enemies, enemies that would tear humanity as you know it apart.

This creature has outlasted even the great race known as the Olympians. Yes, even persevering past hardships that the huntress and wisdom could not. You are more fortunate than most if you have seen this strange figure, for you have seen the Protector of Hope, the Woodland Warrior, the last of the people left from the Land of Old, and the greatest warrior to walk the earth alongside today's Modern World as you call it.

You have been blessed indeed, for the one you have seen is none other than the Shadow Warrior herself

Acknowledgements

Many thanks to my editor, Kristine Terrell who helped me immensely, my photographer and cover artist, Anna Sojka, my parents for their support, and of course, my wonderful pony, Freedom's Stormy Night. Lastly, many thanks to my middle school English teacher, Proal Heartwell. If it weren't for his guidance, I never would have discovered my love for writing. He always said, "Don't be a wish I had, be a glad I did," and now I can finally say that I did it.

Elizabeth Davis is a sophomore at Western Albemarle High School. In her free time, when she is not doing homework, she can be found hanging out at the barn or playing soccer. She enjoys being outdoors and finds inspiration for her stories in the company of her pony and her friends.

90774920R00224

Made in the USA
Columbia, SC
09 March 2018